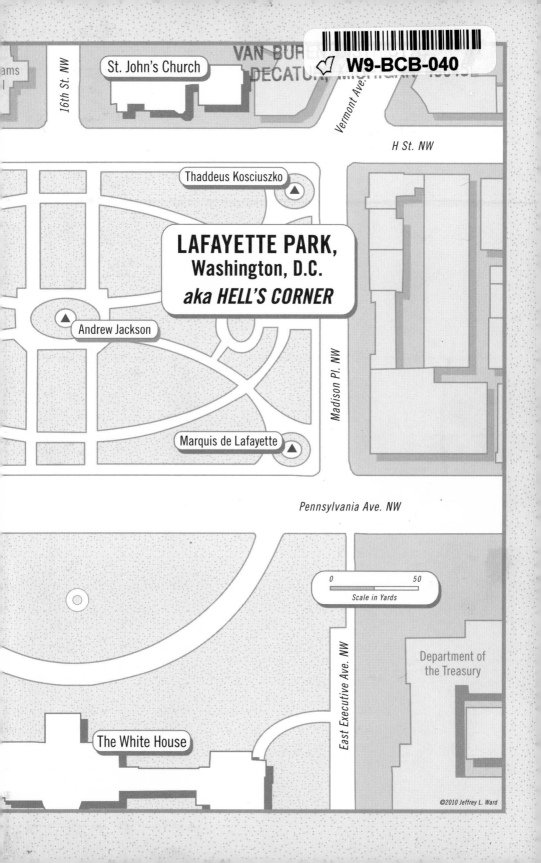

DAVID BALDACCI

HELL'S CORNER

GC

GRAND CENTRAL
PUBLISHING

LARGE PRINT

This book is a work of fiction. Names, characters, places, and incidents are the product of the author's imagination or are used fictitiously. Any resemblance to actual events, locales, or persons, living or dead, is coincidental.

Grand Central Publishing
Hachette Book Group
237 Park Avenue
New York, NY 10017

www.HachetteBookGroup.com

Printed in the United States of America

First Edition: November 2010
10 9 8 7 6 5 4 3 2 1

Grand Central Publishing is a division of
Hachette Book Group, Inc.
The Grand Central Publishing name and logo is a trademark of
Hachette Book Group, Inc.

Library of Congress Cataloging-in-Publication Data

Baldacci, David.
Hell's corner / David Baldacci.—1st ed.
p. cm.
ISBN 978-0-446-19552-2 (regular edition)—
ISBN 978-0-446-57369-6 (large print edition)
I. Title.
PS3552.A446H46 2010
813'.54—dc22
2010030909

To Michelle
Twenty years of marriage and twenty books.
A ride of a lifetime with the woman I love.

HELL'S CORNER

CHAPTER

1

OLIVER STONE WAS COUNTING SECONDS, an exercise that had always calmed him. And he needed to be calm. He was meeting with someone tonight. Someone very important. And Stone didn't quite know how it was going to go. He did know one thing for certain. He was not going to run. He was through running.

Stone had just returned from Divine, Virginia, where Abby Riker, a woman he'd met, lived. Abby had been the first woman Stone had feelings for since he'd lost his wife three decades prior. Despite their obvious fondness for one another, Abby would not leave Divine, and Stone could not live there. For better or worse, much of him belonged to this town, even with all the pain it had caused.

That pain might become even more intense. The communication he'd received an hour after returning home had been explicit. They would come for him at midnight. No debate was allowed, no negotiation suffered through, no chance of any compromise. The party on the other end of the equation always dictated the terms.

A few moments later he stopped counting. Car tires had bitten into the gravel that lined the entrance to Mt. Zion Cemetery. It was a historical if humble burial site for African Americans who'd gained prominence by fighting for things their white counterparts had always taken for granted, like where to eat, sleep, ride in a bus or use the bathroom. The irony had never been lost on Stone that Mt. Zion rested high above fancy Georgetown. It was not all that long ago that the wealthy folks here only tolerated their darker brethren if they wore a maid's starched uniform or else were handing out drinks and finger foods and keeping their obedient gaze on the polished floors.

Car doors opened and car doors closed. Stone counted three clunks of metal against metal. So a trio. Of men. They wouldn't send a woman for this, he didn't think, though that might simply have been the prejudice of his generation.

Glocks or Sigs or perhaps customized models, depending on whom they'd sent to do the deed. Regardless, the weapons would be chambering efficiently lethal ordnance. The guns would be holstered under nice suit jackets. No black-clad storm troopers rappelling from the skids of go-fast choppers in quaint, well-connected Georgetown. The extraction would be quiet, no important person's sleep interrupted.

They knocked.

Polite.

He answered.

To show respect.

These people had no personal grudge against him. They might not even know who he was. It was a job. He'd done it, though he'd never knocked beforehand. Surprise and then the millisecond-long pull of a trigger had been his MO.

A job.

At least I thought that, because I didn't have the courage to face the truth.

As a soldier, Stone had never had any qualms about ending the life of anyone who was trying to terminate his. War was Darwinism at its most efficient and the rules were innately commonsensical, kill or be killed chief among them. However, what he had done after leaving the military had been different in a way that left him permanently mistrustful of those in power.

He stood in the doorway, framed by the light

behind him. He would have chosen this moment to fire, if he'd been on the trigger side. Quick, clean, no chance of missing. He'd given them their opportunity.

They didn't take it. They were not going to kill him.

It was actually *four* men, and Stone felt slight apprehension that his observations had been flawed.

The leader of the pack was trim, five-ten, short hair and efficient eyes that took in everything and gave nothing in return. He motioned to the vehicle parked by the gate, a black Escalade. There was a time when Stone would have rated a platoon of crackerjack killers coming for him by land, sea and air. Those days, apparently, were over. A quartet of suits in a Cadillac on steroids was enough.

There were no unnecessary words uttered. He was expertly searched and ushered into the vehicle. He sat in the middle bench seat, a man on either side of him. He could feel each of their muscled arms as it lay against his. They were tensed, ready to block any attempt by Stone to get to their weapons. Stone had no thought of making such an attempt. Now, outnumbered four to one, he would lose that battle ten times out of ten, a blackened tattoo painted on his forehead, a third eye his reward for the fatal miscalculation. Decades ago it was probable that four men far better than these would lie dead as he walked away to fight another day. But those days were long in the past.

"Where?" he asked. He never expected a response and didn't get one.

Minutes later he stood alone outside a building virtually every American would recognize. He didn't stand there for long. More men appeared, better and higher-ranked than the ones who had just dropped him off. He was now in the inner ring. The personnel became more skilled the closer one approached the center. They escorted him down a corridor with numerous doorways. Every single one of them was closed, and it wasn't simply the lateness of the hour. This place never really slept.

The door opened and the door closed. Stone was alone once more, but again not for long. A door opened in another part of the room and the man entered. He didn't look at Stone, but motioned for him to sit.

Stone sat.

The man settled down behind his desk.

Stone was an unofficial visitor here. Normally a log was kept of everyone passing through this place, but not tonight. Not him. The man was dressed casually, chinos, open-collared shirt, loafers. He slid glasses over his face, rustled some papers on his desk. A single light burned next to him. Stone studied him. The man looked intense and determined. He had to be to survive this place. To manage his way through the world's most impossible job.

He put down the papers; slid up the glasses onto the lined forehead.

"We have a problem," said James Brennan, the president of the United States. "And we need your help."

CHAPTER

2

STONE WAS MILDLY SURPRISED but didn't show it. Registering surprise was never good in situations like this. "A problem with what?"

"The Russians."

"All right." *Nothing new there,* thought Stone. *We often have problems with the Russians.*

The president continued, "You've been there." It wasn't a question.

"Many times."

"You speak the language." Again, not a question, so Stone remained silent. "You know their tactics."

"I used to know them. That was a long time ago."

Brennan smiled grimly. "Just like hairdos and clothes, if one hangs around long enough, things come back in style, including, apparently, espionage techniques."

The president leaned back and put his feet up on the *Resolute* desk that had been a gift from Queen Victoria to America near the end of the nineteenth century. Rutherford B. Hayes had been the first sitting president to use it, and Brennan the latest.

"The Russians have a web of spy rings entrenched in this country. The FBI has arrested some of them, infiltrated others, but more are out there of which we have no information."

"Countries spy on each other all the time," said Stone. "I would be stunned if we didn't have intelligence operations going on over there."

"That's beside the point."

"All right," said Stone, who actually thought that *was* the point.

"The Russian cartels control all the major drug distribution pipelines in the eastern hemisphere. The monies involved are truly enormous."

Stone nodded. This he knew.

"Well, now they control it in the western hemisphere as well."

This Stone didn't know. "I understand the Colombians had been muscled out by the Mexicans."

Brennan nodded thoughtfully. Stone could sense in the man's weary expression the mounds of briefing books he had no doubt pored over today to understand this and a dozen other critical matters thoroughly. The presidency would suck up every ounce of energy and intellectual curiosity one cared to give the job.

Brennan said, "Pipeline trumps product, they finally figured that out. You can make the crap anywhere, but getting it to the buyer is the real key. And on this side of the world *Americans* are the buyers. But the Russians have kicked our southern neighbor's ass, Stone. They have killed and clawed and bombed and tortured and bribed their way to the top, with the result that they are now in control of at least ninety percent of the business. And that is a major problem."

"I understood that Carlos Montoya—"

The president brushed this comment aside impatiently. "The papers say that. Fox and CNN broadcast that, the pundits fixate on it, but the fact is Carlos Montoya is done. He was the worst of the scum in Mexico. He killed two of his own brothers to win control of the family business, and yet he proved no match for the Russians. In fact, our intel leads us to believe that he's been killed. The Russians are about as ruthless as they come in the drug world."

"All right," said Stone evenly.

"So long as the Mexican cartels were the

adversary it was manageable. Not ideal, of course, but it didn't reach national security status. We could battle it on our borders and in the metro areas where the cartels had infiltrated primarily through gang ranks. It's different with the Russians."

"Meaning a connection between the spy rings and the cartels?"

Brennan eyed Stone, perhaps surprised he'd made the connection so fast. "We believe there is. In fact, our belief is that the Russian government and their drug cartels are one and the same."

"That's a very troublesome conclusion," said Stone.

"And the correct one, we think. Illegal drug sales are one of the leading exports from Russia. They make it in the old Soviet labs, and ship it all over the world through various means. They pay off the people they have to and kill the ones they can't bribe. The monies involved are enormous. Hundreds of billions of dollars. Too enormous for the government not to want its share. And there's more to the equation."

"You mean the more drugs they sell to America the weaker we become as a nation? It drains dollars and brain cells. It increases the level of both petty and major crime, taxes our resources, shifts assets from productive areas to nonproductive ones."

Again, Brennan looked surprised at Stone's nimble articulation. "That's right. And the Russians know something about the power of addictions. Their populace certainly abuses both drugs and alcohol. But we have detected a purposeful, enhanced effort by the Russians to basically overwhelm America with drugs." The president sat back. "And then there's the obvious complicating factor."

"They're a nuclear power," replied Stone. "They have as many warheads as we do, in fact."

The president nodded. "They want back in the top tier. Perhaps they want to be the sole superpower, supplanting us. And on top of that they are vastly influential in the Middle and Far East. Even the Chinese and Israelis fear them, if only for their unpredictability. The balance is getting out of whack."

"All right. Why me?"

"The Russians have gone back to old-school tactics, Stone. From your era."

"I'm not that old. Aren't there spies from my era still at the Agency?"

"No, there's really not. There was a hiring freeze before 9/11 and a lot of voluntary and involuntary retirements of older personnel. After those planes hit the buildings, there was considerable ramp-up.

The result is that three-quarters of the CIA is comprised of twenty-somethings. The only thing they know about Russia is they make good vodka and it's cold there. You *know* Russia. You understand the trenches of espionage better than most of the people sitting in the executive offices at Langley." He paused. "And we all know you have special skills. Skills this country spent good money instilling in you."

The guilt factor. Interesting.

"But all my contacts there are gone. Dead."

"That is actually an advantage. You go in with a blank slate, an unknown quantity."

"How will we start?"

"By you going back in unofficially, of course. There will be training, getting you up to date on things. I suspect you will be ready to leave the country in a month."

"Going to Russia?"

"No, Mexico and Latin America. We need you on the ground where the drugs are coming through. It'll be rough work. And dangerous. I guess I don't need to tell you that." He paused and his gaze flicked to Stone's close-cropped white hair.

Stone easily interpreted the observation. "I'm not as young as I was, obviously."

"None of us are."

Stone nodded, his mind racing ahead to the logical conclusion of all this. He really only had one question. "Why?"

"I already told you why. In many respects you're the best we have. And the problem is very real and getting worse."

"Can I hear the rest of it?"

"The rest of what?"

"Why I'm really here."

"I don't understand," the president said irritably. "I thought I had made myself clear."

"The last time I was here I told you some things and intimated other things."

The president made no reaction to these words.

"Then I was offered the Medal of Honor."

"And you turned it down," Brennan said sharply. "A first, I believe."

"You have to turn down what you don't deserve."

"Bullshit. Your actions on the battlefield more than earned it."

"On the battlefield, yes. But in the greater scheme of things, I didn't deserve it. And with an honor like that, *all* things have to be considered. Which I think is why I'm really here."

The two men stared at each other across the width of the *Resolute* desk. By the look on his face the president very clearly understood what "all things" meant. A man named Carter Gray. And a man named Roger Simpson. Both prominent Americans. Both friends of this president. And both dead. Directly because of Oliver Stone, who'd had good reason to do it, but he'd still killed them. And there was really no legal or even moral excuse for that. Even as he'd pulled the trigger on each man, Stone had known that.

But it still didn't stop me, because if anyone deserved killing those two did.

"You saved my life," Brennan began in an uneasy tone.

"And I took two others."

The president abruptly rose and walked over to the window. Stone watched him closely. He'd said it. Now he was just going to let the other man talk and let the chips fall.

"Gray was going to kill me."

"Yes, he was."

"So your killing him didn't bother me as much as it ordinarily would have, to put it bluntly."

"But Simpson?"

The president turned to look at him. "I did some research on that. I can understand why you would have wanted to eliminate the man. But no man is an island, Stone. And cold-blooded killing is unacceptable in a civilized world."

"Unless it's been authorized by appropriate parties," Stone pointed out. "By people who have sat in the chair in which you now sit."

Brennan snatched a glance at his desk chair and then looked away. "This is a dangerous mission, Stone. You will be given every asset you require to succeed. But there are no guarantees."

"There are never any guarantees."

The president sat back down, made a steeple with his hands, possibly an impromptu shield between himself and the other man.

When Brennan didn't say anything, Stone did. "This is my penance, isn't it?"

The president lowered his hands.

"This is my penance," Stone said again. "In lieu of a trial that no one wants because too many unpleasant truths will come out for the government, and the reputations of certain dead public servants will be tarnished. And you're not the sort to order my execution because, as you said, that's not how a civilized people resolve their differences."

"You don't mince words," Brennan said quietly.

"Are they true words or not?"

"I think you understand my dilemma."

"Don't apologize for having a conscience, sir. I've served other men who held your office who had none at all."

"If you fail, you fail. The Russians are as ruthless as they come. You know that better than most."

"And if I succeed?"

"Then you will never have to worry about your government knocking on your door again." He leaned forward. "Do you accept?"

Stone nodded and rose. "I accept." He paused at the door. "If I don't make it back, I would appreciate it if my friends were told that I died serving my country."

The president nodded.

"Thank you," said Oliver Stone.

3

THE NEXT NIGHT STONE STOOD where he had for decades, in seven-acre Lafayette Park across from the White House. It had originally been called President's Park, but now that title encompassed the White House grounds, Lafayette Park and the Ellipse, a fifty-two-acre parcel of land on the south side of the White House. Once part of the White House grounds proper, Lafayette Park had been separated from that august property when President Thomas Jefferson had Pennsylvania Avenue plowed through.

The park had been used for many purposes over two centuries, including as a graveyard, a slave market and even a racetrack. And it was also notable for having more squirrels per square inch than any other place on earth. To this day, no one knew why. The place had changed dramatically since Stone first planted his sign in the ground, the one that read *I Want the Truth.* Gone were the permanent protestors like Stone, their ragged tents and their boisterous banners. Majestic Pennsylvania Avenue in front of the White House was closed to vehicular traffic and had been ever since the Oklahoma City bombing.

People, institutions and countries were scared, and Stone couldn't blame them. If Franklin Roosevelt had been alive and occupying the White House once more he might have invoked his most famous line: "The only thing we have to fear is fear itself." But even those words might not have been enough. The bogeymen appeared to be winning the war of perception in the hearts and minds of the citizenry.

Stone glanced to the center of the park, at the equestrian statue of Andrew Jackson, the hero of the Battle of New Orleans and America's seventh chief executive. Jackson sat on a pediment of majestic Tennessee marble. It was the first statue of a man on horseback ever cast in the United States. The monument was surrounded by a low wrought-iron fence, with a scattering of ancient cannons inside this space. Four other statues memorializing foreign Revolutionary War heroes anchored each corner of the green space.

North of Jackson were rows of colorful flowers

and a large newly placed maple. Yellow tape was wound around flex poles set in the ground ten feet out from this tree because of the open hole several feet deep and three feet wider than the huge root ball. Next to the hole were blue tarps with the displaced dirt piled up on them.

Stone's gaze rose to elevated points where he knew the countersnipers were stationed, although he couldn't see them. He assumed that many of them were probably drawing practice beads on his head.

No trigger slips please, gentlemen. I like my brain right where it is.

The state dinner at the White House was winding down and well-fed VIPs trickled out of the "People's House." One such guest was the British prime minister. His waiting motorcade would carry him on the brief trip to Blair House, the residence for visiting dignitaries, which was located on the west side of the park. It was a short walk, yet Stone supposed government leaders could not safely walk anywhere anymore. The world had long since changed for them too.

Stone turned his head and saw a woman sitting on a bench near the oval-shaped fountain on the east side of the park midway between Jackson and the statue of Polish general Tadeusz Kościuszko, who'd helped the fledgling English colonies free themselves from British rule. The irony that the leader of that same monarchy was now staying at a place overlooking this monument was not lost on Stone.

The woman was dressed in black slacks and a thin white coat. She had a large bag next to her. She appeared to be dozing.

That's odd, thought Stone. People did not doze in Lafayette at this time of night.

She wasn't the only person in the park. As Stone looked toward the trees on the northwest side of the park he spied a man in a suit carrying a briefcase. His back was to Stone. He'd stopped to examine the statue of German army officer Friedrich Wilhelm von Steuben, who'd also helped the colonists kick Mad King George's royal behind more than two centuries ago.

And then Stone noticed a short man with a large belly entering the park from the northern end where St. John's Church was located. He was in jogging attire, though he looked incapable of even walking quickly without collapsing from a coronary. What looked to be an iPod was strapped to a belt around his ample middle, and he had on earphones.

And there was a fourth inhabitant of the park. He looked like a street gang foot soldier, dressed in prison shuffle jeans, dark bandanna, muscle shirt, camouflage jacket and stomp boots. The ganger was walking slowly right through the middle of the park. This too was odd since gangers almost never came to Lafayette Park because of the heavy police presence. And that presence was strengthened and even more vigilant tonight for a very simple reason.

State dinners put everyone on edge. A spring in the step of a patrolling sentry. A lawman's hand a smidge closer to the trigger. A heightened tendency to shoot and pick up the pieces later. If a leader went down, no one escaped responsibility. Heads and pensions rolled.

But Stone had not come here to think about those things. He had come here to see Lafayette Park for the last time. In two days he would be leaving for his monthlong training session. And then it was off to Mexico. He had already made up his mind. He would not tell his friends, the members of the Camel Club. If he did they might sense the truth, and nothing good could possibly come out of that. He deserved to be sacrificed. They didn't.

He drew one more long breath and looked around. He smiled as he saw the gingko tree near the Jackson statue. It was across from the maple that had just been installed. The first time he'd come to this park it had been fall and the gingko leaves were a gloriously bright yellow. It was magnificent.

There were gingko trees all over the city, but this was the only one in the park. Gingkoes could live well over a thousand years. Stone wondered what this place would look like in ten centuries. Would the gingko still be here? Would the big white building across the street?

He was turning to leave this place for the final time when his attention focused on what was coming down the street right toward him.

And his beloved park.

CHAPTER

4

IT WAS THE SOUND of muscular engines, flashing lights and sirens that had put Stone on alert. He watched as the prime minister's motorcade pulled out from the west side of the White House and set off toward Blair House. The building, which was actually three town houses stitched together, was deceptively large. It had more square footage than even the White House and was located to the immediate west of the park and facing Pennsylvania Avenue across from the monstrously large Old Executive Office Building where parts of the president's and vice-president's staffs maintained offices. Stone was surprised the Secret Service hadn't cleared the area before the motorcade left.

He glanced around again. The lady was now awake and talking on her cell phone. The man in the suit was still lingering around the von Steuben

statue with his back to Stone. The jogger was nearing the statue of Jackson. The ganger was still
stamping through Lafayette, although the park
wasn't that large. He should have managed it by
now.

Something was clearly off.

Stone chose to head west first. Though he was no
longer a protestor here, he had come to view Lafayette Park as his turf to defend against all threats.
Even his imminent departure to Mexico had not
changed that. And while he didn't yet feel threatened, he had a sense that that status might abruptly
change.

He eyed the jogger diagonally across from him
on the other side of the park. The man had stopped
and was fiddling with the controls on his iPod.
Stone's gaze flicked to the lady on the bench. She
was just putting away her cell phone.

Stone next approached the statue of the French
general Comte de Rochambeau at the southwest
corner of the park. As he did so, at the adjacent
intersection of Jackson Place and Pennsylvania Avenue security teams were arrayed into walls of Kevlar and submachine guns awaiting the arrival of the
prime minister. As he continued on, Stone met the
ganger face-to-face. The man seemed to be walking
in quicksand, moving but not getting anywhere.

And there was a gun under his jacket; Stone could see the awkward but familiar bump in the material even in the darkened conditions. That was ballsy, thought Stone. You didn't come down here armed, unless you wanted a rooftop countersniper to assume the worst, with the result that your next of kin *might* receive an official apology after your funeral. So why would the man risk his life?

Stone gauged the potential shot trajectory from the ganger to where the prime minister would be entering Blair House. There was none, unless the ganger had a weapon that could defy the laws of physics by bending its bullets around corners.

Stone let his gaze drift to the man in the suit at the northwest corner of the park. The fellow was still examining the statue, an act that normally would take at most a minute or so. And why come here at this hour to do so anyway? Stone eyed the soft-sided briefcase the man carried. Because of the distance between them Stone could not see it clearly, but it appeared bulky enough to contain a small bomb. However, the distance between the bomber and the prime minister essentially doomed any assassination attempt.

The motorcade continued down West Executive Avenue toward Pennsylvania. Sirens and guards galore for what amounted to a half-block-long slow jog on armored wheels. They would hang a left on Pennsylvania and pull in front of the curb next to the famous long green awning that capped the main entrance to Blair House.

Stone spotted movement to the right of him from across the park. The jogger was on the go once more. Stone couldn't be sure, but he thought the fat man was looking in the direction of the suit.

Stone's attention next shifted to the woman. She had risen too, slipped the bag over her shoulder and set off to the north side of the park toward St. John's Church. She was tall, Stone noted, and her clothes hung well on her long frame. He gauged her age at closer to thirty than forty, though he'd never gotten a clear look at her face because of the poor light, the distance and the many trees in between them.

His gaze swiveled again. On the other side of the park the suit was finally moving, heading northwest toward the Decatur House Museum. Stone looked behind him. The ganger was watching him now, not moving at all. Stone thought he saw the man's index finger twitch as though on a trigger pull.

The motorcade made the turn onto Pennsylvania and stopped in front of Blair House. The door to the lead stretch popped open. These types of limo exits tended to happen fast for obvious reasons. You only remained exposed to a possible bullet fired at long or short range for as brief a time as possible. Tonight, though, swiftness did not happen.

The stocky and elegantly dressed prime minister got out slowly and, with the assistance of two aides, gingerly limped up the steps under the awning that had covered the heads of many world leaders. A bandage was wound thickly around the man's left ankle. As he made his entrance into the building a wall of eyes looked outward to every crevice for threats. There were some British security personnel in the mix. However, the heavy lifting on this protection detail was being handled—as it always was for visiting heads of state—by the U.S. Secret Service.

Because of where Blair House was situated, Stone could not see the prime minister exit the limo on his injured limb. His focus remained on the park. The jogger was walking toward the center of the grass. Stone's gaze shifted. The woman was nearly clear of the park. The suit was already on the sidewalk that fronted H Street.

Five more seconds passed. Then the first shot hit.

The impact of lead with the ground sent up a little geyser of dirt and grass four feet to the left of Stone. That was followed by more rounds, the slugs digging into the grass, ripping up flowerbeds, smacking against statues.

As the gunfire continued everything slowed down for Stone. His gaze rotated through the field of fire as he dropped flat to the ground. The suit and the woman were gone from his line of vision. Ganger was still behind him, but on his belly too. The poor jogger, however, was running for his life. And then he simply disappeared from Stone's view. Vanished.

The firing stopped. Seconds of silence. Stone slowly rose. As he did so, he didn't tense, he relaxed. Whether this saved his life or not was anyone's guess.

The bomb detonated. The center of Lafayette Park was engulfed in smoke and flying debris. The enormously heavy Jackson statue toppled over, its Tennessee marble base cracked in half. Its reign of more than a hundred and fifty years in the park was over.

The concussive force of the explosion lifted Stone off his feet and threw him against something hard. The blow to his head made him dizzy, nauseous. For a fleeting instant he sensed debris being blown all around him. His lungs sucked in smoke, dirt and the sickening smell of the bomb residue.

As the sound of the explosion subsided it was replaced by screams, sirens, the screech of tire rubber on asphalt and more screams. But Oliver Stone never heard or witnessed any of this. He was lying facedown on the ground, his eyes closed.

CHAPTER

5

"OLIVER?"

Stone smelled the antiseptic and the latex and knew he was in a hospital. Which was far better than being dead in a morgue.

His eyelids fluttered open. He saw her face. "Annabelle?"

Annabelle Conroy, unofficial member of the Camel Club and its only known con artist, clutched his hand. She was lean and a couple inches shy of six feet with long reddish hair.

"You have to stop getting blown up," she said.

Her tone was flippant, her look was not. She used her free hand to sweep the hair out of her face and Stone could see her eyes were puffy. Annabelle did not cry easily, but she had shed tears over him.

He touched his head where the bandage was. "Not cracked, is it?"

Annabelle said, "No. Mild concussion."

As Stone looked around he noted that the room was fairly bursting with bodies. There was NFL-sized Reuben Rhodes on the other side of the bed, with diminutive librarian Caleb Shaw next to him. The tall Secret Service agent Alex Ford was on Annabelle's right and looking equally concerned. Behind them Stone saw Harry Finn.

Finn said, "When I heard about the bomb going off at the park, I knew you had to be in the middle of it somehow."

Stone slowly sat up. "So what happened?"

Alex answered. "They're still trying to figure it out. Gunfire and then the explosion."

"Anyone else hurt? British PM?"

"In Blair before the explosion. No one was shot."

"With all the gunfire it's remarkable no one was hit."

"More like a miracle."

"No theories?" Stone asked, looking at Alex.

"Not yet. The park is a mess. Locked down tight as I've ever seen it."

"But the PM?"

Alex nodded. "Preliminarily, he was the target."

"But a pretty poor attempt, then," said Reuben. "Since the explosion and gunfire happened at a park he wasn't in."

Stone eyed Alex again. "Rebuttal to that?" he asked slowly. With each word he spoke his head hurt even worse. Thirty years ago he could have shrugged this off and kept moving forward. Not now.

"Like I said, it's early yet. But I'll admit that's a major puzzler. Not a good day for the PM all around."

"What do you mean?" asked Stone.

"He twisted his ankle. Moving pretty slow."

"You know this firsthand?"

"He took a tumble on some interior steps at the White House before the dinner started. Little embarrassing for the guy. Fortunately, media cameras don't roll inside that part of the building."

Annabelle asked, "What were you doing at the park last night? I thought you were still in Divine, Virginia, with Abby."

Stone looked out the window and saw that it was morning. "I came back," he said simply. "And Abby stayed there."

"Oh," said Annabelle in a disappointed tone, but her look was actually one of relief.

He turned back to Alex. "There were four people in the park last night besides me. What happened to them?"

Alex looked around the room before clearing his throat. "Unclear."

"Unclear as in you don't know or you can't tell us?" said Stone.

Annabelle gave the Secret Service agent a fierce look. "Oliver was almost killed, Alex."

Alex sighed. He had never mastered the art of balancing professional secrecy with the Camel Club's constant demands for intelligence on mostly classified matters. "They're reviewing the video feeds and debriefing the human eyeballs on the park last night. They're trying to put the picture together."

"And the four other people in the park?" Stone persisted quietly.

"Four people?"

"Three men and one woman."

"I don't know anything about them," replied Alex.

"Where exactly did the explosion happen? I couldn't really tell."

"Roughly middle of the park. Near the Jackson statue, or what's left of it. Pieces of it along with the fence and the cannon were blown all over the park."

"So there was significant damage?" asked Stone.

"All parts of the park were affected, but the major bomb damage was in a fifty-foot radius. Looks like a war zone inside that ring. Whatever it was, that bomb packed a wallop."

"There was an overweight man in a jogging suit in that vicinity when the shots started," Stone noted. He frowned and tried to remember. "I was watching him. He was running for his life from the bullets, and then he just vanished. But that would have put him right at the epicenter of the blast."

They all looked at Alex, who seemed uncomfortable.

"Alex?" said Annabelle again in a scolding tone.

"Okay, it looks like the guy fell in a hole where they were installing a new tree. The explosion happened at or near that spot. But nothing has been confirmed."

"Do we know who he was?" asked Caleb.

"Not yet."

"Origin of the bomb?"

"Unknown as yet."

"Source of the shots?" Reuben asked.

"Nothing that I know about."

"I hit something," said Stone. "As I was falling. There was a man watching me."

"Could be," said Alex warily.

"The nurse told me they dug a tooth out of your head, Oliver," said Annabelle.

"A tooth? Then I hit the man when the explosion happened?"

Annabelle nodded. "Looks to be. If so, he's missing an incisor."

"Have you seen any of the video surveillance, Alex?" asked Stone.

"No. I'm technically not part of the investigation, which is why I don't have a lot of answers. I'm in protection detail, which means my butt, along with a bunch of others, is in the professional wringer right now."

"Secret Service taking its lumps?" said Reuben.

"Yeah. This is a little more serious than party crashers."

"I was surprised there were so many in the park last night," said Stone. "And had read about the dinner, but the papers said the PM was staying at the British embassy as he usually does. What happened there?"

"Late change of plan. He and the president had planned an early working session the next morning. Far easier logistics getting the PM from Blair to the White House." Alex added, "But it wasn't made public. And yet you still knew he was going to Blair last night?"

Stone nodded.

"How?"

"I passed the motorcade on the way to the park.

It only had one motorcycle officer in the lead, which meant they weren't going a great distance and thus traffic control wasn't critical. The D.C. police chief isn't going to waste valuable resources if she doesn't have to. And the defensive cone was in place around Blair. As many guns as they had there meant it was a top-level dignitary. The PM was the only one who fit that bill."

"Why were *you* at the park at that hour?" Annabelle asked Stone.

"Reminiscing," he said casually before turning back to Alex. "So why so lax about security last night?"

"It wasn't lax. And it *is* a public park," countered Alex.

"Not when safety is an issue. I know that better than anyone," rejoined Stone.

"I just do what I'm told, Oliver."

"All right." Stone looked around. "Can I leave?"

"Yes, you can," said a voice. "With us."

They all turned to look at the two suits standing in the doorway. One was in his fifties, stocky and big-boned with broad shoulders and a gun hump under his suit. The other was in his thirties and lean, under six feet and with a Marine Corps haircut. He was similarly armed.

"Right now," added the older man.

CHAPTER

6

"Not here," Stone muttered to himself as the black Town Car pulled into the campus-style setting of the National Intelligence Center, or NIC, in northern Virginia. They passed the lush taxpayer-funded landscaping and headed to the main low-level building that housed a big chunk of America's intelligence operations.

One wall of the entrance lobby was lined with photos of terrorist attacks perpetrated against the United States. A plaque at the end of this line of devastating images read "Never Again."

The other wall held the official photos of the men who'd held the position of intelligence czar at this agency. They were few in number, as NIC had only been created after 9/11. The most prominent former director had been Carter Gray, a public servant with many high-ranking government positions to his credit. Gray's portly face stared out at the men as Stone and his escorts walked by.

Decades ago Stone had worked for the man, when Stone was known under his real name, John Carr. As his country's most efficient assassin, Carr had used every ounce of courage and cleverness he possessed to serve his country. His reward for that had been the destruction of all the people he had ever cared about carried out by the very same folks he'd so faithfully served. That was one reason Stone had ended Gray's life. And that reason alone would have been enough.

Burn in hell, Carter, thought Stone as the door closed behind him.

And I'll see you when I get there.

Five minutes later Stone was seated at a small wooden table inside a windowless room. He looked around the confines of the space even as he slowed his breathing and tried not to think about his pounding head. An interrogation room clearly.

And that's what's about to happen to me.

The room suddenly went dark and an image appeared on the wall opposite, projected there by equipment housed discreetly in the ceiling.

It was a man sitting in a cushy chair behind a polished desk. From the view Stone had over the man's shoulder it was clear he was on a jet. He was fifty and tanned with pointy hair cut nearly to his scalp and a pair of energetic green eyes.

Before the man could speak, Stone said, "I don't warrant a face-to-face?"

A smile edged across the fellow's face. "Afraid not, but you do get *me*."

Me was the new director of NIC, Riley Weaver. He'd taken over for the deceased Carter Gray. Those were big shoes to fill, and the word in government circles was that Weaver was slowly but surely finding his way. Whether or not that was a good thing for the country was as yet unknown.

At the sound of Weaver's voice, the door to the room opened and two other men filed in and leaned against the wall behind Stone. Stone never liked having armed men behind him, but there was nothing he could do about that right now. He was the visiting team and the home squad made the rules.

"Debrief," ordered Weaver, looking at Stone.

"Why?" replied Stone.

The smile slipped off Weaver's face. "Because I asked, politely."

"Do I work for you? I don't remember getting that memo."

"Just exercise your civic duty."

Stone said nothing.

Weaver finally broke the silence. He leaned forward and said, "I understand you have fair winds and following seas at your back."

Weaver, Stone now recalled, had been a Marine. Marines were part of the navy, and his nautical reference showed that he was tighter in the loop than Stone had expected. The president of the United States represented Stone's "fair winds and following seas," which in nautical parlance meant very favorable navigating conditions. But did Weaver know about his meeting with the president? About his being shipped off to Mexico to deal with the Russians? If not, Stone had no intention of enlightening him.

"Civic duty," said Stone. "Just so we understand each other. It goes both ways."

Weaver sat back. His features showed that while he might have underestimated Stone initially, that miscalculation had been quickly remedied. "Agreed."

Stone succinctly gave his account of the attack in the park.

When he was done Weaver said, "All right. Now look left and observe closely."

CHAPTER

7

A MOMENT LATER STONE WAS WATCHING the prior night's video feed from Lafayette Park. They had slowed down the frame speed so that Stone could view every detail closely and unhurriedly. As the gunfire commenced, Stone watched as people started running in all directions. Perimeter security took defensive positions and looked for the source of the shots. The jogger started to run in the feeble way of a man unaccustomed to exercise. His strides were really short, increasingly weakened hops. His path carried him through the yellow tape and a few moments later he fell or he might've jumped into the hole where the big maple was being planted.

Now Stone could make sense of what he had seen, namely the man seemingly vanishing into thin air. It was like a foxhole, thought Stone. To get away from the bullets.

Then the explosion happened. Stone saw himself lifted off his feet and slammed into the ganger. They both went down. The tooth in his head. He rubbed the spot.

A second later, the cameras went to static. The concussive force of the blast must have jammed the signal somehow. The wall became blank again.

Weaver said, "Observations?"

"Run it again," Stone requested.

He watched the feed twice more.

Stone thought about what he'd just seen. The jogger had tumbled into the open hole around the maple and the explosion had happened seconds later.

"So what was the source of the detonation? The jogger?"

"Not sure yet. It may have been something in that hole."

Stone looked skeptical. "In the hole? No gas lines under the park?"

"None."

"Then you know what you're suggesting? A bomb planted in Lafayette Park?"

Weaver's expression grew even darker. "The implications of that are downright paralyzing, but we can't discount the possibility."

"So you're saying maybe the guy jumped into

the hole to avoid the bullets and gets blown up instead by a bomb previously placed there?"

"If so, it's really bad luck for him. He gets away from the bullets and still dies."

"Who's on the scene?"

"ATF and the FBI as we speak."

Stone could understand that. The ATF handled all investigations involving explosives until it was determined that the act was one of international terrorism. Then the FBI would take over. However, Stone assumed a bomb going off across from the White House would be classified de facto as a foreign terrorist act. That meant the Bureau would take the lead. It probably already had.

Stone asked, "Okay, let's pass over the explosion for now. Do we know the source of the shots? On the video they appeared to be coming from the northern end of the park. From the direction of H Street or perhaps past that."

"That's the prelim conclusion at least, yeah."

"So running north-south. There were no muzzle flashes on the video," Stone pointed out. "That must mean they were hidden from the camera's eyes."

"Behind trees," offered Weaver. "Lot of them at the northern end of the park. But the surveillance cameras are positioned mainly for ground-level observation. So in any event they might not have picked up the flashes if the shooters were really high up."

"Well, the shots had to come from elevated angles," Stone opined.

"How do you figure?" asked Riley in a way that made Stone believe the man already knew the answer but was simply testing him. Stone decided to play along, for now.

"If they were fired from behind the trees at street level they most likely would have carried past the park and across Pennsylvania Avenue to the White House."

"How do you know they didn't?"

"Because you would have already told me if they had or I would have heard about more casualties. There are a lot of people on the White House side. Vehicles lining Pennsylvania Avenue. Sentries doing perimeter patrols. It's inconceivable that someone would not have been hit. So high ground to low. Fits with my observations. From what I could see, the slugs were all plowing into the dirt. And if they passed through tree canopies first, they had to be fired from at or above that line. And a lot of those trees are pretty tall with thick canopies." Stone added, "Anyone on the northern end of the park see anything helpful?"

"There was security. Park Police, couple of

uniformed Secret Service agents, bomb-sniffing canine. They're still being debriefed, but preliminarily they didn't have much on the source."

Stone nodded. "And why wasn't the park cleared last night?"

Weaver's expression showed his displeasure with this query. "I really just want your observations from watching that video."

"I like to have a fuller understanding of what's going on before I extend myself."

Weaver's gaze lowered to a file on his desk. "John Carr?"

Stone remained silent, staring at the digital image of the man on the wall.

"John Carr," Weaver said again. "Your file is so classified even I still haven't seen all of it."

"Sometimes even a government can be refreshingly discreet," noted Stone. "But we were talking about the origins of the shots and the park security, or rather lack thereof."

"Origin of the shots is still being investigated. The park security is really Secret Service jurisdiction and I haven't received a briefing from them."

"Of course you have," countered Stone.

Weaver looked intrigued. "What makes you say that?"

"Security of the president trumps all other

things, which gives the Secret Service interagency heft it might not otherwise have. What looked to be automatic gunfire and an explosion happened right across from the White House over fifteen hours ago. You provide the president with his daily national security briefing at seven every morning. If you haven't talked to the Secret Service yet, then you couldn't have briefed the president on the matter this morning. And if you didn't brief the president this morning about an attack that happened in his front yard, you would no longer be employed as NIC director."

A twitch at Weaver's right eye showed that this conversation was not going according to plan. The two men leaning against the wall moved uneasily.

Weaver said, "The Service said that there were thoughts of clearing the park, but plans changed. Since the PM was going directly to Blair, they felt the park would not be a valid threat point. In sum, they thought they had it covered. Does that answer your question?"

"Yes, but it prompts another one."

Weaver waited expectantly.

"Exactly what plans changed?"

In response Stone received a long Marine stare. "Just give me the rest of your observations if you have any."

Stone looked at the man, reading the intent behind the blunt words. He could play this any number of ways. Sometimes you pushed, sometimes you didn't.

He said, "Too many people in the park doing things they shouldn't have been doing at that hour."

Weaver settled back in his comfy chair. "Go on."

"I've spent a lot of time in Lafayette. Eleven o'clock at night usually the only people there are security. Last night there were four people who shouldn't have been there. The ganger, the guy in the suit, the lady on the bench and the jogger."

"They all could have been there legitimately," Weaver pointed out. "It was a warm evening. And it is a park."

Stone shook his head. "Lafayette Park is not a preferred destination to sit or kill time at night. And the Service doesn't like people lingering there. They'll tell you the same thing."

"They actually have already," volunteered Weaver. "So what are you thinking?"

"Ganger had a gun. I could easily see it without the benefit of optics, so the countersnipers should have already seen it and relayed that to ground forces. Guy should have been nailed as soon as he set foot into the red zone. But he wasn't."

Weaver nodded. "Okay, keep going."

"Lady was dressed nicely. Maybe an office dweller. She had a bag. But sitting on a bench at that hour makes no sense. She talks on her phone, then gets up about the time the motorcade pulls in. Fortuitous for her since she missed the gunfire."

"Keep going," encouraged Weaver.

"The suit was checking out a statue and took a long time to do it. Then he made his move toward Decatur House at the same time as the woman was leaving the park. When the shooting started they were both out of my line of sight. After that I picked up on the jogger, who was running toward the Jackson statue. He seemed to simply vanish, but now I know he actually jumped in the hole to avoid the bullets."

Weaver said, "And got blown up for his troubles."

"That doesn't mean that one or more of the other people in the park last night were also not involved."

Weaver shook his head. "I believe that's a stretch. You got raking automatic fire in the park and then a bomb that had already been planted there and gets triggered probably accidentally by the poor sucker trying to duck the bullets. I think the guy did us a favor. Ferreted out a bomb before it could have done real damage. Now we have to figure out who, how and why on the gunfire and the bomb." Weaver studied him. "You have anything you'd care to add to the mix? Because quite frankly, I'm disappointed in the little you've had to tell me. I thought you were hot stuff and you've really given me not much I hadn't figured out on my own."

"I didn't think it was my job to do your job. But here's another observation for free." Stone added, "The ganger was really a cop, right?"

On that, the screen went immediately to black.

CHAPTER

8

WITHOUT ANY INSTRUCTIONS FROM HIM the car dropped Stone off at Mt. Zion Cemetery. This was intentional, Stone knew. It was as if to say, "We know exactly where you live. We can come for you anytime we want."

Stone walked past the wrought-iron gates that enclosed the cemetery and into the small caretaker's cottage that was his home. The furnishings were spartan and secondhand and fit Stone's personality and limited resources perfectly. There was one large room divided between a small kitchen and a sitting area. Against one wall was a large shelf of books on esoteric subjects in multiple languages that he'd collected over decades. In front of that was Stone's scarred wooden desk that had come with the cottage. A few threadbare chairs sat in front of a blackened brick fireplace. In an alcove behind a tattered curtain was the army cot he slept on. That and a tiny bathroom formed the extent of the premises.

Stone took three Advil, washed them down with a glass of water and sat down in the chair behind his desk while he rubbed his head. Whether he was still leaving for Mexico or not he didn't know. But for now at least he would proceed on the assumption that he was staying until the men came for him.

He held up four fingers on his right hand and stared at them.

"Four people," he said to himself. Although perhaps now only three since the video had made clear the jogger was no longer among the living. Yet they still didn't know who he was or why he was there. So Stone kept the fourth finger up.

"So was the jogger in the classic wrong place, wrong time or was he involved?" he asked himself. "And where are the suit and the woman? And are they connected?"

And there was the ganger who was probably a cop. Stone had realized that was the only reason the man would have come to Lafayette with a gun. He had a badge and authorization to be there armed. The screen going black on him back at NIC was all the affirmation Stone needed. Riley Weaver didn't play any nicer with people than Carter Gray had.

What was bothering Stone was that *both* the

suit and the woman had left just before the gunfire began. Coincidence? Both just as lucky as the jogger was unlucky?

He closed his eyes and pushed his mind to reach back to the night before. His temples were still throbbing and his scalp still burned from having a pointy tooth rammed into it, but slowly the pictures and sounds returned.

"MP-5s or possibly TEC-9s," he said out loud. In reality there could be lots of possibilities for the hardware. "Set on full auto. Probably thirty-round magazines that could be configured for fifty or more. So how many shots had been fired? He had not been able to count every round, of course, but he could make an estimate from the time expired. Full auto, assume thirty-round mags, two to three seconds to empty the ammo box. Firing lasted about three to four times that, or twelve to fifteen seconds. Hundred rounds or so. But only if there was only one weapon being fired. If more than one, they were talking *hundreds* of rounds. A lot of firepower. Since most of the slugs had apparently ended up in the dirt, the FBI would be able to get a fairly precise number. But that didn't answer the far more important question. How exactly had anyone gotten that close to deliver that level of attack?

Stone rose and looked out the window and

assembled in his mind the topography of the area around the park. To the north and west along H Street were the United States Chamber of Commerce building and the venerable Hay-Adams Hotel. To the northeast was St. John's Church. Behind all these locations were federal government and office buildings. He recalled that the Hay-Adams had a rooftop garden area. And it was a taller building than the church. And height was important here to explain the trajectory of the bullets.

He moved on to the next question. *Why did they take me to NIC? Just for my observations? There were other people there who could have told them the same things I did. There had to be another reason. Fair winds and following seas?*

Stone looked out the window and saw the black Town Car pull up to the gates. As the occupants climbed out Stone eyed the men. FBI, he thought. Bureau agents tended to spend a little more on their clothes. Stone doubted that they were here to escort him to a plane destined for Mexico. The president would not have involved the FBI in something like that. Too many legal roadblocks. The Bureau tended to follow the letter of the law. And the FBI director had the clout to tell the president no. So perhaps the equation had changed once more.

And maybe this time in my favor.

As the four people drew closer, Stone could see that his initial observation was correct. He had just spied an FBI Academy ring on one of the men's fingers. There was also a woman with them, and Stone didn't think she was FBI. Assessing every feature from her teeth to her facial structure to her walk, she was a Brit, he concluded. MI6 most likely. Tasked for external intelligence, security and investigations.

This certainly made sense if the British PM was the target. She was either in country traveling with him, stationed here, or she had taken a day flight over, leaving at around two and getting in at about the same time. By the looks of it Stone opted for the latter.

And it was very clear why they were here. The bullets were one thing, but that bomb had been meant to blow somebody up and Stone didn't think it was an overweight jogger. And they thought Stone could somehow help them find the truth.

Ironic, he thought. *The truth.*

He kept watching them as they approached his cottage.

CHAPTER

9

THE WOMAN WAS INDEED WITH MI6. Her name was Mary Chapman. Up close she turned out to be in her mid-thirties, about five-eight, with shoulder-length dirty blonde hair held back with a clasp. Her eyes were intense and shining. She had a compact jaw, thin lips and a slender, wiry build, though her bare calves were muscled. Her fingers were long and her grip was a vise. In Stone's opinion the Brit's features were classically attractive without being overwhelming. Chapman's eyes were deeply green and active. She would never be described as "cute," thought Stone. Confident, intimidating even, but never cute.

"How was the flight across the pond? Little jet-lagged?" Stone said after everyone had been introduced and they'd taken up seats in front of the empty fireplace.

Chapman gazed at Stone and then made a show of smoothing out a wrinkle on her suit jacket. "No bloody beds in coach, even on dear old British Air." Within her accent and words Stone detected a sense of humility along with a potential for broad humor.

"You must be highly thought of for them to fly you nearly three thousand miles here. MI6 has a permanent footprint in D.C., doesn't it?"

Chapman eyed the shabby interior of the cottage before settling her eyes back on Stone's threadbare clothes. "And I thought the Yanks paid their people better."

One of the FBI agents cleared his throat. "Agent Chapman is here to assist the Bureau with its investigation."

Stone turned his attention to the man. He was beefy though strongly built. A desk jockey, Stone assumed, by the size of his waist and perspiring forehead. He was clearly only the messenger and note taker. He wouldn't be doing any of the heavy lifting on this.

"I've already been to NIC. They beat you to it. They came to the hospital. You were slower, if classier."

Beefy looked chagrined by this but plunged on. "And was the meeting helpful?"

"I thought you were into cooperation and sharing these days."

Beefy gazed stonily back at him.

Stone said, "They weren't particularly forthcoming. I'm hoping you can do better."

Chapman crossed her legs and said, "Sorry if I seem a bit nitpicky, but I didn't see your credentials."

Stone replied in a pleasant tone, "I don't have any to show you."

She looked at Beefy quizzically.

He said stiffly, "A formality that needn't interrupt the progress of the investigation."

Chapman hiked her eyebrows at this but remained silent.

"Good," said Stone. He sat back in his desk chair and his features grew serious. "The park." He gave them a minute-by-minute account of what had happened. When he was finished he added, "There are three people out there unaccounted for." He gazed at Beefy. "And do we know the name of the unfortunate jogger?"

"There were human remains found. Everywhere," Beefy added, his mouth curled up with distaste.

"Identifiable?"

"It won't be an easy one, but it's also not

insurmountable. Clearly DNA at this point. If he's on a database somewhere we'll get a hit. We've posted his picture from the video feed on our Web sites and given it to the media to splash around. Someone will hopefully come forward or at the very least report him missing."

"The other three?"

"With the man in the suit and the woman we're running the video feed taken at the park through facial recognition databases, although the man never looked in the direction of the surveillance cameras. No hits as of four minutes ago. We've also placed the images with the media, asking for the public's help."

"Do you see them as perhaps connected to this?" asked Stone.

"Too early to tell. Maybe they were just lucky they left the park when they did."

"And the ganger? Was he a cop?"

"Did NIC tell you he was?"

"Not in so many words. But they didn't deny it either."

"I won't deny it either, then."

Stone said, "His tooth was sticking in my head until the doctors removed it. You can get a dental match on that, and possibly a DNA hit." He held up his sleeve. "And this is his blood. Do you have a kit in the trunk of the Bucar? You can swab for it right now."

"That won't be necessary," said Chapman.

Stone turned to her. "And why is that?"

"Because the tooth belongs to one of our security people who was patrolling the park. The doctors didn't return it to you, did they? See, my man would actually like it back."

"And why was your man in the park last night?"

"Because before he turned his ankle after tripping on some steps at the White House, my prime minister was scheduled to walk across Lafayette Park on his way back to Blair House, at precisely two minutes past eleven. Lucky for him he didn't, since he would have had his damn head blown off."

CHAPTER

10

AFTER THE FBI AGENTS and MI6 Chapman left, Stone puttered in the cemetery for a half hour, righting tombstones toppled by a recent heavy rain and cleaning debris caused by the same storm. This manual labor allowed him to think clearly. And he had a lot that was puzzling him and no answers. As he was bagging some sticks and small branches, he stiffened and slowly turned around.

"I'm impressed."

He turned to see Mary Chapman come out from behind a bush. "I never moved. What, you have eyes in the back of your head?"

"Sometimes." Stone tied up the bag and deposited it next to a wooden storage shed. "When I need to."

Chapman walked over to him. "This is amazing cover for an agent. A cemetery worker."

"Caretaker, actually. This cemetery isn't used any longer. It's a historical site."

She stopped, lifted one leg and rubbed some dirt off her plain black low-heeled pump. "I see. And do you enjoy taking care of the dead?"

"I do."

"Why?"

"They never argue with me." He headed back to the cottage. She followed. They sat on the front porch. A minute of silence passed as they listened to the chirps of birds mingled with the sounds of passing cars. Stone stared straight ahead. Chapman's gaze continued to flick at him like an erratic beam of light.

"So Oliver Stone?" she said at last, with mirth in her eyes. "I've enjoyed several of your movies. Are you here scouting another film?"

"Why did you come back?" he asked, finally turning to her.

She rose and surprised him by saying, "Got time for a spot of coffee? I'll buy."

She had a car, so they drove to lower Georgetown and found a parking spot on the street, an almost unheard-of event in the congested area.

Stone told her so.

"Right," she said, clearly unimpressed by this. "Try parking in London."

They carried their coffees and sat outside at a small table. Chapman took off her pumps, hiked her skirt to mid-thigh, put her feet up on an empty chair, leaned back, closed her eyes and let the sun fall fully on her pale face and bare legs. "England rarely has sun this strong," she explained. "And when it does it's usually immediately interrupted by clouds and then rain. Makes a lot of us seriously suicidal. Particularly if it rains in bloody August and you have no holiday abroad planned."

"I know."

She opened her eyes. "Do you now?"

"I lived in London for two years. It was a long time ago," he added.

"Business?"

"You could say that, yes."

"John Carr?"

Stone drank his coffee, said nothing.

She sipped her coffee and let the silence linger.

"John Carr?" she said again.

"I heard you the first time," he said politely, glancing sideways at her.

She smiled. "Would you like to know where *I* heard that name for the first time?"

Stone didn't answer, but his silence apparently constituted enough of an assent for her to continue.

"James McElroy. He's a good bit older than you are." She ran her eye over his tall, spare frame. "And not in nearly as good shape."

Stone again said nothing.

"He's a legend in British intelligence circles. Ran MI6 for decades. But I believe you know all that. Now he has some special title, I'm not really sure what it is. But he does what he wants. And bloody good for the country too, I can tell you that."

"Is he well?"

"Yes. Apparently somewhat due to you. Iran, 1977? Six fanatics sent to place his head on the sharp end of a spear? Six *dead* men after you finished with them. He said he didn't even have time to pull his weapon to help you. Then you were gone, just like that. Never had a chance to properly thank you."

"I didn't require any thanks. He was our ally. It was my job."

"Well, irrespective, he said that for decades he wanted to buy you a pint for saving his arse, but you never turned up again. He still wants to, as a matter of fact."

"Again, not necessary."

Chapman stretched, put her feet back on the pavement, edged her skirt down and slipped her pumps back on. "By sheer coincidence he's here in town."

"Is that why you came back?"

"Yes and no."

He stared at her expectantly.

"Yes, in that I knew he would want to see you. No in that I had my own reasons."

"Which are?"

She leaned forward and Stone saw the Walther PPK pistol hanging from her black leather shoulder holster revealed through the gap between her jacket and shirt.

He inclined his head at the pistol. "Tough trigger pull, isn't it?"

"You get used to it." She paused, swirling her remaining coffee with a wooden stirrer. "Let's face it, this has been a cock-up from start to finish. The Americans have so many agencies I can't get a straight answer from any of them. My boss feels the same way. However, America is our chief ally and we intend to do nothing to disrupt that relationship, of course. But it was our PM put at risk and we have an obligation to see it through."

"And you've come to me? Why?"

"James McElroy trusts you. Ergo, I trust you. And you *were* there last night. That makes you valuable."

"Maybe. But Iran was a long time ago, Agent Chapman."

"Some things don't change. McElroy said you were one of them."

"That's assuming that I really am John Carr."

"Oh, you are, I have no doubt of that."

"How can you be so sure?"

"When I was here earlier I lifted a set of your prints from a glass in your loo when I went to take a pee. With my boss's weight behind me, I was able to get a priority search on NIC's database. Still, it took passing through eight levels of security, a few burned-out computers and two high-level authorizations before the hit came back." She hiked her eyebrows. "John Carr. Of the CIA's late and lamented Triple Six Division."

"Which officially never existed," he said quietly.

"No matter to me. I was just a nipper when it pulled its last trigger, official or not." She stood. "Ready to go see the man whose life you saved? He really does want to buy you that pint, *Mr. Carr.*"

CHAPTER

11

JAMES MCELROY WAS SITTING in his suite at the Willard Hotel when Stone and Chapman were ushered in. The Brit spymaster was now seventy-four years old, gray and bowed. His substantial belly poked through the front of his jacket. When he rose from the chair, his arthritic knees quivered a bit, yet the man's roaming and intelligent eyes clearly showed that while age had decimated him physically, his mental agility remained completely intact. Though he was once over six-two, gravity and infirmity had shaved a couple of inches from his frame. His hair was thinning and slicked back, revealing lines of pink flesh underneath. Flecks of dandruff clung to the shoulders of his blue jacket.

When he saw Stone, his eyes lit up. "You haven't changed a jot," said McElroy. "Except your hair is white." He lightly smacked Stone's flat, hard belly before extending his hand and then gripping Stone in a bear hug. "And I'm fat and you're not."

When they separated, McElroy waved them both into chairs. "How the hell have you been, John?"

"I've *been*," said Stone simply.

The Brit nodded in understanding, his expression growing somber. "Yes, I actually have some knowledge of what you mean by that. Events became particularly trying for you."

"One way to describe it."

McElroy's eyes narrowed. "I heard about…you know. And I'm sorry."

"More than I got from my own side. But thank you."

Chapman looked at Stone and McElroy and said, "Care to share, sir?"

"No," said Stone. "He wouldn't."

McElroy didn't take his gaze off Stone but said to her, "John and I are of a generation that will carry our professional secrets to the grave. Understood?"

"Yes sir," she replied quickly.

"John, will you join me for a drink?"

"Little early for me."

"But it's already quite late in London, so let's pretend, shall we? Special occasion and all? Two old friends."

An attendant brought drinks for all three. Stone

had a beer, Chapman a Beefeater martini and McElroy a slender finger of scotch. He looked at Stone over the rim of his glass. "Gallstones. Bloody things driving me mad. But it's said a small measure of good scotch can kill them dead. At least I believe I heard that somewhere. In this case a rumor will suffice." He lifted his glass. "Cheers."

They all drank and McElroy dabbed his mouth with his pocket kerchief.

"The PM?" prompted Stone, and Chapman drew a little straighter in her chair as she bit into a fat olive from her drink.

McElroy looked pained, rubbed his side and nodded in a perfunctory manner. "Yes, the PM. Solid chap. I actually voted for him. Between you and me he's a bit dodgy on some things, but what politician isn't?"

"Dodgy enough to be blown up?" asked Stone.

"Don't think so, no. Not homegrown, in other words."

"Lot of enemies out there." Stone glanced at Chapman. "Our closest ally. It's put a bull's-eye on your little island."

"Quite so, yes. But we soldier on, don't we?"

"Who knew he'd be walking across the park?"

"Limited circle," answered Chapman as McElroy

continued to rub his side while finishing his scotch. "They're all being checked out as we speak."

McElroy looked uninterested in this detail, and Stone was quick to pick up on that. "Another theory?"

McElroy sniffed. "I'm not sure it actually rises to the level of a theory just yet, John."

"I go by Oliver now."

He looked chagrined. "Of course you do. I read the briefing papers. Afraid my memory's just not what it was. Well, Oliver, it's just a thought."

"Which is?"

Just as Stone had done earlier, McElroy held up four fingers of his right hand. "A quartet of people in the park last night." He lowered one finger. "Our man was the one whose tooth you were briefly in possession of."

"Agent Chapman told me he was one of yours and that he was patrolling the park. But why, if the PM wouldn't be there?"

"No elaborate explanation. He'd been assigned to patrol the park when the old walk-through plan was still in place. When the PM turned his ankle, we simply left him there to provide a wider berth of security." McElroy held the three fingers up even higher. "But the bloody thing is, John—excuse me,

Oliver—the bloody thing is my counterparts over here can tell me absolutely nothing about the other three."

"I saw the video feed. One of them is dead."

"Not particularly helpful. Then there's the man and the woman. Perhaps they were just there by coincidence. But perhaps not. In either case, I need to know for certain."

"Why were there any people in the park last night? "I'm there at all hours, and the security detail knows me. But late at night the park doesn't typically have visitors."

"Good question. Happened to have asked it myself. Have you found an answer? Because I haven't."

"No, at least not a satisfactory one. No immediate threats against the PM?"

"Nothing particularly credible."

"What line will you be taking, then?"

"Remove him from the threat." McElroy checked his watch. "The PM should be wheels down at Heathrow in twenty minutes, in fact."

"And after that?"

McElroy noticed a fleck of dandruff on his shoulder and brushed it away like he might an unappealing conclusion. "We can't leave it, Oliver.

It happened on American soil, so our reach is limited, but we really can't leave it. Awful sort of precedent if we do. Can't have folks taking potshots at our PM without any consequences."

"If he was the target."

"Have to assume he was until facts prove otherwise."

Stone looked over at Chapman and then back at his old acquaintance. "Agent Chapman seems well capable."

"Yes, she is, otherwise she wouldn't be here. But I believe she will be infinitely more capable with you at her side."

Stone was already shaking his head. "My plate is full."

"Yes, your little trip to NIC. I understand Riley Weaver is marking his territory at an extraordinary clip over there. He'll make mistakes, of course, and let's just hope not too many people die when he does. And the FBI also wants a piece of you, I understand."

"Popular gent," added Chapman.

McElroy and Stone exchanged a knowing gaze. McElroy said, "I'm not sure 'popular' would be my first choice as a description. Short leash, Oliver?"

"Could be."

Stone gave the older man a lengthy gaze.

I wonder if he knows about my meeting with the president, about me going back in?

Stone had no reason to think that McElroy wished him any ill will, but in this business simply saving someone's life did not ensure a permanent allegiance. And Stone was also quite certain that the PM and hence James McElroy would sacrifice him if requested to do so by the Americans.

And then something else occurred to Stone. *That's why I'm here. McElroy was told to deliver the message directly to me from the president.*

He decided to verify this speculation. "I already have an assignment. I'm supposed to leave tomorrow, in fact."

"Yes. Well, plans are fluid aren't they? One has to account for recent events."

"Does one?"

"A new arrangement is possible because of what happened in the park," McElroy said bluntly.

"Why? Simply because I was there?"

"Partly. Plus, in the circles in question, I'm not without influence. And I thought you could be better deployed here than in more southern parts of this hemisphere."

So he does know about the Russians and the Mexican pipeline.

"You became my advocate? That's dangerous."

"So was Iran in 1977. Didn't stop you, did it?"

"My job. You owe me nothing."

"Actually, you're not telling the truth."

Stone cocked his head slightly.

McElroy continued, "I did some investigation afterwards. You had already been authorized to return home. In fact you were technically off duty. The actual team that was supposed to come to my aid was ambushed en route. Killed to a man. Why do I think I'm not telling you anything you didn't already know?"

With this observation Chapman eyed Stone with even deeper interest.

"You were in trouble. I was there. You would have done the same for me."

"Not, I'm afraid, with the same successful results." He added quickly, "Not for lack of will. But I could never shoot that straight."

"So just give me the basic outline."

"You investigate. You succeed. Then..." McElroy shrugged. "What you were promised before will remain unchanged."

"And if I don't succeed?"

McElroy said nothing.

"Okay," said Stone.

"Okay, you'll do it?"

"Yes."

"Excellent."

"So how is this all going to play out?" asked Stone. "I've been on the outside a long time. You don't just jump back in."

"I pulled some professional strings, with the PM's blessing. He and your president are wonderful friends. They golf, they go to war together. You know how that is."

"So you're saying?"

"I'm saying they decided it would be spot-on brilliant for you and Mary here to poke around a bit on this."

"Just so we're clear, I'm not what I once was."

McElroy studied his old friend. "Some remember you only for your extraordinary feats of physicality, for the aim that never missed, the courage that never wavered. But I also remember you as one of the cagiest operatives that ever wore the stars and stripes. Many tried to get you, some close to home. But no one ever succeeded. I'd say you are just what the doctor ordered. And I think it would be personally beneficial for you too. And not just for the obvious reasons."

"So keep my enemies closer?"

"*Friends* and enemies closer," corrected McElroy.

Stone looked at Chapman. "How do you feel about this?"

She said flippantly, "My boss has spoken. And I play by house rules."

"That's not what I asked you," he said sharply.

Chapman lost her playful look. "I need to find out who wanted my PM dead. And if you can help me do that I'll go the last mile with you."

"Well put," McElroy said as he rose, clutching the armchair for support. "I can't tell you what a pleasure it is to have seen you again. It has really done my old heart good."

"One thing. Weaver showed me the video feed of the park surveillance. Unfortunately, it cut off after the explosion. Went to static."

"Did it now?" McElroy peered at Chapman. "Mary, perhaps you can provide Oliver with the *full* video."

"I thought there might be more."

McElroy smiled. "There's always *more*."

Stone's mouth edged upward. "Been back to Iran?"

McElroy smiled. "I wouldn't dream of it unless you went with me. Mary will provide you with our files to date. Good luck." A few seconds later he'd disappeared into an interior room, leaving Chapman and Stone alone.

"I need a ride back to my place," he said.

"And then?" she said.

"And then we'll go over your files."

"Okay, but we may be running out of time."

"Oh, there's no question about it. We *are* running out of time."

12

WHEN HE AND CHAPMAN RETURNED to the caretaker's cottage, Stone put on a pot of hot water for tea while the MI6 agent took the files from her briefcase and spread them out over Stone's desk. She also loaded a DVD into her laptop.

With a frown she said, "You know I would prefer to meet in a more secure place. These files are all classified."

Stone looked up from the stove and said cheerfully, "Not to worry, I don't have any security clearances, so as soon as I look at them they'll be immediately declassified."

"Bloody hell," murmured Chapman.

Teacups in hand, they sat at the desk and began to go over the documents and reports. Stone's gaze flew swiftly over the papers and photos, his agile and experienced mind separating the important from the trivial.

After he was finished Chapman said, "Would you like to see the full feed?"

He nodded. "I'm wondering why I was shown the edited version at NIC."

"Don't ask me. It's your blokes' doing, not mine."

"I'm also wondering if the edited version is the only one they have."

To this, Chapman simply stared stoically at the screen.

They watched the feed. It was picture only, no audio. After the explosion happened, the feed went to static, but only for a second as though the detonation had momentarily disabled the electronic surveillance's signals. When the video resumed, Stone saw the remainder of the feed. Flames and white smoke covered Jackson's statue, or where it used to be. The fence and cannons had also been flung away like feathers. It was a miracle no one had been killed. Luckily, at that time of night the park had been nearly deserted, and the security teams typically kept to the perimeter of the park.

Stone saw himself lying on the ground unconscious while the British agent slowly rose and staggered away.

"Your man looks all right. Except for his tooth."

"He's a tough chap, but he did say colliding with you was like hitting a brick wall."

Stone continued to focus on the feed. The suit and woman were no longer visible. He saw people running; the security bollards on Pennsylvania retracted into the street and police cars and Secret Service vans raced away. Blair House was quickly sealed off.

"Can you show me the last thirty seconds again?"

She hit a couple of keystrokes and Stone watched the explosion happen again. He sat back puzzled.

"What's the problem?" said Chapman as she stopped the video.

"Can you slow it down even more?"

"I'll try." She worked some keystrokes. "This is the best I can do, I'm afraid."

They watched it again with everything in ultraslow motion.

Stone followed the path of the jogger as he passed by a pair of uniformed Secret Service officers and a canine before entering the park.

"Fat chap to be in trainers," noted Chapman. "Doesn't look like a runner, does he?"

"People who wear jogging suits aren't always runners. He might have just been out for a walk."

"If you say so."

"Bomb could have been on that iPod."

Chapman nodded. "I was thinking the same thing. C-4 or Semtex. Or something even more powerful. If so, there will be evidence of that in the debris field."

"Yes and no. Yes, the iPod will be blown apart, but it would be regardless of whether it was part of an explosive device or not."

"But they'll be able to tell," said Chapman. "From scorching marks, from the deformity angles of the parts, outward as opposed to inward, and so on."

Stone turned to her. "You know about explosives?"

"Another reason they sent for me. I spent three years chasing some nasty Irishmen who didn't believe the IRA had actually signed a peace treaty. They liked to make things go boom. Learned a lot."

"I'm sure." Stone looked back at the screen. "He dove into the planting hole."

"And the explosion happened a few seconds later. Maybe a suicide bomber, then."

Stone looked skeptical. "Who kills only himself by diving in a hole?"

"So what do you think the lay of the land is, then?"

He looked at her curiously. "Lay of what land?"

"Your land of too many bloody American agencies. I've only been on this case less than a day and already I feel claustrophobic."

"Ever heard of Hell's Corner?"

Chapman shook her head.

Stone leaned forward and tapped the frozen screen, which showed Lafayette Park. "This is Hell's Corner," he said. "Pennsylvania Avenue, the actual street, belongs to the D.C. metro cops. The sidewalks around Lafayette Park are the Secret Service's turf and the park itself comes under the jurisdiction of the Park Police. Secret Service agents are actually taught to grab a person of interest from the street or park, carry him to the sidewalk and then arrest him there to prevent a pissing contest over jurisdiction."

"Okay," Chapman said slowly.

"Hell's Corner," he said again. "The Feds and cops hate it, but they all have to dance to the same song. The explosion is a case in point. The Park Police will control the scene, but the FBI, and the ATF, because an explosive was involved, will control the investigation. And Homeland Security, Secret Service, NIC and CIA will be hovering like vultures."

Chapman took a sip of tea. "So what now?"

"We'll have to go to the park, talk to the investigators and track down the jogger's identity and that of the woman and the guy in the suit too." He gazed at Chapman. "Your guy? Where is he?"

"Available for questioning. But we have his full report. He saw less than you."

"All right."

She reached for her jacket. "So on to the park?"

"Yes."

"You want to use my car?"

"I think we should, since I don't happen to own one."

CHAPTER

13

ANNABELLE CONROY RODE THE ELEVATOR up to the second floor, stepped off, turned and entered the Rare Book Reading Room in the Jefferson Building of the Library of Congress. She surveyed the large room and spotted Caleb Shaw at his desk in the back. She caught his eye and he quickly came forward.

"Annabelle, what are you doing here?"

"Can you take a break? I've got Reuben and Harry Finn out front. We want to talk."

"About what?"

"What do you think? Oliver. Those guys took him from the hospital and we haven't seen or heard from him since."

"If anyone can take care of himself it's Oliver."

"But he might need our help."

"All right, give me a minute."

As they rode down in the elevator Caleb said, "This has been quite an exciting day for me."

"Why's that?"

"We just got in an F. Scott. And not just any F. Scott. *The* F. Scott."

"The F. Scott what?" asked Annabelle.

Caleb gazed at her in horror. "F. Scott Fitzgerald. One of the greatest American writers of all time." He sputtered, "My God, Annabelle, where have you been all these years?"

"Nowhere near a library, I guess."

"The book is *The Great Gatsby,* arguably his greatest achievement, and certainly his most well-known work. And it's not just any *Great Gatsby,* of which we have several. It's a first edition, first state, of course. But it has the very rare, scarcely obtainable dust jacket cover." Annabelle looked at him blankly. "You know, the one with the haunting pair of female eyes? It is one of the most uniquely famous covers in classic literature. You see, the cover was actually conceived before Fitzgerald finished writing the book. He loved it so much he wrote a scene in the novel that included that image."

"Very interesting," said Annabelle politely, but her tone actually showed little interest. She had once shared a van with Caleb for nearly two days, during which he had regaled her nearly nonstop with literary scuttlebutt. She had never really recovered from the onslaught.

They got off the elevator and walked toward the exit.

Caleb continued, "And that's not the best part. The best part is that it's Zelda's copy. The provenance is absolutely certain."

"Who's Zelda?"

"Who's Zelda?" sputtered Caleb again. "His wife, of course. Scott and Zelda. A more tragic couple you would be hard pressed to find. She died in an asylum and Fitzgerald drank himself to death. He inscribed the book for her. What a coup for the library. A one of one," he added. "We love those."

"Totally unique?"

"Absolutely."

"How much did you pay for it?"

Caleb looked taken aback. He blustered, "Well, I mean, that is not for public—"

"Come on, just an estimate."

"It was well into the six figures, I'll have to leave it at that," he said, a bit pompously.

Annabelle now looked interested. "My grandmother left me her personal copy of *Wuthering Heights*. I wonder how much it might be worth. It's in excellent condition."

Caleb looked intrigued. "*Wuthering Heights*?

First editions of those in pristine condition are rare. Where did she get it?"

"At a bookstore eight years ago. It's a paperback, is that a problem?"

Caleb gazed stonily at her and said stiffly, "Funny."

Outside they met up with Reuben and Harry Finn. Finn was a decades-younger version of Stone, lean and lethal. Unless he needed to move fast, he never seemed to even flinch, as though storing his energy for when a crisis occurred. Reuben had changed from his loading-dock uniform into his usual garb of jeans and a sweatshirt with moccasins on his feet. They sat on the broad steps leading into the library.

Annabelle said, "So what are we going to do?"

"What can we do?" said Reuben.

"Oliver may be in trouble," she replied.

"Oliver is often in trouble," responded Caleb.

"Those men who took him from the hospital," began Annabelle.

Finn cut in. "NIC. Riley Weaver's boys. Heard it from a buddy of mine. It was a catch and release. I doubt Oliver gave them what they wanted."

"Then he is in trouble," said Annabelle. "And we have to help him."

"Why don't we wait for him to ask for that help?" said Caleb.

"Why?" Annabelle shot back.

"Because every time I help him I get in trouble here," he said, looking back at the enormous library building. "I'm actually on probation, a positively horrendous situation for someone of my age and level of experience."

"No one's asking you to risk your job, Caleb. But I did find something out. In fact, it's why I wanted to meet with all of you today."

"What did you find out?" asked Reuben.

"That Oliver was leaving to go somewhere."

"How do you know that?"

"I found a packed bag in his cottage. Along with several books written in what I think is Russian."

"You mean you broke in his cottage and found it," said Caleb heatedly. "You have absolutely no respect for property rights, Annabelle Conroy. None. It's outrageous. It really is."

She slipped a book from her pocket and showed it to the librarian.

"Yes, it is Russian," said Caleb as he glanced at the title. He looked more closely at the title. "It's a book on Russian politics, but it's decades old. Why in the world would he be taking that with him?"

"Maybe he was going to Russia and he needed to bone up on his language skills," suggested Finn. "One way to do that is read the language."

"Why would Oliver be going to Russia?" asked Reuben. "Wait a minute, how would he even get there? He doesn't have a passport. He doesn't have any ID at all. Not to mention money for the trip."

"There could only be one way he could go," said Annabelle.

"You mean on behalf of the U.S. government?" replied Finn.

"Yes."

"On behalf of the government!" exclaimed Caleb. "He doesn't work for the government. At least not anymore."

"Maybe that status has changed," said Annabelle. "I mean, they offered the man the Medal of Honor."

Reuben mused, "Oliver going back inside. After all these years, I can't believe it."

"And after all they did to him," added Finn quietly.

"Why would he do that?" asked Caleb. "If there's one thing we know about Oliver, it's that he really doesn't trust the government."

"Maybe he really didn't have a choice," said Finn.

"But it's not like he's twenty anymore," retorted

Annabelle. "He was almost killed last night. If he goes to Russia, he may never come back."

Reuben said, "He may be older but he's also wiser. I wouldn't discount how much he has left in the tank."

"He almost died in that prison in Divine, Reuben," she reminded him. "And Milton did die," she added with brutal frankness.

Reuben, who'd been very close to Milton Farb, glanced down at his hands. "Maybe we're all too old for this shit anymore."

Finn said, "So how do you want to play this with Oliver? We all know he won't ask for our help. Not after what happened in Divine."

Caleb said, "That's right. He'll do nothing that puts us in any danger."

"Then maybe we don't wait for him to ask for our help," said Annabelle. "Maybe we just become proactive."

"Meaning what exactly?" asked Reuben. "Not spy on him?"

"No, but we can show a united front and tell him what we think."

"I'm not sure that's a great idea," Reuben said.

Annabelle stood. "Fine. If you guys want to wait for his death notice, great. I'm not." She turned and walked off.

"Annabelle!" Reuben called after her.

She never turned around.

"She's very stubborn," grumbled Caleb. "Like most women. It's probably why I never got married."

Reuben glowered at him. "Oh, I think there were a few other reasons for that, Caleb."

CHAPTER

14

TRAFFIC IN D.C. WAS MUCH WORSE than normal, and all because someone had detonated a bomb across from the White House. At least that's probably what some frustrated commuters were thinking. For blocks in all directions the street barriers had been thrown up, making the nation's capital resemble a hodgepodge of corrals. Metro police cars and black Secret Service SUVs were dovetailed in front and behind these barriers to further discourage anyone from approaching.

Stone and Chapman, despite her credentials, were forced to abandon her car and walk. Phone calls were made at every checkpoint as the MI6 agent's documents were scrutinized and her incremental passage authorized by off-site higher-ups. Stone could understand that none of the street cops or agents were willing to fall on the sword because they'd passed them through in error. This was why supervisors cashed the larger paychecks and had the slightly bigger offices. Their asses would be fried if someone further up the food chain decided to throw his weight around.

They finally cleared the last hurdle and approached ground zero, Lafayette Park. To Stone, who knew it perhaps better than anyone else, it was nearly unrecognizable. The center of the park was a blackened mass, trees and plants destroyed, the grass burned, the dirt piled up in mounds. The Jackson statue lay in ruins. A cannon wheel had nearly reached the sidewalk on the Pennsylvania Avenue side. A section of fence was embedded in a tree a good seventy feet away.

The ATF had set up its mobile command post in the middle of Pennsylvania Avenue. The FBI's counterpart unit was set up in Jackson Place to the west of the park. Dogs and armed security were everywhere. All the businesses and government offices located on Jackson Place and across the park on Madison Place had been shut down.

While the park looked like a cop's convention, the people in uniform were still outnumbered by the swarm of suits. Stone and Chapman passed by a large Alcohol, Tobacco and Firearms National

Response Team, or NRT, truck. Stone knew that there were only three NRT vehicles in existence. The NRT members constituted the best bomb experts in the country and could go into any scenario and within a couple days tell what had gone boom and how.

Stone caught sight of some techs in hazmat suits parsing through the explosion site. He also eyed people in hermetic gear who looked like surgeons preparing for the OR. They were scrounging the area, looking for trace evidence. Small colored tents were scattered everywhere. He assumed each one marked a bit of evidence that had been found.

The men in some of the suits clearly represented the FBI. This was not a guess, since they were also wearing their FBI windbreakers. Other jacket and ties beyond that inner circle were members of the Secret Service, this given away by their ear buds and dour expressions as these "outsiders" trod their turf.

Stone and Chapman walked toward the group of FBI agents. However, before they reached the circle of investigators a tall man intercepted them.

"Mr. Stone?"

Stone eyed him. "Yes?"

"I need you to come with me, sir."

"Where?"

The man pointed directly across the street.

"The White House? Why?"

"I believe you know Special Agent Alex Ford. He's waiting there for you."

Stone gazed at Chapman. "She's with me."

The man looked at her. "Agent Chapman?" She nodded. "ID please."

She produced it.

"Let's go."

They were escorted through the front gates, although Chapman had to surrender her gun.

"I want it back," she said to the confiscating officer, "in the exact same condition. I'm very partial to that weapon."

"Yes ma'am," responded the man politely.

They passed by a backhoe and a crew of men in green-and-khaki uniforms who were removing the stump of a tree inside the White House grounds. One of the men winked at Chapman. She scowled in response. As they entered the building and were led down the hall, Chapman whispered, "So *this* is the White House, eh?"

"Never been here?" Stone asked.

"No, you?"

Stone didn't answer.

At that moment Alex Ford stepped from a

doorway and joined them. He nodded to the agent escort. "Chuck, I've got it. Thanks."

"Okay, Alex." Chuck broke off and headed back the way they had come.

Stone made introductions and then said, "Why are we here?"

"I understand you met with Sir James McElroy earlier?" said Alex.

"*Sir?* He didn't tell me he'd been knighted."

"Didn't really want it," remarked Chapman. "But you don't turn down the queen, now do you?"

Stone said, "Yes, I met with him."

"Just so you know, the decision for you to come back inside has not been very popular with certain other agencies."

"Including yours?"

"And including some other folks here."

"Who are we meeting with?"

"Chief of staff and the VP."

"I'm impressed."

"I think the VP is there to give it a bit more gravitas."

"Have they been fully briefed?"

"Don't know. Above my pay grade."

They arrived at a door. Alex knocked.

"Enter," a voice said.

"Ready?" said Alex, and Stone nodded.

Chapman adjusted her cuffs and whipped back a stray bit of hair. She muttered, "What the hell have I got myself into?"

"I was thinking the same thing," commented Stone.

CHAPTER

15

From the anteroom they were admitted into the office of the vice president. He was a tall, white-haired and well-fed man with a reassuring smile and a strong handshake, no doubt built up over thousands of campaign stops. The chief of staff was short and wiry with eyes that continually swept the space around him, like a radar array.

It suddenly occurred to Stone that the VP being here made sense beyond providing gravitas. He was on the president's National Security Council. Still, Stone was actually surprised the man would agree to meet with him directly and not through an underling. But then again, it was hard to refuse your president.

The pleasantries were made and quickly dispensed with. Alex Ford stood by the door, a security presence now and not a friend.

The VP said, "The president asked that we meet with you." He nodded in Chapman's direction. "With you both. We obviously want to get to the bottom of this, uh, delicate matter as quickly as possible."

In his mind Stone translated this into plain English. What the VP had actually just communicated was, "This is not my idea, and though I'm being somewhat loyal to my president I won't take the blame if it blows up. That's why the chief of staff is here. My boss might go down, but not me."

Stone wondered if either man had been made aware of the original plan to ship Stone off to Mexico to help deal with the Russian cartel nightmare. American vice presidents often had been kept in the dark by the chief executive. Chiefs of staff typically knew everything the president did.

The VP inclined his head at the chief of staff, who held out a black leather card case to Stone. "Your credentials," said the man.

Stone slowly took the offered item, opened it and gazed at his face, which was staring back at him from the depths of the official photo that was part of his new commission. He wondered when they had taken his picture. Perhaps when he was sitting in the room at the NIC, which meant that Riley Weaver knew all about this. He had to smile when he saw his typed name:

Oliver Stone.

Next to the photo was his ID card. On it, he had officially become a field agent of the national coordinator for security, infrastructure protection and counterterrorism. This all made sense, Stone thought. The national coordinator worked within the National Security Council and reported to the president through the national security advisor. There was a link to the White House, but with one step in between. The president was covering all the bases. Just as his savvy VP was now doing. He flipped to the next sleeve in the case and there was his shiny badge with the agency insignia.

He said, "Interesting choice of agencies."

The VP smiled his winning and inscrutable smile. "Yes, isn't it?"

Yet Stone had managed to read a thousand such inscrutable faces. And the VP's was no exception.

He believes this is all insane, and he's probably right.

The chief of staff added, "It carries the same weight as DHS and the FBI. If not a bit more, actually. There are few doors that won't open. And most of them are in this building."

Well then, let's hope I won't have to try and open any doors here, thought Stone. He said to the chief of staff, "You serve at his pleasure." Before the startled man could say anything, Stone turned to the VP. "And you obviously trust your running mate's judgment, or at least hope he's not making a serious miscalculation by conferring this authority on me."

Both men now appeared to look at Stone in a different light.

The VP nodded. "He's a good man. So I hope that his trust is justified when this is all said and done. I assume you feel the same way."

Stone pocketed his new credentials without answering.

The chief of staff said, "You will be sworn in after this meeting by a representative of the national coordinator's office. Thus you will also have arresting authority. You are also entitled to a sidearm. If you so choose," he added in a dubious tone.

It was clear the chief of staff too thought it was madness to be handing over this much authority to a man like him. Stone briefly wondered how long the chief of staff had argued with the president over this decision before the latter had won out.

Stone glanced at Chapman. "My friend from MI6 here has a very nice Walther PPK. I think that will do for now."

"All right." The VP rose, signaling an end to the meeting. Stone knew that his working hours were measured in fifteen-minute increments and he had added incentive to have this particular encounter over.

Wait much longer and the smell of all this might permanently attach to you, sir.

They all shook hands. The VP said, "Good luck, *Agent* Stone."

As they followed Alex back down the hall, Chapman said wryly, "Hell, if I knew it was this easy to become an American agent I would've come over here a long time ago."

"It did go a bit too smoothly," said Stone as he eyed Alex.

The Secret Service agent said, "Things have changed in the last fifteen years. We've got more contractors walking around with guns and badges than you can imagine. Both in force protection in overseas military campaigns and right here at home. Just the nature of the beast."

Out of Chapman's earshot he added, "Look, you need to understand that people know John Carr is back."

"I'm aware of that."

"You have a lot of secrets, Oliver. Too many for some."

"Yes, that had occurred to me too."

"You don't need to do this."

"Yes, actually I do."

"Why?" demanded Alex.

"For a number of reasons."

Looking highly disgruntled, Alex said nothing.

Stone said, "After we finish here we're going back over to the park. Can you come with us?"

Alex shook his head. "I'm on protection duty here. And like I told you before, I'm not allowed anywhere near this investigation. They've built a Chinese wall around this sucker for obvious reasons."

Stone studied him. "Because someone believes there's a mole in the Service?"

The other man looked uncomfortable about this observation but nodded. "I think it's a load of crap, but you have to cover all the bases."

In another room of the White House Stone was sworn in. Next, Chapman got her beloved gun back and they left the White House. She and Stone headed to the park.

"Pretty nice to have the president of the only remaining superpower on your side."

"Maybe."

"Am I ever going to hear the full story on that?"

"No, you're not."

16

STONE AND CHAPMAN flashed their badges and passed through the gauntlet of security at the park.

"What first?" she asked.

Stone pointed to a man encircled by suits. "Let's go right to the top."

They again showed their IDs. When the man saw Stone's agency he motioned the pair over to a clear space.

"Tom Gross, FBI," he said. "I'm the case agent. Out of WFO's Domestic Counterterrorism Unit." Gross was in his late forties, a bit shorter than Stone, stockier, with thinning dark hair and a serious expression that had probably been permanently stamped on his features one week after joining the Counterterrorism Unit.

Stone began, "We're here because—"

Gross interrupted. "I got a phone call. You can

expect the Bureau's full cooperation." He looked at Chapman. "Really glad your prime minister was unhurt."

"Thanks," replied Chapman.

Stone asked, "Has any group claimed responsibility?"

"Not yet."

Gross led them to the point of origin of the explosion while Stone explained that he had been at the park last night. The small colored tents marking where evidence had been found had increased greatly in number while they had been across the street.

Gross said, "The media's been all over this thing, of course, even though we've kept them well back from the crime scene. Damn mess, really. We've had to shut down everything within a full-block radius with the park as the center. Lot of pissed-off people."

"I'm sure," said Stone.

"The director has held a press conference in which he said very little, because we don't know very much. The ADIC will handle the rest of the media through the MR Office," he added, referring to the assistant director in charge and the FBI's Media Relations Office. "We're taking the lead over

ATF, but they're handling the heavy work on the bomb piece."

Stone eyed Gross. "So you've concluded it's international terrorism as opposed to domestic?"

"Can't say that, no," admitted Gross. "But because of the geographic proximity and the PM's presence."

"Right," said Stone. "Have you seen the surveillance video of the park from last night?"

"Got it all set up at the mobile command post. Unfortunately, the damn cameras were knocked out by the blast. Surprised about that, because there's about a dozen recorders stationed all around here and manned by probably five different agencies. The bomb might have been designed to jam them, though, for some reason."

Stone's face was inscrutable at this comment. The FBI had clearly not been privy to the unedited video. Stone filed that one away for now. "Source of the gunfire?" he asked.

Gross pointed to the northern end of the park. "Rooftop garden of the Hay-Adams Hotel. We found lots of shell casings. TEC-9 rounds."

"Interesting choice of weapon," said Stone.

"Why?" asked Gross.

"Limited range. About twenty-five useful meters.

Which is shorter than the height they were firing down from. And it's hard to hit anything with a TEC-9 that's not standing right in front of you."

"Well, they *didn't* hit anything."

"But you found no guns?" Stone asked.

Gross shook his head.

"How was that possible?" asked Chapman. "Do people just walk around in the States carrying machine guns? I thought the British press was making that up."

"Not sure yet. And no, people do not walk around here carrying machine guns," Gross added indignantly. "The hotel folks are cooperating fully. The garden is popular but not incredibly secure. Of course we shut the hotel down until the investigation is over. We kept all the guests on premises and are interviewing them right now."

Stone asked, "Were the guns set up remotely or were human fingers pulling the triggers?"

"If they were operated remotely all traces were removed. For now I think we have to assume human involvement."

"You said you locked the hotel down?" Stone said.

"Yes, but there was a time gap," Gross conceded.

"How long?"

"It was pretty much chaos down here for a couple

hours. When the source of the gunfire was confirmed, that was when the lockdown was set up."

"So, easily enough time for the gunners to slip out, taking their hardware with them?"

"Multiple machine guns wouldn't be exactly inconspicuous," Gross pointed out.

Stone shook his head. "If you know what you're doing you can break down a TEC-9 very quickly and fit it inside a briefcase."

"We shut things down as fast as we could. But it is what it is."

"Hopefully, someone at the hotel will remember seeing people leaving, perhaps with a bulky case?" noted Chapman.

Gross didn't look too confident. "An event they had there was just letting out. Lots of people with briefcases leaving about that time, apparently."

"That wasn't a coincidence," said Stone. "That was good prep work."

A guy in a hazmat suit walked over to them. He tugged off his head covering. He was introduced as an agent from the ATF, Stephen Garchik.

Gross said, "Good to go?"

Garchik nodded and grinned. "Nothing that'll kill you."

Stone looked at the tent markers. They were divided between orange and white. The orange were far more numerous and were spread out relatively evenly around the park. The white markers were almost all on the western side of the park.

"Orange is bomb debris and white are locations of found slugs?" Stone ventured.

Garchik nodded approvingly. "Yep, obviously there were far more bomb bits than bullets, emanating from the blast seat."

"What kind of explosive device was it, Agent Garchik?" Stone asked.

"Just make it Steve. Too early to tell. But by the size of the debris field and damage to that statue, it was some powerful stuff."

"C-4, or Semtex maybe?" asked Chapman. "They can both do serious damage in relatively small footprints."

Garchik said, "Well, this is a lot of damage for a stick of TNT or even a pound of Semtex. Maybe it was a cocktail of components. Maybe HMX or CL-20. That stuff is scary powerful. They're all in the family of most potent non-nuclear high explosives. But it most likely wasn't military ordnance."

"How do you know that?" asked Stone.

Chapman answered. "White smoke on the video. Military grade is oil-based, leaving a black smoke trail. White is usually commercial."

The ATF agent smiled appreciatively. "You

know your stuff. We're bagging and tagging now. Taking residue from the blast seat." He pointed at two burly black Labradors being walked around the grounds by their handlers. "Roy and Wilbur," he said. "Those are the dogs' names," he added. "Dogs are the cheapest, most reliable bomb detectors in the world. One of my dogs can screen an entire airport in a couple hours. So they'll burn through this whole park in no time. Find bomb residue my guys won't even be able to see with all our fancy technology."

"Impressive," said Chapman.

Garchik continued with enthusiasm. "There aren't even any machines in existence that can measure accurately the power of a dog's nose. But I can tell you that people have about 125 million smelling cells in their nasal passages. Our Labs have twice that. We'll run all the evidence up to our Fire Research Center in Maryland. We can torch a three-story building up there and have a hood large enough to capture every molecule of the burn-off. Be able to tell you exactly what was used."

Stone said, "Anything left of the guy in the hole?"

Garchik nodded. "Bombs throw debris three hundred and sixty degrees. We've pulled body parts out of tree canopies, off surrounding rooftops. Two, three blocks away. Found a piece of a foot on the White House lawn. A partial index finger on the roof of St. John's Church. Then there was tissue, brain matter, the usual stuff. DNA field day. Guy's on a database somewhere we'll know soon enough." He nodded at the NRT truck. "Of course, the first thing we did was shut down the area and send in our dogs."

"Secondary strikes," noted Chapman.

"Right. They've made that a fine art in Iraq and Afghanistan. Trigger off a bomb, everybody rushes in to help, and they pop the secondary strike to take out the first responders. But we found nothing." Garchik added in a proud tone, "And our Labs are exceptional. They're mostly service-dog-school dropouts that can sniff out nineteen thousand different explosives based on the five major explosive groups, including chemical compounds. We train them with food. Labs are land sharks, do anything for food."

"They can never be fooled?" asked Chapman.

"Let me put it this way. Roy over there found a four-inch-square C-4 block that was covered in dirty diapers and coffee, packed in Mylar bags in cement-lined crates, sealed in foam and locked in a storage room. And he did it in about thirty seconds."

"How is that possible?" asked Chapman.

"Smells occur at the molecular level. You can't seal them up, no matter how hard you try. Plastics, metals, pretty much any container or cover-up method can't trap molecules because those materials are still permeable. They can hold solids and liquids, and even gases, but smell molecules are something altogether different. They can pass right through those substances. If the detection method is sensitive enough it really doesn't matter what the bad guys do. Trained bomb detection canines have an olfactory capacity that is humanly impossible to fool, and believe me, lots of people have tried."

"How do you think this bomb was detonated?" asked Gross.

The ATF agent shrugged. "Basic rule of three. To make a bomb you have to have a switch, power source and the explosive. Bombs are just basically something that can violently expand at extremely fast speeds while trapped in a confined space. You can detonate a bomb any number of ways, but the basic two are via a timer and by what we call command detonation."

Chapman said, "Meaning the person doing the detonation is present?"

"Either the bomber or someone else. And the 'someone else' is usually to safeguard against the bomber getting cold feet. Probably half the sui-cide bombings in Iraq are detonated by third par-ties for that very reason."

"I take it you've been there," said Gross.

Garchik nodded. "Four times. And to be frank, I hope I don't have to go back."

"So *where* was the bomb?" asked Stone. "On the blown-up jogger?"

"Nope, don't think that's possible," said Garchik.

"Why?" asked Stone.

"He went to the dogs."

"What?" said Gross.

"I'll show you. Come on."

CHAPTER

17

GARCHIK LED THEM to the ATF's command unit. Inside he fired up an array of electronic equipment. Moments later they were watching some of the video feed from the night before. When a particular scene came up he froze it and pointed his finger at the screen.

"There. Like I said, he went to the dogs. Or *dog,* in this case."

The image was of the man in the jogging suit. He was entering the park from the north. He was frozen right next to two uniformed officers, one of whom had a dog. The jogger was perhaps a foot from the canine.

Chapman said, "Is that a bomb detection canine?"

"Yes, it is. Secret Service's. Now, I don't think their dogs are better than ours, but I can tell you any person carrying an explosive walking that close to a bomb detection canine trained in this country is gonna get busted. I don't care how he tried to hide it. That dog would be going nuts or else doing a passive alert, meaning he'll sit right down on his butt. This dog was doing neither."

"And you'd think if he was carrying a bomb on his person he wouldn't have walked right next to the dog in the first place," said Stone. "He couldn't assume it wasn't a bomb sniffer."

Gross added, "Which means this wasn't a suicide bomber. The guy jumped into the hole to avoid the gunfire. Looks like the bomb was in that hole."

"Well, that's progress anyway," said Stone. "Ruling out the jogger."

"Was it a pressure switch?" suggested Chapman. "Jogger hit it and boom."

"That's possible," conceded Garchik, though he didn't look convinced. "Accidental detonation, you mean."

"Maybe. Did you find any evidence of another type detonation switch?"

"There's a million pieces of stuff lying around here and we're still looking. But to complicate matters a bit, Lafayette Park is home to a lot of static electricity."

"And static electricity can set off a bomb," said Chapman.

"That's right."

"But if you go to all the trouble to get a bomb into Lafayette Park, why would you build the bomb in such a way that it might trigger off accidentally?" asked Gross.

Garchik said, "Might be as simple as the folks who managed to get the bomb in here were better than the guy building the bomb. That's not as implausible as you might think. Or it could have been on a frequency switch and something interfered with it."

"The jogger was wearing an iPod," Gross pointed out. "That could have interfered."

"That's possible, yes."

"But are we really sure the tree hole was the source of the bomb?" asked Chapman. "We're sort of jumping to conclusions here that it was."

"We haven't finished our analysis, but it's a safe bet that was the bomb seat," said Garchik.

Stone said, "Then are we sure that the bomb going off was an accident?"

They all looked at him curiously.

Gross said, "It had to be. Otherwise why would they set off a bomb that had no chance of killing the prime minister?"

"Unless it was set on a timer," said Chapman. "The PM was supposed to be in the park last night.

If it was set on a timer there's no way to take that back."

"And it was a coincidence that the man jumped in the hole and it went off when it did," added Garchik. "That works."

"No, it doesn't work," countered Stone. "You're forgetting the gunfire. Why have both the gunfire and the bomb? And if the gunfire wasn't done remotely, then the shooters would've known the prime minister wasn't in the park."

"That's not necessarily true," said Chapman. "I'll show you."

She led them back outside, where she pointed to the trees in front of the Hay-Adams Hotel. "If they were on the rooftop garden back there then the trees would've hidden the park from their view. They hear the sirens and the motorcade coming. They wait for it to pull in, the prime minister to get out and walk to the park. Then they start shooting."

Stone did not look convinced. "So you're saying this elaborate plan was put together and the gunners were firing blind?" He shook his head. "If I were going to do this, at the very least I'd have one spotter with a clear view of the PM's movements stationed somewhere near the park with a secure line of communication. I'm not shooting blindly through tree canopies. And if the PM doesn't come to the park, I call off the mission. But if he does set foot in the park I can't afford to miss."

"And they did miss everyone," Gross pointed out.

The ATF agent nodded. "It's a puzzler all right."

Stone turned to him. "So if you were going to pull off this bombing, how would you detonate, Steve?"

"Pressure switches can be problematic, particularly under these conditions. I mean, you've got a tree in a hole and a bomb somewhere near it. Maybe in the root ball, maybe under the tree. That's a lot of weight. And people moving stuff around, digging. Chances are that pressure switch gets tripped accidentally. And once you cover the bomb up with dirt, what's going to trigger it? Something has to cause the switch to engage. It's called a pressure switch for a good reason. No, if I were going to do it I'd use a command control device, meaning remote detonation. Now, if they did that they might have used a cell phone, which would make our job a lot easier. Cell phones have a SIM card and all the components are serialized, so we can reconstruct the phone and maybe track down where and who purchased it. Of course if a cell phone was used, you actually have two phones. One planted on the bomb as the switch and the other to call that phone.

We did find some bits of wire, corner of a transistor, plastic shell casing, leather—"

"Leather?" Stone exclaimed.

"Yeah, tiny patches of it. About a dozen pieces. Had some black markings on them, so the probability lies with it being part of the explosive. Still trying to determine what it is. But we will. And then we have to definitively determine if it was tied to the explosion. Not all the junk we find out here will be."

"Could have come off the jogger's trainers," suggested Chapman. "His shoes were made of leather, right?"

"Yes, but the color's off. I saw the video feed and the guy's shoes were blue."

"The black marks could be scorching from the bomb," Chapman pointed out.

"No, the rest of the leather was brown. Probably has nothing to do with anything."

"So right now," Gross said, "you still can't tell us how the detonation was done?"

"That's right."

"Why are you thinking the bomb was in the tree hole in the first place?" Gross said. "Apart from the location of the damage?"

Garchik said, "Follow me." He led them to the site of the detonation and pointed into the hole.

"Unless I'm reading this wrong, this is ground zero. Blew that tree right out of here, and it wasn't light."

They all stared down at the hole, which had become even wider and deeper because of the explosion.

"Okay, so what are we looking for?" asked Gross.

"Well, there was already a crater here. The excavation for the tree."

"Okay," said Gross. "So?"

Garchik made a fist and swung it downward. "When you smack the water with your fist, a certain amount of water shoots up on both sides of the hand. Simple concept of volume displacement. Same thing happens with a bomb. If the bomb is aboveground it acts like the fist. It'll push downward, sideways and also up. But a bomb buried in the ground has a different effect. It will propel *mostly* upward because it's covered by looser dirt. Path of least resistance. It still deepened the existing hole."

"Causing a crater. A bigger crater than if the bomb had been aboveground," said Stone slowly.

"But the bomb in this case was buried in the dirt, right?" said Gross. He looked at each of them as though waiting for their collective affirmation.

"I wish I could tell you for certain," said Garchik. "Normally, making that determination is one of the easiest parts of the equation. But here we have a complicating factor. There was already a big crater here before the bomb went off."

Gross looked confused. "I'm not exactly following you here."

Stone said, "He means he can't tell if the bomb was buried in the dirt or may have been in the root ball or even under the tree." He looked at the ATF agent. "Right?"

"That's right."

"Does it matter?" asked Chapman. "In any case the bomb was placed in the park in that hole."

Gross said, "That's true. The question is, how did they do it? This is Lafayette Park, not some back alley in Baghdad."

Stone looked around. Guns and bombs right across from the president's house. There could only be one answer. "We've got a traitor somewhere," he said.

Chapman added, "And if the PM hadn't turned his ankle he'd be dead."

Stone looked at her. "But more to the point, they got a bomb into Lafayette Park. Across from the White House. The most heavily guarded piece of land in the world. How?"

CHAPTER

18

AFTER A MINUTE OF SILENCE as they each thought
about this question, Gross said, "I just don't see
how anyone could have managed that. This place is
under surveillance 24/7."

"That's true," said Garchik.

It is very true, thought Stone. "But all the evidence seems to point to that being the case. A bomb
was planted in that hole."

Gross looked at Chapman and then at Stone.
"Do you realize how many people would have to be
potentially involved in something like that?"

Stone said, "Well, for starters we need a list of
anyone involved with the process of digging that
hole and planting that tree. The National Park Service handles all that, but there would have been
others involved too."

Gross pulled out his phone and walked off a few feet as he punched in a series of numbers.

Stone turned to the ATF agent. "Once you determine what sort of bomb it was, what then?"

"We'll put it on BATS. Bomb and Arson Tracking System. ATF maintains it. It has worldwide reference. Bombers don't like to deviate from their formula, so they develop signatures. Pretty practical reason. Once they find a method that works, they don't change it."

"Because they might blow themselves up with a new method," said Chapman with a knowing look.

"You got it. Bombers typically like to test out their stuff beforehand, and that's another way we catch them. Blowing stuff up in the woods and somebody reports them. They never think to realize that they can check all their connections and switches without detonating. Because the bomb materials themselves *will* go off. The only weak points are the connections and the power source."

"Maybe these guys like to blow stuff up for the hell of it. Like to see the boom," observed Chapman.

"I do think that's part of it," replied Garchik. "So anyway, we'll run it through BATS to see if the same signature appears on there. Then maybe we'll know who our bomber is. I know a lot of signatures from memory, but nothing about this one is striking me as familiar."

"Anything else?" asked Stone.

"Not right now."

"Okay, thanks. And let Agent Gross know as soon as you have anything."

After Garchik walked off, Gross rejoined them, slipping his phone back in his pocket. "All right, I just set off a shitstorm back at WFO."

Stone eyed the blast seat. "Getting back to basics. Who was the target?"

Gross glanced at Chapman and said, "Pretty clear. British PM."

"He wasn't in the park," replied Stone.

"But he was scheduled to be. At just about the time the bomb went off. It was probably on a timer, despite what Garchik said. It got accidentally triggered, probably when that guy jumped in the hole."

Stone shook his head. "A mission like this requires precision. By detonating, even accidentally, they give away their whole plan. They won't get a second shot. They put everyone on alert for no reason at all. And your theory doesn't explain the gunfire."

"It doesn't make much sense when you explain it like that," admitted Gross.

Stone looked at Chapman. "You keep saying he was scheduled to walk across the park? Who told you that?"

"Got it from the PM's office."

Stone looked toward the northern edge of the park and tried to recreate in his mind exactly what he'd seen the previous night. But for some reason the most vivid details just wouldn't come. Maybe it was his concussion. Or maybe, he admitted to himself, *I'm just getting old.*

They joined Gross in examining the rooftop garden at the Hay-Adams Hotel. The trees did block the line of sight into the park.

"They *were* firing blind," said Gross. "Because if they had a spotter in the park they would've known the PM wasn't there."

There were markers on the floor showing where all the casings had been found.

Gross said, "TEC-9s, like I said before. Over two hundred rounds. So it was probably multiple guns."

"Agreed," said Stone as he gazed at the floor. "And no one below or in the hotel heard or saw anything?"

"I think lots of people heard and saw lots of things. But whether they can remember it correctly and communicate that to us effectively is a whole other question."

"You'll obviously match the casings to the slugs found in the park," said Stone.

"Already done," replied Gross. "Not that there was much doubt about that."

"Good, because there's plenty of doubt about everything else," noted Stone.

CHAPTER

19

LATER THAT NIGHT Stone and Chapman drove back to Stone's cottage. When he opened the door he glanced to his right when he saw her.

Annabelle was sitting in a chair by the fireplace. He ushered Chapman in as Annabelle rose to greet him. After introducing Chapman to Annabelle, Stone was about to say something when Annabelle held out the book written in Russian. "I guess you'll be wanting this back. Are you still planning to go on your . . . trip?"

Stone frowned as he looked down at the book. "There are personal boundaries, Annabelle. And I've always respected yours."

"You're not going to make me feel guilty about this, Oliver, so don't even try. I haven't known you all that long and I think we've nearly lost you about five times at least by my count."

Chapman gazed at Stone in surprise. "I didn't think you were working anymore."

Annabelle answered. "He wasn't. So just think what his mortality rate will be now."

Stone laid the book down on his desk. "I think I'm clearly old enough to make that decision for myself. And to answer your question, my trip has been postponed."

"What trip?" asked Chapman.

Stone ignored her.

Annabelle said, "But you are back working for the government?"

"Like I said, I'm old enough to make that decision."

"Why, Oliver, why would you? After all they did to you."

"Yeah, why? I think we deserve an answer, said a voice."

They all turned to see Reuben Rhodes, Harry Finn and Caleb Shaw at the door to the cottage. It was Reuben who'd spoken.

"I feel like I'm at bloody Waterloo Station," muttered Chapman as the men came forward.

Stone looked down. "It's not easily explained."

"At least tell me you're not working this damn park explosion case," said Annabelle.

"That's exactly what he's doing."

This came from Alex Ford as he walked into the cottage.

"Blimey," said Chapman. "I think you need to change the locks on your door."

Alex stood near the fireplace. "Should I tell them or are you going to?"

"Tell us what?" said Annabelle.

"That Oliver was presented with a commission and badge today. He is now a duly sworn in member of the federal government working with Agent Chapman here from MI6. They've been tasked to find out who tried to blow up the British PM."

Stone looked coldly at his friend. "Thank you for maintaining confidences, Alex."

Reuben said, "Since when the hell are there confidences among us? How many times have I covered your back, Oliver? Risked life and limb? And you the same for me?"

"The same for all of us," added Annabelle.

"This is different," replied Stone.

"Why, because you've got a badge now?" growled Reuben.

Annabelle added, "You've joined up with the same folks who hurt you so badly. Don't you see why we're all stunned? Especially after what happened in Divine. They were just going to let you rot in that prison."

"And I would have except for all of you, I know that," Stone said quietly.

"So why?" Annabelle asked again.

"As I said, it's hard to explain. Actually it may be impossible to explain."

"We're all waiting for you to try."

Something seemed to stiffen in Stone's features. "You're assuming that I owe you an explanation. I don't."

Annabelle looked like Stone had slapped her. Even loyal Reuben seemed stunned, and Caleb gaped.

"Well, I guess that's all the explanation I need," said Annabelle. She turned and walked out.

Reuben glanced at his old friend. "She didn't deserve that, Oliver. None of us do."

"This is just the way it has to be. I'm sorry, Reuben."

"Fine. I'll be sure and come to your funeral."

Reuben also left. Caleb started to follow behind, paused and looked back at Oliver. "This is the only time I've been relieved that Milton isn't alive. To hear this."

Harry Finn said, "I hope you know what you're doing." Then he followed Caleb out.

Now only Alex was left except for Chapman.

Stone gazed at the Secret Service agent. "Do you want to tell me I'm wrong too?"

"No. I figure you know what you're doing, even if I don't particularly like it. But there's a problem with your bomb plant scenario."

"How do you know what our theory is?" asked Stone. "I didn't think you were involved in the investigation."

"Technically, I'm not. But you still hear things."

"So what's wrong with our theory?" Chapman asked.

"The Secret Service canine unit did a sweep of the park earlier."

"When exactly?" asked Stone sharply.

"I'm not sure of the precise time. But you probably noticed a canine unit at the north end of the park?"

"We did, on the video," said Stone.

"They don't bring the dogs out for their health."

"Would they typically cover the entire park?" asked Stone.

"Yes. With a dog it doesn't take that long."

"So the dog would have detected a bomb?" said Chapman.

"That's sort of the point," answered Alex.

"Well, it's also sort of the point that a bloody bomb did go off in the park," she shot back.

"I'm just telling you what I know. I guess I'll be going now."

"Alex, this is not how I wanted things to go down," said Stone.

"Yeah, but they did, didn't they? I hope you make it, Oliver, I really do."

A moment later he was gone. A few seconds later they heard his car start.

"Nice group of mates you have. Seems like they really care about you."

"And I care about them."

"Who are they really?"

"Not important."

"Who was this Milton bloke the little fellow mentioned?"

"A friend."

"But he's dead. How? Accident?"

"No, large-caliber rifle round."

Chapman was about to say something when Stone's cell phone buzzed. It was FBI agent Gross. Stone listened and then clicked off.

"The woman from the park last night has turned up."

"You mean they caught her?" asked Chapman.

"No, she walked into the FBI all on her own."

CHAPTER

20

"I'm Marisa Friedman," the woman said as Stone and Chapman took seats opposite her and Tom Gross in an interior office at the FBI's Washington Field Office, which all agents referred to as the WFO. Stone took a few moments to study her. In good light and with only a few feet separating them he decided she was closer to thirty than forty. She was Chapman's height or a bit taller, with blonde hair that curled around her neck. It was not her natural color, Stone could tell. Her eyes were blue and striking, her face interesting with elegant bone structure, the chin sharply angled and the two sides of her jaw forming perfect bookends for the expressive mouth. Her clothes were clearly expensive but she wore them in a casual manner; minimal jewelry and makeup completed the attractive package.

Gross added, "Ms. Friedman voluntarily came

in when she learned we were looking for anyone who was in the park last night."

Friedman shook her head and looked troubled. "I have to tell you I was shocked at what happened. I'd just gotten to H Street when the gunfire started. And then the explosion." She shivered uncontrollably.

"How did you find out the FBI was looking for you?" Stone asked.

"A friend of mine saw an item on the news and phoned me."

Stone looked at Gross, who said, "In situations like this we call in the media and ask for their assistance in getting the word out. Usually very effective."

"Well, it certainly was in my case," said Friedman.

"In any event you probably would've assumed the police would want to talk to you," said Stone.

"I guess so, yes, although I don't have any experience in things like this. My home was broken into years ago, that's really the only contact I've ever had with the police."

"Can you tell us what you saw?" asked Gross.

"Smoke and people running and screaming." She looked at Stone and her voice shook. "I've never been that frightened in my life."

"But before all that you were sitting on one of the benches in the park?" said Stone.

"Yes, that's right."

"Little late at night for that, wasn't it?" asked Stone.

"My office is located in the line of town houses on the west side of the park."

"Jackson Place?" said Stone.

"Yes. Most of the offices there are linked to the White House, but I was able to snare one of them for my business through more luck than skill. I was working late. Left the office. The night was so nice I sat down and might've even dozed off. I don't usually do that, but I did last night. It was a long day and I was tired. And I know the park is about the best-protected space in the city, so I felt very safe." She gave a hollow laugh. "That turned out to be quite ironic. It really was bad timing all around," she added with another little shiver. "Nice relaxing time in the park that turned into a war zone. For a minute there I thought I'd stumbled onto a movie set."

"Only the bullets and bomb were real," said Stone.

"Yes."

"What *is* your business?" asked Gross.

She flashed a smile. "In this town, that close to the White House you're one of the two Ls."

"Lawyer or lobbyist," answered Stone.

"You win the prize." She crossed her legs and flicked at the hem of her skirt, revealing briefly a glimpse of her pale bare thighs. From the efficient way she did it, Stone deduced this was a tactic of hers during a meeting, at least a meeting with men. He glanced at Gross and saw that it had gotten his attention too. When he looked at Chapman she was just finishing rolling her eyes at this same act.

Mars, Venus, thought Stone.

"So which are you?" he asked Friedman. "Lawyer or lobbyist?"

"Both, actually."

Gross cleared his throat. "And who do you lobby on behalf of?"

Her gaze shifted to the FBI agent. "Lobbyists are the most regulated beasts on earth, so my client list is a matter of public record. But it has no relevance to last night. If I hadn't decided to sit on the bench instead of going right home I wouldn't even be here."

"We still need to check," said Gross.

"Check away. It's all part of the public record. There's nothing particularly remarkable about them, the usual businesses, trade associations. I have some foreign clients, but their businesses are mainstream."

"Who were you calling last night?" asked Stone.

She seemed surprised by the question.

"I was in the park last night," he explained. "And the park is also under video surveillance 24/7. You were seen on the phone."

"Wow, Big Brother is alive and well," she said casually, but her long forehead bunched into neat rows of skin. "Can I ask why it's relevant who I was talking to?"

Gross said, "We can easily enough get that information. But you can save us time by cooperating. However, if you don't..."

She looked at him with a weary expression. "I know, I know, then you think I'm up to no good. Look, it was just a friend."

Gross poised his pen over his notepad. "Your friend's name?"

"Do you really have to check that out? I mean, it seems silly. It was just a friend."

Gross said, "Ms. Friedman, a bomb exploded across from the White House. No detail is too small in an investigation like this. And the question is not *silly*. Now, your friend's name and the subject of your conversation?"

"It's just a man that I know."

"Name?" Gross said again, this time with a

harder edge to his voice. This obviously would be the last time the FBI agent would ask politely.

She sat forward and her voice dropped. "Look, this friend I was talking to is married."

"Okay," said Stone.

"And so?" prompted Chapman with a malicious look.

"And not to me, obviously. And maybe we're more than just friends."

She did the leg cross, skirt flick again, but this time her hands jerked and she didn't seem nearly as confident.

Stone saw Chapman shoot the woman a contemptuous look at this bungled ploy to distract. Even Gross didn't drop his gaze to her legs this time.

Gross said, "We're not really concerned with your, um, friend's marital issues."

Friedman sat back, relieved. "Okay, thank you."

"But I still need his name and what you were talking to him about."

She sighed resignedly. "Fine. Willis Kraft. He lives in Potomac. We were just talking about... personal stuff."

"And his wife doesn't understand him?" said Chapman, still gazing at the woman in disgust.

Friedman's gaze hardened and she and Chapman did a brief staredown that the Brit ended up winning.

"I didn't voluntarily come down here to be judged on my personal choices," Friedman said to Gross as she broke off looking at Chapman.

"And that's not what we're concerned about," said Gross quickly.

"So does it all have to come out?"

"As I said, your friend's marital issues don't concern us and we can be very discreet. Give me his contact information and we'll take it from there," said Gross.

She did so, and then Stone said, "The guy in the jogger's suit in the park?"

"Yes, I saw him," she replied. "What about him?"

"Did you get a good look at him?"

"Not really." She wrinkled her nose. "He was so overweight I remember thinking he was the last person you'd expect to see in workout clothes."

"Did you see the man in the suit with the briefcase?" asked Stone. "He was over near the statue of von Steuben in the northwest corner."

"No, I don't think so. There are some trees there. And even with the park lights it was dark."

"Yes, it was," agreed Stone. "But you left about the same time heading toward H Street."

"I wasn't aware of his movements. I was fumbling in my bag for my metro card."

"McPherson Square?" asked Stone quickly. "Or Farragut West station?"

"McPherson. It's a bit closer to the park. I live in Falls Church. I don't own a car, so I always take the metro."

"So you didn't actually see the explosion?" asked Gross.

"No, I wasn't facing the park, obviously. When the guns started firing I instinctively ducked and ran. Hell, everybody did."

"Did you have any sense of where the gunfire was coming from?"

She thought for a few moments. "It all happened so fast. I was just trying to get low and out of the way. It was somewhere above me, at least I think so."

Stone said, "Did you look back toward the park when the bomb exploded?"

She nodded.

"What did you see, exactly?"

Friedman sat back, furrowed her brow again and pursed her lips in concentration. "A lot of smoke, some flames shot up, really high. It was near the Jackson statue in the middle of the park. It was hard to tell at night and because of the trees in the way, but at least that's where it seemed to be."

Chapman asked, "Did you see anyone running away from the scene?"

"Like I said, everyone was running once the gunfire started up. And they ran faster when the bomb went off. There were a couple of cops and a dog I remember seeing. The dog was barking and the cops pulled their guns and I think they headed toward the park. I couldn't swear to that because I was going the other way, fast."

"And the man in the suit?" asked Gross. "He must've been somewhere close to you at that point."

"He might've been, but I never saw him."

"Okay, anything else?" asked Stone.

"I felt the ground shake a bit. It must've been a very powerful bomb. It seems ridiculous that with all the police down there no one noticed an explosive somewhere in the park. I mean, how did that happen?"

Gross sat back. "What did you do after that?"

"Grabbed a train home. I got lucky. I heard they closed the metro station a few minutes after I got on."

Gross rose and handed her a card. "If you think of anything else let us know."

After she left Gross looked at the other three. "Well?"

"She didn't add much to what we already knew," said Stone.

"What a simpering sot," snapped Chapman. "I was surprised she didn't pull her bloody dress up over her fake blonde hair."

Stone ignored this barb and said, "Okay, we have gunfire that should have never happened. A bomb that shouldn't have gone off. And a target that wasn't even there."

Gross's phone rang. Ten seconds later he clicked off. "Okay, this sucker just got even more complicated. A group in Yemen has claimed responsibility for the attack."

CHAPTER

21

THE NEXT DAY STONE WATCHED on TV along with Tom Gross from the latter's office as the media reported that a group based in Yemen had opened fire on Lafayette Park and also set off a bomb there. It was done to show that it could reach inside the very heart of the American government. At least that's what the loose translation of the group's message released to the Western media had implied. Afterward there was a brief press conference at which the FBI director spoke, and then the ADIC answered a few questions from the media, without really telling them anything at all.

Stone asked, "Are we sure the Yemen message is authentic?"

Gross nodded. "Whoever called it in had the proper authorization codes."

Stone added, "But that just authenticates the group making the statement. It doesn't prove they actually did it."

"That's true. And they sometimes lie."

"I don't suppose they gave any helpful details on how they managed the guns and the bomb right under our noses?" asked Stone.

"No. What scares the crap out of me is that if they can hit Lafayette Park successfully, what's next? What place is safe? It's like they said, it's symbolic. And you know every American is right now thinking the same thing."

Stone said, "And can the terrorists hop across the street and hit the White House?"

Gross nodded. "That possibility is on the mind of every person in this building."

"In lots of buildings," added Stone.

Gross said, "Where's your British sidekick?"

"Not really sure," said Stone.

"What's your take on her?" asked Gross.

"She's one of their best or she wouldn't be involved in this."

"A good asset for us, then?"

"I think so. Any hits on the jogger, or the suit?"

"None. Unlike Marisa Friedman, the images on the video of the guy in the suit weren't really clear.

I'm not surprised no one has recognized him. He was never looking at the cameras. Just was sort of staring at the ground."

"You think he knew where the cameras were posted?"

"Not even I know where all the cameras are posted," replied Gross. "But we did put out a notice to the media outlets for all people in the park that night to come forward. That's how Friedman came in. So I am surprised we haven't heard from him."

"Well, we *wouldn't* hear from him if he were involved in this somehow," Stone pointed out.

Gross sat down at his desk and fiddled with his stapler. "How close a look did you get at him?"

Stone searched his mind. "Five-seven, balding, slightly stooped shoulders. Never really saw his face. His skin color might have been more dark than light. Whether that was race, ethnicity or a tan I couldn't tell. Obviously no turban, kufi or Palestinian keffiyeh. You would have clearly seen that on the video."

"Your description tallies with what we have of him on the feed."

"Heard from Agent Garchik?" Stone asked.

"I've been harassing the guy every half hour. He did say he was going to go back out to the park today for some follow-up searching."

"When exactly was he going back out?" Stone asked.

"He said this afternoon."

Stone rose.

Gross gazed up at him. "Going somewhere?"

"Running down a few things."

"And you'll share whatever you find?"

"I play fair."

"I looked you up on the official database. But didn't find anything."

"I would be surprised if you had."

"Why?"

"Because officially, I don't exist."

22

THIRTY MINUTES LATER Stone was back at Lafayette Park. The area was still shut down and security was the tightest he had ever seen, tighter even than after 9/11. Someone had penetrated the very heart of the national leadership, and in the stunned countenances of the security forces Stone could sense anger, embarrassment and fear.

He had just reached ground zero when Chapman joined him. She was dressed in black slacks and a matching short jacket that was cut a bit large to accommodate her shoulder holster.

Stone said, "All female agents I've ever met use a belt holster."

"Is that right? Well, I find I get a quicker pull from the shoulder. And that means I don't have to stuff my damn gun in my pantyhose when I'm using the loo. And I have an extra layer of material sewn into my blouses at that spot."

"Why?"

She gave him a fierce look. "Because I have breasts, Stone, in case you hadn't noticed."

"Actually, I was trying to remain gender neutral, Agent Chapman."

"Very PC of you. So Yemen?" said Chapman.

"You believe it?" asked Stone.

"Bloody convenient for some."

"And your boss?"

"He doesn't believe much anymore, actually."

"That comes with age," noted Stone. "Agent Garchik is coming here later today to do some follow-up."

"Follow-up? Didn't he get enough the first time round for his super-duper debris analyzer?"

"I believe his follow-up means he actually has some concerns."

"Oliver?"

Stone immediately turned when he heard the voice. It was distinctive, unforgettable, really. And he hadn't heard it in a very long time.

"Adelphia?"

The woman was standing behind the barricades on H Street. She had four police officers and two Secret Service agents in her face.

Stone hurried over to her while Chapman followed.

One of the agents said, "The lady said you asked to meet with her here. Or else she wouldn't have gotten this far."

"Adelphia?" he said again as he stared at her.

The agent said, "So you do know her, sir?"

"Yes, I do."

"Still can't let unauthorized persons inside the tape. The scene hasn't been released yet."

"Right," said Stone. "I'll step out and escort her from here."

He passed through an opening in the barricades, took Adelphia's arm and led her in the direction of St. John's Church. There was a bench near the entrance. Stone knew this bench had been used years ago to teach rookie CIA agents how to conduct signaling assignments for dead drops of clandestine information. Now it was just a place to rest.

They sat while Chapman hovered nearby but out of earshot, in deference to Adelphia's hurried request to talk to Stone alone.

Oliver Stone and Adelphia shared a common history. She had been a protestor at Lafayette Park even before him. They had become friends. She had helped Stone during some critical times in his life. And then one day she had not come back to her small tent near the edge of the park. After a few days he went to her tiny apartment above a dry cleaning business in Chinatown to check on her. The place was empty. No one could tell him where she had gone. He had not seen her again until right now.

She looked older, her hair full of gray. Her face, wrinkled when he had last seen her, was even more drawn and withered; the pouches of skin under her eyes had inflated. He remembered her as pugnacious and difficult. And secretive. But he had learned enough of her background to suspect that she had led an extraordinary life before settling in Lafayette Park.

"Adelphia, where have you been all this time? You just disappeared."

"I had to, Oliver. It was time."

Her voice was not nearly as accented as it was before. Her command of the English language, always a bit ragged, had improved markedly.

"What do you mean it was time?"

"I need to tell you something."

"What?"

"A question first. Are you once more working for the government?"

"Once more? How do you know I ever did?"

"There are many things I don't know about you,

Oliver. But there are some things I do know about you." She paused and added, "Such as your real name is John Carr."

He sat back and studied her in a new light. "How long have you known?"

"You remember when that man attacked you when I was trying to give some money to that poor homeless person?"

"I remember."

"You defended yourself using a technique that I had only seen once before. When some elite Soviet commandos came to Poland to round up dissenters."

"Did you suspect me of being a spy?"

"The thought did cross my mind, but events proved otherwise."

"You were made aware of certain events?"

"I know that your country betrayed you. But you once more work with them?"

"Yes."

"Then I can help you."

"How?"

"The man in the suit that was here two nights ago?"

He leaned closer. "You know where he is?"

"Yes."

"And do you know why he was at the park that night?"

"Yes."

"Was he there to meet with someone?"

"Yes." She paused. "He was there to meet with me."

23

"HIS NAME IS DR. FUAT TURKEKUL," said Adelphia, before Stone could even ask the question.

"A doctor of what?"

"Not medical. He's a Ph.D. Of both political science and economics. He is a very well-known man in elite academic circles. He is multilingual. He spent years at Cambridge. The London School of Economics. The Sorbonne. Now he's a visiting scholar at Georgetown."

"Turkekul? Where is he from originally?"

Adelphia snagged a bit of hair out of her eyes. "Why does it matter?"

"Adelphia, you know what happened here."

"And Fuat being a foreigner he goes to the top of the suspicion list?"

"Why was he meeting you in the park that night?"

When she didn't answer he said, "There are many things I never knew about you. Would one of them be the real reason why you were in the park all those years?"

"I knew who you were while I was still at the park," she said. "What does that tell you?"

"That you were not working with or for the Americans. Otherwise I would have been taken away."

"My allegiances were to another country. But one that was an ally of America."

"Which one?"

"Does it matter?"

"Perhaps not to me, but it will to others."

"Her?" she said, indicating Chapman.

"Not so much, no."

"Your best ally in the Middle East," she said finally. "That was my master."

Stone slowly nodded. "All right, that I can understand. But getting back to Turkekul?"

"He is not simply a scholar. He has other interests. But again, these interests are in line with the Americans' goals."

"So you say. But what happened two nights ago doesn't make me believe that."

"He had nothing to do with that attack," she said sternly. "As I told you, he was there to meet me. If he hadn't left when he did, he would've been killed."

"Yes, his timing was very fortuitous," said Stone in a skeptical tone.

"I tell you he had nothing to do with it."

"Why didn't you meet with him, then? You weren't there, that I know for sure."

She appeared nervous. "It is not easy to say why. But I couldn't. The time for me to come passed and so he left. We adhere to an exacting schedule."

"You've talked to him since then?"

She looked warily at him. "I didn't say that."

"Adelphia, I need to speak with him. Now."

"I'm sure he knows nothing about any of this."

"If that's the truth he has nothing to fear."

"Famous last words coming from you."

"You don't trust me?"

"You've gone back in, you said so yourself. I may trust you, but not *them*." She glanced once more at Chapman as though she represented "them."

"If Turkekul had no connection to the attack he has nothing to worry about."

Her look was clearly one of skepticism. "I saw you yesterday with the FBI agent. I will not take them to Fuat. Nothing can make me do that."

"Your words are not assuring me as to his innocence."

"There are many agendas out there, Oliver. And most of them have nothing to do with pure guilt or innocence. You know that."

"All right, then take me, just me."

She nodded at Chapman. "And what of her?"

"Just me, Adelphia. But I need to speak with him now."

She drew a long breath. "This is not easy, Oliver."

"We've known each other a long time. You can trust me. Just as I've trusted you. And after all, you came to me."

"Let me make a call," she finally said with great reluctance.

CHAPTER

24

ON THE WAY Adelphia told Stone that Fuat Turkekul was staying on the Georgetown campus at the residence of a full-time faculty member who was away on a sabbatical overseas.

Stone looked where they were headed. "This is not the way to Georgetown," he remarked.

"I would not take you to where he is staying," she replied. "In case we're being followed. He will meet us near the George Washington University campus."

"All right."

"Your friend did not appear pleased to be left behind," said Adelphia as they walked along. Stone had asked Chapman to stay back at the park.

"I wouldn't either. Tell me more about Turkekul."

"What do you want to know?" she asked in a

cautious tone. The car horns arose from the snarled traffic as they slowly made their way west of the White House and toward GW University.

"Everything."

"That is impossible."

"You said he's a scholar and a friend of this country. You said he is also far more than an academician. And that he was meeting with you at the park that night for a reason you won't disclose."

"See, I have already told you much."

"You have really told me nothing," he countered.

"I didn't have to come to you at all," she replied crossly.

"But you did. Don't let it be for nothing."

"I will let Fuat decide what to tell or not to tell. It is up to him really."

And she would say no more. They arrived on the GW campus and Stone followed Adelphia to the place where Turkekul would meet them.

They were let into the building after Adelphia pushed a buzzer and identified herself to a man Stone assumed was Turkekul. They walked up one flight of stairs. Turkekul was waiting for them at the open door to an apartment. He wore a white dress shirt with a cardigan over it, and gray slacks. He was taller than Stone had gauged, about five-ten, and bald, as Stone had correctly remembered.

Up close Stone could now see that Turkekul was his age or slightly older.

Adelphia introduced them and Stone showed his badge to the man. Turkekul studied the credentials and then closed the door and motioned them to take seats on the white couch in the main room of the apartment. As Stone looked around he was intrigued by the piles of books and typewritten pages scattered everywhere. From some of the titles he was able to read it became clear that Turkekul was a man of diverse intellectual interests who was versed in at least four languages.

"From what Adelphia told me you're not staying here, but rather at Georgetown."

"I also maintain a flat here. Just in case. One can never be too careful," said Turkekul.

"I'll never argue with that."

He offered them hot tea. Adelphia accepted. Stone declined. Turkekul fetched the tea and settled across from them.

"Adelphia has told me some of the situation, and she let me make the decision to meet with you. For that I thank her." Turkekul's voice was firm, commanding. He was obviously used to lecturing. Stone tried to diagnose the underlying accent and inflection to determine the man's origins. Though normally quite adept at that, he came away with no definitive answer.

"Why do you thank her?" asked Stone. "From the way she told it, you didn't want to meet at all."

"Then you misunderstood her. I thought it better to clear the air now, instead of having what you call the loose threads."

"You knew the park was under video surveillance," said Stone. "And also where the cameras were arrayed?"

Adelphia clenched her teacup a bit more tightly while Turkekul finished a sip of his drink before setting the cup down and carefully wiping his mouth with a handkerchief pulled from his sweater pocket.

"Why do you say that?"

"You kept your back to them. You stooped over, your face pointing down. I remember that. That maneuver threw off my estimate of your height. And you were pretending to read the plaque on the statue, to give you some reason to not look toward the bank of cameras." He glanced at Adelphia. "Did you tell him where the cameras were located?"

Before she could answer Turkekul said, "You are mostly correct. However, I was not *pretending* to read the plaque. I did in fact read it. The German von Steuben has long been of historical interest to me."

"Why?"

"My maternal grandfather was German. He was also in the military."

"German and in the military?"

"The Third Reich, yes. But with a twist."

"What twist?"

"He was a Jew."

Stone said nothing.

"And he was a spy. They discovered his real identity in 1944. They didn't bother sending him to a concentration camp to join his fellow Jews. They simply executed him on the bombed-out streets of Berlin. The incensed and war-weary crowd of Germans tore his body apart, I was told. It was indeed tragic. A few more months and the war in Europe would be over."

"He died a hero," added Adelphia, though she was looking at Stone.

"Adelphia told me you were meeting with her at the park that night, only she never showed up. She also told me that you have interests outside of academia."

"That is true."

"What are those interests?"

"I cannot see how they have relevance to what you seek."

"I'd like to be the judge of that."

"I can see that."

"But we can start with what you saw that night in the park."

Turkekul spoke in great detail for the next ten minutes as he patiently laid out what he had observed. "I was past the Decatur House when I heard the guns commence firing," he added.

"And what did you do?"

"What any sensible person would have done. I ran in the other direction."

"So you could tell from where the gunfire was coming?"

"Yes and no. Yes in that I saw the bullets ripping through the trees in the park. Thus I assumed that the origin was coming from H Street or thereabouts. I did not stop to look and gauge exactly the shots' origins. I have some nerve, but not enough to stand pat when guns are firing."

"And the woman who left the park about the same time you did?"

"I saw her once. She too was running across the street."

Stone glanced at Adelphia. "So what were you two planning to meet about?"

"If we refuse to tell you, I suppose you will turn us in," said Turkekul.

"No."

Turkekul looked surprised. "Why not?"

"Because Adelphia is an old friend of mine. She's helped me in the past. She kept secrets about me to herself. I don't betray my friends."

"Even though, as I understand it, you now work for your government."

"I don't betray my friends," Stone said again.

"An admirable trait," opined Turkekul. He remained silent for a few seconds, his index finger tapping absently on the arm of the chair.

Finally he sat forward. "I have been given a mission, Agent Stone. A very difficult one. One that no one else has been able to accomplish."

"Which is?"

"To help us find Osama bin Laden."

The voice did not belong to Fuat Turkekul.

Stone turned to see Sir James McElroy stroll into the room.

CHAPTER

25

McElroy sat down across from Stone.

Stone said, "It's comforting to see that you still lie as well as ever."

"A necessary skill in our line of work, as you well know."

"So how big a lie was it?"

"I have known about Fuat here for some time now. We actually worked with the Americans to bring this whole mission up to snuff."

"I can tell you that your keeping me in the dark forced me to waste an incredible amount of time, but then you already know that."

"Without seeming to make excuses, Oliver, I also have a higher authority to answer to."

"And they wanted to keep the truth from me?"

"Yes. However, I decided to bring this charade to

an end for two reasons. One, it wasn't fair to you. And second, it's inefficient."

Stone looked at Adelphia. "I take it he asked you to come to me?"

Adelphia nodded. "But I've wanted to for a long time. I miss our chats. Our friendship."

Stone looked back at McElroy. "Are you here simply to say you're sorry and pat me on the head, or do you intend to fill me in? And is Chapman aware of this?"

McElroy blew his nose into his handkerchief and shook his head. He had on the same blue blazer but a fresh shirt and pants. His face was pinched and the eyes evidenced the physical pain he was suffering. "No, she's not."

"All right," Stone said warily.

"To get back to your first query. We decided to tell you because you might've figured it out on your own. I know how tenacious you can be. It was the most extraordinarily unfortunate timing that Fuat was in the park when it happened."

"And you see no connection?" Stone asked.

"Actually, I wish I did. It would at least make some sense out of what so far is inexplicable."

"You're sure about that?"

"That Fuat was not the target? Reasonably sure.

The mission has hardly begun. And Fuat is not in the front lines. It would be counterintuitive to expect a man to be hunting Osama bin Laden from the United States. It's merely in the planning stages, a delicate operation between several like-minded countries, but it does involve a fresh approach with new assets on the ground, hence the need for secrecy. Adelphia represents one such entity. My interests are self-evident."

"And what are your interests, Mr. Turkekul?" Stone gazed at the other man.

Turkekul said, "After the end of World War II my German mother left for Turkey where she met my father. I don't believe he knew of her ethnicity. The war destroyed the official records of millions of people. I only found out when I was an adult. I was born in Turkey, just outside of Constantinople. But I grew up in Pakistan, although for a time my family lived in Afghanistan. I am a Muslim like my father but I despise the people behind 9/11. They have taken the concept of jihad and twisted it into something ugly and indefensible in furtherance of their own hatred for others."

"Fuat is our ace in the hole, as it were," said McElroy. "He has intimate contacts not only within the Muslim community but also in the area of the world where we believe our quarry to be."

"The mountains between Pakistan and Afghanistan?" replied Stone.

Turkekul smiled. "You will not get the man with a Predator drone strike. He is too cunning for that. And perhaps he is in those mountains, and perhaps not."

"And it was decided to deploy you now and not before?" asked Stone.

Turkekul was about to say something in response when McElroy broke in. "Not something that we need to go into, Oliver. Just take my word on that."

"All right, but if you are so well-connected, Mr. Turkekul, there are those who would suspect you may be of help to the West. They may have attempted a preemptive strike."

"Machine guns and bombs and they missed poor Fuat standing out in the open? Hardly credible," said McElroy.

"I don't disagree. But the Yemen group taking responsibility?"

"In my eyes equally incredible, but the Yanks, I have to admit, see it differently."

"Why a meeting in Lafayette Park?"

McElroy glanced at Adelphia, who said, "No one expects you to go to so conspicuous a place to conduct a clandestine rendezvous."

"Dark alleys and darker pubs," chimed in McElroy

with a fake shudder. "Like in the cinema. Rubbish, actually. That's where all the coppers are looking for the spies between pints."

"Why didn't you show up that night, Adelphia?" Stone asked again.

"It was called off by my superiors. I was not given a reason. I knew that when I did not appear by a certain time Fuat would leave by prearrangement." Adelphia added, "Do they know the source of the bomb?"

"No, not yet."

"Was it a suicide bomber?" asked Turkekul. "That is their preferred choice of attack, other than an IED. I know of this group in Yemen. They stick to that playbook religiously."

Stone eyed McElroy, who made a slight shake of the head. Stone shifted in his seat. "It's an ongoing investigation."

"Will you have to report this contact to your superiors?" Turkekul said.

McElroy cleared his throat. "Oliver, I cannot officially tell you what to do. But I would ask that you think about that question carefully. A report at this juncture, even a censored one, could well lead to the termination of this mission before it's ever had a chance to succeed." McElroy bowed his head and seemed to be waiting for an answer.

Stone didn't deliberate for long. He turned to Turkekul. "I'll say nothing, for now. However, despite what you've said, if it becomes apparent that you were the target I would assume you would want to know that?"

Turkekul said, "You assume correctly. And I thank you for that."

"I'll fill Chapman in."

"Actually, she needn't know," McElroy said quickly.

Stone shook his head. "I don't keep things from my partner. I know, she knows."

McElroy looked indecisive. "I'll leave it up to you, then."

Stone rose from the couch. "One last question. Adelphia. How was the communication made between you two as to the location?"

"I left a message up on the main notice board in the middle of Georgetown campus," said Adelphia. "It was in a code that Fuat and I worked out."

"The same code we used to use when we both were at the park?"

"Very close to it," she admitted.

"Don't trust secure electronic communications?" asked Stone.

"There are no such things, my friend," said

Turkekul. "Several of my colleagues have found that out to their great detriment."

McElroy added, "The insecurity of electronic systems has forced us all back in some ways to the old spy dodges. A bit less efficient, but we all get to use our ingenuity instead of relying on machines to do it for us. I actually like it a lot better. But then I'm an old Cold War relic."

McElroy walked Stone out. "I'm sorry it had to be done this way. I would have preferred otherwise, Oliver. It wasn't fair to you."

"Life is rarely fair."

"I understand the investigation proceeds slowly."

"If at all."

"It has to make sense, somehow. If it doesn't, much of what I believe in life goes up in smoke."

"Can I expect any more surprises along these lines?"

"I hope not. As for Chapman?"

"I'm going to tell her. And you won't convince me otherwise."

"You're probably right."

"Take care, *Sir* James."

"Oliver, watch your back." He paused and added, "And your front too."

"You know something I don't?"

"No, but the old relic's antennae are tingling something fierce."

"One more time," said Stone. "Are you withholding anything else from me?"

"Good luck, Oliver. And please take my advice."

CHAPTER

26

"So what did you learn?" Chapman asked Stone when he returned to Lafayette Park.

Stone led her off to the side and away from the other investigators in the park. He told her everything that had happened, including her boss's appearance and Fuat Turkekul's mission.

"Good God," she exclaimed. "I can't believe it."

"What, the underlying facts, or that you weren't in the loop?"

"Both, I guess." Her gaze was downcast, her look one of lost confidence.

Realizing what she was thinking, Stone said, "McElroy plays things very close to the vest. And he compartmentalizes. And he withholds when he deems it necessary. I expect you know that."

"I do, it's just..."

He gripped her arm. "Don't let this destroy the

faith you have in yourself. That will help no one, least of all you. Keeping you in the dark is not a reflection on your ability. It's just the way it is. We've all had to suffer through that."

She looked up, drew a breath and her resolve seemed to stiffen. "You're right." She put a hand on his shoulder. "I do appreciate you telling me, though." She removed her hand. "Did he ask you to do that?"

"Do you want the truth?"

"Yes, please," she said firmly. "It would be refreshing, actually."

"Initially he didn't want you to know. But when I told him I don't keep things from my partner he agreed with my decision to tell you."

Chapman studied him closely, evidently trying to determine if *he* were telling the truth. "Good, enough said on the subject."

"So where were you this morning?" asked Stone.

She looked sheepish. "I was actually having a lie-in. I've had about two hours' sleep in the last forty-eight, and the jet lag really kicked in. I was a bit knackered. And I didn't think I could manage to be much help when I could barely stay awake."

Stone glanced over and saw Agent Garchik striding toward them. "Maybe he'll have some answers."

They met him at the barriers and followed Garchik back to ground zero. The ATF agent's expression was both curious and concerned.

"You have some developments?" prompted Stone.

Garchik nodded as he stared down at the crater. "You could say that. Those pieces of leather we found came from a Wilson basketball."

"A basketball!" exclaimed Chapman.

"You're sure it was involved in the explosion?" Stone asked.

"I can't think of another reason why bits of a basketball would be in Lafayette Park. And the scorch marks showed they were quite near the blast seat. You could say right on top of it."

They all looked down at the hole.

"Your conclusion?" Stone asked.

"I think the bomb could very well have been in the basketball and the ball was placed inside the root ball of the maple. That location would tally with the debris field and other indicators we found."

"A bomb in a basketball?" said Chapman.

"It would work," said Garchik. "And it's been done before by a few people, all dead now. Cut it open, put the bomb inside, reseal it, pump it up so that if anyone held it, it would feel legit. I wouldn't advise dribbling the sucker, though."

"How was it detonated?" asked Stone.

"Remotely would be my best guess, right now. Not a timer."

Stone said, "But we have information that the bomb dogs had patrolled the site the night of the bombing. Wouldn't they have sensed it? You said they couldn't be fooled by anything."

"They can't. But they do have limits."

"What exactly are those limits?" asked Chapman.

"Typical scent radius for the dogs is about three feet in all directions aboveground. And they can sniff out explosives buried up to roughly the same distance belowground." Garchik pointed at the crater. "This hole before the bomb went off was over four feet deep and well over eight feet across."

"But uncovered," Stone pointed out.

"Yeah, but the root ball was huge. Six feet wide by over three feet high."

Stone realized something. "And there was yellow warning tape up cordoning off this area. So the dogs might not have gotten within ten feet of it."

"That's right," said Garchik. "So whether the bomb was here when they made their pass or not, chances are good they wouldn't have detected it unless their handlers took them past the tape and let them climb right on top of the root ball. Which I sort of doubt was the case."

Stone's gaze immediately swung toward the White House. "Then we need to talk to the people who installed it as soon as possible. But first we need to look at the video."

"Video?" said Chapman.

"The video feed will show when that tree went in and who did it. It will also show if anyone went back in there afterward. And what they had with them. Like a bag big enough to place a basketball in."

Garchik said, "It would be pretty hard to slip a basketball inside a root ball and not have someone see you. There's a burlap sack around it to hold the dirt and roots together, but it would still be complicated. You'd have to get the ball there somehow, get down into the hole, slit the sack, put the ball in and somehow patch the sack back up."

Chapman added, "And he couldn't exactly waltz it past the White House guards. I'm assuming the workers have to go through checkpoints."

"Yes, they do," answered Stone. "And I would imagine an X-ray of the basketball would reveal the bomb inside?"

"Absolutely," said Garchik.

"Then if one of the groundspeople was involved he didn't take the ball through White House security." He looked around. "But he could have come directly to the park to begin work on the tree.

Someone could have given him the ball then. The White House wouldn't be involved at all."

"Which would be captured on the video," said Garchik. "We'll have to check that angle, but it seems way too easy to detect on our part."

Stone said, "Which means we're missing something." He looked down at the crater. "Let's check that video feed. Right now."

CHAPTER

27

A FEW MINUTES LATER they were standing in the FBI's command post on Jackson Place. They had called in two Secret Service agents, who huddled with them around the large TV screen. The feed they would be looking at had come from the Secret Service's archives.

"We keep the images for a minimum of fifteen years," explained one of the Secret Service agents.

"You're not the only agency with electronic eyes on the park, though," said Stone.

The same agent smiled. "We all have peepers on our little slice of Hell's Corner. In an ideal world we all share what we see, but this is far from an ideal world."

"What exactly are you looking for?" asked the other agent.

Stone explained about the tree being planted, and also about the bomb dog going near the tree.

Agent Garchik had stayed behind in the park to keep going over the crime scene, but Tom Gross had joined them after being called by Stone. The FBI agent said, "We need to see the entire feed from the time the tree was delivered to the moment the bomb went off."

They were shown this feed from three different angles. It took a long time, even though the security guard was able to speed up the frames without any significant detail being missed. At the end they stared at the screen with the same unanswered questions.

Gross said, "The dogs did make a pass, but they stayed outside the tape line. That was a big hole in the security wall. Secret Service is going to get dinged for that."

The two agents exchanged glances and grimaced but said nothing.

"And there wasn't even a hint of anyone planting anything in that hole," added Chapman.

Stone said, "You're sure this is all the footage?"

One of the agents said, "That's it."

Gross, Stone and Chapman left the command center. On the way back to the park Gross said, "I can't remember the last case I had where not only haven't I taken a step forward, I keep taking steps back."

Stone closed his eyes and recalled what he had seen on the video. A crane had lifted the large tree up into the air. Then a crew of National Park Service personnel in their green-and-khaki uniforms had moved in and helped direct the placement of the maple into the hole.

He opened his eyes. "There had to be a staging area for the tree. Where it was kept before being installed? That wasn't on the video."

"That's right," said a hopeful-looking Gross.

Chapman added, "And the time stamp on the video shows that the tree was put in a day before the bombing happened. So why was the hole still uncovered?"

Gross said, "I think we need to find answers to those questions."

A moment later his phone rang. He talked for a few moments and then clicked off. "We got a hit on the jogger. Missing persons report was phoned in a few hours ago. Family member. Matches the description, and he was in the vicinity of the park."

"Why so long to call it in?" asked Stone.

"Something we'll have to find out when we talk to them."

"I think we should split up," said Stone. "You

and your men can handle the groundspeople and Chapman and I can talk to the family members. You have the address?"

Gross gave it to him. As they were parting company the FBI agent said, "Now we've only got the suit to track down."

Stone never turned around. "Yeah," he said over his shoulder as Chapman marched along beside him.

When they got to her car she said, "You know you could be charged with withholding vital evidence in an investigation. With obstruction even."

"If you think that's the case, feel free to report me."

The two looked across the width of the rental at each other.

Chapman finally sighed. "I don't think it would further my career to pull the rug out from under my boss. So just get the hell in the car."

When the doors plunked closed she threw it into gear. "Where to?"

Stone gazed down at the slip of paper that Gross had given him with the address. "Anacostia. Make sure you keep your gun handy."

"Is it dangerous, then, this Anacostia?"

Stone thought for a few moments before replying, "I guess less dangerous than Lafayette Park, actually."

CHAPTER

28

CARMEN ESCALANTE lived in a duplex a few blocks from the river. The neighborhood was within sight of the ballpark of the Washington Nationals, but had not benefited from the gentrification that was going on in other areas around the stadium.

They reached Escalante's address and Stone knocked on a door that was scarred by at least three old bullet pocks by his quick count. They heard curious sounds approaching. Footsteps and something more. Something that clunked. When the door opened they were looking down at a petite woman in her twenties who had metal braces on each arm to support her twisted legs. Hence the strange sounds.

"Carmen Escalante?" Stone asked.

She nodded. "I am Carmen."

Stone and then Chapman showed her their badges.

"We're here about your report of a missing person," said Chapman.

"You don't sound American," said Carmen curiously.

"I'm not."

Carmen looked confused. Stone said, "Can we come in?"

They followed her down a short hall to a tiny room. The furniture was thirdhand, the floor littered with junk. Stone could smell rotting food.

"I haven't had a chance to clean up lately," Carmen said, but her tone was unapologetic. She dropped onto the couch and stood her braces against the arm of the furniture. On either side of her was stacked what Stone could only politely describe as crap.

Stone and Chapman remained standing because there was nowhere else to sit.

"I'm sure you've been worried about...?" Stone said in a prompting manner.

"My uncle, Alfredo, but we call him Freddy."

"We?"

"The family."

"Are they here?" Stone looked around.

"No, they're back in Mexico."

"So you live here with him?"

She nodded.

Stone said, "And his last name?"

"Padilla."

"When was the last time you saw him?" asked Chapman.

"Two nights ago. He went out for dinner."

"Do you know where?"

"At a place on Sixteenth Street, near F. He come from España originally, my uncle. My father's family, the Escalantes, they come from España too, a long time ago. Good paellas in España. He liked his paellas, my uncle. And this place he goes to, it has good paellas."

Stone and Chapman exchanged glances, obviously thinking the same thing.

That would have put him close to Lafayette Park.

"Can I ask why you waited so long to call the police about him?" Stone asked.

"I have no telephone here. And I cannot get around too good without Uncle Freddy. I think he will come home anytime. But he does not. I finally ask a neighbor to call for me."

"Okay. Do you remember what he was wearing when he went out?"

"His blue sweatsuit. He liked to wear it, but he didn't like to work out. I thought that was funny."

"Was he not in good shape?" asked Chapman.

Carmen made a motion with both hands to indicate a large belly. "He liked his *comida* and his beer," she said simply.

"How would he usually get home? Did he have a car?" asked Stone.

"We have no car. He use bus or train."

"Did he tell you he might go for a walk after dinner?" asked Chapman.

Carmen's face started to tremble and she pointed to the little TV perched on a particleboard stand. "I see what happened. The bomb. Uncle Freddy, he is dead?" A tear slid down her cheek.

Stone and Chapman again exchanged a look. "Do you have a photo of your uncle here?"

Carmen pointed to a lopsided bookshelf against one wall. There were a half dozen framed photos on it. Stone went over, checked them out. Alfredo "Freddy" Padilla was in the third from the right. He wore jeans but also the same blue warm-up jacket in which he had been blown to bits. Stone picked it up and showed it to Chapman, who nodded, instantly recognizing the man from the countless times she'd watched him on the video. Stone put the photo back down and turned to Carmen.

"Do you have any family who could come and stay with you?"

"Then he is dead?"

Stone hesitated. "I'm afraid so."

She put a hand up to her mouth and started to quietly sob.

Stone knelt down in front of her. "I know this is a really bad time, but can you think of any reason why your uncle would have wanted to take a walk through Lafayette Park that night?"

The woman finally composed herself, finding some internal strength that Stone was frankly surprised she possessed.

"He love this country," she said. "We only recently come here. Me for the medicos to help with my legs. Uncle Freddy he come with me. My parents are dead. He get job. It not pay much, but he was doing the best he could."

"Your English is very good for only recently coming here," commented Chapman.

Carmen smiled. "I take it in school from when I was little. And I travel to Texas. My English is best in *mi familia*," she said proudly.

"So Lafayette Park?" prompted Stone.

"He liked to go and look at your White House. He would tell me, 'Carmen, this is greatest country on earth. A person he can do anything here.' He had me go one time. He carry me on his shoulders. We look at the *grande casa blanca*. He say your president lived there. And that he was a great man."

Stone stood. "Again, I'm very sorry."

Chapman asked, "Is there anyone who can come and stay with you?"

"It is all right. I have been by myself before."

"But do you have other relatives?" persisted Chapman.

Carmen sniffled but nodded. "I have people who can come and take me back to Mexico."

"Back? But what about your doctors?" asked Stone.

"Not without Uncle Freddy," she replied. "My parents were killed in a bus accident. I was also on the bus. That was how my legs came to be like this. Uncle Freddy, he too was on bus. They take out his spleen and other things, but he got well. And he was like a father to me." She stopped. "I...I don't want to live here without him. Not even if this is the greatest country in all the world."

"If you need any help will you contact us?" Stone wrote his phone number down on a piece of paper and handed it to her. He paused. "If you could give us something of your uncle's? A comb or a toothbrush. So we can..." His voice trailed off.

They left with a couple of articles containing

Alfredo Padilla's DNA to compare to the man's remains. They sealed them in evidence bags Chapman had brought. Stone was certain it was the man. But the DNA would be conclusive.

As they were walking back to the car Chapman said, "Okay, I'm an old cynic, but I want to start crying my bleeding eyes out."

"Alfredo Padilla was clearly in the wrong place at the wrong time," said Stone. "And she has to pay the price."

"He paid a pretty big one too," Chapman reminded him.

They got back in the car. She said, "What now?"

"We hope Agent Gross has better luck than we did. But something tells me not to count on that."

CHAPTER

29

THEY LEFT A MESSAGE for Gross and grabbed some Chinese takeout on the way back to Stone's cottage. The weather was nice so Stone carried his little round kitchen table and two chairs out to the front porch. He laid out two plates and utensils and pulled two beers from the small refrigerator in his kitchen.

They sat down and Chapman held up her beer and clinked it against Stone's.

"Cheers. You know how to treat a lady."

"You bought the food. And I have no idea how old the beer is."

She took a spoonful of wonton soup, extra spicy that made her eyes water, and retreated once more to her beer.

"Too hot for you?" said Stone as he eyed her with some amusement.

"Actually, I'm into pain. One of the reasons I do this job, I reckon."

"I worked with MI6 back in the day. Didn't know any female agents then."

"Still aren't that many. Testosterone world plain and simple."

"Clear career path or did you stumble onto it by accident?"

"Bit of both, I suppose." She took a mouthful of chicken and rice. "My dad was a copper and my mum was a nurse."

"That still doesn't explain the MI6 connection."

"Sir James McElroy is my godfather."

"Okay," said Stone slowly as he lowered his fork.

"He and my grandfather were in the army together before Sir James went to the intelligence side. I guess he took a fancy to me. Really became a father figure to me when my dad was killed."

"How did your father die? In the line of duty?"

Chapman shrugged. "That's what they said. I never really found out the exact details."

"And that's how you came to be part of law enforcement?"

"I guess Sir James was grooming me all that time. Right schools, right training, right contacts. It seemed inevitable."

"In spite of what you wanted, you mean?"

She took a sip of the beer, holding it in her mouth a moment before swallowing. "I ask myself that from time to time."

"And what's the answer?"

"It changes. And maybe I'm right where I need to be. Maybe I can even find out what really happened to my poor dad." She pushed her plate away and sat back, put her feet up on the porch railing. "What about you? You and Sir James obviously go way back. And he knows things about you I guess I never will."

"They would mean nothing to you."

"What did it feel like, to do what you did?"

Stone rose and stared out at the tombstones in the fading light. The weather in D.C., miserably hot and humid in the summer, and uncomfortably raw in the winter, could suddenly evolve to times like this, when the climate was perfect and you wished the day would never end.

She stood next to him. "Look I won't push it," Chapman said quietly. "It's really none of my business."

"It got to the point where I didn't feel anything anymore," Stone said.

"But how did you get out?"

"I'm not sure I ever did."

"Was it your wife?"

Stone turned to her. "I thought your boss was more discreet."

"It wasn't him," she said hastily. "I just made a guess based on my own observations."

"What observations?" Stone said sharply.

"Of you," she answered simply. "Of things that matter to you. Like friends."

Stone turned away. "Good guess," he said.

"So why did you come back in the fold? After that?"

"I guess I could say I had no choice."

"I think someone like you would always have a choice."

Stone didn't speak for a long time. He just kept staring at the graves. A breeze rippled over them and Chapman wrapped her arms around herself.

"I have a lot of regrets," Stone said finally.

"So this is about making amends?"

"I don't think I can ever make amends, Agent Chapman."

"Please, just call me Mary. We're off duty now."

He glanced at her. "Okay, Mary. Have you ever killed anyone? Intentionally?"

"Once."

Stone nodded. "And how did you feel?"

"Happy at first. That it wasn't me dead. And then I felt sick. I'd been trained to do it, of course, but—"

"No training can prepare you for it."

"I guess not." She clenched the porch railing. "So how many people do you reckon you've killed?"

"Why does it matter to you?"

"I guess it doesn't. And it's not morbid curiosity. I...I don't know what it is, exactly."

Before Stone could answer his cell phone buzzed. It was Tom Gross.

"We're back on duty, *Agent Chapman*," said Stone.

CHAPTER

30

THEY MET GROSS NOT AT HIS OFFICE at the FBI, but at a coffee shop near the Verizon Center. The federal agent was dressed casually in khaki pants, a polo shirt and a Washington Capitals zippered jacket. They bought coffee and sat at a table in the back. Gross looked pale and nervous, his gaze flitting around the small space, as though he suspected he was being followed.

"I'm not liking how this is shaking out," Gross said. His hand went to his jacket pocket and then pulled back.

"You used to smoke?" said Stone.

Gross nodded. "Right this minute, sorry I gave it up."

"So talk to us."

Gross hunched forward and bent his head low. "First tell me how it went with Carmen Escalante?"

Stone and Chapman alternated filling him in about the bereaved and crippled young woman.

"Sad stuff, but then she's a dead end?"

"We never had high hopes for that line anyway," said Stone. "She's a victim, just like her uncle."

"Wrong place, wrong time. Poor sucker. Loves America and look what happens to him."

"How'd things go on your end?" asked Chapman.

Gross shifted in his seat and took a swallow of coffee before answering. "I decided to cut to the chase and snagged the whole National Park Service crew that worked on the installation, including their supervisor, and sat their butts down at WFO. Supervisor's named George Sykes. Career government service; guy has six grandchildren. Background clean as anyone's. He was with his team the whole time and swore on a stack of Bibles that none of them were involved. And I tend to believe him. There were like seven people around the entire time from the moment the tree was delivered to the staging area. No way they all got bought off."

"So why was the hole still uncovered?" Stone asked.

Gross smiled. "Got a real education on that. The National Park Service is very particular about the plantings in Lafayette Park. Apparently only specimens available during George Washington's era are installed there. Those guys are really historians who dig the occasional hole. I learned a lot more about that today than I needed to. But the reason they left the hole open was because they had to prepare special dirt, an arborist was going to look at the tree to make sure the transition hadn't damaged it, yada, yada. They were scheduled to close the hole the next day."

Chapman spoke up. "So the bomb was in the tree's root ball before it was even delivered to the site. That has to be it. The National Park Service folks aren't involved at all."

Stone looked from her to Gross. "Do we know the timeline with the tree? Where it came from? Who was involved on that end?"

"Running that down as we speak. The thing is, I don't see how a tree gets from that point to Lafayette without it being checked for a damn bomb. I mean, at the very least you'd think they'd let a canine take a sniff when it got to the staging area. That tree was big. As you saw on the video, they had to crane the sucker in."

Stone said, "Well, is there a record of a dog going over it for explosives?"

"Not that I can find. And none of the installation crew recalls that happening."

"Another big hole in security if that's true," said Chapman.

"Yeah, but a bomb in a root ball?" said Gross. "Who'd figure that one?"

"Yeah, like jumbo jets flying into skyscrapers," said Stone. "Or explosives in underwear or shoes. We have to start being ahead of that curve or more innocent people will die."

Gross took another swallow of his coffee, his brow a mass of wrinkles.

"Something else?" prompted Stone, who was studying the man carefully.

When Gross spoke he lowered his voice to a level where Stone and Chapman had to lean forward to hear. "I can't believe I'm saying this, but I think our side is watching us. Screwing with us, I mean. That's why I asked to meet you two here."

Chapman said, "Our side? Why do you think that?"

Gross looked at Stone warily. "I know you're with NSC, and frankly I've pulled too many years to blow my career, but I'm also not going to sit pat and pretend everything is fine either."

Stone leaned forward more. "My loyalties run to the people at this table. Now tell me why you suspect that your own side is against you."

Gross looked irritated and sheepish at the same time. "I think my damn phone is being bugged, for one thing. At my office and my house. And it's like when I ask questions, there're more fingerprints down the line than there should be." He eyed Stone and then Chapman. "Tell me something. And I'd like the truth."

"All right," said Chapman quickly, but Stone remained silent, waiting.

"The video feed from the night of the explosion? I mean after the detonation took place? I gotta tell you I'm not buying the company line that the blast screwed the cameras permanently. Like the Secret Service said today, there are lots of eyeballs on that park. But they all don't share." He stopped speaking and eyed them. "So is there more?"

Chapman shot Stone a glance.

Gross frowned. "Yeah, I thought so. So you guys are screwing with me too. How the hell can I run an investigation with both hands tied behind my back? You know what? The only person I trust right now is my wife. And that's the God's honest truth."

"I can understand that."

"And why the hell were you two privy to the full video and I wasn't?" He scowled at Chapman. "Hell, you're not even an American."

"There's no good reason why you were kept out of the loop," admitted Stone. He looked at Chapman. "Your laptop in the car?"

She nodded.

"Go get it."

A minute later she was back and fired her computer up. Seconds later they were looking at the video feed. The *full* video feed.

After they finished Gross sat back, apparently mollified. "Okay, I'm still pissed that I got the rug pulled out from under me, but I didn't see anything on there that deserved to make it off-limits to the FBI."

That was true, thought Stone. But in light of what he had learned, was there something there he just wasn't seeing?

He said to Chapman, "Run it again from the point where everyone starts walking off from the park. And do it in slow motion."

She did as he asked. After a minute Stone said, "Freeze it there." He stared at the motionless video. He was angry for not having seen it before, particularly after what he had learned today.

"Can you enlarge the frame?"

She clicked some keys and the picture morphed larger in front of them.

"Can you swing the frame to the left?"

Chapman manipulated the built-in mouse and the image moved to the left.

Stone put his finger on one spot on the screen. "Do you see it?"

Gross and Chapman looked closer.

"What?" they both said together.

"That car's headlights flicked against the window there. You can see a face clearly reflected in the darkened glass."

The other two leaned closer. "Okay," said Chapman, "I can see it now."

Gross nodded. "But who is it?"

"It's the man in the suit. *That's* why you didn't get this part of the feed."

"Wait a minute," said Gross. "How do you know it's the guy in the suit?"

"Because I met him today."

Gross's face turned red and he stood. "You know where he is? Son of a bitch. You guys keep holding shit back from me. Maybe you're the ones bugging my phones."

Stone stared up at him. "Agent Gross, keep your voice and your temper in check. And sit down. Now."

There was something in Stone's manner that made the federal agent obey. He sat, though his expression was still angry.

Stone continued, "The man in the suit was in the park that night to meet with someone about a very high-priority mission for this country."

"And how do you know that?"

"I'm telling you what I was told earlier today

from a source that I trust. As I said, I met the man whose face is reflected in that window. His mission involves tracking down someone who is the enemy of this country. Perhaps its greatest enemy," Stone added.

Realization slowly spread over Gross's features. He said, "Damn, do you mean...?"

Stone held up his hand. "A highly secret mission. Secret enough for the FBI to have been given an incomplete video feed of a major crime scene to keep his features off the video. Let's leave it at that."

Gross exclaimed, "But then this guy might've been the target."

"No. If he were they wouldn't have missed him."

"And where is this guy?"

"Nearby."

"Okay," Gross said. "And where does that leave us?"

"With not much," said Chapman grumpily. "With not bloody much."

CHAPTER

31

CHAPMAN DROPPED STONE OFF at his cottage and then went on to her lodgings. Stone walked around the cemetery tidying up things at the same time he was thinking about the day's events. They had hit dead ends pretty much in every direction. Each person in the park that night had been checked and found to have nothing to do with the bombing or the gunfire. Alfredo Padilla had been blown up by mistake. Marisa Friedman worked nearby and had been calling her lover. Fuat Turkekul was there to meet Adelphia to discuss their very important operation. The British cop had been there on orders from MI6. Four promising leads turned out to be worth nothing.

Stone went inside and sat behind his desk. It was late and he should sleep, but he wasn't tired; his mind was working too fast to rest. He attempted to read a book to try and relax, but his mind kept coming back to what had happened in Lafayette Park.

Someone had carried off an incredible feat of terrorism smack in the middle of one of the most protected areas in the world, and they had done so for no apparent reason. He did not believe the statement from the organization in Yemen. This operation had to have taken a long time and required enormous resources. While Islamic terrorists had a lot of both, their assets were not infinite. They could not afford to waste them. Therefore, you did not undertake all that for symbolic reasons, any more than you would go to all the trouble of hijacking a jumbo jet and "symbolically" flying it close to a tall building instead of directly into it.

And he also didn't buy the theory that he had seen some pundits bandying about on TV. That people would be scared to come to D.C. now. So what? The government wouldn't be crippled because busloads of tourists from Iowa or Maine decided to go somewhere else on vacation. It was not a "replicable act," as some counterterrorism specialists liked to say. This wasn't a shopping mall or an airport ticket counter. You detonate in one of those places and you terrify people all over the county, who will stay away from their malls and airports. That would severely disrupt the economy. But there was only one White House. Only one Lafayette Park.

If it doesn't make sense the way I'm thinking it through, it means I'm thinking it through wrong. But then what way is right?

He was about to try a different tack when he sank down in his chair after putting out the desk lamp with a flick of his hand.

There was someone outside.

He dropped down and smacked a part of the plank floor in the kneehole section of his desk. The short board spun on a swivel. Inside a holster clipped to the underside of the plank was a custom pistol that he had carried for many years on the job. Back then it was as much a part of his body as his hand. Stone gripped it and swung the board back into place.

He crawled to the rear window and peered out. There was a moon, and even though the men were moving stealthily through the underbrush, Stone still saw them because he knew where and how to look.

He slipped his cell phone from his shirt pocket and was about to text a message when he heard the voice.

"Stone? I'd like to talk to you."

Stone's finger was poised over the send button. He recognized the voice. His mind was moving swiftly over the possible reasons why the man would have come here to see him.

"What about?" he called back.

"I think you know. I'm sure you have a gun and I've been told how well you wield one. And I'm sure you've spotted my men despite their best efforts. So that no one gets hurt, I propose that I come inside and meet with you. Just one-on-one. Does that work?"

"And if it doesn't?" Stone shot back.

"I could say we would just leave."

"Why don't I believe that?"

"We're both on the same side here."

"It doesn't feel that way right now."

"I give you my word. I just want to talk."

"Then why come late at night with a strike team?"

"It's just the way I travel. Don't take it personally. But I do just want to talk."

Stone thought rapidly. He really had no leverage here at all. And information could be a two-way street.

"Just you," he called back. "And I *do* have a gun. If I see even one red dot floating in the air, things will get ugly very fast. Understood?"

"Understood. I'm coming in."

"Slowly."

"Right. Slowly."

A few moments later Riley Weaver, the head of NIC, appeared in the doorway of Stone's humble cottage, which was surrounded by the dead and also now at least a half dozen armed men.

CHAPTER

32

"CLOSE THE DOOR BEHIND YOU," instructed Stone. "And move away from it to your left."

He rose from behind the desk, keeping out of the line of fire from the window.

"Open your jacket."

"I'm not armed."

"Open your jacket."

Weaver did so. He was startled when a hand swiftly searched him.

"You're light on your feet," said Weaver.

Stone stepped back from the man, keeping his gun aimed at him.

"Can we turn on a light?" asked Weaver. "I'm walking blind here."

"If you hadn't shown up with a platoon of fire-power I might treat you with more courtesy." All the time he was talking Stone had kept moving, circling the man. He assumed the former Marine would have excellent night vision too, and he was not proved wrong.

"Okay, I can see you now and I know you can see me," said Weaver. "How do you want to do this?"

"You see the chairs by the fireplace?"

"Yes."

"You on the left."

"And where will you be?"

"Somewhere else."

Weaver moved forward and sat in a rickety wooden chair. He turned his head slightly to the right. "I can't see you anymore."

"I know. What do you want?"

"Our last meeting ended too abruptly."

"Entirely your doing."

"I know. I admit that. You're working with NSC now. And the FBI."

"So?"

"So how would you like to be part of a joint effort with NIC?"

"I already have enough alphabet letters, thanks."

"You guys are no closer to solving this than from the moment that bomb detonated."

"Okay, you have your interagency spies in place.

The man you replaced did the same thing. Not always to positive effect."

"I'm not Carter Gray. I know you two went way back and not in a good way."

"He was excellent at what he did. I just didn't happen to agree with all he did."

"I read up some more on John Carr."

"Good for you. Why are you here? And it's not just to offer me a job you know I wouldn't take."

"You have the president's backing. I know why."

Stone stared across at the man in the dark. He was ten feet from Weaver, behind and slightly to the man's right. A perfect killing angle since most people were right-handed and to fire back they normally wouldn't turn to their right, it was too awkward. They would turn to the left. And then of course it would be too late.

"And where does that get us?" he said.

"I'm not one to dwell on ancient history. A bomb and machine guns in Lafayette Park are what I'm focused on."

"Some are calling it symbolic."

"Do you believe that?" asked Weaver.

"No. Terrorists are only into symbolism so long as there are lots of casualties."

"I agree. Too much time and assets went into this. There had to be a reason."

"I was just trying to think of one when you showed up."

"If we work together we might just get there sooner rather than later."

"I told you, I already have a team on this one."

"We're all on the same team."

"You snatched me from my hospital bed before the FBI could get to me, played the bully at NIC, ridiculed my attempt to tell you what I knew or thought and then turned out the lights when I asked a question. If that's your version of foreplay you'll never get lucky."

"Okay, I deserved that. I played the heavy with you and it backfired. I realize that now."

"And you're here now to play nice?"

"Is that too hard to believe?"

"Yes, it is. This is Washington, where they eat their young *and* their old. So one more time, why are you here?"

Stone counted ten seconds off in his head and the silence persisted. He lined up the silhouette of Weaver along his gunsight. He strained to hear the sounds of black boots moving in on him.

He can't be that stupid, thought Stone. Acting as a distraction. It didn't matter to Stone that the men outside worked for the same government he did. He had enough experience to know that citizenship was no protection when you were in the middle of someone else's agenda. Or conspiracy. Which in Stone's mind were one and the same.

"I'm scared, Stone."

This unexpected comment caused Stone to glance up from his sightline.

"Why?"

"Because something is going to happen. Something big, and I'm clueless about what it might be. And if the nation's intelligence chief is clueless, well, it's not good. I don't want to be remembered for missing the big one."

Stone relaxed a bit more. "Something big. Based on what? Chatter?"

"That and my gut. How did that bomb get in that hole? Why machine guns that hit nobody? And I've got another question that I don't even think you've thought of."

"What?"

"What happened to the original maple tree in the park? My sources tell me it just died, overnight. That's why it had to be replaced. It'd been there for decades, hale and hearty, and then it just up and died and no one knows why."

Stone seemed paralyzed by this statement. He'd been gone from Lafayette Park for some time. Still, he remembered that maple, tall, huge canopy, beautiful specimen. It had seemed healthy.

And then it just died. And no one knows why.

He sat down next to the man and slipped his gun in his waistband. When Weaver eyed the weapon, Stone said, "I'm authorized to carry one now."

"No arguments from me. And you're probably going to need it before this is over."

"So you think the tree was deliberately sabotaged?"

"Either that or it's a pretty big coincidence. No new tree needed, that bomb ain't getting to Lafayette Park. Because it came inside that tree. I think we all realize that now."

"Agent Gross with the FBI said they were tracking down that angle. But they aren't finding much."

"That's interesting."

"You're telling me you didn't know that already?"

"FBI has always gone its own way. I keep my ears to the ground, though. And I think what they'll continue to find on that end is a big zip."

"Why? Tracks too well covered?"

Weaver gazed over at Stone through the darkness. "They didn't X-ray that root ball. It's going in the park, in the dirt. It's not the Christmas tree for the White House."

"Canine sweep?"

"Not sure. But don't think so."

"Why not?"

"No definitive answer on that."

"ATF thinks it was a remote detonation setup."

"Hmmph."

"You disagree?"

"Let me put it to you this way. No bomb is fool-proof. I almost got my hand blown off once dealing with a 'foolproof' explosive when I was in the Corps."

"So what's your theory?"

"Can we turn on some lights? I feel like I'm back in high school sneaking some of my old man's hooch."

"I prefer the dark."

"Okay, suit yourself. The bomb goes in with a remote detonator. Probably a cell phone. Tree hole gets covered up. Then it's detonated at the precise time they want. But instead we got a guy running from gunfire who jumps in a hole to save his ass, and boom."

"But how did the bomb detonate?"

"Like I said, bombs are tricky things. Fat guy jumps and lands right on it, or maybe one of the slugs hits it. Detonates."

"We'd actually discussed that possibility."

"So I'm here wasting your time?"

"No, I hadn't thought of the tree being killed on purpose. That's one for you."

"It only occurred to me tonight."

"ATF thinks the bomb was in a basketball and then placed inside the root ball."

"Doesn't matter, still could have gone off accidentally."

"But that makes no sense. The only reason the guy jumped in the hole and, according to your theory, prematurely detonated the bomb was because he was running from the gunfire. Why go to all the trouble to get a bomb there and then screw it up by shooting off the guns?"

"It makes perfect sense if you look at it in a different way."

A few seconds later Stone said slowly, "You mean if the gunners and bombers were different."

"Exactly. And if so, the bombers are pretty pissed off right now at whoever started shooting."

Stone said, "The Yemeni group?"

"Those guys claim credit for lots of shit they had nothing to do with. Maybe they did the guns, okay. But then the bomb goes off and they figure, 'Hell, let's take credit for that too.' Raises their profile with other terrorists. More street cred equals more funding. That's how it works. Sort of like turf and budget wars in D.C."

"Then that means the bomb was meant to kill someone else at the park at a completely different time."

"That's right. Only the question is who?"

CHAPTER

33

Two hours after Weaver and his men left, Stone could still not fall asleep. Weaver was obtaining a list of events to be held at Lafayette Park in the upcoming months and told Stone that he would share that information with him. For his part, Stone told Weaver all that they had uncovered about the jogger's background and the other information he had learned from ATF and the FBI's inquiries. He did not tell Weaver about Fuat Turkekul. If the NIC chief was meant to know about the operation to catch Osama bin Laden, people other than Stone would have to so inform him.

Stone lay on his cot thinking all of this through while the night burned onward to dawn. Finally his thoughts turned to the Camel Club. Caleb and Reuben had been friends of his for years. They had literally been through hell and back together. Alex

Ford had been a more recent arrival to the ranks of the club, but he had twice saved Stone's life and risked his career on at least five other occasions to help him and the others. Annabelle had blown into their lives only a short time ago but had quickly proved her loyalty to Stone. And Harry Finn had stood shoulder to shoulder with Stone in a firefight with a team of trained assassins even though Stone had killed Finn's father more than three decades ago.

And I basically told all of them that I didn't trust them. That I didn't need their help. But that's not the whole story.

Only a handful of people knew that Stone had taken his old rifle and killed two prominent Americans who had destroyed his life, costing him his wife and child. Stone had killed many people on behalf of his country. He had dutifully followed orders. Yet these two men he'd killed on his own. Judge, jury and executioner. He felt he was justified for what he'd done. He felt no remorse for ending their lives.

But still. He had a conscience. All those years of killing had never managed to totally rid him of one. And with his strong sense of justice, Stone knew that he would have to make payment one day. It was only right. But he was not going to take his friends down too. They didn't deserve that. He was living on borrowed time. His friends were not. The Camel Club, he knew, was coming to the end of its run. At least with him as its de facto leader.

He showered, dressed and headed out as the sun was just starting to creep upward. He stopped at the front door when he saw Chapman sitting on the hood of her rental just outside the wrought-iron gates sipping on a Starbucks coffee.

He zipped up his jacket against the cool morning air and walked over to her. She was dressed in jeans, a heavy black sweater and boots, looking very unlike a proper MI6 agent. Her hair was tied back revealing a small mole near her temple. She slipped off the car hood, reached through the driver's window for a second cup of coffee in the holder and handed it to him.

"Figured you for an early riser," she explained as he drank down some of the java.

"Thanks," he said curtly.

"Interesting night?" she asked.

"Why do you ask?"

"Just wondering."

"Wondering enough to watch my place last night?"

"Could be. Late-night visitor?"

"Are you asking or confirming?"

"Just asking."

"Riley Weaver. NIC. Wanted a chat. Had some interesting theories."

"Can I hear them?"

"Let's head on to the park."

Chapman put the wheels in gear and they drove off. On the way down to M Street Stone explained to her what Weaver had to say.

"Pretty good stuff, actually," she said. "Weaver seems to be on top of this."

"If he can narrow down who the target was it'll be even better."

"Shouldn't be too difficult. How many events are there at Lafayette Park?"

"More than you might imagine. And it's not just government folks like the president. Private groups can apply to be there. For a special event or to protest. It can be quite a lengthy list."

"Still, we should be able to narrow it down. And at least the threat has been removed."

"No it hasn't."

"What do you mean?"

"Because we don't really know what the threat is yet. We have to assume they'll try again. Getting the bomb in the park took a lot of work. The target has to justify that level of effort. They won't leave it like this."

They arrived near the area, and after passing through various security checkpoints, they walked onto the grass of Lafayette Park. Stone looked around. It was still early and there were few folks about, all of them authorized, of course. The park and vicinity were still shut down to the public.

Stone sat on a bench and finished his coffee while Chapman hovered in front of him. "Is it true you used to sort of live in the park?" she asked.

"Yes."

"Why?"

"Why not?"

"Okay, this is going nowhere."

"I was protesting. You're allowed to do that in this country."

"What were you protesting about?"

"Everything, pretty much."

"What, taxes and stuff?"

"No, I never made enough money to pay taxes."

"So what, then?"

Stone stared over at the White House. "Just things that I thought weren't right."

"Are they right now?"

"I doubt it."

"But you stopped protesting?"

"Just because I'm no longer at the park full-time doesn't mean I'm not still protesting."

"Do you trust Weaver? From what you said, the man was pouring his heart out to you. Seemed legitimately concerned."

"He *was* legitimately concerned. That somebody was going to perpetrate another 9/11 on his watch. I'm sure he will do all he can to stop that from happening. And I'm sure he will try and capture all the credit for doing so while leaving the rest of us in the dark if he can."

"No honor among thieves or spies?"

"I see that as a case of splitting hairs, actually."

Chapman threw her empty coffee cup away in a trash can and sat down next to him. "So we're waiting on the FBI's follow-up on the trail of the tree and who had the opportunity to put a bomb inside it. And Weaver is going to find out who might've been the real target at the park. Doesn't leave a lot for us to do."

"Why inside a basketball?" asked Stone suddenly.

"What?"

"If the bomb is inside the root ball why bother to put it in a basketball? It would take up more room and any hump through the burlap might've raised suspicions. So why not just wedge the bomb in the root ball."

"I actually think I have the answer to that. Moisture."

He looked at her. "Go on."

"That tree is obviously going to be planted in the dirt. And watered. Probably soaked since it's a new planting and they want to get it established. Unless it's a completely encased mechanism meant for underwater use, presumably military in nature, explosive devices do not much like water. In fact, a little bit of liquid seeping in can foul a switch in no time, or even render the explosive element useless. You put it in a basketball, it's sealed watertight. Or at least watertight enough."

"Okay. But would a basketball be the first thing that occurs to you as far as a watertight compartment?"

"I don't play the game, so no, it wouldn't for me." She sat up straighter. "But you're thinking the choice of the basketball might be a clue as to the bomber's identity?"

"It's certainly a possibility. And since clues have been particularly hard to come by with this case, we can't afford to ignore any possible ones."

"Then you've bought into Weaver's theory that the guns and the bomb were done by two separate organizations? Guns possibly by the Yemeni group and bomb by person or persons unknown?"

"I won't go so far as to say I agree with it, but it's intriguing enough to check out."

"So why did they fire all those bullets and not hit a damn thing?"

"I wish I could tell you the answer to that. In my mind it's critical."

"This basketball thing is not so popular in my part of the world."

"True. Though I can't imagine a bunch of millionaire NBA players have banded together to blow someone up at Lafayette Park."

"But the bombers might have some other connection to the game."

Stone pulled out his phone and made a call. "Agent Gross, Stone here. I'm down at the park and I have some information for you and a question." He told Gross about his meeting with Weaver and the NIC chief's theory of the case. Then he told Gross about his basketball idea.

Gross said, "Okay. I'll pick you up in twenty minutes and we'll go talk to the folks where that tree came from."

Stone clicked off and looked at Chapman. "He's coming to get us. We're going to check out where the tree came from."

"Good. I'm getting bored doing nothing."

Stone rose and looked around. He started pacing off in different directions in the park as Chapman watched him curiously. Some of the damage from the blast had been cleaned up. And the small-tented markers were still laid out, giving the effect that both white and orange snow had fallen on the park. Weeks from now they would probably continue to find things. Possibly even years from now. He imagined a tourist happening on a bit of ear. Nice souvenir from their visit to the capital.

He finally ended up at the crater. Chapman joined him at the edge.

"So what's going on in that noggin of yours?" she asked.

"I'm missing something. Something obvious, but I don't know what."

CHAPTER

34

"DIDN'T KNOW YOU AND RILEY WEAVER were so tight," said Gross as the FBI agent deftly handled the wheel of his Crown Vic on the way out of D.C.

Stone sat next to him; Chapman was in the backseat.

"Only met the man twice in my life. And neither time voluntarily. That doesn't constitute 'tight' for me."

Gross shot him a glance. "So why'd he come to you? And not me?"

"You're his competitor. I'm just the man in the middle."

Gross made a face. "We've got to cut this competitive shit out if we're really going to protect this country."

"Sounds good to me," voiced Chapman. "You blokes are on the same side, after all."

"It's a little more complicated than that, Agent Chapman," said Gross as he glanced at her in the rearview mirror.

"Just because you say it's complicated doesn't make it so," she replied.

"Anyway, if NIC would cooperate with us, it would make all of our jobs easier."

"And you don't think every agency out there doesn't say the same thing about the FBI?" said Stone.

Gross gave a resigned laugh. "I guess you're right."

"Weaver is still learning his way over there," said Stone. "He doesn't want the hammer to come down on his watch. He's probably working this thing 24/7 using all conceivable methods. I was just one of them."

"So where are we headed?" asked Chapman after a few seconds of silence as the nearly empty streets of D.C. flew by.

"Pennsylvania," answered Gross. "That's where the maple came from. A tree farm up near Gettysburg."

"Do they know we're coming?" asked Stone.

"No."

"Good."

"Shouldn't you surround the place with agents?" said Chapman.

"Whoever was involved in this won't be sticking around. We go in with heat, the people left behind might clam up. I want some answers and a bit of finesse never hurts."

Many miles later they pulled past the gates of the Keystone Tree Farm. The paved road led them to a long one-story building painted white with a green metal roof. In the background were various outbuildings both small and large with several big enough to accommodate fifty-foot-tall trees. The parking lot held a few dusty pickup trucks, a compact car and a black Escalade SUV. The three climbed out of the Vic and headed to a door marked "Office."

A plump woman in too-tight jeans directed them back to a small room where a large man sat behind a metal desk, a phone to his ear. He waved them in and pointed to two chairs. When Gross flashed his badge the man said into the phone, "I'll have to call you back."

He put down the receiver, rose, tucked in his shirt where it had ridden out and said, "Can I see that badge again?"

Gross moved closer and held his commission and badge out to the man for several long seconds. Even after the man looked away Gross held up the FBI shield as though to convey the significance of their presence.

"What can I do for you?" said the man uneasily.

Gross said, "A name would be good for starters."

The man cleared his throat, "Lloyd, Lloyd Wilder."

"And you run this place?"

"I'm the foreman, yeah. Ten years now. What's this about?"

Gross perched on the edge of the man's desk while Stone leaned against one wall and Chapman sat in a chair. All of them peered at Wilder, who swallowed nervously and nearly fell back into his chair.

"Look," Wilder began, "those guys told me they were legal. Okay, maybe they didn't have all the paperwork, but do you know how much red tape there is? Take me all day every day just to read through the stuff, and I can't find anybody else willing to do this sort of work and—"

Stone, catching on to this before Gross did, said coldly, "We're not with Immigration. The shield said FBI, *not* ICE."

Wilder looked from one to the other. "FBI?"

Gross leaned down so his face was uncomfortably close to Wilder's. "FBI. That fellow over there is with the counterterrorism folks. The lady with MI6 out of the UK."

Wilder eyed Chapman with an incredulous look. "MI6. Like James Bond?"

"Better than Bond, actually," said Chapman. "Like dear James on steroids."

Gross added, "And we could give a crap about your illegal aliens, but if you don't cooperate ICE sure will be interested."

Wilder's face sagged. "But if you ain't here about them, what are you here about?"

"You watch the news?"

"Yeah, I check out ESPN every night."

"I mean the real news."

"Oh, I mean some days. Why?"

"Explosion at Lafayette Park?" added Gross. "You hear about that?"

"Hell yes. It's all over the place."

They all stared at him pointedly and he looked back, puzzled.

"But what's that got to do with me?" he finally blurted out.

"We believe the bomb was planted in the tree that came from this place of business."

"Come on, you got to be kidding me." Wilder grinned weakly. "Wait a minute. You guys ain't really Feds, right? This is some kind of joke, ain't it?"

Gross moved closer to him. "When a bomb goes off that close to the president of the United States, I can't find anything remotely funny about it, Mr. Wilder. Can you?"

The smile faded. "So this is the real thing? You guys really are cops?"

"We really are. And we want to know how a bomb got in one of your trees."

As the full weight of what was happening descended on him, Wilder appeared to be hyperventilating. "Oh Jesus. Oh sweet Jesus." The man started rocking back and forth.

Stone moved around beside him and placed a calming hand on his shoulder. "We're not accusing you of anything, Mr. Wilder," he said. "And from your reaction, it seems clear you don't know anything about it. But you may be able to help us nonetheless. Now take a couple of deep breaths and try to relax." He squeezed the man's shoulder.

Wilder finally calmed and nodded. "I'll do whatever I can to help you. I mean that. I'm a patriot down to my bones. I've been NRA all my life. Hell, my daddy was a union man."

Gross sat down across from him while Stone remained standing. Stone said, "Tell us about each of the people who work here."

For the next twenty minutes, Wilder pulled out employment records and went over each worker with them.

"That's it," he said when he'd finished. "And there's not one on that list that's smart enough to do anything with no bomb. Hard enough to get them to hold the right end of a shovel. Although that may be because my *español*'s not too good."

Stone put his finger on one name on the list. "John Kravitz. He doesn't sound Latino."

"Well, he's not, of course. But you're barking up the wrong tree there. No pun intended," he added hurriedly.

"Why?" asked Stone.

"He's college educated."

"I thought you intimated they were all stupid. And nothing against your line of work, but why is a college grad digging up trees?"

"We do more than that here. John's degree's in landscape design, horticulture, stuff like that. He's a good arborist. Sees stuff no one else does. Why we hired him."

"How long has he been with you?" asked Chapman.

"About seven months. Didn't expect him to stay that long, but he seems content."

"Has he been in to work this week?"

"Every day like clockwork."

"Where is he now? Here?"

Wilder checked the clock on the wall. "He'll be here in about thirty minutes. He only lives about five miles down the road in a little trailer park off the highway."

"What else can you tell us about him?" asked Gross.

"He's about thirty, thin, tall as you," he said, pointing at Stone. "With brown hair and a goatee."

"He get along with everybody?"

"Look, the other guys can barely put two words of English together and I'm not sure they're even literate in their own language. Like I said, John is a college boy. He usually spends his lunch hour reading."

"Know anything about his personal life? Political beliefs?" asked Gross.

"No. But I'm telling you John is no bomber."

"Does he play basketball by any chance?" asked Gross.

"What's that got to do with anything?"

"Just answer the question."

"He told me he played in high school. We have a hoop out back. Boys play at lunchtime if they're not out making a delivery."

"Whose ball do you use?" asked Stone.

"Ball? We've got a couple around here. John I know has one." Wilder looked flustered. "What's a basketball got to do with a damn bomb?"

"We're going to wait for John. When he gets here you have him come back to your office, okay?" said Gross.

"Do we really have to—"

"Okay?" Gross said firmly.

Wilder managed to whisper, "Okay."

CHAPTER

35

WHILE THEY WERE WAITING for John Kravitz to arrive, Stone and Chapman explored the grounds. A few Latino workers watched them warily from a distance, probably fearing they were from ICE. Stone didn't pay much attention to them. But something did capture his interest. Over a building behind the office, there were some holes in the wood and the outline of what once had been bolted there. Stone pointed to it, but Chapman only looked quizzical.

"Basketball hoop," said Stone. "Or where one used to be."

"So someone took it down?"

"But didn't fill in the holes or paint over it."

When they went back inside and asked Wilder about it, he professed to know nothing about the missing hoop.

"I know it was up yesterday. Some of the guys were playing."

Thirty minutes passed, and while a half dozen other people arrived for work, Kravitz was not among them.

"We'll need his address now," said Gross.

"I'm sure it's nothing," said Wilder.

Stone pulled Gross to the side. "Chapman and I will pay him a visit while you stay here with Wilder."

"You think he's in on it?"

"I'm not sure what to think right now, so we have to assume he is."

Wilder said, "I can call him at home, see if he's okay. Tell him to come on in."

"No," said Stone. "No calls. Just sit tight with Agent Gross."

Stone nodded at Gross and the FBI agent's hand dipped to the butt of the gun in his belt holster, while Wilder, seeing this, started hyperventilating anew.

Gross said, "You want me to get some LEOs as backup for you?"

"Some local cops wouldn't hurt," said Stone. "Just tell them no sirens and to stay back until we signal them."

Gross nodded. "Good luck."

A minute later Stone and Chapman were in the Crown Vic on the way to the trailer park. Stone was driving. The sedan streaked down the highway. They passed a police cruiser going the same way. The cop driving was about to hit his lights at the speeding car when Stone slowed, dropped back and held his badge out the window. The cop in the passenger side slid down his window.

"You the LEOs they called in for us as backup?" Stone asked.

The cop nodded. "Possible suspect in the Lafayette Park bombing?"

Stone nodded. "Just follow our lead. Okay?"

"Yes sir," said the obviously excited young deputy.

Stone rolled his window back up and hit the gas.

Chapman glanced over and saw the gun in a shoulder holster Stone was wearing.

"What are you carrying?" she asked.

"You wouldn't recognize it."

"Why not?"

"For starters, it's older than you are."

"I know most of the major makes. American and European, Chinese, Russian."

"It's not a major one."

"I know some of the lesser-known models."

"It wasn't mass-produced."

"Limited run?"

"You could say that."

"How many were made?"

"One."

When they got to the trailer park, Stone left the car by the side of the road and they made their way to Kravitz's trailer on foot. The park had about twenty-five trailers mounted on permanent foundations and was bracketed by thick woods. The cops were ten paces back and on either side of the narrow gravel road that constituted the only ingress and egress.

"If he is the bomber he might have his trailer wired with a booby trap," noted Chapman.

"That thought had occurred to me."

"So are we going to just knock on his door, then?"

"We'll play it by ear."

Chapman looked put off. "Okay, pleased to see you have the plan all formulated."

"In a situation like this plans usually are for shit. You react professionally to what comes at you. That's the best plan of all."

The trailer was set off by itself, a small patch of gravel in front. An ancient and battered Chevy pickup was parked in front, its metal corroding, its paint disintegrating. They checked to make sure the truck was empty and then took cover behind it.

Stone eyed the two cops and motioned with his hand where he wanted them to take up position. When they were in place he called out, "John Kravitz?"

There was no answer.

"John Kravitz? Federal agents. We need you to come out, hands in clear view. Right now."

Nothing.

Chapman looked at Stone. The two cops stared at him too.

"What now?" she asked.

"We do it the hard way," said Stone.

"Which is?"

Stone eyed the white tank attached to the front of the trailer. He took out his gun. "Kravitz, you have five seconds to come out or I'm going to put a round into your propane tank and blow you right to hell."

"Are you mental?" hissed Chapman.

The two cops looked at Stone like they were debating whether to arrest *him*.

"Two seconds, Kravitz," called out Stone.

He assumed his firing stance and lined the tank up in his sight.

"Stone!" said Chapman. "You could blow us all up."

"One second, Kravitz."

The door to the trailer opened and Kravitz came out, his hands in the air. He looked like he'd just gotten out of bed. "Don't shoot," he said in a pleading voice. "Don't shoot, I don't have a gun. Hell, what do you want with me? I just overslept. Do they send the Feds out for that now?"

Stone saw the flash of light in the reflection of the trailer window. Immediately realizing what it was, he screamed, "Everyone down! Now!" He grabbed Chapman's arm and pulled her to the ground. From the corner of his eye he saw the two cops hit the dirt. Kravitz still stood upright looking stunned. Stone let go of Chapman and whirled around, pointed his gun at the woods and fired. At the instant he did so a bullet was fired from somewhere deep in the woods. The two shots together sounded like a mini-explosion. Following his lead, Chapman had her gun out in a second and fired off six rounds from her Walther in the same direction.

The round fired from the woods hit Kravitz squarely in the chest, exiting out the back and smacking into the side of the trailer. Kravitz stood stock-still for about a second, his eyes wide, as though he didn't even realize he'd been shot. And killed. Then he toppled to the ground. Stone knew he was dead before he hit the gravel. Long-range rifle ordnance was almost always fatal with a center chest shot.

Before anyone else could move, Stone was up and sprinting toward the woods. He scanned the tree line and called over his shoulder, "See if he's still breathing. If he is, do what you can and call an ambulance. Then secure the crime scene and call in backup. Chapman, with me, keep low."

She raced after him as he entered the woods.

"That was a long-range rifle round," he called out. "Look for any movement, five hundred yards and out."

"How'd you even know anyone was out here?"

"Saw the optics signature in the reflection on the trailer window. I had no chance of hitting the sniper with a pistol round. I was just hoping to screw up his shot."

After several minutes of searching and coming up empty they ran back toward the trailer. On the way there Chapman said, "You probably saved my life."

"You weren't the target."

"But still."

"You're welcome."

When they got back to the trailer Stone said to the cops, "Anything?"

One cop shook his head. "Dead. We called in backup."

"Okay, set up roadblocks and search teams along a mile perimeter. It's probably too late, but we have to try."

The cop grabbed his radio to do this.

Stone said to Chapman, "Keep low and follow me."

They made their way stealthily up to the body. Kravitz was lying on his back, his arms and legs splayed, his eyes open and staring lifeless up at a blue sky. A patch of crimson was on his shirt where the bullet had gone in.

"Single tap," observed Stone. "LV."

"LV?"

"Left ventricle. For torso shots I preferred the aorta myself."

"You're kidding, right?"

Stone didn't even glance at her; his gaze was skimming over Kravitz. "Working knowledge of the human body is part of any good sniper's curriculum."

"Well, I guess we know now that Kravitz was part of the bombing plot."

"And somebody shot him to keep him from

talking to us. That seems clear. The part that isn't so clear is how they knew we were coming for him this morning."

Chapman looked around. "I see what you mean. We haven't told anyone. Gross picked us up at the park on the spur of the moment. Wilder couldn't have called anyone because Gross is with him."

Stone stiffened. "Damn it!"

"What?"

Stone didn't answer. He punched in the number for the FBI agent. The phone rang and rang and then went to voice mail. Instructing the cops to stay at the crime scene and wait for their backup, Stone did a hundred on the way back to the tree farm while Chapman white-knuckled the armrest. Along the way he called in more LEOs to meet them at the tree farm. When they pulled in the parking lot, he knew something was wrong. He pointed to the tread marks on the parking lot asphalt. "Those weren't there when we left. Somebody got out of here in a hell of a hurry."

Stone didn't wait for the other cops to arrive. He pulled his gun and kicked open the door to the office. The woman who'd ushered them in to see Wilder was lying on the floor, a bullet hole in the middle of her forehead. Stone motioned to Chapman to cover him as he approached the door to the interior office. Crouched down, and using the wall as a shield, he turned the knob with his free hand and pushed the door inward. Then he backed away and took up position where he had a clear firing line into the office.

From her vantage point Chapman had already seen it. She caught a quick breath as Stone moved next to her.

Wilder was on the floor just inside the office. Even as far away as they were, Stone and Chapman could see that a good portion of his face was gone.

"Shotgun," said Stone.

He moved forward, keeping his gun trained straight ahead, ready to fire in an instant if something came at him. A few seconds later he gave the all clear.

Chapman joined him as he gazed down at the body of Special Agent Tom Gross where it lay behind the desk, his gun in his hand. There were two bullet holes in his broad chest. Stone knelt and checked the man's pulse. He shook his head. "He's gone. Shit! Damn it!"

"What the hell is going on?" said Chapman as she stared down at the dead man.

Stone looked around. "They split us up and played us out," he said. "It's like they know what we're going to do even before we do." He knelt down and touched the barrel of the gun. "Warm. He fired it, very recently."

"Maybe he hit one of them."

"Maybe." He scanned the room for other signs of blood but found none. He pointed to the opposite wall where a bullet had lodged. "Probably Gross's one shot before he went down. At least he died fighting."

"What the hell do we do now?"

They heard sirens coming.

"I don't know," said Stone. "I don't know."

CHAPTER

36

"Whose idea was it to leave Special Agent Gross alone?"

Stone and Chapman were at the FBI's WFO, where they sat on one side of a long table and four grim men and one dour woman sat on the other side.

Stone said, "It was my idea. Agent Chapman and I went to the trailer to find John Kravitz and Agent Gross stayed behind with Lloyd Wilder."

"Did you know whether any of the other workers at the tree farm were involved in the bombing conspiracy?" asked the woman, who had identified herself as Special Agent Laura Ashburn. She was dressed in a black suit and her brown hair was pulled back in a ponytail. About forty, she was of medium height, had pleasant features and a trim figure, but her eyes were black dots that bored through everything in their path. And right now the only thing in that path was Stone.

"We didn't know that. And we still don't."

"And yet you left him there with no backup?" said one of the male agents.

Before Stone could answer another man said, "You left with Agent Chapman and you also had LEO support. And yet Tom Gross had none of that. He was alone."

"I should have had Agent Chapman stay with Gross and then called in backup for them while I went to the trailer park," conceded Stone.

Chapman interjected, "There was nothing stopping Agent Gross from doing that."

All five FBI agents looked at her. One said, "When you're trying to control a potential hostile situation and you have one potential bomber in your presence, you don't really have time to yak on your phone."

This same man turned back to Stone. "I understand that you are a recent hire by the adjunct agency to NSC."

"I am."

"But you're a little old to be jumping into the game, aren't you?"

Stone said nothing to this because what could he say, really?

Ashburn opened a file and added, "Can't find much on you, Oliver Stone. Other than an illustrious film career." The derision in her voice was mirrored in the expression of her four colleagues.

"Pretty rookie mistake for such a man of your years," added the agent at the far left of the table. "Leaving an agent in a vulnerable situation." He leaned forward. "What would you suggest that we tell his wife? His four kids? Got any suggestions? Love to hear them, *Agent* Stone."

"I would tell them that her husband and their father died fighting. As a hero. That's what I would tell them."

"I'm sure that'll make it all better," sneered Ashburn.

Another agent said, "Have you ever been left all alone on assignment? I doubt it, since a guy like you probably covers himself at all times. Plenty of firepower at your back."

Chapman spoke up. "You have no idea what you're talking about. He saved my life and the lives of two police officers today. He figured out there was a shooter in the woods while we were standing around with our thumbs up our arses. And if you knew half of this man's history you wouldn't be sitting here grilling him for—"

"I don't care about his history. I'm only concerned with the present," Ashburn shot back.

"Well then, maybe you need to check with your superiors because—"

Stone put a hand on her arm. "Don't," he said quietly.

Ashburn closed her binder. "We'll be filing a detailed report on this, the chief element of which will be a strong recommendation that you be removed from this case and a full investigation launched to see if any disciplinary or criminal charges should be imposed against you."

"This is utterly ridiculous," snapped Chapman.

Ashburn leveled a withering gaze on her, the black dots resembling hollow-points about to be launched. "I don't know how it is across the pond, but this is America. Here we have accountability for our actions." She glanced at Stone. "Or inaction, as the case may be." She looked back at Chapman. "Piece of advice? I'd find a new partner if I were you."

The agents all rose as one and filed out of the room.

Chapman glanced over at Stone. "Do you blokes routinely beat up on each other like that?"

"Usually only when it's deserved."

"And you think it is here?"

"A good man is dead. He shouldn't be. Someone has to be blamed for it. And I'm as good a selection as anyone." He rose. "And maybe they're right. Maybe I am too old for this."

"You don't really believe that, do you?"

Stone didn't answer. He just left the room, left the WFO, hit the streets and kept walking. The night air was crisp, the sky cloudless. There was snarled traffic and honking over near the Verizon Center because some event was going on there.

As he walked along, Stone thought of the last few moments he'd been with Tom Gross. He hadn't really focused on the man's safety. He'd wanted to go after John Kravitz. In truth, he'd believed that he was keeping Gross safer by going after the alleged bomber at his home berth and leaving Gross behind. It had never occurred to him that they would attack at the tree farm *and* kill Kravitz. They definitely had manpower and intelligence and nerve. A formidable combination.

A sudden thought struck him and he called the number Riley Weaver had left for him. He wanted to know if Weaver had a list of the events that had been scheduled at Lafayette Park. If there was a lead in that list, Stone wanted to run it down. Someone answered the phone. Stone identified himself and asked for Weaver. The man put him on hold but was back within ten seconds.

"Please don't call this number again."

The line went dead and Stone slowly put his phone back in his pocket. The explanation for that brusque putdown was easy. Weaver knew that Stone had screwed up and cost an FBI agent his life. Because of that, Stone was off the cooperation list with NIC now. And forever.

As he passed block after block, his focus continued to deepen, even as the D.C. nightlife went on all around him. Runners along the Mall, tourists with maps in hand, partiers packed in groups heading to the next entertainment and office-dwelling men and women in suits lugging thick briefcases and burdened with weary countenances as they trudged home, probably to keep working.

Taking out Kravitz made perfect sense if he were involved in the bombing. One less mouth to betray the people behind it. They must have staked out the trailer park and were there ready to kill the man when Stone had shown up. But there was an alternative theory that if true was far more disquieting.

They knew we were coming.

In order to do that, they either would have needed to follow them or been ahead of them. Both scenarios carried serious implications and also the possibility of a mole in their ranks. But why the tree farm? Had Lloyd Wilder been involved as well? If so, the man was a consummate actor. The woman in the office? A long shot.

Tom Gross? But why take him out? He was the lead investigator, but he would simply be replaced with another. And the murder of an FBI agent would only result in the formidable Bureau tripling its already heightened effort to find those behind the Lafayette Park incident. It made no sense at all. None.

He arrived at his destination, flashed his badge to gain admittance and entered Lafayette Park. At least his credentials hadn't been pulled. Yet. He sat on a bench, surveyed the surroundings where the investigative work was still going on. His mind swirled with recent events, not one bit of it solidifying into something useful. It was just mist, vapor. As soon as he focused on something promising, it vanished.

His gaze shifted to the White House across the street. The bombing had no doubt popped the president's bubble of safety that he believed he had here. Every security force involved in defending this bit of earth had suffered a hard blow to their professional egos.

Hell's Corner, Stone thought, was indeed living up to its name.

When he looked up he saw the man approaching. A part of him was surprised, but another part was not. He drew a long breath and waited.

CHAPTER

37

THE CAMEL CLUB MINUS ITS LEADER sat around Caleb Shaw's condo in Alexandria, Virginia, overlooking the Potomac River. Caleb had just finished serving tea and coffee to everyone except Reuben. The big man had brought his own hip flask with something presumably stronger in it than Earl Grey or Maxwell House.

Annabelle was dressed in a black skirt, loafers and a jean jacket. She spoke first and her tone was blunt. "How bad is it, Alex?"

Alex Ford, still wearing a suit and tie from his workday, leaned forward on the hassock, took a sip of coffee and said, "Pretty bad. An FBI agent is dead along with three other people, including at least one bombing suspect."

"And they're blaming Oliver?" asked Caleb with an air of indignation.

"Yes," Alex said. "Whether rightly or wrongly. I told Oliver that there were many people unhappy with him being involved in this case, and now it's come home to roost."

Harry Finn was leaning against the wall. He'd finished his coffee and put his cup down. "Meaning making a scapegoat out of Oliver is a great way to kick him off the case?"

"Right. Although knowing Oliver, he probably does blame himself for what happened."

Reuben growled, "You go after terrorists, people can get hurt. And they damn well asked him back into the fold, not the other way around."

"That's what's so infuriating, Alex," said Annabelle. "He didn't have to do this at all. Now he's in there risking his life and they blame him for someone getting killed."

Alex spread his hands. "Annabelle, don't be naïve. This is Washington. There's nothing fair about any of it."

She flung her long hair out of her face. "That makes me feel so much better."

Caleb spoke up. "But what will happen now?"

"An investigation is being conducted. Two of them, actually. The search for the terrorists goes on, obviously. But now there will be a secondary inquiry regarding what happened that led to the death of

Agent Gross and the others. To determine if there's any evidence of negligence or wrongdoing."

"With respect to Oliver, you mean," interjected Annabelle.

"Yes."

"What might happen to him, worst case?" asked Caleb.

"Worst case? He might go to prison depending on how it plays out. But that's unlikely. He might be kicked off the case. That's far more likely. Even with his friends in high places, no one can stand that heat for long. Especially if the media starts riding that horse right into the ground."

"This is a nightmare," said Caleb. "If the media does enter the fray then they'll start investigating Oliver and his past."

"The man doesn't have a past, at least officially," noted Reuben in a deep grumble.

"Exactly," said Caleb. "That's my point. They will be relentless in trying to find out exactly who he is."

"The government won't want that," said Alex.

Reuben nodded in a knowing fashion. "He knows too damn much. A lot of stuff that would be embarrassing if it came out now."

Annabelle said, "Triple Six stuff, you mean?"

"Exactly."

"You...you don't think the government... might try to silence him?" she said in a halting voice.

Caleb looked incredulous. "This isn't the Soviet Union, Annabelle. We don't assassinate our own people."

Annabelle glanced at Alex, who quickly looked away. She said, "All right. He's helped all of us in one way or another. Which begs the question of why we're here debating whether to help him or not."

"That's not the question," Alex said. "The question is, by trying to help him will we make it even worse for him?"

"How is that possible?" she asked. "Right now he has everyone against him. He needs us. We're all he has left."

"He made his position on that pretty clear," said Alex. "He doesn't want our help."

"Only because he doesn't want us in danger," she shot back. "And speaking for myself, that's not a good enough reason."

She rose. "So I'm going to help him, whether he wants that help or not."

38

JAMES MCELROY SAT DOWN next to Stone on the bench while the Brit's security team hovered in the background. He leaned his cane against the edge of the metal armrest.

"Chapman has filled me in on the particulars," said McElroy.

"I'm sure."

"She said you saved her life."

Stone didn't answer.

"Still, not a particularly good day for any of us."

"You could say that."

"And do you blame yourself?"

Stone looked at him. "And why wouldn't I?"

McElroy considered this. "I suppose I would've been disappointed if you'd answered any other way. I've grown used to finger-pointing over the years, accepting it as just the way the world works now. But I know it doesn't work that way for you and never has. And neither does it for me."

"So am I going to be pulled from the case?"

"Do you want to be?"

"I don't like unfinished business."

"I wish I could give you a definitive answer, but I can't."

"The president wavering on me? He's done it before."

"He's a politician. It's never easy. That's mostly why I never threw my hat into the ring. A spy's life is a bit easier in that department."

"So until I get the word either way am I free to continue my investigation?"

"The answer to that would be yes."

"That's all I needed to know."

"I understand that Riley Weaver came to visit you."

"He did."

"He's scared, as I understand it. Sees something big coming over the horizon. And he thinks that what happened here plays into it somehow? That it was merely a first step?"

"I think he believes that, yes."

"And do you?"

"Since the attack at the park made no sense, then it seems likely that it was part of something else."

"Bigger than exploding a bomb and scattering machine-gun fire across from your president's humble abode? Goodness, we might be in serious trouble."

The man's words were said in a jesting tone, but it was apparent from the look of concern in his eyes that McElroy too had a sense of foreboding. "Any inkling as to what that something else might be?"

Stone turned to him. "Fuat Turkekul."

"What about him?"

"I don't believe in coincidences."

"Meaning his being in the park at the same time of the attack."

"I think someone in your food chain knows something about it."

"So why didn't they kill him, then?"

"That would make the answer simple. This isn't simple." He eyed the security team. "Feel like a bit of a walk?"

"If you'll lend me a hand, yes. Knees aren't what they used to be, and what they used to be was never much, I'm afraid."

The two old allies walked along the brick path. Stone supported McElroy with a firm hand under his elbow as the spy chief made his way slowly along using his cane.

"Theories?" said McElroy.

"They know everything before we do. And more to the point, they seem to know what we're going to do at the same time we decide to do it."

"So a traitor assuredly?"

Stone nodded. "Any possibilities?"

"I've looked that issue up one side and down the other and I can't find a viable suspect. Damn infuriating."

"So you suspected something like that too?"

"I always suspect something like that. And it usually turns out to be true. I agree with you that the other side seems to be always ahead of us. But I don't know how they're doing it."

"We could lay a trap. Channel information through one source only and see if it ends up in the wrong hands."

"I don't think whoever it is will fall for that."

"Worth a try?"

"Then we warn them we suspect."

"If they're as good as I think they are, they already know that we suspect."

"I'm afraid I'm going to have to sit down, Oliver."

Stone helped his friend to another bench and then sat next to him. "Tell me something," said

Stone. "Did what happened at the park cause Turkekul to change his plans in any way? Was the mission altered at all?"

McElroy didn't answer right away. "Of course it would have been completely altered if Fuat had been killed," he pointed out. "Altered to the point of being abandoned. One would think that would have been the goal of the attack."

"Since the man didn't die, we have to think of alternative reasons."

"I can think of none."

"For now, but we have to keep trying."

"It won't be easy for you. The FBI is looking to crush you. Its director has already had a meeting with your president. I have also had the pleasure of your leader's company, and have done my utmost to dissuade him from giving in to the entreaty that you be removed from the case."

"Until they make me stop I'll keep going."

"Pretty much sums up our professional lives, Oliver."

"Yes, it does."

"I wish you luck."

"I'll need it."

"You'll also need this."

McElroy took a memory stick from his pocket and handed it to Stone.

"What is it?"

"The FBI's preliminary report on the attack at the tree farm." As Stone looked uncertainly at the USB stick, McElroy added, "By the by, I had a computer delivered to your cottage earlier." He paused. "You do know how to work a computer, don't you?"

"I can manage. And thanks."

"Cheers."

McElroy rose on stiffened legs and slowly walked off.

CHAPTER

39

STONE SAT BACK, RUBBED HIS EYES and yawned. He poured out a last cup of coffee and surveyed the miniscule interior of his cottage before his gaze alighted once more on his shiny new laptop computer. It looked almost as out of place in his dingy surroundings as a Picasso hanging on the wall would have.

What was on the memory stick McElroy had given him was far more interesting than the computer itself. The FBI, motivated no doubt by the murder of one of its own, had done an intensely thorough investigation of the tree farm and the trailer. What they had found was incriminating if not wholly surprising.

Stone ticked off the points in his head.

A sharp-eyed agent had noticed that a narrow section of the cement blocks forming the foundation of

Kravitz's trailer home was of a slightly lighter color. They had removed this stack and entered the open space underneath and found bomb-making materials, along with two basketballs, both of which had been cut in half.

A review of John Kravitz's personal history had found him to be a college graduate as his boss Lloyd Wilder had noted. But what Wilder hadn't told them, or more likely didn't know, was that Kravitz had been arrested twice in the past during rallies against the government for items ranging from antiwar protests to stem cell research. Also found on his cell phone were names and addresses of certain people on government watch lists.

His neighbors had reported that Kravitz had acted suspiciously over the last few weeks, though Stone discounted that as witness bias since there had been no specific examples from any of these neighbors as to why they thought that other than the police and FBI showing up at the man's door.

From the records at the tree farm and the accounts of those working there, Kravitz had full access to the maple tree before it was loaded on a truck and sent to D.C. This included during after hours, because he had a key to the special storeroom where the tree was being prepared for shipping. The insertion of a bomb in the root ball of a tree that large, even housed inside a basketball, would not be difficult for an experienced hand like Kravitz, the report had found. Any disturbance at the site of entry could be easily covered up and then further disguised by the burlap container.

Kravitz had been shot with a rifle round that had ripped through his heart, killing him instantly. Stone had to admire the skill of the sniper, since the person would have had to make that shot with the distraction of Stone and Chapman shooting at him. The secretary at the tree farm had succumbed to a .45 round from a handgun, Lloyd Wilder from a shotgun blast to the face and finally Tom Gross had taken two .45 rounds to the chest. He had fired his weapon once, hitting the wall.

Two different guns used in the attack meant two different attackers, at least. A shotgun was problematic. It was unfailingly deadly at close range but very noisy. The handgun could be used with a suppressor. Yet no one had heard anything, the report added. This was not so unlikely as it seemed. When Stone had traveled there with Gross and Chapman he'd observed that the tree farm was set far off the road. So probably no cars passing by would've heard the shots. And the other people working there at the time were far away in the fields. The office building was low and long. It would have blocked the view of any vehicle coming there from anyone working in the fields or other buildings. And tree farms were noisy places with machinery on for much of the time. Still, everyone there had been interviewed and professed to have heard or seen nothing. There were only three people in the office and they were all dead.

Stone leaned back and drank his coffee as outside the dawn began to emerge.

So Kravitz was part of the bombing plot and he was killed when the cops moved in. Short, sweet, made sense. Evidence all there. Signed, sealed, delivered. Check off the box. But why the attack at the tree farm in the first place? Was Lloyd Wilder part of the conspiracy? There was no evidence to point to that. And Stone had seen the man's face when they told him why they were there. Stone had seen many liars. Wilder, he believed, had not been lying. The secretary? No connection. No evidence of wrongdoing.

Stone heard the footsteps outside the cottage. He quickly closed the laptop, sending the room into darkness. Just as he had with Riley Weaver, he pulled his gun from his desk drawer and crouched down in the kneehole with his eyes barely above the top edge. He was getting a little tired of late-night unannounced visits.

The silhouette at his door was that of a woman. He could tell by the hair, the shape of the face and torso.

Agent Chapman? Too tall. Hair too long.

"Oliver?"

He moved his finger away from the trigger and rose.

A few moments later he was staring at Annabelle Conroy as she walked into his cottage and plunked down in a chair by the fireplace, crossed her arms and scowled up at him.

"Annabelle, what are you doing here?"

"We need to talk."

"About what?"

"About everything. But let's start with you being in trouble and needing our help."

He said wearily, "I can handle this. And I don't want all of you—"

"What!" she snapped. "You don't want us to what? Care about what happens to you? You want us to just come to your funeral and wonder what if? Did you really think that was going to work?"

He sat down next to her and slid his pistol into his waistband. "No, I guess I didn't expect that."

"Good, because I'm here to tell you that we're going to help, whether you like it or not."

"How? You can't meddle in an FBI investigation."

"I wouldn't call it meddling. And since when are you against becoming involved in official investigations? From what I know, you've made a career out of doing just that."

"It's different this time."

"Why, because you're now working for the government? I don't see how that really makes a difference. And since the *government* isn't happy with you right now, I would think you'd need some unofficial help."

"But still I'm not sure what any of you can do."

"That never stopped us before." She turned to him and her tone became less aggressive. "All I'm saying is we want to help. Just like you did with me, and everybody else in the good old Camel Club."

"But you've already paid me back for helping you. I'd be dead in Divine, Virginia, but for you."

"This isn't a tit-for-tat contest, Oliver. I'm your friend. I would be here for you at any time."

Stone let out a sigh. "Where are the others?"

"Out in the car."

"I thought so. Would you like to get them? I can put some more coffee on."

"Don't bother. We brought breakfast too."

She rose as he looked up at her in mild amusement.

"Camel Club forever," she said.

40

IT TOOK THE BETTER PART of three hours, but Stone finally brought them all up to speed on the case. Finn, Reuben and Caleb sat in chairs ringed around Stone's desk while Annabelle perched on top of the desk. Alex Ford was not with them because he was on duty.

"So the bomber, at least one of them, has been caught," said Caleb.

"Seems that way," answered Stone.

"Only you don't look convinced," said Finn. He had on a dark blue windbreaker, jeans, dusty boots and his Glock.

"All the evidence is there," said Stone. "In fact, too much."

"FBI see it that way?" asked Reuben.

"I don't know, seeing as how I'm a bit out of favor with them right now."

"If not this tree guy, who then?" interjected Annabelle. "If you're saying he was set up, it's a hell of a setup."

"Agreed." Stone was about to say something else when someone knocked on his door.

It was Chapman. She stepped inside and saw the others.

Stone said bluntly, "I've finally come to my senses and asked my friends to help us out."

Chapman looked around at them. "Help us how?" she said in a skeptical tone.

"In the investigation."

"And what agency are they with?"

Caleb volunteered, "I'm with the Library of Congress."

Chapman stared at him, openmouthed. "The bloody hell you are."

He looked taken aback. "I beg your pardon?"

She turned to Stone. "What the hell is going on here?"

"I spoke with McElroy last night. He gave me the FBI file on the incident in Pennsylvania. I've gone through it. With them."

"With your friends? Who are going to help us?" she said slowly, as though not believing her own words. "A bloody librarian!"

Caleb said with dignity, "I'm actually a rare

book specialist. In my field that's like being James Bond."

Chapman drew her pistol with enviable speed and placed it against Caleb's forehead. "Well, in my field, little man, that means shit."

She put her gun away while Caleb looked like he might have a stroke.

"Do I have a choice?" asked Chapman.

"In what?" asked Stone.

"In working with them?"

"If you want to continue to work with me, you'll have to work with them."

"You lot do things a bit peculiarly over here."

"Yes, we do," agreed Stone. "So would you like me to fill you in on the FBI's report? Unless McElroy has done the honors already?"

Twenty minutes later Chapman was fully informed both of the content of the report and Stone's skepticism with its conclusions.

"So if Kravitz might not have done it, who did?" she asked.

"That's what we have to find out. But I may be wrong and the FBI right."

"And we'll be doing this how, with the FBI's knowledge and cooperation?"

"I would say with neither their cooperation nor knowledge," Stone replied.

Chapman pulled Caleb from his chair and plopped down in it. "All right. Do you have any whiskey here?"

"Why?"

"Well, if I'm going to break the law and my oath of service I'd like to do it in a bit more relaxed frame of mind, if you don't mind."

"You don't have to do it at all, Agent Chapman," said Stone. "This is my plan and my responsibility. Your boss will understand fully once I talk to him. Then you can back out gracefully."

"And then what, I get my arse shipped back to the good old UK?"

"Something like that."

"I don't think so. Unfinished business bothers the devil out of me."

Stone smiled. "I can understand that."

She sat forward. "So where do we go from here?"

"With a plan, an ever-evolving one, but one that involves no one else getting hurt," said Stone firmly.

"I don't think you or anyone else can guarantee that, Oliver," said Annabelle.

"Then at least a plan that allows maximum protection for all of you."

"Doesn't sound all that much fun, really," said Reuben.

Chapman eyed him with interest. "So you're willing to die for the cause?"

He faced her with a defiant gaze. "I'm willing to die for my friends."

"I like your way of thinking, Reuben," said Chapman, giving him a wink.

"Well, there's a lot more of me to like, MI6."

Caleb had watched this exchange with growing frustration. He turned to Stone. "So is there something we can do now?"

"Yes," Stone said. "I actually have something for each of you to do that will utilize your strengths."

Caleb looked at Chapman. "I usually get the dangerous stuff."

"Really?" she said, looking bemused.

"It's my lot in life, I suppose. You should take a drive with me sometime. I think that will explain everything. I'm a real daredevil. Just ask Annabelle."

"Oh yeah," said Annabelle. "If you want to drive yourself nuts spend a couple days zooming around country roads with Mr. Speedy while he drones on and on about some dead writer no one but him has ever heard of."

"Sounds delightful," replied Chapman. "Sort of like gnawing off one's arm for sport."

"Caleb," said Stone. "I'd like you to research at

the library all events to be held at Lafayette Park over the next month."

Chapman's lips twitched as she stared at a red-faced Caleb. "I'd go in with at least two machine guns for that one, mate."

Stone proceeded to give out the rest of the assignments to the others. Before they left, Annabelle gave him a hug.

"Good to be back where we belong."

Chapman was the last to leave.

Stone said, "I'll meet you at the park in three hours."

"Do you really trust these people?"

"With my life."

"Who are they? I mean really."

"The Camel Club."

"The Camel Club? What the hell is that?"

"The most important thing in my life," answered Stone. "Only I forgot that for a little bit."

CHAPTER

41

"You look puzzled, Agent Garchik."

Stone and Chapman walked up to the ATF agent as he was staring over the grounds of Lafayette Park.

Startled, he turned to them. "I was sorry to hear about Tom Gross," he said as they joined him. "He seemed like a real good guy."

Stone nodded, while Chapman simply stood there frowning. Her hair was unkempt and she looked like she'd slept in her clothes. And she had, for all of two hours. Stone, on the other hand, had shaved, showered and pressed his pants and shirt.

"He also believed that his own side was watching him. Do you have the same feeling?"

Garchik looked nervously around. "How did you figure that?"

"I think of the highly unlikely, then push it to

the practically impossible, and I often find I arrive at the truth, particularly in this town." He studied the man. Garchik's eyes were bloodshot and his clothes were as wrinkled as Chapman's. "But that isn't all that's bothering you, is it?"

Chapman added, "You were bragging before that you could tell us what sort of bomb it was very quickly. We haven't heard a peep from you since. Did your state-of-the-art facility fail you?"

"Can we talk somewhere else? This place is starting to give me the creeps."

The three of them walked a couple of blocks to a bagel shop. Stone and Chapman each had a large cup of coffee. Garchik twisted plastic stirrers into knots and ignored the bottle of orange juice he'd purchased.

After swallowing a mouthful of coffee Stone said, "Do you feel comfortable talking here?"

"What? Yeah, I guess."

Chapman said, "You can trust us, Agent Garchik."

He gave a dull laugh. "That's good to know. I'd thought I'd run plum out of people I can trust."

"What happened to make you feel that way?" asked Stone.

"Little things. Reports not coming back. Pieces of evidence not where they should be. Clicks on my phone when I pick it up. Funny shit on my computer at work."

"Is that all?" asked Stone.

Garchik snapped, "Isn't that enough?"

"It would be for me. I'm just wondering if there's more."

Garchik drank some of his juice. He put the bottle down and took a breath. "The bomb."

"What was it?"

"Some components we don't usually see in an explosive device."

"What do you mean?"

"I mean some unique combinations that were a surprise."

"You mean undetectable?" asked Chapman quickly.

"No. That would be impossible. Bombs have to have certain elements. Blasting caps for starters. This bomb had all that, at least we found pieces that showed that."

"So what, then?"

"We also found some other stuff."

"What stuff?" said Chapman, her irritation growing.

"Stuff that nobody has figured out what the hell it is yet, which is why I'm just referring to it as *stuff*."

Stone said, "You mean you found debris from the explosive that you are unable to identify?"

"That's more or less what I'm saying, yeah."

"What is ATF's official position on it?" he asked.

"Official position?" Garchik chuckled. "Their official position is that they are officially baffled and scared shitless. We're actually getting NASA involved to see if they can figure it out."

"NASA! So what are the implications for this?" asked Chapman.

"I don't know. None of us knows. That's why we're keeping this on a tight need to know. I probably shouldn't even be telling you. Correction: I know I shouldn't be telling you."

Stone thought about this as he fingered his coffee cup. "Did Agent Gross know?"

Garchik eyed him warily. "Yeah, he did. I told him myself. He was the lead investigator, after all, thought he had a right to know."

"And what was his reaction?"

"He told me to keep him apprised. I think he had other things on his mind."

"Did you tell anyone that you'd told him?"

Garchik saw where this was going. "You think he was killed because of what I told him?"

"It's possible."

"But who would've known?"

"Hard to say since we don't know if he told anyone or not. So did you tell anyone you'd informed him of that?"

"Maybe a couple people at ATF. I have people I have to report to," he added defiantly.

"I'm sure you do. Have you been out to the trailer owned by John Kravitz?"

"Yeah. We checked the bomb material found there."

"And did it match the debris in the park?"

"Yes. Although it was a strange place to keep the stuff."

"Under the trailer, you mean?" said Stone.

"Yeah."

"Moisture," said Chapman. "Not good for that sort of stuff."

"Right," agreed Garchik. "And not to mention it was difficult to get to." He shifted uneasily in his seat. "Look, I'm no chickenshit. I've infiltrated militias and gangs and come out alive. But what I'm not used to doing is watching my own side. That freaks me out."

"It would me too," said Stone.

"What do you think is going on?"

"There's a traitor out there somewhere," answered

Stone. "And people are aware of it. So they're trying to ferret the spy out."

"So they're basically watching all of us."

"Right. The only problem is if one of the watchers is actually the traitor."

"God help us if that's the case," said Garchik. "So what should I do?"

"Keep your head down, limit your conversations on your phone and with your colleagues, and if any other agency strolls into your space, play stupid."

"There are a lot of us at ATF. I'm not the only one who knows about this new stuff."

Stone rose. "Given the circumstances, I wouldn't necessarily count that to be a good thing."

They left a troubled-looking Garchik in the bagel shop and headed back out.

Chapman said, "So what about your fabled Camel Club? Have they started their work yet?"

Stone checked his watch. "Right about now, in fact."

Harry Finn walked along like he had not a care in the world. Wraparound shades, jeans and a sweatshirt, sneakers, bedhead, he looked like a college student. Which was what he wanted considering he was on the Georgetown University campus. It had stone buildings that looked craned in from Cambridge or Oxford, nice green spaces, students hurrying here and there or else lounging in between classes. Finn walked confidently among them all. He sipped on a cup of Starbucks, shifted the weight of his backpack over his left shoulder.

He picked up the trail of Fuat Turkekul within five minutes. He did so by good prep work. This involved a little computer hacking onto the college's database, a couple of discreetly placed questions and a thorough recon of the campus.

The Turkish-born scholar walked along, books cradled under one arm, in deep discussion with another faculty member while a trail of students brought up the rear. They went into a building near the western end of the campus. Finn did too.

Stone's instructions had been explicit. Watch this man. And it wasn't entirely for Turkekul's protection. Stone had been clear that he was not convinced of his loyalties yet.

"It could go either way at this point, Harry," he'd said. "If someone tries to get to him, stop it. But if he does something that suggests he's working for the other side, document it and let me know right away."

Turkekul was teaching a class on the second floor of the building. It had thirty-two students. Finn slipped in as the thirty-third, set up his recorder as did many other students, took out his book and laptop and settled back. If Turkekul noticed him he gave no indication of it. Unlike some of the other students there, Finn listened to every word the man said, and also how he said it, which was often even more important than the actual words spoken.

And unlike any of the students there, Finn assessed the room for threats and came away not entirely satisfied. One door in and out. Little cover. Turkekul would be a sitting duck at the front of the class.

Finn touched his chest and felt the Glock nestled there in the holster. If he'd been an assassin Turkekul would already be dead. He wondered how a man tasked to hunt down Osama bin Laden was allowed to live so cavalierly. It made no sense at all. And things that didn't make sense bothered Harry Finn. They bothered him greatly.

Caleb settled into his desk at the Rare Book Reading Room and eyed his other colleagues as they moved around doing assorted tasks. He nodded and smiled to several.

"Morning, Avery," he said to one portly fellow.

"Caleb. Congrats on acquiring the Fitzgerald."

"Thanks," Caleb said, beaming. He really was

proud of that one. When things had settled down in the room he lifted his glasses to his eyes, pecked some keys on the keyboard and worked his way through several government databases, hoping with each click of a key that he would not run into insurmountable interference. His dear friend Milton Farb could have accessed the necessary database in seconds, but Milton had been one of a kind. Yet Caleb had gotten better over the years with electronics, and he approached the task Stone had given him with deliberation and calm. And he was an employee of the federal government and thus had requisite passwords and authorizations. And it wasn't as though events at Lafayette Park were classified. At least he hoped they weren't.

Within a half hour he breathed a sigh of relief. He hit his print button and the two-page single-spaced document slid into the catchbin of his printer. He picked it up and studied it. There were a lot of events on here. And some of them would be attended by some real Washington heavyweights. If his friend was hoping to narrow his search down by consulting this list, Caleb knew at once that it would not be all that easy.

He slipped the papers in his briefcase and returned to work.

CHAPTER

42

ANNABELLE AND REUBEN reached Pennsylvania around three that afternoon. They drove first to Keystone Tree Farm. It was obviously still secured by the FBI. Barricades and black SUVs were everywhere. And Pennsylvania state troopers were there to support the federal agents.

Annabelle, who was driving, said, "No surprise there. That place will be out of circulation for a long time. Let's keep rolling."

"You want to try the trailer park?" asked Reuben.

"Might as well, but I have to believe it'll be the same crime scene scenario there."

And it was. Cops and Feds in abundance. The road into the trailer park was completely closed off.

"Want to bluff our way in?" asked Reuben. "If we say we live there?"

"Something tells me that's way too risky for the potential reward. But I have another idea."

"Good, because Oliver wants information and I'm not sure how we're supposed to get it."

"There's always a way, Reuben. We just have to find it."

At four-thirty that afternoon, Annabelle found it. Parked outside the tree farm, they watched as a pickup truck pulled out with four of the Latino workers from the farm inside.

"Quitting time," said Reuben.

"No. I doubt there's much work going on there. Feds probably interviewed all of them and then let them go. If they try to leave the area, they'll probably be really sorry. Let's see if they're keeping them under surveillance."

The truck pulled onto the road and sped off. They waited for thirty seconds but no other car followed.

Annabelle put her car in gear. "Okay, the Feds are very trusting. And we're not."

"Where do you think they're headed?" asked Reuben.

"There's a bar in that direction. Let's hope they pull off for happy hour after all that interrogation."

They did go to the bar. And Annabelle and Reuben waited for them to go inside before slipping out of the car and heading in.

"You speak Spanish?" Reuben asked.

"I spent a long time in L.A., so yeah, pretty fluently. You?"

"I know more Vietnamese than Spanish."

"Then order your beer in English and let me do the talking."

"And my role?"

"If a guy who we're not interested in hits on me, take him out."

"Great, thanks. Nice to use my finely honed skills."

Inside, the four Latinos were huddled around one table, beers already in hand. They were talking in low voices and casting furtive glances at the few other people in the bar.

Annabelle and Reuben sat at a table near them and then Annabelle put some money in the jukebox. On the way back she dropped her car keys near the table. One of the men bent down to pick them up. When he handed them back, she thanked him in Spanish. Then she pulled a map from her pocket and asked him directions, explaining that she and her friend were trying to find a tree farm. The man told her that he and his friends worked at this very same tree farm.

Annabelle smiled and pulled up a chair, motioning Reuben to stay where he was. She sat down and said, "We're looking to buy a dozen cypress and were told that your place had some excellent specimens. I work for a landscaping firm in Delaware," she explained. All of this was spoken in rapid Spanish and seemed to put the men at ease.

The first man told Annabelle that they indeed had such trees, but she could not get them.

"Why not?" she asked.

He explained about what had happened.

"Oh my God," she exclaimed. "That's awful. I read about it in the paper, of course, but they didn't say the name of the tree farm, so I never associated it with yours. I hope they caught who did it."

The men shook their heads.

"And was this John Kravitz a friend of yours? His name was the one I was actually given when I was coming up here."

Kravitz had not been a close friend, and the men seemed stunned to learn that he had been involved with the bombing in Washington.

"That's really a shame," said Annabelle.

One of the men said that he believed John Kravitz to be innocent.

"But I heard on the news that they found

bomb-making material at his home. That's pretty serious."

Whether the man had heard this too wasn't clear. He insisted that Kravitz was innocent.

"And were you all there when the people were killed?"

They nodded.

"That must have been horrible. I guess you're lucky you weren't killed too."

They had been out in the fields, they told her. They had heard and seen nothing.

"I guess the police have questioned you," said Annabelle.

The surly looks on the men's faces confirmed that.

"Well, it looks like whoever did it might get away. Too bad," she said. Annabelle left that comment hanging out there to see what reaction it might inspire. One of the men whispered something to the first. He looked at Annabelle.

"The police didn't ask about the basketball hoop," he said.

"Basketball hoop?" Annabelle feigned ignorance even though Stone had told her about the missing hoop.

"We had a basketball hoop up at one of the outbuildings. We would play ball there at lunch. John played too sometimes. He was good."

"And what happened to the hoop?"

The first man glanced over at his companion who'd whispered to him.

"What's up?" Annabelle asked innocently.

"Miguel saw something that night."

"What night?"

"The night before the people were killed. He came back to pick up his sweater he left there."

"What did he see?"

"He saw someone taking down the basketball hoop."

"Taking down the hoop? Did he see who it was?"

"No. But it wasn't John. It was a smaller man. And older. Then another man came. Another stranger. They talked."

"Miguel, did you hear what they said?"

Miguel shook his head. "They spoke a funny language. I didn't understand it."

"Did you try and talk to them?"

"No. I was afraid. I was hiding behind another building."

"Did you tell the police this?"

"They didn't ask."

"Okay," said Annabelle. "Well, I guess we'll have to look somewhere else for the trees. Thanks."

She returned to the table with Reuben and filled him in on the parts he hadn't overheard.

"Taking down a basketball hoop. And speaking a funny language, huh?"

"Well, it obviously wasn't Spanish."

When they left the bar a man who had been sitting near the jukebox sipping on a beer followed them. When their car pulled out, so did his. And then he clicked a number on his phone and spoke into it. A half mile away another vehicle started up and sped toward the direction Annabelle and Reuben were traveling.

CHAPTER

43

STONE WAS SITTING AT A DESK in Chapman's room at the British embassy listening to the sound of the shower running. A minute later Chapman walked out of the bathroom wrapped in a white terrycloth robe, her feet bare. She was drying her hair with a towel.

"Getting a bloody night's sleep and bathing with regularity is a little tough around you lot," she said.

"I'm sure it's the time difference," he said. Stone was going over some documents on the table and occasionally glancing at the laptop computer set up on the desk. He paused to look around the room.

"MI6 takes good care of its agents."

"The British embassy is known for its first-class accommodations," noted Chapman as she sat on the couch. "And a hotel just doesn't cut it when one is examining classified documents and carrying a laptop with highly secret data." She rose. "Give me a sec to dress and we'll have a spot of tea."

She left the room and Stone could hear drawers and doors opening and closing. A few minutes later she came out dressed in a skirt, blouse, no hose and no shoes. She was just finishing buttoning her blouse. He glanced away when she looked up at him.

"Feel better?" he said casually.

"Loads, thanks. I'm famished." She picked up the phone, ordered tea and some food and joined Stone at the desk.

"Any word from your friends, the Camel Club?"

"Caleb called during his lunch hour. He faxed the list over of upcoming events at the park." Stone picked up two sheets of paper. "Here they are. There are lots of potential targets on there, unfortunately."

Chapman ran her eye down the list. "I see what you mean. Any of them stand out among the others?"

"A few. Two that the president was going to be attending. Other heads of state, congressmen, celebrities. But narrowing it down will be difficult."

"But my PM isn't in the mix." She put down the papers and looked thoughtful. "You know, chances are very good that I'll be pulled off this little caper."

"Because of no proven threat against the PM?"

"That's right. MI6 doesn't have unlimited resources."

"But the implications of what is being planned here could have global repercussions that reach to the UK."

"That's what I'll say in my next report. Because I'd like to see this through. But I wouldn't be surprised if you have to carry on without me."

Stone didn't say anything for a few moments. "I hope that's not the case," he said.

She looked at him closely. "I'll take that as a compliment."

"It was meant as one."

When the tea and food came they ate and drank while going over the evidence once more.

"Nothing from Garchik and his mysterious debris?" Chapman asked as she took a bite of a hot scone.

"No. Weaver from NIC has cut me off. FBI too, obviously. ATF may be next." He looked at her. "Guilt by association, I'm afraid. You won't be too popular either."

"I've dealt with worse. Got on the wrong side of the queen once."

Stone looked intrigued. "How?"

"Misunderstanding that was more her fault than mine. But she's the queen so there you are. But it eventually got sorted out." She took another bite of scone. "But from what I've learned about you, you're a man who's used to rocking the boat."

"That was never my intent," Stone said quietly.

She leaned back in her chair. "You expect me to believe that?"

"I did my job, even when I didn't agree with it. In that regard I was weak."

"You were trained to follow orders. We all are."

"It's never that simple."

"If it isn't that simple our world goes to hell in a hurry."

"Well maybe sometimes it should go to hell."

"And I guess it did for you."

"You ever been married?"

"No."

"Ever want to be?"

Chapman looked down, "I guess most women want to be, don't they?"

"I think most men do too. I did. I was married. I had a woman I loved and a little girl who meant everything to me."

Stone grew silent.

Chapman finally broke the quiet. "And you lost them?"

"And the fault was entirely mine."

"You didn't pull the bloody trigger, Oliver."

"I might as well have. You don't voluntarily leave a job like mine. And I shouldn't have married. I shouldn't have had a child."

"Sometimes you can't control those things. You can't control love."

Stone looked at her. Chapman was staring directly at him.

"You can't," she repeated softly. "Not even people like us."

"Well, considering how things turned out, I should have tried."

"So you're going to blame yourself forever?"

He looked surprised by the question. "Of course I am. Why?"

"Just asking." She put down the rest of her scone and refocused on the reports in front of her.

Stone hit the TV remote and the news came on. They were just in time to hear a female reporter broadcasting near Lafayette Park.

"And late-breaking developments have Alfredo Padilla, originally of Mexico, dying in the blast. Apparently there was a bomb planted in a tree hole at Lafayette Park, and Mr. Padilla, unfortunately running away from the shots being fired in Lafayette, fell into the hole and accidentally detonated the bomb planted there. A memorial service is being planned for Mr. Padilla, who is being hailed as a hero, even if unwittingly. FBI special agent Thomas Gross, a veteran with the Bureau, was killed during a shootout at the tree farm where the tree with the bomb in it was procured. He will be honored at this same memorial service in what some are calling a political move to mend relations between the two countries. Another man, John Kravitz, who worked at the tree farm and was allegedly involved in the bombing conspiracy, was killed by an unknown person at his home in Pennsylvania as police closed in. We will bring you more details as they become available."

Stone turned off the TV.

"Someone has been shooting off his mouth," he said. "Back in the old days we never would've revealed that much about an ongoing investigation."

"That was before the days of the Internet and frothing media that have to deliver content every second of every day," remarked Chapman.

"I wonder if they'll let me attend Gross's memorial service."

"I wouldn't count on it if I were you."

Five minutes later Chapman said, "Hold on."

"What?" Stone said, glancing at her.

She held up a piece of paper. "Evidence listing from the crime scene at the park."

Stone looked at it. "Okay. What do you see?"

"Read down that column," she said, indicating a list of numbers and corresponding categories on the left side of the sheet.

Stone did. "All right. So?"

She held up another sheet. "Now read this."

Stone did so. He flinched and looked back at the first sheet. "Why didn't anyone put this together before?"

"Most likely because it was on two separate reports."

Stone looked between the two documents.

"Two hundred and forty-six slugs found in the park and environs matching the TEC-9s," he said.

"Right."

He looked at the other piece of paper. "But the casings found at the Hay-Adams Hotel only numbered two hundred and forty," he said.

"Right again."

"You would expect to have more casings than slugs, because some of the slugs might never be recovered," Stone began.

"But you would never have fewer casings than found slugs," Chapman said, finishing his thought.

"Unless the bad guys took a few with them and left the rest. Which they never would. They would either take none or all."

Stone looked up. "You know what this means?"

Chapman nodded. "The casings were planted at the hotel and someone miscounted. The shots came from somewhere else."

CHAPTER

44

"WE HAVE COMPANY, ANNABELLE," said Reuben.

She glanced in the rearview mirror. "The black SUV with the tinted windows?"

"Yep."

"It was parked at the bar when we pulled up," she noted.

"I know. I think someone is interested in our conversation with the Latinos."

She said, "So what do we do? We're in the middle of nowhere. And I don't want to call 911, because then we'll have to explain things I don't want to."

"Keep driving. There's a bend coming up. They'll make their move there."

"And what will our move be?" Annabelle asked.

"Still thinking of it. Just drive. And hit the curve fast. I want the driver focused on the road, not me."

Annabelle accelerated and drove into the bend in the road at speed.

"Punch it more," instructed Reuben.

She did so, fighting to keep the car on the road.

Reuben had turned in his seat and was looking back. He pulled a large handgun from his pocket and aimed it out the window.

"I didn't know you were armed," Annabelle said.

"Well now you do."

"Do you have a permit for that thing?"

"Yeah, but it expired about fifteen years ago."

"Wait a minute, what if those are cops back there?"

"We're about to find out."

The SUV came into view. There was a man hanging out the side of the truck holding a submachine gun.

"Don't think they're cops," said Reuben. "Keep it steady."

The submachine gun fired about the same time Reuben did. The sub was aimed at the car. Reuben was aiming at the front tire. The sub hit its target, blowing out the back window of their car. Annabelle hunched forward and down, her head near the steering wheel.

Reuben fired once, twice and then a third time as the guy holding the sub reloaded. The front tires on the SUV shredded. The car shot across the road, hit the shoulder and flipped on its side.

Annabelle sat back up. "Jesus."

Reuben turned back around. "Look out!" he screamed.

A second SUV was coming from the opposite direction and heading right for them. Annabelle cut the wheel hard and her car lurched across the road, cleared the shoulder and landed in the dirt. She gunned the engine and steered the car toward a stand of trees. They reached it. She slammed the car to a stop and they jumped out and ran for the trees as the SUV bore down on them.

Reuben turned and fired a few shots in the truck's direction, causing it to veer off. The second they reached the trees, bursts of submachine-gun fire hit. Reuben grabbed Annabelle's arm and threw her into the cover of the woods.

He wasn't as fortunate. A round slammed into his arm.

"Shit!"

"Reuben!"

He wheeled around and fired at the now stopped truck. The windshield splintered and the men inside took cover.

Reuben turned and stumbled into the woods along with Annabelle. She held on to his other shoulder and helped him along. Between gritted teeth Reuben said, "Now might be a good time to call the cops, Annabelle. I'd rather have to explain things to them instead of lying in a box after these guys finish with us."

She slipped the phone from her purse and hit 911. Nothing happened.

"Damn it. No bars."

"Great."

"But I had reception around here before."

"Maybe they're jamming the signal."

"Who the hell are they?"

"People we do not want to meet up close."

They heard running feet behind them.

They took cover behind a tree. Reuben fired off the rest of his ammo in the direction of their pursuers. A volley of automatic fire came back at them.

"Load my pistol for me," said Reuben between gritted teeth. "Extra clip in my right pocket." She did so and handed it back to him. He studied the terrain around them. "Submachine guns against a pistol only has one outcome," he said.

"So we're dead?"

"Didn't say that."

"I wonder what Oliver would do."

"What Oliver would do is the unexpected."

"So exactly what does that mean in this situation?"

Reuben fired three more shots, then they took cover behind a large oak as the machine-gun fire raked across it.

Reuben said, "When the rounds stop, you run that way." He pointed behind them. "Cut to the left and get back to the road. You should be able to make a call there or flag down a car."

"And what about you?" she said fiercely.

The firing stopped as the men reloaded.

Reuben grabbed Annabelle's arm and pushed. "Go."

"There has to be another way."

"There is no other way. We can't con our way out of this."

"Reuben, I can't leave—"

He gripped her arm so tightly that she winced. "You will do what I tell you to do. One of us has to get out of this."

"But—"

The next moment he was running flat-out right at their pursuers.

Stunned, Annabelle turned and ran in the opposite direction. Tears streamed down her face as she heard the firing start up again.

Annabelle ran. But she couldn't outrun the tears as the gunfire continued.

CHAPTER

45

IT WAS DARK IN THE CITY. Stone watched carefully from a spot he'd chosen in Lafayette Park. He checked his watch. Ten seconds to go. He counted down in his head. The light started blinking from a distance. This was a little demonstration he and Chapman had come up with. She was clicking a high-powered red-beamed laser off and on to simulate the muzzle flashes of a weapon.

She was standing in the rooftop garden of the Hay-Adams. The light was barely visible from where he was standing. And the trees were blocking any real sightline. He called Chapman and told her the results of his observations. She moved to the next spot in their experiment, a building behind and to the left of the hotel.

Stone had chosen that building using the hotel as a base marker, because of the bullet pattern in the park and also because the windows in that building actually opened. He had recalled that all the markers denoting found slugs were on the left-hand or western side of the park. That didn't seem unusual at first, but now coupled with the revelation that the shooters had not been at the Hay-Adams, it was not simply unusual; it was enlightening.

While Stone was waiting for Chapman to reach the next location, he felt a presence behind him. He turned. It was Laura Ashburn, the female FBI agent who had interrogated him over the slaying of Tom Gross. She was dressed all in black except for her blue FBI windbreaker with the gold lettering on the back. She wore an FBI ball cap and was staring at Stone.

"Agent Ashburn," he said. "Anything I can do for you?"

"I wanted to talk to you," she said.

"All right."

"We filed our report."

"Okay."

"It wasn't very flattering for you."

"After our meeting I didn't expect it to be. Is that all you wanted to tell me?"

"I'm not sure," she said hesitantly.

He smiled.

"You think something's funny."

He said, "Let me tell you what I think is funny. After all the assets that have been thrown at this case no one knows what the hell really happened here or why. You're all running around pointing fingers at everyone else, withholding information, spying on your own people."

"What the hell are you—"

Stone talked right over her. "Spying on your own people and doing your best to try and get ahead of the other guy. The only thing that's lost in the process is actually solving the case, and maybe saving some lives down the road."

"Well, that won't help Tom Gross."

"You're right, it won't. What might have helped Tom Gross was a little trust and cooperation from his own agency."

"What exactly did he tell you?" Ashburn asked, her features full of confusion.

"Basically that if he couldn't even trust his own side how the hell would he ever solve the case?"

Ashburn looked down and then cast furtive glances around the park where the investigation was proceeding, albeit at a more subdued pace. "I finally got some background on you," she said, her gaze still avoiding his.

"I'm sure that will make its way into your amended report."

"Did you really turn down the Medal of Honor?"

Stone glanced at her. "Why do you want to know?"

"My son is in Afghanistan. Marines."

"I'm sure he'll serve his country well, just like his mother."

"Look, you can be pissed at me, but leave my son—"

"I don't play that game. I meant exactly what I said. You're just doing your job. I don't fault you. If I were in your shoes, I'd be upset too. I'd want to strike back too. And if you want to use me as a target that's fine. There's plenty of blame on my end. I won't deny that."

With this brutal self-judgment hanging out there the woman's features softened.

"I've actually been going over things again, about what happened in Pennsylvania, I mean. That's really why I came here to find you."

"Why would you be going over things again? You already filed your report, as you said."

"Look, I *am* pissed. Tom was a friend of mine. I do want a target. And you seemed like a very handy one."

"All right," Stone said evenly.

"The thing is, I'm not sure you actually did

anything wrong. I interviewed the state cops. They said you probably saved their lives. Acted before they even knew what was happening. That you got shots off at the shooter and were after him while they were still wondering what was going on."

"I've probably had a bit more experience than they have in those types of situations."

"So I understand," she said frankly. "And Tom could have called in backup when he contacted the LEOs. In fact he should have."

"I honestly thought the dangerous part would be at Kravitz's place, not the tree farm."

Ashburn let out a resigned breath. "I believe you."

"And I hope you believe me when I tell you I won't rest until I find out who did it."

She stared at him for a long moment. "I do."

The two agents exchanged a firm handshake and then Ashburn disappeared into the darkness. A few moments later Stone gazed out at the red blinking light and then over at imagined points on the grass where he gauged that the "bullets" would be "hitting" based on his roughly estimated trajectory. He punched in the number for Chapman. "Go up one floor," he said.

A few minutes later the lights commenced again.

He called her. "I think that's it. Any evidence of
the guns having been fired from there?"

"No casings, but I've got a patch of what looks
like oil or grease. I'll collect some of it for examina-
tion. And when I opened the window, there was no
squeak or creak."

"Like it had been opened recently."

"Yes, but, Oliver, you didn't tell me this place
was a U.S. government building undergoing
renovation."

"I was hoping I was wrong."

CHAPTER

46

STONE AND CHAPMAN RETURNED to his cottage. They had just settled in to talk over this latest discovery when Chapman hit the light on Stone's desk, plunging the space into darkness.

"What is it?" hissed Stone.

She didn't have time to answer.

The door burst open and Stone counted at least three men hurtling through it.

They were masked, dressed in black and carried MP-5s. They moved as one unit, an unstoppable force.

They were just about to meet the proverbial immovable object.

Chapman hit the first man with a crushing blow to his knee, pushing it in a direction no knee was designed to go. He went down screaming and grabbing at his destroyed limb. Stone grabbed his gun from his desk drawer, but he didn't even have time to aim before Chapman cartwheeled across the space, dodging a wall of submachine-gun rounds launched from the last two men in the unit.

It was soon to be one left.

Her fist drove up and through the man's throat at the same time that she cantilevered her body to a seemingly impossible angle, whipping around him like he was the pole and she was the dancer. She kicked his legs out from under him and delivered a crushing blow to the back of his neck. He coughed once and lay still.

Not missing a beat, Chapman launched herself at the remaining man, who was already halfway to the door, in full retreat.

When he saw what the man had thrown Stone screamed, "Look out." He fired. His rounds ripped through wood, plaster, but unfortunately not flesh.

The mini-explosion ripped through the place. The flash-bang completed half its mission, the blinding flash. Stone had covered his eyes just in time.

Chapman caught it full in the face and yelled in pain.

Stone stuffed his shirt collar in his ears and then covered them with his arms. An instant later came the bang. *Now they'll regroup with reinforcements and come back to finish the job,* thought Stone.

What they hadn't counted on was Stone not being paralyzed. He rolled right, snagged Chapman's Walther off her, and held it in his left hand. He grabbed Chapman by the arm and slid her behind his desk. He gripped his customized pistol in his right hand and waited.

The first man came through the door, his submachine gun on full auto. Stone ducked down, slid sideways, and fired through the opening under the desk. His rounds hit their target: the shooter's knees. No Kevlar on legs. The man went down screaming. The second man started to hit the opening, but Stone fired three shots through the gap.

A few moments of silence. Then, a siren in the distance.

Stone called out: "I'll make a deal before the police get here. I'll let you take your wounded buddies out. You have five seconds. After that, we all take our chances. And from what I've seen, you're good, but I'm better."

The siren drew closer.

"All right," a voice said.

The men were slid out. A few moments later Stone heard a vehicle start. Then silence again.

The siren also faded away. Going somewhere, apparently.

He rolled Chapman over, checked her pulse. She was alive. He cradled her in his arms.

A minute later she opened her eyes, stared up at him. "Bloody hell," she exclaimed. She looked around. "I know I got two of them. I think I killed one of them. Where the hell are they?"

"We came to an understanding."

They both jumped up as something slammed against the remains of the front door.

Stone aimed his gun at the doorway and Chapman leapt to her feet as Stone tossed her the Walther.

"Oliver?"

"Annabelle?" he said, when she appeared in the doorway.

A second later Reuben fell into the room, landing on the wooden floor.

"Reuben," exclaimed Stone.

Annabelle helped Stone get the big man up and over to a chair. Blood was seeping down his forearm and his face was pale.

"What happened?" said Stone.

"We were followed in Pennsylvania. Got into a gunfight. Reuben was shot. He needs a doctor."

Reuben put a hand on Stone's arm and pulled him downward.

"I'll be okay," Reuben said weakly. "One in the arm went clean through but it hurts like hell. Other one nicked my leg."

Stone looked down at the hole in Reuben's pants leg.

"You need to go to the hospital. Right now." He looked angrily at Annabelle. "Why haven't you already taken him?"

"He insisted on coming here. Reuben wanted me to run for help, but when I heard all the shooting I had to come back and make sure he was okay."

Stone glanced at Chapman before looking back at Reuben. "Did you see anything that might identify the men?"

"They were good, Oliver," he said. "Trained very well. That's what I wanted to come and tell you. I don't know how I got the jump on them. Better to be lucky than good. Got hold of one of their weapons, opened fire and they all took off."

"Trained very well? Meaning?" said Stone.

He turned to Annabelle. "Go get it from the car."

"But Reuben, we need to get you—"

"Get it and then I'll go quietly."

She ran out to the car and was back in a few seconds. She was holding something. She handed it over to Stone.

He looked down at it and then glanced at Reuben. "Do you know what this is?"

Reuben nodded. "Figured you would too."

Chapman looked at it over Stone's shoulder. "That's a 9mm Kashtan submachine gun."

"Yes, it is," said Stone. "Russian made."

Reuben grimaced and clutched his arm. "That's right. Russian made." He glanced up at Annabelle. "The weird language those guys were talking when they took down the hoop?"

"You think it was Russian?"

"I'd bet a year's pay it was. Not that that's a lot of money, but still." He grimaced.

"Weird language?" asked Stone.

Annabelle started to explain what had happened, but Stone stopped her. "You can fill me in later. We need to get him to the hospital." Stone put an arm under Reuben's shoulder and helped him to his feet. He turned to Annabelle. "Stay here and call Harry and make sure he's okay and then do the same with Caleb. Then join us at Georgetown Hospital."

"Right."

Chapman got on the other side of Reuben and the three made their way slowly to Chapman's car. The ride to the hospital was quick, and while Reuben was being checked out Stone sat in the waiting room with Chapman and Annabelle, who had just gotten there.

"Did you get ahold of them?" asked Stone.

She nodded. "Both okay. Finn is still on assignment. Caleb is at his condo. I told Harry to be extra careful and Caleb to stay put."

"Good, now tell us what happened in Pennsylvania."

She explained what had happened in the bar and afterwards. When she gave him the exact location of the attack, Stone hurried off to make a call. When he came back she picked up the story again. "So after I found Reuben we circled back to the highway. Guy in a truck stopped, asked no questions and let us hop in the back. I managed to get the bleeding to stop, but I was afraid Reuben was going to pass out on me. The guy dropped us off at a car rental place. I got us another ride and drove back to D.C. as fast as possible. I wanted to stop and get him medical attention, but he wouldn't let me. Said we had to get to you. And show you that gun."

"Did you get a look at any of them?"

Annabelle took a deep breath. "Not really, but one of their trucks flipped over. Some of them have to be hurt or even dead. If you get some people up there to check on it. I gave you the location."

Stone said, "I already made the call. They're heading there right now."

Twenty minutes later Stone got a response. He listened, asked a few questions and then put his phone away.

"The truck is gone."

"That's impossible. It flipped over. I saw it. The people had to have been hurt, maybe killed."

"But you can have all that cleaned up in less than thirty minutes. They did find some shell casings and an indentation in the dirt where the truck rolled and a few bits of wreckage, but that was all."

Annabelle said, "These people are good."

Stone looked at Chapman. "Yes, they are. They clean up after themselves really well."

"Submachine guns," said Chapman. "Heavy firepower. And he had what, a pistol?"

"That's right. But he said he was going to do what you would do, Oliver. Be unpredictable. So he waited for them to start reloading and then he charged their position. I guess they didn't expect that." She shuddered and let out a gasp. "I thought for sure he was dead."

Stone squeezed her hand. "But he's not. The doctors said he's going to be fine. He's just out of commission for a while."

Annabelle said, "But since it's a gunshot wound won't the hospital have to report that to the authorities?"

Stone took out his shield and held it up. "Not after I showed them this and told them Reuben was working with me."

"Oh."

"But if the blokes were Russian, how does that connect with what we found out tonight?" said Chapman.

Annabelle looked at her wide-eyed. "What did you find tonight?"

Stone told her about the possible origins of the shots from a U.S. government building. "It's undergoing renovation so it's empty, but it's supposed to be secure nonetheless. We talked with the guards there. None of them remembered anyone coming to the building that night, certainly not carrying automatic weapons."

"Is there only one entrance into the building?" asked Annabelle.

"The very question I put to them. They said not if one had a key card with the necessary authorizations. With that someone could access other entrances."

"Do we know if someone did that?"

"Checking it out now," said Stone. "But I'm not hopeful."

"Why?"

"Either the card will have been stolen or cloned or something else. And yet the next question is, why go to all the trouble of leaving evidence behind at the Hay-Adams and not actually do the shooting from there? What did the office building have that the hotel didn't?"

"Well, the building was empty. The hotel wasn't," pointed out Annabelle.

"They still had to get to the rooftop garden. And it was empty that night. No, they wanted us to think they were at the hotel. They needed that building. Why?"

Chapman said, "Just add it to all the other questions we don't have answers for."

"But it is important," Stone said.

"Why?" asked Annabelle.

"Because right before you and Reuben got to the cottage, someone sent a team to kill us. They almost succeeded, and would have except for my friend here." He indicated Chapman. "How did you learn to move like that?" he asked her.

"I took ballet as a lass. Hated it back then, but I have to admit, it does come in handy when someone is trying to murder you."

"You think the attack had something to do with what you found out?" asked Annabelle.

"I think it had everything to do with the fact that we discovered the gunfire came from a supposedly secure federal building."

CHAPTER

47

THE NEXT MORNING CHAPMAN was at Stone's cottage by seven o'clock, and she wasn't alone. James McElroy slowly made his way into the cottage and took a seat in front of the fireplace. He'd changed his jacket and wore no tie. His open-collared shirt had a checked pattern. His hair was neatly combed and his slacks pressed. But his reddened eyes and saggy face spoke of the stress he was enduring.

"Chapman told me about your little adventure here last night." He looked at the damaged door and eyed the bullet holes. "Not quite as civilized as a nightcap," he pointed out.

"No," agreed Stone.

"U.S. government building, eh?"

"Yes."

"Complicates an already overly complicated situation."

"But it's the first time we've gotten under their collar, so to speak."

"Well, that is something, I suppose." His expression changed. "Spoke to the PM this morning, Oliver," he began.

"And?"

"And he's not pleased."

"Well, for what it's worth, neither am I. But we've only been on the case a few days. And in that time four people have died and my friends nearly made it six."

"Yes, Agent Chapman filled me in on your decision to use your, what was it again?"

Chapman said, "The Camel Club."

"Right, this Camel Club group to help. I have to say I find the name quite imaginative."

"And do you disapprove of my use of them?"

"Personally I've found the utilization of irregular forces a stroke of genius, particularly when the paid troops are lacking. Whether that was the case here or not, I'm not prepared to say. But that's not the issue."

"So what exactly is the problem?"

"I understand that you put a man on Fuat Turkekul?"

"Yes. Harry Finn. Former Navy SEAL. He now works for a red cell team testing the security of sensitive facilities in this country and abroad. But he's taken some time off. And he's elected to use that time off to help me."

"I of course know all about his mother, Lesya, and the fate of his father, Rayfield Solomon."

Stone looked stunned. "I wasn't aware that was public knowledge."

"It's certainly not," replied McElroy. "I would not have been advised of it except that Solomon was a friend of mine from years back. We had done some joint operations together in both Asia and South America. And I knew Lesya from her days with the former Soviet Union. I was actually one of the first Western intelligence officers to know that she was a double agent."

"Then you know the whole story? About me, I mean? What I did to Rayfield Solomon?"

"Orders are orders, Oliver. You were following them. If you hadn't you wouldn't have been simply put in the clink for insubordination. You would've been shot for treason. I know how the Yanks operate on that score, which is similar to how we do things."

"I could still have refused."

"But you can't change that fact now, no matter how much you may want to."

"Then you also know about Harry?"

"Not everything, no."

He and Stone exchanged a long glance.

McElroy said, "But you do trust him?"

"He's proven his loyalty to me beyond doubt."

"May I ask how you managed that? With what happened between his father and you?"

"We worked it out. That's all I can say on the matter."

"I see." McElroy did not look convinced. "Still, making him privy to Fuat's presence and role? That was a reach, wasn't it? I have to say I'm surprised."

"I can't ask a man to risk his life without telling him why. Harry knows what Fuat Turkekul means to this country. He will do everything in his power to safeguard him."

"Which begs the question of why you think Fuat needs additional protection."

"Agent Gross believed his own people were spying on him. Agent Garchik thinks the same. And we found out last night that the park shooters were not in the hotel but in a government-owned building that required a special security card to access."

"I see," McElroy said, nodding his head.

"Did you know that ATF found something in the bomb debris that they can't ID? That they've had to call in NASA?"

"Yes, Chapman reported that to me. Bombs to

outer space? Of all the agencies you folks have, why that one?"

"Maybe the substance is something that looks like it might be from a space program. Other than that I don't know."

"You folks and the Russians are really the only ones with any space program to speak of other than a few stray private entrepreneurs with lots of money."

Chapman and Stone exchanged a glance. If McElroy noted this he made no reaction.

"For all I know, NASA won't be able to determine what it is either," said Stone.

Chapman spoke up. "Or they may know but won't say. Or aren't allowed to say," she amended.

McElroy looked between them. "Well, we seem to be in an appalling sticky wicket. I've had to look over my shoulder for my enemies before, but I'm not sure there's a degree on the compass right now that's safe."

"So what does your PM want?"

"Assurances that we won't make a bad matter even worse."

Chapman said, "Can it get much worse?"

"Anything can become worse," said McElroy. "Oklahoma City to 9/11? The underground bombings in London to the attacks in Mumbai? This could be the tip of the iceberg, as Director Weaver intimated to you earlier."

"And I haven't heard from him since. I take it what happened with Agent Gross triggered that?"

"If I had to speculate, I think our Mr. Weaver is truly running scared. Afraid to turn to anyone. So don't take it personally."

"That's a hell of a situation to have with the head of our intelligence umbrella."

"And yet it's exactly the one we do have. It's like when the global financial collapse occurred. Credit markets were frozen. No one trusted anyone else. That's where we are in the intelligence world right now."

"And the bad guys keep plugging away," said Chapman hotly.

"Precisely."

"And we can't control what the bad guys do," said Stone.

"It depends on who they are," replied McElroy.

Stone thought about this for a moment. "Are you suggesting what I think you are?"

"What do you think I'm suggesting, Oliver?"

"That we back off because certain folks might not like what we find?"

"I think that captures the spirit of the thing, yes."

"And that's what you want us to do?"

With difficulty McElroy rose on shaky legs. When Chapman got up to help him he waved her off. "I'm fine. He straightened his jacket and turned to Stone.

"I'm telling you no such thing. As far as I'm concerned, it's full speed ahead. And damn the torpedoes, I believe, is how your Admiral Farragut put it."

"But the PM?" said Stone.

"Nice enough fellow, but he's out of his depth in the intelligence field. And so long as he sees fit to entrust me with the security of the British people I will act as I see fit. I refuse to be paralyzed. I trust you. I presume you trust me. That's good enough."

"Bucking the command carries a price."

"I'm too old to care, really. But don't forget my earlier warning. I believe that very little of what we've seen so far is actually what it appears to be."

"Which means that all of our conclusions are wrong too."

"Perhaps not all. But the important ones, probably yes."

He looked at Chapman. "You two make a good team, unless my instincts have totally deserted me. Watch out for each other." He turned to leave. "Oh, and Oliver?"

"Yes?"

"I'm actually quite glad you have these Camel Club people on your side."

"So am I."

"Remember, all the king's horses and all the king's men."

"I remember."

"One more thing. There's a car waiting outside to take you to the WFO. The FBI wants to talk to you two." McElroy twirled his cane in the air. "Good luck."

CHAPTER

48

THE RIDE TO THE WFO was made in silence; the two agents in front didn't look at or speak to them. They were escorted into an elevator once they arrived and rode it up to a higher floor. They got off and followed two other agents to a large conference room with a table that would accommodate a dozen. There were only three people sitting at it, though. One was the FBI director, the other his second in command. And the third was Agent Laura Ashburn, who'd approached Stone in the park the previous night after grilling him about Tom Gross's death.

The director was a short man with a pugnacious face and a brisk manner. Of all the bureaucrats in Washington, the FBI director was the one with real independence. His tenure did not end with an election result. It continued on for the full ten-year term no matter who won the Oval Office.

He asked them to sit, shuffled some papers in front of him, adjusted his glasses and looked up at them.

"Agent Stone. Agent Chapman. I am trying to come fully up to speed on this thing, but the more I get into it the more confusing it becomes. I would like you to start from the beginning and tell me all that you've discovered, all that you've deduced and all that you are currently speculating about."

"Does this mean I'm not going to be taken off the case, sir?" Stone asked.

The director glanced at Ashburn and back at Stone. "I've read the report. The *amended* report filed by Agent Ashburn here. Suffice it to say you won't be taken off this investigation. Now I'd like to hear both of your reports."

"It may take a while," Stone advised him.

"This is my top priority." He settled back in his chair.

Three hours later they finished talking. Ashburn and the ADIC had taken copious notes on their laptops. Even the director had scribbled down some key points.

"My God," said Ashburn. "Attacked at your home? Why didn't you report it?"

"Since I don't know who ordered the hit I wasn't comfortable reporting it to anyone."

The director grimaced. "You can trust the FBI, Stone."

Stone looked at Chapman with an uneasy expression. She gave a slight nod.

Stone turned to the director. "There's one more thing, sir."

The agents focused on him.

"What is it?" asked the director.

"My friend who was attacked in Pennsylvania managed to salvage a bit of evidence from the crime scene."

"More than what our people found?"

"A bit more, yes. It was a Russian-made submachine gun."

The trio of agents sat back as though connected by wire.

"And the Latino workers they talked to at the bar before they were attacked saw two men taking down a basketball hoop at the tree farm. According to them the men were speaking an unusual language. It might've been Russian."

The director eyed his two colleagues, put down his pen and stroked his chin.

When he didn't say anything, Stone said, "I had a conversation previously with someone you know very well."

"Who was that?"

"He lives in the *casa blanca*."

"All right. Go on."

"He told me that the Russians had taken over the drug business in the western hemisphere, ripping it out of the Mexicans' hands."

"That's true, they have. Carlos Montoya and the others are, in essence, out of business in their own country."

Ashburn spoke up. "But what motivation would the Russian cartels have for exploding a bomb in Lafayette Park?"

"The president said that as far as this country was concerned the Russian government and the Russian cartels were one and the same. Do you agree with that assessment?" Stone looked at the director expectantly.

He looked uncertain but finally said, "I would not disagree with it." He tapped the table with his pen. "So what would be their possible motivation to explode that bomb and then do all the rest?"

"To show that they can, perhaps," said Stone.

"I don't buy that. And the Yemen terrorist group that claimed responsibility?"

"Easily manipulated. And I don't believe that the Russians did it just to show they could."

"What then?"

"I spent some time in Russia decades ago. The

one thing I learned is that the Russians are some of the most cunning people on earth. They never do anything without a very good reason. And just because they're no longer a superpower doesn't mean they don't want to be again. The president has the same opinion."

"So this is some plot by the Russians to gain global prominence again," said the director.

"We certainly can't discount that possibility." Stone folded his arms over his chest and said, "And why does none of this seem to surprise you?"

The director didn't flinch at this blunt remark. He picked up another piece of paper. "We got some forensics tests back. The substance Agent Chapman found on the floor of the government office building has been found to match a certain weapon."

"It was the lubrication oil for the TEC-9 submachine gun, wasn't it," said Chapman.

"Yes."

"So they did fire from there."

"Appears to be the case."

A few seconds passed. "Is there something else?" asked Stone. The director was looking off and seemed to have forgotten there were other people in the room.

"John Kravitz."

"What about him?"

"He also spent time in Russia."

"When?"

"When he was in college. He was already on a couple of our watch lists. We believe he went over there to hook up with a group that specializes in mass disinformation campaigns on the Internet."

"But nothing violent?" asked Chapman.

"No, but the nonviolent can quickly become violent. We've all seen that."

"The U.S. government building," added Stone. "Someone had access to that, and I don't believe it was John Kravitz."

The director nodded thoughtfully. "And Special Agent Gross actually told you that he feared his own people were spying on him?"

"Yes sir."

Chapman nodded in agreement.

Stone added, "An agent from the ATF told us the same thing."

The director said, "Garchik."

"Yes. Have they found out what this mysterious component to the bomb is yet?"

"Not to my knowledge, no."

Stone's mouth opened slightly and he sat forward. "To your knowledge, sir?"

The director looked nervous for the first time since they'd arrived in the room. He glanced at the

ADIC and nodded to the door. The man did not seem pleased by this unspoken directive, and then looked positively put out when the director stopped Ashburn from joining him. After the door had closed behind the ADIC, the director leaned forward. "Something is going on here that is unprecedented in my experience."

"There's a traitor in the ranks," Stone said.

"More than that, I'm afraid. Worse than that."

Stone started to ask how anything could be worse than having a traitor in your midst, but then he remembered what McElroy had told him.

Things can always be worse.

The director cleared his throat. "There is something going on inside our government that... that does not mesh very well with the way we do things."

"Meaning what exactly, sir?" asked Stone.

The director rubbed his hands together.

"Some of us appear to be working at cross-purposes."

"Some of us?" asked Chapman blankly.

"Agent Garchik is missing."

"What?" Stone said sharply.

"And the mysterious debris component that he found at the park has also gone missing."

"How is that possible?" asked Chapman.

"I'm not sure. It was outside our chain of command."

"But the Bureau is the lead agency," pointed out Stone.

"But ATF was taking the lead on the bomb forensics."

"But an agent and evidence going missing is very unusual," said Stone.

"Yes, of course it is," the director said sharply.

"Any leads?" asked Chapman.

"No, we just found out about it, actually. We have teams going over the scene."

"Where was he taken from?"

"Not exactly sure. He's divorced, lives alone. His car is missing."

"Signs of a struggle?"

"Not definitive."

"No communications?"

"Neither from Garchik nor from whoever might have taken him."

"Might have?" asked Chapman.

"We can't rule out that he left voluntarily."

"Who reported him missing?"

"His supervisor."

Stone said, "Who reported the evidence missing?"

"His supervisor as well. When Garchik didn't make his routine check-in, he became worried.

One of the things he did was examine the evidence locker."

"Garchik told us that NASA was being called in to try and ID the debris."

"I wasn't aware of that."

Stone sat back as Ashburn said, "This is all really stunning."

"The media can't get wind of any of this," said the director firmly. "All statements will go through my office. Is that understood?"

"I don't talk to reporters," said Stone, as Chapman nodded in agreement.

The director motioned to Ashburn. "Agent Ashburn will be taking over the lead on the investigation. You will work directly with her."

Ashburn and Stone exchanged a glance. Stone thought he saw the woman attempt a smile.

"That's fine," said Stone. "I look forward to it."

"Agent Ashburn here told me you were up for the Medal of Honor for your service in Vietnam."

"I was offered it, yes."

"But turned it down. Why?"

"I didn't think I deserved it."

"But your country did. Isn't that enough?"

"No sir, it's actually not."

49

"Reuben?"

The large man opened his eyes and stared straight up.

Stone gazed down at him. "Docs say you'll be leaving soon."

"Great. I don't have health insurance. So let me just declare bankruptcy right now. Oh, that's right. Bankruptcy is for people who actually have property."

"I can see you're feeling better already."

This came from Annabelle, who had been planted in the chair ever since Reuben had been admitted. She rose and stood next to the bed.

Stone said, "Your bill is being taken care of."

"By who?"

"Uncle Sam."

"Why? Did he bail out the loading dock where I work too?"

"Just get some rest."

"Did you find those guys?"

Stone shook his head. "The area had been pretty well sterilized."

Annabelle said, "So you're still on the job?"

"For now."

"What else can we do?"

"I think you've both done enough."

"We didn't learn very much that was new," she said.

"No, you actually helped shine a whole new light on everything."

"Russians?" said Reuben. "Are the bastards really behind this?"

"Looks to be the case."

"Why?" asked Annabelle. "I thought they were our ally now."

"Allies come and allies go. And it might not be the Russian government, per se."

"I called Harry and Caleb. They're coming over later to see Reuben. Well, Harry said he would if you thought it was okay to take some time off his assignment."

"I think that would be fine. Please let him know."

As he turned to leave, Annabelle put an arm

around his shoulders and said in a low voice, "Please take care of yourself. We almost lost Reuben." Her eyes glimmered and Stone touched her cheek.

"I will, Annabelle."

Chapman was waiting for Stone in the hospital lobby. They walked to her car and drove off.

"Well, the meeting with the FBI really gob-smacked me," she said.

"The fact that we're still on the case, or something else?"

"The fact that your director seemed very much out of the loop."

"And I'm wondering why."

"What do you think happened to Garchik and that evidence?"

"I don't know, but I think where we'll find one we'll find the other."

"You think he's a bad cop?"

Stone didn't answer right away. "No, I don't. I think he may have been in the wrong place at the wrong time."

"Lot of that going around. Look at Alfredo Padilla. And Agent Gross."

"Right."

"So the question becomes, if someone is keeping things from the director of the FBI, who could have that kind of clout?"

Stone looked at her. "I need to try and see someone today."

"Who?"

"Just someone."

"Is it important?"

"Yes."

"Where is this person?"

"Well, he lives right across from Lafayette Park."

CHAPTER

50

It was not an easy thing to get in to see the president of the United States without an appointment. In fact, it was virtually impossible. The man's work schedule would put anyone else's in the world to shame. On Air Force One he could cover multiple countries in one day and be home in time for a state dinner and then some late-night phone lobbying with his cohorts on Capitol Hill.

Thus Stone was very surprised to be sitting in a helicopter as it was flown across the Maryland countryside. It touched down in the craw of the Catoctin Mountains where a three-car motorcade took him the rest of the way to Camp David, perhaps the best-protected parcel of land in the world.

This did make sense, thought Stone. Meeting at Camp David was far more private than walking the halls of the White House. As the motorcade entered the confines of Camp David and a ramrod-straight Marine in dress blues met him, Stone wondered exactly how he was going to broach the subject with the man. And what his reaction would be.

Well, I'm just about to find the answers to those questions.

He stood in a small wood-paneled room alone. But not for long. The door opened and there was the president dressed casually in corduroy pants and a checked shirt with loafers on his feet. He held a pair of glasses in one hand and a BlackBerry phone held up to his ear in the other.

He glanced at Stone standing there and motioned for him to take a seat. The president finished his call in low murmurs, slid the phone in his shirt pocket, poured a cup of coffee from a pot set up on a side table and poured one for Stone too. He handed him the cup and sat down, sliding his glasses over his face.

"Lost a contact," said Brennan. "Backup glasses until they get my other pair. Can't face the public in glasses. They don't like that."

Stone thought about that and it did occur to him that he couldn't remember seeing a president with glasses on during a public event.

"I appreciate you taking the time to see me on such short notice, sir."

The president leaned back and scrutinized him. "I'm sure you know why I did. The sense of urgency is compelling. We seem to be spiraling right out of control on this. Every day there's a new crisis. Made any sense of it yet?"

"Some. But there are a lot of new questions."

"Give me a quick debrief."

Stone did so, leaving out nothing, including the attack at his cottage and about Fuat Turkekul.

"I know I'm not telling you anything you aren't aware of," he said.

The president nodded. "The PM and I are very close."

"James McElroy also plays by the rules."

"An impressive man. Always seems to know more than anyone else, myself and his prime minister included, I think."

"The mark of a good intelligence officer," commented Stone. "But keeping me in the dark on that did cost us time."

"I'm aware of that, but it couldn't be helped," he said brusquely.

"I understand."

"Some good has come out of this," said Brennan.

"Sir?" asked Stone with a questioning look.

In response the president picked up a remote and

hit a button. A part of the wall slid open, revealing a flat-screen TV. The president touched another button and the TV came on. "This was recorded earlier," he explained.

Stone watched as the image of Carmen Escalante appeared. She looked even smaller and her leg braces even bigger on the screen than in person. She was being interviewed about the death of her beloved uncle and her own personal plight with her medical issues.

"Word has really spread about this, causing two things to happen. We're holding a joint memorial service for Mr. Padilla and Agent Gross. The president of Mexico is flying up for the ceremony. And, second, private donors have stepped in to pay for Ms. Escalante's operations for her legs."

"That's very nice."

"As you probably know, relations with Mexico have been strained due to the immigration issue among other things. However, things have thawed a bit with what happened to Padilla. I know he's an accidental hero, but he still lost his life. And we need heroes wherever we can find them. The story has gotten favorable play in Mexico and here. The people of our two nations have come together a little bit more. It's positive, or so my aides tell me. Something to build on for the future. That's one of the major reasons we're holding the joint memorial service."

He hit more buttons and the TV turned off and the wall slid back into place. He put the remote down and leaned back in his chair, sipping his coffee.

"Which brings us to today."

"Yes sir."

"All right. I think it's now time for me to ask why you wanted to meet."

"I know you're a busy man so I'll get right to it." Stone paused, but only for a moment. "Could you tell me where Agent Garchik is? And what happened to the evidence that went missing with him? Because I know you have the answers to both those questions."

CHAPTER

51

PRESIDENT BRENNAN AND OLIVER STONE stared at each other for an uncomfortably long time. Stone had engaged in such protracted battles of will before with people he considered his employers. The key was never to break eye contact. If you did they interpreted that as a sign of weakness and would pounce. They all had this skill; that was why they were in leadership positions.

"I beg your pardon?" the president said, but there was a slight hitch in his voice that was compelling in its disclosure of what the man was truly thinking.

Stone didn't answer. He just kept staring at the man, as though he could see the content of every synapse firing. Stone had to convey through this silence that he knew everything, though some of it was only speculation.

He waited.

Brennan said nothing else, his gaze intensifying briefly, but then slowly the burn faded. He stood.

"Let's take a walk, Stone. I think we need to come to an understanding, and I need to stretch my legs."

Stone followed him outside after the president slipped on a jacket. The security detail accompanied them, keeping both men encircled at the center of a hard diamond formed by the Secret Service agents. The men and women of the security detail were dressed casually in deference to their boss's clothes and the rustic surroundings.

The president spoke in a low voice as they made their way along a trail in the woods over which many past presidents had trod.

"Love it up here. Recharge. Forget my troubles, so to speak, at least for a little while."

Stone's gaze drifted right and left and up ahead as the agents kept to their marks precisely. Camp David in truth was even better protected than the White House. It was in the middle of rugged terrain, and its perimeter defenders, a large detachment of highly trained Marines, would be able to see any adversary coming long in advance.

The president drew so close to Stone that their elbows touched. Stone automatically looked around to see if the Secret Service agents had an issue with that. However, since their boss had initiated the proximity, the security detail just kept trudging along.

"Stone, we have a problem."

"The debris. Do we know what it is yet?"

"Have you ever heard of nanobots?"

"Nanotechnology? I've read about it in the newspapers. That's about the extent of my knowledge."

"Damnedest things. It's already in our clothes, foods, cosmetics, appliances, lots of things. And most people have no idea it's even there. Half the scientists think it's perfectly safe. And the other half say we don't know enough and it could have unforeseen and possibly disastrous long-term consequences."

"So they found some of these nanobots in the debris? But I thought they were microscopic?"

"They are. They were only revealed after being put under the scope."

"Why would they have been there? What would be the purpose in the context of a bomb?"

The president smiled resignedly. "There's the rub, Stone. We don't know. What we think is that someone out there has come up with a new application that uses nanotechnology in ways that were never intended."

"You mean for criminal or terrorism purposes?"

"Yes."

"What are people speculating? I mean, for why the nanobots were there? There must be some theories."

"There are. The most popular one is also the most chilling. That theory involves some sort of contagion being grafted onto the explosive. When the bomb exploded it released this contagion that is now in the system of everyone who's been at that park. And they've unwittingly carried it on to others."

Stone flinched and moved away from the man. "I've been to that park. I was knocked over by the blast. I could be contaminated. You shouldn't be near me."

"I've already been exposed, Stone. Through Agent Gross, Garchik and others. Hell, the FBI director was out there too. But I can tell you that I've had every test known to the doctors and they've given me a clean bill of health."

"Is there any evidence of the existence of such a contagion on the debris?"

"Not that we know. But you know what they're telling me now? That the damn nanobots have the ability to invade and actually change certain molecular structures of other substances. This 'transformation' can leave the substances in their original form, but it can change them subtly enough to make identifying them much harder. So right now we don't believe there's a contagion problem, but the truth is we don't know for certain. We're not even sure what to test for. So all the things the doctors checked me for may be worthless. And furthermore, they could have used nanobots to produce a totally new contagion. It's like my grandkids playing whack-a-mole. You hit at one hole and the damn thing shows up in another."

"And Agent Garchik?" he said.

"We thought it best to remove him from the field for a while. He's currently at an ATF safe house in—"

Stone put up a hand. "I'd prefer not to know the exact location."

"You mean?"

"In case someone tries to get it from me. Yes."

"Dangerous times, Stone. Uncertain times."

"Enemies closer."

"Right. If only we knew exactly who they were anymore. It's getting harder and harder on that score."

"I think every soldier deployed to Iraq and Afghanistan would agree with you on that."

"It's ironic, actually," said Brennan.

"What's that?"

"I originally sought you out to go fight the Russians in Mexico. Now I find them much closer to home. Possibly right across the street from the White House."

"You know of course about the gun found and Kravitz's ties to Moscow?"

"Yes, yes, all of that, but there's something else."

Stone waited expectantly.

"When the Soviet Union was a world power they had an immense scientific discovery program. Labs all over the place and tens of billions of dollars to fund those efforts."

"So nanobots?"

"Nanobots. There are few countries or organizations with the wherewithal to pull something like this off. The Russians are near the top of the list."

"What do you want me to do now, sir?"

"Your job, Stone. And I promise you that I'll have your back."

Stone gazed hard at the man. The president seemed to sense Stone's doubts.

"I mean that, Stone. You survive this, the slate is clean. You have my word. No more blowbacks against you." He put out his hand. Stone shook it.

Brennan added, "Why do men like you do the job you do? It can't be for the medals. And it's certainly not the money."

Stone said nothing.

"Why then? God and country?"

"Both simpler and more complex, Mr. President."

"What then?"

"So I can look at myself in the mirror."

CHAPTER

52

STONE WAS FLOWN BACK to D.C., where he met
Chapman by prearrangement at Lafayette Park.

"How did it go?" she asked anxiously.

"Informative."

"In a helpful sort of way?"

"That remains to be seen."

"Come on! Any revelations? You met with the
president, for God's sake."

Stone explained about the unknown bits of
debris possibly being connected to nanotechnology.
And also about the whereabouts of Agent Garchik.

"Did you know all that when you asked to meet
with the president?"

"Let's say I suspected it."

"And you told him of your suspicions?"

"I thought the direct way was best."

"Pretty ballsy. So nanobots? Bloody hell. What's

the world coming to when they stick stuff in stuff we can't even see that could come back and kill us all?"

"I think some folks would call that progress, actually," said Stone dryly.

"So the Russians are playing around in their laboratory again. Ominous development."

"Drug trafficking is worth hundreds of billions of dollars. That's one motivation. Couple that with science that could make Russia's enemies wastelands, that's something you can't measure in mere treasure."

"Russia's enemies, meaning my country and yours."

"Despite détente, Gorbachev and Yeltsin, things have never really been rosy among the three nations."

"But why would they detonate a bomb in Lafayette Park that didn't kill anyone?"

"I don't know."

He moved over toward ground zero and looked down at the crater.

"Riley Weaver's questions are also still unanswered," he said.

"What do you mean?"

"How did the tree suddenly die? And why was the hole left open after the tree went in?"

"The arborist and stuff. Agent Gross told us about it."

"Well, I guess we need to check it ourselves."

"But what about Ashburn? Isn't she on the case now?"

"I'd prefer to handle it."

"Just in case we lose another agent?" she said quietly.

Stone didn't answer.

An hour later they were standing in front of George Sykes, who was wearing the uniform of the National Park Service. He was the supervisor previously identified by Tom Gross who'd overseen the installation of the tree. Sykes was a fit man with a crushing grip. Chapman discreetly rubbed her sore fingers together after shaking the man's hand.

"The maple had shown no signs of disease or any other problem," he said. "We did a survey of the park one morning and found that it was nearly dead. No way to save it. Broke my heart. That tree had been there a long time."

Chapman said, "So you pulled it out, ordered a new one and installed it?"

"Right," replied Sykes. "We're very careful about the materials that go into the park. They have to be historically accurate."

"So we understand. And the tree farm in Pennsylvania was one of your vetted suppliers?" said Stone.

"Yes. I told all this to Agent Gross."

"We understand. But in light of what happened to him we needed to go back over this."

"Absolutely," said Sykes quickly. "What a nightmare. And they think one of the men at the tree farm was involved?"

"Apparently," said Chapman vaguely. "What can you tell us about when the tree was delivered?"

"We kept it in a secure staging area a few blocks from the White House."

"And then you had it craned in here?" asked Stone.

"That's right," said Sykes.

"And the tree was installed but the hole remained uncovered?" said Chapman.

"That's right," said Sykes.

Stone said, "Why not cover it up right away? In fact it was a hazard, wasn't it? You had to put tape around it to keep people away."

And keep the bomb detection dogs away from it, was Stone's unspoken thought.

"Transplanting a tree of that size creates a lot of stress for the specimen. You have to do it in stages and check the health of the tree along the way. Craning it in and putting it in the hole was only one step in a series of them that started when it was dug up at the farm in Pennsylvania. The key is to take it slow and easy. We put it in the hole and left it uncovered to measure its health. The maple was to be examined the following morning by our arborist. He'd give us a report and tell us the correct mixture of fill dirt and nutrients the tree would need for this transition period."

"Sounds complicated," said Chapman.

"It can be. You're talking about a living thing that weighs tons. And proper watering is very important to help establish the roots."

"Okay," Stone said slowly. "But you still don't know what killed the first tree?"

Sykes shrugged. "It could be a number of things. While it is strange to see it die so quickly, it's not unheard of."

"Could it have been deliberately sabotaged?" asked Chapman.

Sykes looked at her in amazement. "Why would someone want to kill that tree?"

Stone explained, "Well, if the tree didn't die, there would have been no need to replace it. No new tree, no bomb in the tree."

"Oh," said Sykes, looking thoroughly appalled. "You mean they killed the first tree and then blew up the second? Those bastards."

Stone could sense he was far more upset about the demise of the trees than the human being who had been blown up.

"Well, thank you for your help," Stone said.

Chapman and Stone walked back to her car. She said, "Clearly the bomb was in the root ball before it got here. And the fact that the hole wasn't covered up isn't that significant. Even with dirt in there the remote detonation presumably would have worked. Radio signals can certainly penetrate a few feet of dirt."

"So it seems, despite my misgivings, that the tree farm was the key and any connection there was lost when Kravitz died."

"They've certainly tidied up the trail behind them," noted Chapman. "Wait a minute, were these nanobot things found at Kravitz's trailer?"

"Not to my knowledge, no."

"Well, wouldn't they have been?"

"I don't know. But that's something we have to find out."

Chapman checked her watch. "I need to go report in and also debrief Sir James."

"I'm going to the Library of Congress to talk to Caleb."

"Your intrepid researcher?"

Stone smiled. "He is quite good if you know his strengths."

"How about dinner tonight?" she asked suddenly.

Stone turned to look at her. "All right," he said slowly. "Where?"

"Restaurant on Fourteenth Street called Ceiba. Been wanting to go there. We can compare notes. Say around seven?"

Stone nodded and walked off while Chapman hurried back to her car and drove not to the British embassy but to a hotel in Tysons Corner, Virginia. She rode the elevator to the sixth floor. She opened the door to a room and went in. It was a large suite made up of a spacious living room, bedroom and dining area. She looked out at the views from the window, took off her jacket and shoes and rubbed her feet as she sat on the couch. She pulled her gun and studied it. When the knock came she put the Walther away.

She padded across the room and opened the door.

The man entered and she resumed her seat and looked up at him.

"I don't bloody well like this," she snapped. "Not at all."

NIC director Riley Weaver stared down at her.

"It doesn't really matter what you like or not. And the authorization goes to the top on *both* sides."

"How do I know that for sure?" she snarled.

"Because it's true, Mary," said James McElroy as he limped in from the bedroom.

53

STONE MADE A STOP FIRST at the hospital to check on Reuben. He heard his friend's voice long before he got to his room. Apparently from the little Stone could make out, Reuben wanted to leave but the doctors were unwilling to release him for several more days.

Annabelle met him at the doorway to Reuben's room. "Maybe you can talk some sense into him," she barked.

"I doubt it," said Stone. "But I'll try."

"I'm fine," bellowed Reuben as Stone came into his line of sight. "It's not like this was the first time I've been shot. But I'll take a damn bullet over Nurse Ratchet here poking me with needles in places I don't want to be poked."

The nurse taking his vitals merely rolled her eyes

at Reuben's comment. As she turned to leave she whispered to Stone, "Good luck."

Stone looked down at Reuben. "I take it you want to leave?"

"What I want to do is get the assholes who did this to me."

Stone pulled up a chair and sat down at about the time Caleb wandered in with a vase of flowers.

"What the hell are those?" snapped Reuben.

Caleb frowned at the man's ungrateful attitude. "They're peonies. Very hard to get this time of year."

Reuben looked mortified. "Are you saying you brought me flowers?"

"Yes. To brighten up this very depressing room. Look, it's all gray and blah. You'll never get well because you'll be too depressed."

"I think they're beautiful," said Annabelle as she took the flowers from Caleb and smelled them.

"You would think that. You're a girl," said Reuben. "But guys don't bring guys flowers." He suddenly leveled a ferocious gaze at Caleb. "Did anyone see you bring those in?"

"What? I... Well, I suppose. A few. The people at the nurses' station were admiring them."

Reuben, who had been sitting up in bed, collapsed back. "Oh great. They probably think we're dating."

Caleb exclaimed, "I'm not gay."

"Yeah, but you look like you are," shot back Reuben.

Caleb scowled. "*I* look like I am? How exactly do gay people look, Mr. stereotyping Neanderthal?"

Reuben moaned and put a pillow over his face. From under it they heard him grumble, "Next time bring me a beer, for Chrissakes. Or better yet, a *Playboy.*"

While Annabelle went in search of a vase for the flowers, Stone turned to Caleb. "I received your list of events coming up at Lafayette Park. I wanted to see you about it."

Reuben took the pillow off his face and said, "Where are you going with that?"

Stone quickly explained things to him and added, "But there are a lot of events."

"There are," agreed Caleb. "But I've been doing some digging and I've been able to narrow it down." He pulled some slips of paper from his pocket and laid them out on the end of the bed as Stone leaned over to see them.

Caleb explained, "I started with the assumption that this must be really big. Otherwise why go to all the trouble at Lafayette Park."

"Agreed," said Stone.

Annabelle came back into the room with the

flowers in a vase, set it down on a counter and joined them.

"There are five events that I think fall into that category," continued Caleb. "They all occur within the next month. First, there's a climate change rally. Then an antitax protest. Lots of people and lots of potential casualties at each one of those. Next, the president is giving a speech to honor the soldiers killed in the wars in the Middle East, along with the French president."

Reuben piped up, "That gets my vote. Two leaders with one pop. And all that stuff happened at the park when the British prime minister was there. Maybe they're going after the E.U."

Stone said, "Go on, Caleb, and finish the list."

Caleb continued, "Fourth, there's a world hunger protest. And last a demonstration against nuclear weapons."

"I'm telling you, terrorists will go with quality over quantity," said Reuben. "You take out a couple heads of state over killing lots of ordinary citizens."

Annabelle shook her head. "Not necessarily. It depends on who's behind the plot. If it's some anti-war group or people who think climate change is a crock, those events could have been the targets."

Stone said, "I doubt the Russians are all that interested in our tax policies."

"The Russians!" exclaimed Caleb. "They're behind this?"

Stone ignored his friend's query and said thoughtfully, "I wonder how far away one would have to be to remotely detonate a bomb buried in the earth? And, second, how would the bombers know where the podium would be situated with the heads of state? I know they place the stages in different spots. Sometimes even on the sidewalk. This bomb would have done no damage to them in that event."

Reuben said, "I'd ask Alex. If it turns out the stage was going to be set up near the Jackson statue then I think that confirms there's a spy."

Stone replied, "I think you're right."

Annabelle said, "I'll call him. We're getting together later anyway."

Caleb added, "And I have to get back to work."

"So do I," said Stone.

"And what about me?" complained Reuben. "You guys go off having fun while I'm stuck in here."

At that moment an attendant came in with Reuben's lunch. She put the tray in front of him and took off the top to reveal a dark spongy mass that was apparently a piece of meat, some stringy vegetables, a doughy roll and a sippy cup with what looked like pee in it.

Reuben whimpered, "Please get me the hell out of here."

"As soon as possible, Reuben, I promise," said Stone as he hurried out.

"Enjoy your flowers," snapped Caleb. "And next time I'll be sure to bring my Village People's greatest hits collection for all to hear. And I might just wear a very flamboyant scarf *and* my skinny jeans." He stalked out.

Annabelle leaned over and kissed Reuben on the cheek and brushed back his matted hair. "Hang in there, big guy. And just remember we almost lost you. What would I do without my Reuben?"

He smiled at this comment and watched her leave. He waited for a few moments to make sure they were gone and then he picked up the vase. He took a deep sniff of the peonies and sat back with a contented look.

CHAPTER

54

Mary Chapman let the water wash over her, the steam in the shower rising like morning mist over a lake. She slapped the wall of the shower in frustration, ducked her head under the cascading water and took a deep, controlling breath. She turned off the water, stepped out of the shower, toweled off and sat on the bed.

The meeting with Director Weaver and Sir James had been efficient and hit on all relevant points. This was part of the job. She should have no problem with any of it. It was the reason she'd been brought over here. But she did have a problem with it. And she didn't know what to do about it.

She dried her hair, took her time choosing what to wear, slipped on her heels and jewelry, grabbed her bag and gun and walked down to the front of the hotel after calling for her car. She drove into

D.C. fighting the rush-hour traffic. He was already there waiting for her.

She smiled at Stone, who'd changed clothes and was dressed in a pair of slacks and a white long-sleeved shirt that matched the color of his close-cropped hair and offset nicely the deep tan on his square-jawed face. He'd rolled the shirtsleeves up to reveal ropy forearms. At six-two, he looked even taller because of his leanness. Yet when he'd grabbed her arm outside John Kravitz's trailer she had felt the immense strength in his grip. Even at his age the man was still made of iron. She presumed he would be until the day he died. Which might be sooner than anyone expected.

When she thought this Chapman stopped smiling.

"I never thanked you for saving my life back at your cottage," she said. "The flash-bang got me, but not you."

"Well, we'd both be dead except for you. I've never seen anyone move that fast."

"High praise coming from you."

He momentarily put a hand on the small of her back as they were escorted to a table overlooking Fourteenth Street. He was more than twenty years older than her, but still, there was something about him that was unlike any man she'd ever met. How he had survived so long doing what he did. And he had the most intense pair of eyes she'd ever seen.

His light touch made Chapman feel protected and comforted, but when he removed his hand her depression set in once more. She ordered a mojito and he a beer. They scanned their menus.

"Productive afternoon?" he asked, eyeing her over the menu.

She felt her face growing warm as she looked over at him. "A little boring, actually. Reports and briefings are not my strong suits. How about you?"

Stone's cell phone buzzed. He looked at the number and answered it.

He mouthed the name *Agent Ashburn.*

He listened. His eyes twitched. He shot a glance at Chapman. "Right, thanks for the heads-up."

"What's up?" Chapman asked after he put his phone away.

"They just found the Latinos from the tree farm in Pennsylvania."

"What do you mean they *found* them?"

"Dead. Execution style. Bodies dumped in a ravine."

Chapman sat back, her face pale. "But why kill them?"

"The guy saw someone taking down a basketball hoop. He didn't tell the cops. He told Annabelle. And now they're all dead."

Chapman nodded. "They're cleaning up loose ends."

"Looks to be. Probably the only reason they didn't kill everyone at the tree farm along with Gross and the supervisor is because they knew we were coming."

"How?"

"Sniper who killed Kravitz called and told them we'd gone off in a hurry. Where else would we have been going?"

"Right." Chapman looked chagrined at missing such an obvious point. "But again, he saw someone take down a basketball hoop. So what? It's not like he could identify him in a lineup, right?"

"Maybe he could."

"What do you mean? He didn't tell Annabelle that."

"He didn't know Annabelle from Adam. And we know someone was at that bar listening in."

Chapman sipped her drink. "That's right, they came after them later."

"So maybe he was holding that back from someone. Blackmail?"

"He got a bunch of bullet wounds instead of cash. So who do you think he might have seen?"

"Maybe Lloyd Wilder."

Chapman's jaw fell open. "Lloyd Wilder?"

"Possible. Kill him and the others, two birds with one stone."

"So *he* was part of the bombing too?"

"I'm not sure what part if any he played, actually. But the fact that they took him out as soon as we showed up tells me he was expendable from day one."

"So we need to check into Wilder's background?" She shook her head, looking frustrated. "This thing just keeps on growing."

"We'll let Ashburn and the Bureau dig into Wilder's history. They'll probably find some money in an offshore account somewhere."

"And I thought conspiracies were confined to Hollywood films."

"Actually you'll come to see that D.C. is just one big conspiracy."

"That's comforting."

"I also spoke with Harry about Turkekul."

Stone paused as the waiter came over and took their orders. After he was gone Stone resumed. "Nothing out of the ordinary."

"I guess that's good."

"Maybe or maybe not."

"I'm not following."

"The man has been tasked to take out the number one terrorist in the world and he's teaching a course at Georgetown?"

"It's background cover for him."

Stone didn't look convinced.

"But Sir James is aware of this. You trust him, right?" she said, even as she felt her stomach tighten and her skin grow cold.

"I trust you," he said.

"Why?"

"I just do. Let's leave it at that."

CHAPTER

55

As they ate Chapman kept shooting glances at Stone. If he noticed, Stone made no reaction. She downed several more mojitos and a glass of port after the meal was done.

"You have a car?" he asked after the bill was paid.

"Yes, but why don't we walk for a bit? It's a nice evening."

"That's a good idea."

"Really?" she said smiling.

"Yes. You've had a lot to drink. A walk will help clear your head," he added in a strange voice.

They strolled along, passing by restaurants teeming with hungry, boisterous patrons. Car horns honked and people walked past.

"Troubled?" Stone said.

She glanced at him sharply. "Just thinking about things. Why?"

"No reason. Just a lot to think about."

"So Director Weaver never got back to you?"

"I have to assume he never will. That's why I had Caleb research for me."

"And after reviewing his research, what are your conclusions?"

"I don't have any," he admitted. "I just have more questions." He paused. "Weaver did say one interesting thing before he cut me off."

"What?" she said, perhaps a tad too quickly.

"He said things might not be as they seem. I think he meant that we were all looking at this the wrong way. That if we could find the right way to look at things we might make sense out of everything."

"Do you believe that?" she said.

"I don't disbelieve it. At least not yet."

She stopped at a street vendor and bought a ball cap with "FBI" on it. When Stone looked at her, puzzled, she explained, "Got a nephew back in London who's keen on them."

"Does he know you work for MI6?"

"No, he thinks I'm in the computer business. I'd be much cooler to him if he knew the truth."

As they continued to walk along she said, "Okay,

let's go back through what we know. Gunfire and bombing. Maybe unrelated. The Hay-Adams Hotel was a distraction and the gunfire actually came from a U.S. government building undergoing renovation. Padilla runs for his life and triggers the bomb that was probably in a basketball in the tree's root ball. That leads us to the tree and from there to the tree farm."

Stone picked it up from there. "The tree farm leads to John Kravitz, who had bomb-making elements under his trailer. He's killed to prevent him from talking to us. Agent Gross and the other two are killed for reasons yet unknown, but Wilder might've been involved. The bomb had some unusual elements that tentatively have been identified as nanobots. Why they were in the bomb is unknown. Agent Garchik has been 'relieved' of his field duties pending further developments. We have several pieces of evidence that show either the Russian government or Russian drug cartels, or perhaps both, may be behind this."

"And the Latinos were killed because they might have seen something or else they might have been part of the plot."

"Yes. And the actual target of the bomb is still unknown. We have a number of possibilities but no definitive answer."

Chapman stopped walking and looked at him. "Okay, there's the list. We've checked it twice."

"We left out one thing. Fuat Turkekul."

"But his presence has been explained."

"Has it?"

"Sir James explained it. And I know you trust him, despite what you said earlier."

"No, I said I trusted *you*."

Chapman's cheeks reddened slightly. Stone gazed at her for a moment and then looked away. He checked his watch.

"You have another date?" she said with an attempt at a smile.

"No, I was just wondering how long it would take before you told me."

"Told you what?"

"Whatever it is you're keeping from me."

CHAPTER

56

CHAPMAN TURNED and took a few hesitant steps away from Stone. When she turned back he hadn't moved. He was just looking at her.

She came back to him. "What do you want from me?"

"The truth."

"I thought you said you trusted me?"

"All trust has limits. And it has to be constantly earned."

"You didn't tell me that part."

"I didn't think I had to."

"You're putting me in a very awkward position."

"I know."

"I need a drink."

Stone raised his eyebrows at this. "Okay. But it would be nice if you remained sober."

"You should've seen me doing pub crawls whilst at university. I can hold my bloody liquor."

She turned and headed off.

"Agent Chapman?"

She turned back to him. "What!" she snapped.

He pointed behind him. "There's a bar right there."

She looked where he was pointing. "Right. Well done." She pushed past him and into the bar.

Five minutes later she'd downed two vodka tonics while Stone sipped on a bottle of ginger ale and eyed her steadily. "You sure you'll be able to drive home okay?"

"It's a bloody breeze driving here after London."

"Not if you're drunk. A British agent arrested for DUI?"

"I'm not drunk!"

"Okay. Then let's move on." He stared at her, waiting.

"I can't tell you everything. I hope you understand that," she said.

"I don't."

"Well, too bad. That's just the way it has to be."

Stone rose. "Take care of yourself."

She gazed up at him in amazement. "Just like that?"

"Just like that."

"Stone!"

He turned and left.

He walked block after block, his long legs eating up the pavement in great chunks as adrenaline roared through his body. He thought she was different. He was wrong.

Same old shit, he thought. *Same old shit.*

He passed the Capitol building and kept going until he recognized the area he was in. Whether he had meant to come here or not he wasn't sure, but he was a man who almost always followed his instincts. He passed throngs of young men on the street. When several seemed overly interested in him, he stuck his federal badge on his belt and let them see his gun. They immediately backed off.

"It's cool," one said.

Another said with a grin, "Hey, Gramps, ever kill anybody with that gun?"

"No," lied Stone. He held up a finger. "But I have with this."

The young men looked skeptical.

One said, "You killed somebody with just your pinky? Right."

He showed them the finger again. "Not the pinky. This is the index finger. It gives far more leverage against the carotid, so it's easier to crush."

The men shuffled off.

Stone walked on.

He reached the door, knocked.

He heard the clunks as she came to answer it.

The door opened and Carmen Escalante looked up at him with wide, sad eyes.

"Yes?" she said.

"I was here before," he said, showing her his badge.

"Yes, I remember. What is it you want?"

"To see how you're doing."

"That's right," said a voice.

Stone turned and saw Chapman standing a few feet behind him. She came forward. She looked a bit out of breath, and she was holding her high heels in her left hand.

"We wanted to make sure you were okay," she said, getting her breathing under control and slipping on her shoes.

"May we come in?" asked Stone, still staring at Chapman.

"Yes, okay."

CHAPTER

57

They followed Carmen down the hall. They immediately noticed that the home had been cleaned and the stench of rotting food was gone. When they entered the small living room, they saw furniture and a large flat-screen television that had not been there previously.

"What happened?" asked Chapman, looking around.

Carmen smiled sadly. "When people saw on the TV what happened to Uncle Freddy, they come and they help me. Clean my house, buy me things. They are very kind."

"What people?" asked Stone.

"People from the TV station."

"The TV station?" asked Stone.

"Well, they say people donate money. People on the street. And they give me many things." She pointed to the TV. "Like that. Uncle Freddy would have liked that TV very much. He liked to watch football. Not your kind."

"Not mine either. You mean soccer," said Chapman.

"Yes, that is what I mean. And they clean my house and now someone come every day to check on me." She tapped her braces on the floor. "They say they will also help with my medical bills. And buy me a new pair of these."

"That's terrific, Carmen," said Chapman.

"Would you like something to drink?" she asked. "I have many things now to drink," she added proudly.

They declined and Stone said, "Will you stay here, then?"

Carmen sat down and they did too.

"I do not know. I have to think. They have a service for Uncle Freddy. I must go to that. Your president, he will be there. And my president too. From Mexico. Though I don't like him very much. But I will still go. Then I will decide what to do." She looked around at her new possessions. "I like this place very much. And my new things. Very much."

"So maybe you'll stay?" said Stone.

"It is possible, yes." She fell silent for a moment.

"I can go back to school. In Mexico I worked in a doctor's office. I know computers. My English is good. I can type and file things. I can get a job. I can have friends."

"You can do all those things," said Stone encouragingly.

"My family thinks I should come home. They say I do not live in a nice area."

"But you have to think about what you want. It's your life to lead," said Chapman. "And you can always move from here to another place."

She looked uncertain. "And I can take my new things?"

"Absolutely," said Stone. "I'll even come and help you."

"You will do this for me?" she said, looking at him in wonder.

"Yes."

"You are strange government people."

Chapman glanced at Stone. "Yes, I guess we are," she said.

Promising to return to check on her, they left.

"Where did you come from?" Stone asked as they walked down the street.

"I followed you. Bloody difficult in heels, let me tell you. You walk very fast."

"Why did you follow me?"

"Because you were right. And I wanted to tell you so."

"So the truth this time?"

She stuffed her hands in her pockets. "Riley Weaver and Sir James are working together." She took a breath and said, "God, I can't believe I'm telling you this. I've broken just about every professional rule MI6 has."

"That's all right. Most agencies have too many rules."

"Bloody easy for you to say," she replied irritably.

"Why are they working together? To what purpose?"

"It wasn't Sir James's idea, that I know."

"So he was persuaded?"

"As Sir James said, your president and our prime minister get along rather well. And America is the superpower. Everyone else just follows its lead."

"So why keep it from me?"

"Weaver is afraid of you. That's quite clear from what I've seen and heard."

Stone thought, *If he knows what I did to his predecessor, I would be afraid of me too.*

"What exactly is your role in all of this?"

"I've been tasked to investigate and solve this crime."

"Even though your prime minister was clearly not the target? Does MI6 have that much free time on its hands to allow one of their best agents to stay over here and assist us in our criminal investigations?"

She said nothing, just studied the pavement.

Stone turned away. "Don't bother following me this time."

She grabbed his arm. "All right, all right."

He turned back, looked at her expectantly.

"I've also been tasked to watch you."

"MI6 tasked by the American government to watch me?" he said skeptically.

"The world has gotten a lot more complicated, Oliver. Assets are not what they used to be, even for you Americans. Global cooperation, that's the ticket these days. We do favors for the Yanks and they reciprocate. It's not well-known of course, all hush-hush, but it does happen."

He cocked his head. "Watch me why? Do they think I'm involved in what happened?"

"No. But Weaver has some other agenda in mind."

"Has he shared it with McElroy?"

"I don't believe so, at least not completely. But Sir James's hands are tied." She stared at him pensively. "What's in your background that could have prompted this level of attention?"

"I have three decades' worth of answers and not nearly enough time to explain them even if I were so inclined, which I'm not."

"If you tell me what's going on, maybe I can help."

"You? The person who's been tasked to spy on me?"

"I thought we were partners on this thing."

"We are, but only on this *thing*. Nothing else."

"So who's withholding information now?" she said sharply.

"You were withholding things related to the here and now. I've never asked about your past missions. And I expect the same courtesy from you."

"So where does that leave us?" asked Chapman quietly.

"Back where we started," Stone said sharply. "And let's leave it that way."

CHAPTER

58

THEY TOOK A TAXI BACK to Chapman's car at the parking garage.

She said, "I can drop you off at your cottage."

"I feel like walking some more," he replied.

"Look, I'm sorry about not telling you earlier about Weaver. But I have my orders too."

Stone drew close to her. "If that's how you want to operate, so be it."

"Well, how exactly do you operate in that regard?"

"I don't keep things from the people I'm working with in the trenches. That's where my loyalties lie. That's why I told you about Fuat Turkekul even though *your* boss didn't want me to."

Her face flushed. "Okay, okay. I get it. And I am sorry."

"I'll see you tomorrow." He paused. "Are you sure you're okay to drive?"

"I'm fine now. All wide-eyed. A firm verbal spanking does it every time."

After a very long walk Stone reached the George-town campus, which was quiet at this hour. He found the community message board, pulled out a piece of paper and a pen, wrote a note and posted it on the board using a few extra pushpins stuck into the cork. On the way to his cottage he used his cell phone to call Harry Finn.

"Glad Reuben's okay," were the first words out of the man's mouth.

"Me too," said Stone. "He wants to leave the hospital but I think he'll be safer in there."

"You think the folks might try again?"

"Even though he told us what he knew, as did Annabelle, there's no reason not to be careful. Now tell me about Fuat."

Stone stopped and leaned against a tree as he listened.

Finn said, "If he is going after bin Laden, he's taking his own sweet time. He gets up, eats, teaches class. Has lunch. Teaches some more. Has office hours. Goes for a walk. Has dinner, goes to his apartment, reads and goes to sleep."

"No secret communications? No clandestine meetings?"

"Not that I've seen. And I would have."

"I know you would, Harry."

"They may have him lying low because they know we're watching."

"I thought of that too. But it's difficult to know what to do about it. Look, go home and rest."

"And Turkekul?"

"I'm going to try a different angle. I'll keep you posted."

Stone continued the walk to his cottage. On the next block over his internal senses started tingling. Six o'clock and nine o'clock. He could feel them there before he even saw them. A man behind. A woman to his left. They looked innocuous, uninterested in him. That is, they did to the casual eye. Stone hadn't possessed a casual eye in over forty years. His hand drifted to his holster. He picked up his pace just a bit because he wanted to get to the next intersection a few seconds faster. A plan had formed based on knowing this area as well as he did.

As soon as he reached the intersection he suddenly veered to his right. A construction Dumpster was up on the sidewalk because the house located there was being renovated. He took up a defensive position behind it, drew his pistol and placed a bead on the woman.

"Agent Stone?" the woman called out.

Stone kept her in his gunsight and said nothing.

"Director Weaver would like to talk to you."

"I'm sure he would."

"We were assigned to bring you to him."

"I prefer he come to me."

The man appeared next to the woman. He said, "Sir, the director is a very busy person."

"So am I."

A car drove past and the old woman inside peered out at the man and woman before driving on. A few other people were walking up the street, not yet in earshot, but they soon would be.

"He just wants to talk," said the woman, desperation creeping into her voice.

"I'd be glad to entertain him."

"Okay, where?" the man asked.

"The outdoor parking lot down by the river. One hour."

"Sir, the director—" began the woman as she nervously looked over her shoulder at the approaching people.

Stone cut in, "The *director* will be very pleased

to meet me there at that time. Now keep walking so I can put my gun away."

"This is highly irregular," snapped the woman.

"Yes, it is."

"We're federal agents too," added the man. "On the same side as you."

"I'll buy the first part, but not the second. Go!"

They walked off. Stone slipped the gun back in its holster and set out for the river. He wanted to get there first. He had things to get ready. He picked up his pace even as a knot grew in his stomach. It was one thing to risk life and limb trying to solve a complex case. It was quite another to have to do so while watching your rear flank. But apparently that was just how things were now.

And why am I surprised?

CHAPTER

59

THE THREE VEHICLES PULLED UP to the empty parking lot and stopped. It was one o'clock in the morning, and being a weekday, working Washingtonians had long since finished their collective entertainment for the evening and gone home to sleep. The security team piled out first, checking out obvious attack points and sending personnel scurrying into these hidden crevices before signaling that it was safe for Riley Weaver to exit his ride. He was dressed in a suit and striped tie, looking more ready to step in front of a camera and play the pundit's role or host a global conference on terrorism than skirmish with an ex-assassin in an empty parking lot at the edge of the Potomac. The bulge at his chest indicated the body armor he wore. He looked around a bit uncertainly before taking a few steps toward the water's edge.

"Stone?" he called out.

A phone rang. Everyone grabbed cells.

"Sir," said one of the guards as he picked up the ringing phone from the top of a pier piling, right where Stone had placed it earlier. He handed it to Weaver.

"Hello?"

"Hello, Director," said Stone. "What can I do for you?"

His voice was on speakerphone. When Weaver tried to disable it, he couldn't.

"What the hell are you doing?" he exclaimed. "It won't let me off the speakerphone."

"I want everyone to hear this. So again, what can I do for you?"

"You can start by showing yourself." Weaver looked nervously around at the darkness.

"And why is that necessary? I thought you wanted to talk. All we need are voices to do that."

"I wanted to meet at NIC," snapped Weaver.

"And I picked this place instead."

"Why?"

"Frankly, your place gives me the creeps. Never quite sure if I'm going to walk out or not."

"What is wrong with you? You are a federal employee."

"Of an agency unaffiliated with yours."

"What are you afraid of?"

"You brought the SWAT team with you. Again! And you're wearing Kevlar. What are *you* afraid of?"

Weaver performed a 360-degree spin, trying to see where Stone might be lurking.

"I've got long-range eyes, Director, so don't even bother."

"I don't like it that you can see me but I can't see you."

"I like it just fine. And as your messengers said, we're all on the same team."

"Which begs the question of why we have to meet in such a damn fool way," barked Weaver into the phone.

"Depends on what you want."

"Did you speak to Agent Chapman tonight?"

"You know I did. Or else you wouldn't be here."

"What did she tell you?"

"She told me lots of things. You'll have to be more specific."

"About our arrangement."

"Meaning you and her?"

"Come on, Stone, don't play stupid."

"You were a Marine, Weaver."

"Still am. Never leave the Corps no matter what other uniform you put on."

"I was hoping that would be your answer. And in combat who do you rely on?"

"Marine next to you."

"That's right. And did you ever keep secrets about the fight in front of you from the Marine next to you?"

Weaver didn't answer right away. He glanced around at his security detail. Several of them were eyeing him closely.

"This isn't exactly combat, Stone. You know that as well as anyone. You carried a rifle for your country."

"It's looking an awful lot like a battlefield to me."

"So you're saying Chapman told you?"

"I'm saying partners don't keep secrets. If you have a problem with that, then the problem is with me, not her."

"She could get in a lot of trouble for this."

"But she won't."

"How the hell do you know that?"

"Hit the speakerphone button twice, Weaver."

"What?"

"Just do it."

Weaver did so and the speakerphone function was disabled. Weaver held the phone up to his ear. "What the hell are you playing at?"

"Nanobots."

Weaver noticeably stiffened.

"And since you never got back to me with the list of events at Lafayette Park, I had someone do it for me. There's a bunch of stuff on there that could have been the target for the bomb, but something tells me the answer isn't anywhere on that list."

"Where, then?"

"You know about the Pennsylvania adventure my friends had? And the executions of the Latinos?"

"Of course. I am the director of NIC."

"Lot of trouble for a cover-up. Coupled with the fact that those shots into the park were fired from a government office building behind the Hay-Adams that one needed a pretty high security clearance to get into spells 'traitor' with a capital T."

"Nothing new there. We're looking into that angle."

"Your 'looking' will show that the person who accessed the building used a stolen or cloned security card while the real card owner was halfway around the world."

Weaver pursed his lips. "Cloned. Actual holder was in Tokyo."

"And this person was with the State Department?"

"Jesus, Stone, what are you, a freaking mind reader?"

"No. The folks at State have always been lax about security. Thirty years ago half my missions were because they'd screwed up somehow. And I can see they haven't changed."

"Any thoughts on who the inside person might be?"

"Not yet. I need to keep digging. But, Weaver, if I have to spend all my time looking over my shoulder for your boys, that will be very distracting."

"I can see why your superiors had such a hell of a time with you in the army. You don't play well with others."

"Sure I do. My problem was when my superiors said one thing and did another. And I can see that hasn't changed either."

"And when that happens what do you do? Eliminate the offender?"

Stone, who was sitting at the window of a building across from the parking lot that he'd accessed through a never-locked rear door, stared down at the NIC director.

Okay, next question answered. He knows I killed Gray and Simpson.

"The past is past."

"I don't think so."

"Then you're a fool, and more than that you're doing a disservice to the country you were sworn to protect."

"What the hell are you talking about?" barked an enraged Weaver. "I've fought, bled and killed for my country."

"So have I," retorted Stone.

"What exactly do you want?"

"I want you to stop screwing with me. If you want to help, I welcome it. If not, just stay the hell out of my way."

"I am the head of the nation's intelligence service."

"Yes, you are. So start acting like it, Marine."

Weaver flinched. But before he could respond Stone said, "And the next time we meet it might be over a beer talking about old times, because the traitor who's trying to pull something really catastrophic is either dead or awaiting trial. I can't believe you'd have a problem with that."

Weaver nodded slowly as he visibly calmed. "Okay, Stone. We'll play it your way. For now. I guess I understand how you survived all those years."

"I guess so."

"Stone?"

"Yeah?"

"What do you think is going on?"

Stone stood there in the darkness deciding how to respond. "You were wrong. The guns and the bomb were done by the same party."

"How the hell do you know that?"

"There's no way I believe in a coincidence that big."

"Okay, why?"

"Something big, Weaver. On your watch. You were right to be concerned."

"How big?" asked Weaver nervously.

"Big enough to make us forget the bullets and the bomb."

"We have to stop it, Stone."

"Yes, we do."

A minute later Weaver and his security detail were gone. Stone came down from his hiding place. He heard the sound and whirled around in time to see Chapman emerge from behind another building. She holstered her gun and joined him.

"What are you doing here?" he asked.

"I saw what went down on the street with the two agents and followed you here."

"Why?"

"You're my partner. I needed to make sure you were okay."

After a long gaze passed between them, Stone said, "I appreciate that."

"And I heard the essentials. *I* appreciate you covering for me with Weaver."

"It's what partners do."

"Come on, I'll give you a lift home."

This time Stone accepted the offer.

When they got there he said, "You take my cot, I'll sleep in the chair."

"What?"

"Cot and me in the chair."

"I heard you the first time. But I'm okay to drive."

"No you're not. You almost hit two pedestrians and three parked cars on the way here."

"I'll be fine," she said with a bit less confidence.

"The last thing I need is for my partner to be taken from me because she got busted for drunk driving."

"Well then let me take the chair."

He pointed to his cot and said, "Go." He gave her a shove in the back.

Looking bemused, Chapman slipped off her heels, padded to the cot and drew the privacy blanket closed.

CHAPTER

60

THE NEXT MORNING CHAPMAN SLOWLY WOKE, turned to the side, fell off the cot and hit the floor hard.

"Bloody hell!"

She rubbed her head.

She glanced up to see Stone standing in front of her holding two cups of coffee.

"Good morning," he said pleasantly.

She sat on the cot and took the offered coffee. She winced and rubbed her head as she drank some.

"My head feels quite ready to burst."

He said, "Four mojitos, two vodka tonics and a glass of port. And that's just what I saw. I'm stunned you still have a head left."

"I told you I could hold my liquor."

"Why don't you shower and then we can grab some breakfast."

"Wonderful. I'm famished. I know a nice restaurant."

"I know a better one."

"I'll be ready in ten minutes."

Forty minutes later they were in downtown D.C. and in line with a group of construction workers ordering breakfast at a food truck a few blocks from the Capitol. They carried their egg sandwiches and hash browns over to Chapman's car and sat on the hood hungrily eating their meal.

Her mouth full of scrambled eggs, Chapman moaned. "God, this is good."

"It's the lard, I think," said Stone, munching on a hash brown. "And the fact that they never wash their frying pan."

Finished, they climbed in Chapman's ride and drove off.

"Where to?"

"The park."

"Hell's Corner. It's living up to its name."

"I wonder how NIC is doing this morning."

"Based on what happened last night, probably not great." She skimmed her fingers across the steering wheel. "Look, I know what you did last night. You effectively blocked Weaver from taking action against me for telling you about my other mission. It was neatly done."

"I've been in this business long enough to know how it really operates. I needed him to back off, but he has lots of assets. So I also need his help and focus."

"How much do you intend on telling him? I mean about what you've figured out?"

"A lot. Again, he has resources we don't. And the primary objective is the same for us both. To prevent whatever is coming."

"You think it really is in the planning stages?"

"It's past the planning stage. Now it's in the execution stage."

"And the Russians? Pretty formidable foes."

"Yes."

"I've had a few run-ins with them. They can get pretty nasty."

Stone said nothing.

"You spent time in Russia. At least that's what your file says."

"I did."

"Cold War era?"

"Yes."

"How was it?"

"It was what it was."

"Was your mission successful?"

"I came back alive, so I'd say yes, it was."

She drove on.

Twenty minutes later Stone and she were

standing in the office building from where they'd deduced the guns had been fired. He opened one of the windows.

"What are we looking for?" she asked. "This building has the height to give it a direct sightline to the park. But we'd already established that."

"I know. But I think there's something else."

"Like what?"

"If I knew that I wouldn't be here looking out the window."

He continued to gaze down at the park and then onward, south to the White House. There was something in the depths of his mind that he knew was important, but he couldn't recall it. He had seen it, he was sure of that. In fact he had seen it in the park. But it wouldn't come. He'd racked his brain all morning, but that focus had only served to bury the potential answer even more deeply.

Chapman leaned against the window and stared at him.

"It's hurting my brain watching your brain burn itself out."

"Let's go. I need to check the message board at Georgetown University."

"You into social networking with college students?"

"No. My target is a little older."

CHAPTER

61

"Anything interesting?" Chapman asked as she watched Stone gazing over the message board. His eyes focused on one piece of paper set about two inches from where he'd put his message the night before. He read over it, quickly translating the coded response.

"Yes. Let's go."

The trip was short and they soon arrived at the apartment located over a dry cleaner's. Adelphia answered their knock and motioned them in. They sat down. Stone slowly looked around. "I didn't know you had moved back in here."

"I haven't," said Adelphia. She had on a long skirt, a white tunic and a string of green beads. Her black-and-silver hair was pulled together at the nape of her neck. "This is just temporary." She paused. "I was surprised to see your note."

"I'm glad to see that the little code we came up with is still effective."

"What can I do for you?" she prompted.

"How is Fuat Turkekul?"

"Is that why you came here? To get information about him?"

"Is that a problem?"

"I know you are having him followed. That could be very dangerous for Fuat."

"The shots in the park came from a government office building. How dangerous do you think that is?"

Adelphia sat back, her features inscrutable to a stranger like Chapman. But Stone could tell she was both intrigued and concerned.

"You have confirmed this?"

"To my satisfaction, yes."

"And why tell me? I am not part of the investigation. My mission has to do with Fuat, nothing more."

"What if one is connected to the other?"

"I do not think that likely."

Chapman, who had been sitting there silently, blurted out, "But can you just dismiss it like that? You have to account for the possibility. Otherwise you're not doing your bloody job."

Adelphia didn't bother to look at her. "I didn't

expect you to partner with such a nervous person, Oliver."

"*Do* you discount the possibility?" he asked. "To such a degree that you won't prepare for it?"

Adelphia hunched forward. "Fuat is prepared for anything."

"He eats, he teaches classes, he reads. I suppose somewhere in there he works on finding bin Laden, even if he is seven thousand miles away."

"As you were told, the plans are in the preliminary stage."

"Very preliminary. Ever since my colleague has been following him he's done very little prepping."

"It is not always obvious."

"It is somewhat obvious, Adelphia. To the trained eye."

"What exactly are you saying?"

"That what I was told about Fuat may not be true."

"In what way?"

"That he's not actually going after Osama bin Laden."

Adelphia sat back. Stone noted that the fingers of her left hand twitched a bit.

He continued, "It's logical, isn't it? To throw me off stride you tell me Fuat is going after the most sought-after terrorist since Hitler. You probably counted on the fact that the name alone would pre-clude the need for further explanation."

Chapman said, "You mean he's not going after bin Laden?"

Stone kept his gaze on Adelphia. "Well?"

She rose and strode over to the window and looked out.

"There's no one out there," he said. "At least no one connected to me. But maybe that's not what you're concerned about."

She turned back to him. "This is not something you want to become involved in, Oliver. It really isn't. I say this to you as an old friend."

"I'm already involved." He rose. "And I have one more question for you."

"I promise no answer."

"Turkekul wasn't at the park to meet with you that night. So who was he really there to see?"

CHAPTER

62

THEY LEFT ADELPHIA'S APARTMENT without the question being answered.

Chapman said, "How did you figure they weren't going after bin Laden? And that Fuat Turkekul was meeting with someone else that night?"

"I suspected each was true. Adelphia confirmed both for me just now."

"But she didn't say anything."

"That's what confirmed it."

"But why were you suspicious in the first place?" persisted Chapman.

"You don't task a man to chase Osama bin Laden and then plunk him in a teaching position in a university in the West, unless you believe bin Laden is hiding out on the East Coast somewhere. It makes no sense. That's why I had Harry tail him. Not really for protection, but to see what he was doing. Or rather *not* doing."

"And the fact that Adelphia wasn't at the park to meet with him?"

"You don't arrange a meeting like that and then just not show up. They had a message board arrangement. The meeting was late at night. It's a ten-minute cab ride from Georgetown to the park. Turkekul could have checked the board right before he left. If she couldn't make the meeting, Adelphia could have posted that message up until a few minutes before he would leave for the rendezvous. She answered my post promptly, which tells me she checks it often. There was no need for him to stand around in the park waiting for her. That is inefficient and stupid. And potentially lethal."

"But if not her, who? And *did* he meet with anyone?"

"Not that I saw, no."

"What does that tell you?"

"That the meeting might have been off-schedule." He added, "Not something his superiors knew about."

"If that's the case, why cover for him?"

"If Turkekul is a valuable asset he would be protected after the fact. And even if the meeting was off-schedule that doesn't mean it was off-mission and thus could have been important to his superiors."

"Could he have been set up, then?"

"They didn't kill him. They could easily have done it by firing a few minutes earlier. No, he wasn't the target."

Chapman touched her temples. "My poor head is literally swimming with possibilities and none of them unfortunately make any sense."

They returned to the park. Stone walked it from north to south and east to west while Chapman dutifully followed looking alternatively curious and bored.

She finally said, "Are you thinking if you walk the scene of the crime, inspiration will strike?"

"I'm not looking for inspiration, just answers." He gazed back at the building where the shots had presumably come from. "Shots fired. Everyone runs. Padilla jumps into the tree hole. The bomb detonates."

"The bomb was detonated prematurely. And we need to find out who the actual target was. It keeps coming back to that. That bomb was really supposed to go off when this park was filled with VIPs. If we can determine the target we can reverse engineer it back to the people behind the plot. At least hopefully we can."

Stone shook his head. "We're still missing something. The picture is still off. Way off." He paused. "Okay, let's change direction for a minute and do a simple process of elimination."

"How?" she asked.

"If Turkekul wasn't meeting with Adelphia, who was he going to meet with?" Stone looked around the park. "Not your security man. Not Alfredo Padilla obviously. Not me."

Chapman gasped. "Wait a minute. You mean the woman?"

Stone nodded. "Marisa Friedman."

CHAPTER

63

"Why Friedman?" asked Chapman as they walked along H Street.

"She was at the park. As I said, simple process of elimination."

"But she explained what she was doing here. She voluntarily came forward, in fact."

"I would too, if I were guilty of something. Her face was caught on the video feed. If she didn't come forward it would look very suspicious. This way she defused that suspicion and appeared to be an upright, law-abiding citizen."

"An adulterous upright citizen. But she has an office right over there." Chapman pointed to the line of town houses on Jackson Place. "It would make perfect sense for her to be in the park."

"Please put your hand down just in case she's

watching. They've allowed the business owners back in now."

Chapman dropped her hand and looked chagrined at her indiscreet action. "Sorry."

"She said she's a lobbyist, and maybe she is. But maybe she's more than that."

"So she could have been Turkekul's unscheduled meeting?"

Stone said, "If he had such a meeting planned, she was the only one in the park he would be meeting with."

"But if so, he might have told Sir James and the others about it."

"Then perhaps they're covering for her too."

"Because she's part of his mission, whatever that is?"

Stone nodded.

"So her being in the park was because of Turkekul being there?"

"If my theory is right, yes," replied Stone.

"But did they meet?"

"They left at the same time. I saw no interaction between them while they were in the park. She was on her phone but he wasn't."

"And maybe they were going to meet but—"

"But then the guns and the bomb went off."

"What do you think they were meeting about?"

"I have no idea. But I doubt it was about finding bin Laden."

"So what do we do with this fresh angle?"

"If we try to go after her and she is being covered by higher-ups we might get our butts handed to us."

"So we can't touch her?"

"Officially, no. But there might be another way."

"How?"

Stone took out his phone and made a call. "Annabelle? I have another assignment for you. If you're willing."

The next day Annabelle and Caleb walked into the office of Marisa Friedman. They had made an appointment and Friedman was waiting for them. Annabelle had changed her appearance greatly. The hair was short and blonde, her face made up, her clothes European, her accent an authentic mix of German and Dutch. Caleb was dressed all in black and had his thinning hair slicked back. He had on square-cut spectacles and a bit of stubble on his face. He carried an unlit cigarette and explained it by telling Friedman it was the only thing that worked for him in trying to quit.

She lifted up her sleeve and showed him the Nicorette patch on her arm. "I'm kind of in the same boat."

Friedman led them back to her large office on the top floor with windows overlooking Lafayette Park. The space was decorated in a manner that suggested Friedman had traveled widely, had good taste, and the money to exercise those heightened sensibilities.

"We're just now back in our space," she said.

"Why is that?" asked Annabelle.

"There was a bombing in the park. And gunshots."

"My God!" exclaimed Caleb.

"You didn't hear?" said Friedman with a surprised look.

"As you might have deduced from my accent, I am not from this country," said Annabelle.

"And I'm an expatriate myself," added Caleb jauntily.

"But the Americans like their bombs and guns," said Annabelle. "At least that is what we are told." She shrugged. "So it is normal, then?"

"No, it's not normal, thank God." Friedman leaned forward. "I have to say that your phone call has intrigued me. You want to bring green jobs from Europe here? Can I ask why since green has already taken off where you are?"

Annabelle made a face. "It's the bureaucracy. The, what you call, red tape. It is killing us. Our business cuts across many different geographic boundaries. The EU makes all businesses jump through hoops that are often impossible and usually totally ridiculous. Our business model is good. Our technology sound. But if we cannot implement it?" She shrugged again.

Caleb added, "Now, I have some experience over here though I've been gone a long time. My friends tell me that America is the place to be. That you want green jobs. That the red tape is not so bad. That things can be done quickly and that there are also government incentives to do so."

"That's true. What country did you settle in?" she asked suddenly.

"France."

She asked a long question in French. Caleb answered her promptly, throwing in a joke at the end that made her laugh.

Annabelle said something in German and Caleb answered her in German.

"I'm afraid my German is very poor," said Friedman.

"Excuse us," said Annabelle. "That was very rude."

"You Europeans speak so many languages. Makes us Americans feel quite inept."

"Your country is big, ours are small," said Annabelle. "Language skills are a necessity. But your French is very, um, nice."

"How can I help you?"

"We are in need of a presence, a footprint I think you call it, here in Washington. We want to build a factory producing our goods in the United States. We also have IP patent and licensing issues that need political addressing." Annabelle paused. "Is that the proper term? Political addressing?"

"Lobbying, I think," commented Caleb. "And friends in high places."

"I can certainly handle these matters for you," said Friedman. "I have relations with many government people, and energy is one of my specialties. Can I ask how it was you came to me?"

Caleb looked embarrassed. "I'm very much afraid it had nothing to do with your reputation, stellar though I'm sure it is."

Annabelle added, "We based it on proximity." She pointed out the window.

Friedman followed her motion. "The White House?" She smiled. "Interesting due diligence. But I guess that's one reason I settled on this space."

"But then we also checked the records for your client list. It was very impressive and very much in our area of necessity," remarked Annabelle.

Caleb leaned forward and tapped his cigarette on the carved wood of Friedman's desk. "But it would be helpful if you could tell us a bit of your background. We want to get this right. Our business model shows a clear path to a multibillion euro, or dollar, rather, revenue point. We must start on a firm foundation. It is imperative."

"Of course." Friedman gave them an account of her background, education and work experience and items with which she could help them.

As the meeting ended she said, "For the sort of work you require I would imagine a ten-thousand-dollar-a-month fee. Understand this is applied to work done under our normal fee structure. For work outside that scope, more monies will be due. It's all explained in our standard fee agreement.

"Of course," said Annabelle. "That seems logical."

"Where in Germany are you from?"

"Berlin. But I grew up elsewhere."

"Oh, really? Where was that?"

"Many places," said Annabelle abruptly.

Caleb added, "Quite cosmopolitan. And secretive she is."

"Nothing wrong with that in today's world where everyone is watching everyone else," Friedman said in a light tone.

"We'll be in touch," said Annabelle. *"Auf Wiedersehen."*

"Ciao," added Caleb.

CHAPTER

64

JUST IN CASE THEY WERE FOLLOWED, Annabelle and Caleb drove first to a restaurant and then to a hotel. They rode the elevator up and Annabelle opened the door to her room. Stone and Chapman were sitting there waiting for them.

They gave the pair a detailed briefing of their meeting with Friedman.

"Do you think she suspects anything?" asked Chapman.

"If she's really that good she suspects everything," answered Annabelle as Stone nodded in agreement.

"She obviously has a functioning lobbying business," said Annabelle.

"We knew from her client list and checking out her history that she had that set up," said Stone. "But that does not preclude her having a sideline."

Chapman added, "Or from the lobbying being her cover and spying being her main occupation.

Annabelle ran a hand through her hair and pulled off her wig. "Any idea what her angle might be?"

"As I told you, we suspect she might be involved with some plan being headed up by American intelligence."

"And that's why she was at the park that night?" asked Caleb.

Stone nodded. "Exactly. The man I've had Harry following was potentially her contact. It's just my theory. None of it is confirmed yet."

"And the man Harry is following? What's going on with him?"

"It's up to us to find out."

"Through Friedman?"

"Yes. But without her knowledge. I certainly don't trust her."

"But how does this tie into the bombing?" asked Caleb.

"I don't know if it does," admitted Stone. "It could be that it was a coincidence they were both there that night. How did you leave it with her?"

"That we'd be in touch," said Annabelle.

"So what has this really accomplished?" asked Chapman. "I mean, I know you blokes are good at this, but this leaves us nowhere to go with her."

"Actually, it does," said Annabelle. She opened her bag, slipped open a hardshell plastic case and they saw the impression of a key set in a mold. "Got her office key out of her purse when Caleb asked her to show him the painting in the foyer while I excused myself to use the ladies' room. I can have an actual key made in no time."

Caleb said, "She has a security system."

Annabelle added, "But the keypad is by the front door. We watched the office last night. Friedman was the last to leave at seven and she keyed in the number. I got it on my camera from where I was in the park pretending to take pictures of the statues."

Chapman looked at Stone. "So we're breaking into her place?"

"Not you. I am."

"Why not me?"

"You're too official."

"You've got a badge too."

"I've always seen that status as temporary. You, on the other hand, are a lifer."

"When are you going to do it?" asked Chapman.

"Why?"

"So I can tell the cops to be waiting for you."

Annabelle scowled at her. "Whose side are you on, lady?"

"But if you let me go, I won't call anyone," offered Chapman.

Stone said, "I don't like it."

"You keep preaching about partners and loyalty."

"Okay," Stone finally said. "You and me."

Annabelle started to protest. "But—"

Stone put a hand on her shoulder. "Please, Annabelle, just let it go."

Caleb said, "But we did all the hard work and you two get to have the fun of burglarizing the place."

This made Annabelle smile. "You've come a long way, Mr. Librarian. And by the way, I really dug your metrosexual look when we paid Friedman a visit."

Caleb brightened. "Thank you. I've always thought that—" He started and looked at her. "Metro what?"

"Good luck," Annabelle told Stone. She turned to Chapman. "Watch his back, and I mean it."

"I will," promised Chapman.

Stone and Chapman walked briskly down the street. Stone was in a suit and carried a briefcase. Chapman was in a skirt and heels with a shawl wrapped around her shoulders. She carried a large bag. They walked through the park and over to Jackson Place and Stone inserted the key in the door of Marisa Friedman's office. They went inside and Chapman punched in the code on the security keypad and the beeping stopped. Stone closed the door behind them and moved forward into the office space.

There was enough ambient light from outside to allow them to see their way around, though Chapman did bump her leg against a desk.

"According to Annabelle, Friedman's office is up the stairs and at the rear," she said as she rubbed her thigh.

An hour later they stood facing each other, the failure evident on their features.

Stone perched on the edge of Friedman's desk and looked around. They had gone through all the paper files, but Stone figured many things would be kept on the computers. But the system was password-protected, and while they had tried a few, nothing worked.

"Any brilliant ideas?" asked Chapman.

"No. We should've had Harry come with us. He probably could've gotten into the computer."

"We should probably get out of here."

They moved back down the stairs. Stone saw it

first, out the window. He rushed to the keypad and armed the system and then pulled Chapman into an interior office on the first floor of the suite.

A few moments later the door opened and the security system's beep went off. Marisa Friedman hit the appropriate keys and the beeping stopped. She shut the door behind her and climbed the stairs.

Stone edged open the door and peered out, Chapman at his shoulder.

"Do we leave now while she's occupied?" said Chapman.

"No, we wait."

Twenty minutes passed, then he and Chapman heard steps coming back down and Stone eased the door shut. They listened to the security system being set and a few seconds later the door closed.

Stone counted to five and then looked out.

"It's clear. Let's go."

They managed to open and close the door during the delay of the security system arming.

"There!" said Chapman, pointing to the north where Friedman was just about to turn the corner at the Decatur House.

"Oliver? Agent Chapman?"

They turned to see Alex Ford standing there watching them. "What are you two doing here?"

"What are *you* doing here?" blurted out Chapman.

"I'm on perimeter security duty, if it's any of your business," retorted Alex. He looked at Stone. "Oliver?"

"I'm sorry, Alex, no time. I'll explain later."

Stone grabbed Chapman's arm and they hurried off, leaving Alex to gape after them.

"She's getting in a cab," said Chapman a minute or so later.

"Not a problem." Stone hailed another cab that passed by a few moments later. They climbed in and Stone showed his badge and instructed the driver to follow the other vehicle.

The cab turned down one street and then another, steadily making its way west.

"This is looking familiar," said Stone.

"What?" asked Chapman.

"George Washington University. She could have walked. It's a nice evening."

"Do you know where she's going?" asked Chapman.

"I believe so, yes."

"So spill it," Chapman said in exasperation.

The cab pulled to the curb. They watched as Friedman got out.

"She's going to see Fuat Turkekul," said Stone.

"How do you know that?" demanded Chapman.

"Because that's the same building where I met with him."

"Well, let's go see what they're up to."

At that instant an SUV screeched in front of their cab and two more behind. Before they could react, they were surrounded by armed men. Stone and Chapman were pulled from the vehicle and pushed into one of the SUVs, and it started moving before they could even catch their breath. As Stone looked back he saw Marisa Friedman staring after them. She'd obviously played her part to perfection in setting him up. And yet her features didn't speak of triumph. She actually looked a little sad, Stone thought.

Twenty minutes later they were hurried into a building that looked abandoned. Up dimly lit steps to a door. Through the doorway and then another. They were pushed into seats and the men with guns left, shutting the door behind them. The lights came on and someone moved at the front of the room.

Adelphia sat there, her hands in her lap.

Riley Weaver looked extremely upset.

Sir James McElroy simply seemed intrigued.

65

Weaver said, "What the hell are we going to do with you guys? You keep popping up like a really shitty penny."

McElroy put his elbows on the table and made a steeple with his hands. "How did you get onto Marisa Friedman?"

Stone said, "She was really the only one left."

"And you deduced where she was going?"

"To see Turkekul."

McElroy glanced at Weaver and then at Adelphia.

Stone said to McElroy, "So this is why you wouldn't answer my earlier question, after I found out about your connection with him?"

"You mean whether I was withholding anything else from you? In my defense, I came to this a bit late in the game, and the more we delved into it, the more tangled it became. I have to say that this is the most intense chess match of my career, Oliver. It really is. I hope I'm up to the challenge."

Stone turned to Weaver. "And are you up to the challenge?"

Weaver flushed. "We're doing the best we can under very difficult circumstances. One little misstep and we blow everything out of the water. That's what you almost did tonight."

"How did you get onto us?" asked Chapman.

"Easy. We followed Friedman and saw you following her."

"Why follow your own agent?" asked Stone.

"Because she's extremely valuable and we take care of our people."

"I saw her looking at us when you snatched us. She didn't seem surprised."

"When we spotted you, we phoned her, filled her in."

"So she didn't know until then?" asked Stone.

"What's it to you?" barked Weaver.

"So what is the real deal with Fuat Turkekul?" asked Chapman. "He's not going after bin Laden, is he?"

"How long have you suspected him of being a traitor?" said Stone.

Weaver looked surprised, Chapman shocked,

but McElroy nodded thoughtfully. "I thought you might work it out."

"It took me long enough," noted Stone. "Too long, in fact."

"He came to us with much promise," said McElroy. "So much promise, in fact, that Adelphia here, one of our best, was assigned to work with him before we transitioned him principally to Friedman's handling."

Adelphia nodded. "That was one of the reasons I had to go away, Oliver," she said. "To work with Fuat."

"On what exactly?" asked Chapman.

Weaver laughed ruefully. "He came and sold us a real bill of goods. First, he could take us to bin Laden. Then, we had a mole in our midst. And he would help us track it down."

"But it turned out he was the mole?" said Stone.

"A Trojan horse, more like it," noted McElroy. "He came to us in disguise, as it were. And now he has unleashed a virus amongst us."

"A virus? How?" asked Chapman.

"We let him in the door," lamented Weaver. "And he brought other elements with him. Unknown elements."

McElroy added, "Our only recourse now is to let him think we trust him, are working with him and then follow it up to his other connections. Not the preferred way to go about it, but we have few options."

"That's why he wasn't doing much?" said Stone.

Weaver nodded. "That's right. Fuat takes everything very slowly. Wanted to move to D.C. Lot of prep time, build his network, and the next thing we know things are going to hell."

"The incident in the park?" asked Chapman. "That's him?"

"Undoubtedly," said Weaver. "We think it was just a prelude to something much bigger."

"And Friedman? What's her role?" asked Stone.

"She's one of our deep cover agents. A lobbyist and lawyer by day with a plethora of international clients, many of them fronts by our government and our allies. That allows her to travel widely. She sees and reports back. Her Middle Eastern language skills are spot-on. She spent many years there for the CIA and later in joint assignments with NIC. She has solid contacts in the region. She was a logical choice for the assignment with Fuat, to supplement what Adelphia was doing."

"How do you explain that connection? Lobbyist and academic?"

"Easily enough. Friedman represents several organizations in the Middle East that have relationships with Turkekul. Officially they are working on a number of initiatives to strengthen trade relations between Pakistan and the U.S."

"And the phone call she made while in the park?"

"To another agent who provided her cover when the FBI made inquiries," answered Weaver.

"When did you begin to suspect Turkekul?" asked Chapman.

McElroy fidgeted with his tie. "Far too late, of course. He was quite good. Friedman suspected something first, and we followed up on those suspicions and confirmed them. And she did so at great personal risk to herself I might add."

"But you're saying he doesn't know you suspect him?" said Stone.

"He is too wily an operative not to suspect. But we have given him no reason to really suspect, if you understand me. We have given him rope. We have covered for him on several occasions, as you are well aware."

"What do you think his plan is?"

"Nanobot residue in a bomb?" said Weaver. "Scares the hell out of me, and it should you too. I know you talked with the president about something at Camp David. It was about that, wasn't it?"

"Among other things. The president explained

to me about the biological and chemical potential. But he didn't really get into details. Can it also make the bomb more powerful, for example?"

McElroy said, "No, it's still a traditional explosive. We believe it is simply a way to deliver biological and chemical weapons on a far more prodigious scale than ever possible before."

"How can these nanobot things do that?" asked Chapman. "And keep in mind I basically failed science at university."

McElroy nodded at Weaver. "I will leave the essentials to my colleague here."

Weaver cleared his throat. "Nanobots are the next generation of nanorobotics. They occur at the molecular level and have a lot of potential uses, beneficial ones, including the delivery of drugs into the body. It's thought that one day soon nanobots can be released into cancer patients and be programmed to attack and destroy cancer cells, leaving healthy cells unharmed. The possibilities are endless, really."

"And the biological weapon delivery systems?" asked Stone. "A terrorist can put anthrax in a bomb right now. So why does this nanotechnology angle make it more dangerous?"

"At the molecular level anything is possible,

Stone," said Weaver with a trace of irritation. "You can basically build something one atom at a time, outside the normal configurations."

"Meaning the normal configurations that we have systems set up to *detect*," said Stone.

"Point well taken, Oliver," said McElroy. "That really is the entire heart of the matter. Detection. If they can change it so we can't ferret it out, that gives the other side an enormous advantage over us. In fact, an insurmountable one."

"The other side? Meaning the Russians?" said Stone.

"How about the Chinese?" said Chapman. "They have more money than anyone. And their science is not too shabby."

"The Kashtan submachine gun. And talking a weird language," Stone reminded her. "Points at Moscow, not Beijing."

"And we have very good reason to believe that the Chinese are not involved in this," said McElroy. "Principally because they don't have to resort to such tactics to be a superpower. Economically they already are. These days it's not necessarily how large your military is, but how big your bank account is, and the Chinese wallet is fatter than anyone's. The Russians, on the other hand, are not in the same position."

"And the incident in the park was a way of testing the delivery system?" asked Chapman.

"We believe so, yes," said Weaver. "The nanobots were scattered everywhere. There were no bio- or chemical weapons grafted or grown onto them. We've confirmed that. At least the ones we know about. But if there had been? Catastrophic."

Chapman said slowly, "So the nanobots are a way to actually grow or build bio- or chemical weapons, at a microscopic level and in an undetectable configuration? Load them onto a bomb and set them off?"

"That's right," said McElroy. "And if done properly, conventional security forces would be powerless to stop them. So we're hoping that Fuat makes a mistake and leads us to whomever he's working with. And soon. It is not enough to arrest him. We need the others. And he's the only source we have to get there."

"We're trying to get Friedman to put some pressure on him. Hence her meeting with him tonight. A meeting you guys almost blew to hell," Weaver pointed out.

Ignoring this, Stone said, "How did Turkekul get hooked up with the Russians?"

"In your meeting with him he told you that he lived for a time in Afghanistan?" said McElroy.

"That's right."

"The timing of him being there was interesting."

"Let me guess. Late seventies, early eighties. When the Russians were trying to destroy the Afghan freedom fighters?"

"That's right. Fuat I'm sure on the surface pretended to be on the side of the Afghan freedom fighters."

"But he was in the Russians' back pocket," said Stone.

"Of course we think that now," said Weaver. "When he first approached us we thought he was shooting straight. If we knew his loyalties were with Moscow he'd be in jail right now. But we didn't know."

"So our discovery of the Russian gun in Pennsylvania didn't come as a surprise?" said Stone.

"No, it was simply more confirmation of what we already knew," replied Weaver.

"But why have a practice run in the park of all places?" said Chapman. "It allowed us to analyze the debris and discover these nano-things."

"I believe it shows they have great confidence in their technology," answered Weaver. "Arrogant bastards. The Cold War never really ended."

"That may be their undoing, of course. At least

we can hope that is the case," noted McElroy. "At least it provided us with an opportunity to turn the tables."

"So you think Turkekul was there to detonate the bomb remotely?" asked Stone. "After he left the park?"

"He was scheduled to meet with Friedman, that's why they left together," said McElroy.

"Which would have been nice to know before," said Stone.

"Need to know, Stone," growled Weaver.

"Right," Stone snapped back. "I'm getting really tired of hearing that justification for keeping us in the dark."

McElroy said, "To answer your question, Oliver, yes, we do think he remotely detonated it. The excuse of meeting with Friedman there was the perfect cover. She was very surprised when he didn't initiate contact while she was sitting on the bench."

Weaver focused on Stone and Chapman. "And what we don't need are you two screwing all of this up."

"If you had told us about it, we wouldn't have come anywhere near it," Stone said reasonably.

"You didn't require reading in, until now. And

I'm not thrilled about it. So from now on keep clear. Got it?"

McElroy rose, supporting himself with the table-top. "I think they do indeed *get it,* Director."

"One more question," said Stone. The two men looked at him expectantly. "The president knows about the nanobot angle. But does he know that you suspect Turkekul is a traitor?"

McElroy and Weaver exchanged a quick glance.

"Are you keeping it from the president because you let a spy this deeply in the game before realizing it?" Stone was gazing directly at Weaver. "Because if so, that could really come back to bite you in the ass."

The NIC director flushed. "If I were you, I'd just keep that absurd opinion to yourself. I've never understood why you were brought into this in the first place. You've been out of the field for over thirty years, and quite frankly, it shows. To repeat, you are ordered to keep the hell away from Fuat Turkekul. Understood?"

McElroy responded. "As I noted before, Director, I'm sure that Agent Stone understands the situation perfectly."

McElroy looked directly at Stone and gave him a quick wink.

They were dropped off at Chapman's car. As she drove Stone home she said, "Well, at least things are explained now. The Russians are on the prowl once more. Oh goody."

"Why the gunfire?" Stone said abruptly.

"What?"

Stone closed his eyes.

"Tents," he said.

"Tents? What the bloody hell are you talking about? Are you planning on going camping?"

"White tents. All on one side."

This same observation had earlier led him to the government building being the origin of the shots and not the Hay-Adams Hotel. But could there be another reason?

"Stone?" said Chapman. "What are you talking about?"

He didn't answer.

CHAPTER

66

THE NEXT MORNING, after receiving a phone call, Stone and Chapman met with Agent Ashburn at the FBI's mobile command unit. The woman looked excited as she ushered them in.

"We think we know how the tree was poisoned," she announced as she pointed them to the coffee pot and cups set up on one table near the door.

They sat with their coffees and watched as the screen came on.

"What are we looking at?" asked Stone.

Ashburn paused the video. "This is from the DHS video taken of Lafayette Park. The time stamp shows it's from three weeks before the bombing."

"What made you look at the DHS tape?" Chapman asked.

"We look at everything at the FBI," she replied smugly. But then she added in a more humble tone,

"And we were basically getting zip everywhere else. So we looked at this and it has an angle that is really interesting." She hit the play button and the screen once more came to life.

As Stone watched, it was as though he were only feet away from the park; the images were so clear, so close, every pixel vivid and stark. He leaned in as the woman hobbled into view. She was dressed in layers of filthy, ragged clothes, her face and hands blackened with the grime from living on the streets. Her hair was a mess of curls and jagged lumps that hung down past her neck.

"A vagrant," observed Chapman.

"Homeless, yes," said Ashburn. "At least in appearance. But watch what she does."

The woman slowly made her way across the park, even as Stone saw the uniformed Secret Service officers converging on her. The park was a public space, and technically open to everyone. But it was also across from the White House and visited by many tourists, and steps were employed to keep it safe and presentable. Stone had seen the Secret Service remove other homeless people from the park who were either too disturbing in appearance or too aggressive in their manner. The agents were unfailingly respectful and discreet. He'd even seen some of them buy the less fortunate folks food and coffee after escorting them away.

This woman on the screen, though, didn't seem to want the attention. She picked up her pace, stumbling along, her left foot dragging behind. It was only now that Stone could see a plastic bottle clutched in her hand. She reached the maple and fell down on the ground moaning and twitching.

Ashburn froze the screen. "See that?" She used a laser pointer to indicate the bottle of water. It was tipped upside down and its cap was off. In the halted video a stream of liquid was captured pouring out of the bottle and onto the base of the tree. Ashburn played the rest of the video and Stone and Chapman watched as the entire contents of the bottle emptied out and were quickly absorbed into the mulch top around the tree.

The next moment the uniformed officers were helping the woman up and escorting her away.

Stone said, "Did the cops notice a strange odor coming from the bottle?"

Ashburn shook her head. "Asked and answered. We rounded up those uniforms yesterday. They remember the woman, but let's just say her personal aroma was strong enough to cover anything that was in that bottle. And they just figured she accidentally poured her water out on the ground. It was no big deal. And when the tree died some time later, nobody connected the dots. But we did soil samples from around the original tree and actually found pieces of its bark the Park Service had kept. Tests run on them confirm a poison was applied that effectively prevented the tree from absorbing water and nutrients. Death was inevitable."

Stone looked over at her. "Good work, Agent Ashburn. I think you hit on exactly how the tree was sabotaged."

"Still a long way from figuring out the rest of it, though," she said resignedly.

They left her and walked to the park. Chapman pointed up ahead. "They're prepping to plant another tree," she said. The National Park Service personnel were out in force working around the crater.

"Let's just hope they use a different supplier this time," said Stone. "And check it for bombs."

The grounds team was roughly the same one they had interviewed. George Sykes was directing his uniformed troops as they cleared debris and reshaped the crater, filling it with fresh soil.

"Guess the ATF is finished doing their investigation here," noted Chapman.

"Guess so."

"So what was your eureka moment last night?" she asked. "You just said something about white tents and left it at that."

"I would have come down here today even if Ashburn hadn't called." He pointed to the north toward the office building where the shots had come from. "Gauge the sightline."

"I already did that, thank you."

"You remember what the colored markers in the park represented?"

"Orange for debris and white for slugs."

"Do you recall the distribution of each?"

Chapman gazed around the grass. "Orange was everywhere, which is to be expected with a bomb. An explosive is indiscriminate in its distribution of wreckage."

"And the white markers?"

Chapman hesitated. "As I remember it, they were uniformly on the western side of the park."

"Uniformly—that's the key term."

Chapman looked back at the office building and then at the park. "But you told me the bullet distribution was the reason you had me look at that building in the first place."

"Chicken and egg. I was looking at the wrong end of the equation."

"What?"

"I thought they used that building, at least partially, because it was taller than the hotel's garden terrace and they could see over the trees. That way they wouldn't be firing blindly. I was thinking like a sniper. That was an incorrect approach."

Chapman looked confused, but only for a moment. "You mean since there was no actual target in the park, the PM for example, why would they care about firing blindly?"

"Right. They could fire machine-gun rounds right through that tree canopy. Who cares? But the office building allowed them to see over the trees. And in the dark that was a necessity because things look different in the dark and spatial skills deteriorate. They might have been using night optics, but there's a lot of ambient light around here at night. And night optics can be seen by other people using night optics, and there's a lot of that around here with the security forces in place."

"Okay," said Chapman slowly. "That means?"

"The shooters contained their fields of fire to the west side."

"You were on the west side of the park. Along with our man."

"And bullets did hit uncomfortably close to us. I believe that occurred more by accident than intent.

If they'd hit us I don't think they would have cared."

"So why did they confine it to the west side?" wondered Chapman.

Stone was about to answer when Chapman stopped him. "Don't look now, but one of the groundspeople is staring at us with a very strange expression."

"Which one?"

"The young woman. Hang on, I'm going to try something."

"What?"

"Just hang on."

Stone pretended to examine a spot in the grass with investigative interest. Two minutes later Chapman returned to him. "Okay, we wait five minutes and then we walk north and go into the church over there."

"Why?"

"To meet with the lady."

"How did you manage that?"

"Let's just say it was a bit of girl-to-girl signaling that is impervious to male capture and translation."

CHAPTER

67

Five minutes later they were in St. John's Church admiring the embroidered kneelers in the "presidential pew" of the house of worship.

"James Madison. John Quincy Adams," read Chapman as she glanced down at the kneelers. "Impressive list of blokes."

Stone replied, "Your country certainly didn't think that back then. Revolutionaries and even terrorists, they were called."

"Well, after a couple hundred years even the thorniest differences can be overcome."

The woman, dressed in her green-and-khaki uniform, entered the church and slipped off her hat. She spotted them and hurried over.

Chapman said, "I saw you trying to catch our eye. Thank you for meeting with us."

"I really don't know if it's anything. And even

though it's our break time I can't be gone too long."

Chapman asked, "What's your name?"

"Judy Donohue."

"Okay, Ms. Donohue, what's troubling you?" asked Stone.

"Something that was said when you came to interview Mr. Sykes."

"How do you know we did?" asked Chapman. "He was alone."

Donohue looked embarrassed and uneasy.

Sensing this, Stone said, "How long have you been with the Park Service?"

"Ten years. Really love it."

"Are you from the area?" Stone asked.

She smiled wryly. "Nope. About as far from it as you can get from a place like this."

"Where's that?" asked Chapman.

"Grew up in the middle of nowhere Montana. God's country. I've been an outdoor girl all my life." She held up her hand. On the back of it was a tattoo of a bird. "That's the *Sturnella neglecta,* otherwise known as the western meadowlark. It's Montana's state bird. Got that when I was sixteen. My friends were getting hearts and guys' names. I opted for wildlife."

"And about what Mr. Sykes said? I guess you were nearby?"

Donohue dropped her wry look. "I didn't mean to eavesdrop," she said quickly. "I was just nearby working on a project and..."

"And you just heard things," Chapman said pleasantly. "Perfectly understandable."

"So what did you hear that raised questions in your mind?" asked Stone.

"He said we were waiting on an arborist to check the tree. And that we were putting together special soil and nutrients and such."

"That's correct," said Stone. "You mean you weren't?"

"No, we do."

"All right," said Stone slowly. "Then what's the problem?"

"I know I'm not explaining this very well. Why I work with my hands and not at a desk, I guess."

"Just take your time, Judy," Chapman said helpfully.

"Well, you see, the arborist had already checked the tree and given it a clean bill of health. He took another look at it again when it went in the hole, but only to make sure the stress of being craned in hadn't injured it. The soil and nutrient plan was all ready to go."

"So you're saying that there was no need to leave the hole unfilled?" said Stone.

"Not really, no. I remember putting up the poles and tape and thinking it was pretty silly to leave the hole that way. I mean, what if someone fell in it?"

"And someone did," said Chapman.

"Well, anyway, I still thought it was weird."

"What explanation did Sykes give you for leaving the hole open?" asked Stone.

"He didn't give us an explanation. He's the crew chief. We do as we're told."

"When Agent Gross came by were you all present when he asked his questions?"

"For part of the time, but then he went off with Mr. Sykes."

"And I take it the question about the uncovered hole didn't come up while you were all there?"

"I recall the FBI agent getting to that issue, but then Mr. Sykes said it was time to get back to work and he'd finish the rest of the answers."

"Did any of the other crew members have the same questions about the hole being uncovered?" asked Chapman.

"They're a good bunch, real dedicated. But they also follow orders and don't think too much about it. I guess I'm a little more independent. And after overhearing what Mr. Sykes told you, I just thought you ought to know."

"You did the right thing, Judy," said Chapman.

"I have to get back."

"Right," said Stone. "This was very helpful. But don't mention it to anyone."

Donohue nodded, a nervous expression on her face. "Do you think Mr. Sykes did something wrong?"

"We're sure going to find out," said Stone.

CHAPTER

68

THEY LEFT THE CHURCH and walked back to the park.

"So now George Sykes is a suspect," said Chapman. "Is there anyone who's *not* involved in this thing?"

"A conspiracy does require more than one person," observed Stone.

"Oliver?"

They turned to see Alex Ford striding toward them.

"Let me do the talking," said Stone quickly to Chapman. "Hello, Alex," he said, turning to his friend.

"So are you going to tell me anything remotely close to the truth about what's going on?" Alex asked, his voice strident.

"I know I'm being secretive and cryptic, but the

fact is I'm not sure it's a good idea you knowing about any of this."

"So that's how it stands? A member of the Camel Club in name only?"

"No, that's not what I meant. But I have a commission and a shield now and—"

"That didn't stop you from involving Annabelle, Harry and Reuben, did it? They don't have a badge or a commission but I do."

"I know none of this is simple."

"Oh, it's completely simple. You've cut me completely out of the loop. I thought we were friends. And I thought our friendship would rise above everything else."

Stone started to say something but then stopped. He glanced at Chapman and then back at Alex.

"You're right."

This frank admission seemed to drain the anger from the Secret Service agent. "Okay."

"We've made some progress," said Stone. "But not enough, and my sense is that we're running out of time. And if I've been less than candid with you, it's partly due to your being in a very delicate position."

"Partly?"

"Yes, the rest is due entirely to my clumsy handling of our friendship. I'm sorry."

"Can you tell me this? Should I be worried? I mean for the president?"

"I know of no specific threats against him, if that's what you mean. And if I did, you and the president would know too. That I swear."

"I heard you met with him at Camp David."

"I did. I needed to speak with him frankly."

"And did he respond in kind?"

"He did. To a surprising degree, in fact."

"I understand Reuben is still in the hospital."

"Yes, that was close, Alex, too close."

"We pushed you to let us help, Oliver. We're all big boys and girls."

"There is still responsibility at my level. I won't be making that mistake again."

"You can't protect your friends from everything."

"I can at least stop putting them in dangerous situations."

"You said you're making progress. Are you close to finding out what's going on?"

"We are, actually."

"And is it bad?"

Stone glanced at Chapman before answering. "I think it's very bad, yes."

"Be careful, then. And if there's anything I can do to help, I'm here." Alex turned and walked off.

"He's a fine bloke," said Chapman as she joined Stone.

"Yes, he is. Every time I talk with Alex I'm reminded both how lucky I am to have friends like him and also how unworthy I am to have friends like him."

"Well, they probably feel the same way about you."

"You think so? I don't."

"So what do we do about Mr. Sykes? Direct approach or something more subtle?"

"Subtle. And direct at the same time."

"How do we manage that?"

"I'm thinking of a way right now. And something else just occurred to me. You know the Latinos that were killed?"

"Yeah?"

"Lloyd Wilder wasn't involved. The Latinos all were."

"What?"

"The man who told Annabelle he saw the men taking down the hoop was lying."

"But you thought Lloyd Wilder was involved too. What changed your mind?"

"I *suspected* he was involved. I wasn't convinced. But after thinking about it, I'm convinced my suspicions were wrong."

"Why?"

"Annabelle and Reuben were strangers in a bar looking for the tree farm. And these men just happened to volunteer that one of them had seen someone, not John Kravitz, take down that hoop?"

"Well?"

"It was all staged. The man said he was hiding behind a building. As we saw when we were there the building with the hoop was over fifty feet from the next closest structure. And on a ladder and in the dark it's nearly impossible to ID or even tell someone's size and age. So how did he know he wasn't John Kravitz?"

"That's right. And the guy did say he left before the man even came down the ladder."

"And right after they get this 'critical' piece of info Annabelle and Reuben are attacked?"

"So you think it was a setup?"

"I think they knew who Annabelle and Reuben were before they walked in that bar."

"And they tried to kill them?"

"Operative word, *tried*. I know Reuben got shot twice, but they were both nonfatal wounds. Deliberately nonfatal, I believe. He's as brave as they come, but there's no way you're overrunning a position fortified with machine guns by charging at them with a pistol. And they would not have retreated. By all combat logic Reuben should be dead."

"So they let him live, you mean? Why?"

"So Annabelle and Reuben could come back and tell us what they heard. Another red herring, another dead end to run down, wasting time. And then the Latinos end up shot soon thereafter. More smoke and mirrors. More clues to hunt down that will take us farther from the truth."

"And someone is also cleaning house," said Chapman. "By killing them."

"That too."

"If you're right, your country is really letting Turkekul have a lot of rope. He might kill everyone before he hangs himself."

"Maybe."

"So now Sykes?" said Chapman.

"Yes. Now Sykes."

CHAPTER

69

ONLY THEY COULDN'T FIND SYKES. He had not returned from the break and none of his crew knew where he was. They searched the park and the adjacent areas.

Stone got on his cell phone and reported this to Ashburn, along with what they had found out from Judy Donohue.

Ashburn said, "I'll get a BOLO out on him ASAP. He couldn't have gotten far."

Stone put his phone away and looked at Chapman. "I don't like how this is shaking out."

"Meaning they always seem to be one step ahead?"

"Meaning I'm feeling manipulated again."

"He might have seen Donohue slip away to come and talk to us and panicked. Why don't we get in the car and start doing a grid search? Maybe he's somewhere hoofing it on foot."

They drove out and turned onto Pennsylvania Avenue on the east side of the White House. They had gone two blocks when it happened.

The sound of the shot wasn't muffled. It could be heard clearly above the ordinary sounds of the city. People in the streets started running for cover and screaming.

The traffic stopped and horns started blaring.

Stone and Chapman jumped from the car and raced forward.

They heard a siren drawing near.

They ran from car to car, peering inside.

The siren grew louder. Then another one joined it.

Chapman looked behind her. Two cop cars were cutting through the traffic heading their way. Stone saw this too and picked up his pace. He reached in his jacket for his gun. Chapman accelerated on the other side of the line of stalled traffic and mimicked his movements. They finally reached the obstacle in the road—two cars in a fender bender that Stone sensed was much more. An older man was leaning against the car in front looking very shaken and scared. As Stone looked down he could see the man had vomited on the street.

As he approached, Stone held up his badge and called out, "Sir, what's wrong?"

The older man pointed at the car behind his, where the two bumpers were locked together. Stone checked the license plate of this car. Government issue. His spirits sank. He peered inside the car. "Damn."

Chapman was looking in from the passenger window. "Good God."

The two cop cars screeched to a stop and men in blue jumped out. They saw Stone and Chapman holding their weapons and pulled their own.

"Police!" they cried out, their guns aimed at the pair.

Stone and Chapman held up their badges high so the cops could see them.

Stone barked, "Federal agents. Got a homicide here. FBI just put a BOLO out on this guy. But somebody got to him first."

The cops crept forward, checked Stone's creds and looked in the car.

Sykes was lying back against the driver's seat. The windshield was cracked. There was a hole burned into his forehead from the shot. Blood and brain matter were splattered around the car's interior from the exit wound.

It was no wonder the other driver had thrown up after seeing this, thought Stone.

Chapman saw the cell phone on the front seat. Using a handkerchief, she scooped it up and checked the call log. "He got a call ten minutes ago. From a blocked phone. Maybe the techs can dig it out."

Stone nodded, looking around. "Right. Okay, he got the call, made a run for it."

Chapman added, "They set him up. Knew somehow he'd have to take this route. Lined the shot up."

Stone was now looking straight ahead, searching for where the shot had probably come from.

One of the cops said, "What do you need us to do?"

Stone kept looking while he talked. "Call in backup and secure the crime scene."

He pulled his phone and called Ashburn, filling her in.

A string of expletives exploded over the phone. Having sufficiently vented, Ashburn said, "I'm sending reinforcements right now. We'll coordinate with D.C. Metro."

Stone clicked off. "Cavalry's coming."

"How do you want to break down the search?" Chapman asked.

A woman who'd been standing on the sidewalk came running up to them. She was about twenty, with kneeless jeans and an iPhone clutched in her right hand and a shopping bag in her left.

"Sir? Ma'am?"

They turned to her. She pointed to a building farther down the street. "I was looking up at that building as I was walking and I saw a flash of light. Then I heard the car crash. I think that's where... where it came from."

Stone said quickly, "Could you tell which floor?"

The woman looked at the building, silently counting. "Sixth. At least I think."

They could hear other sirens coming as the backup flew toward them. Stone yelled to the two cops first on the scene to follow him and Chapman. As they ran toward the building he pulled out his phone and let Ashburn know about this development, giving her the address.

Stone put his gun away and ran as fast as he could, his gaze darting up to the sixth floor, waiting for another flash of light to appear.

"You don't think the shooter is still in the building, do you?" said Chapman as they reached the entrance and ripped the doors open. Stone had ordered one cop to guard the front of the building and the other the rear.

Stone didn't answer. He held up his badge to the security guard who approached them. "You have a possible sniper in this building. Did you see anyone come in today who looked suspicious or who was carrying an unusually shaped bag?"

The guard shook his head. "No one like that. But I just finished making my rounds, so someone might have slipped in then."

Stone said, "The FBI is on the way. What other exits do you have here beside the lobby?"

"This way." He led them to a door off the lobby.

"Down that hall and to the right. Takes you to the loading dock in the rear."

As they started off the man said, "You want me to go with you?"

"No, stay here. There's a police officer posted out front. Anything happens you get to him."

"Okay, good luck."

Stone and Chapman darted through the door and down the hall. They had only gone about twenty feet when she grabbed his arm.

"What?" he said.

"That security guard?"

"What about him?"

"Do they normally wear gloves?"

Stone flinched, wheeled around and sprinted back the way they had come.

The door was locked now. Chapman shot the handle off and kicked it open. They rushed back into the lobby. There was no sign of the guard.

Outside the cop told them that the man had come out and headed into the alley.

"He said you told him to help secure the rear of the building and—"

Chapman and Stone ran off before he finished.

They found the security guard's uniform next to a Dumpster. Stone and Chapman peered around.

"He can't be more than a few seconds ahead of us," she whispered.

"Thanks to you," said Stone. "If you hadn't figured out—"

She hit him hard, knocking him down an instant before the round slammed into the side of the Dumpster at the spot where Stone's head had just been. Chapman rolled, took aim and fired. Her shots chipped concrete off the side of the building, but the shooter was already gone.

Stone had rolled over on his belly and had his gun aimed at the same spot.

"See anything?" he hissed.

She shook her head. "He's gone."

The cop from the front, obviously having heard the shots, came running.

"Stay down," exclaimed Chapman, and the cop went to his knees and then scuttled forward until he was behind the Dumpster too.

"Backup's here," he said. "You guys okay?"

Stone sat up and looked at Chapman. "Thanks to her I am."

Chapman shrugged. "More luck than skill, really."

"I'll take it. That slug was going right for my head."

The three of them made their way cautiously down the alley. They picked up their pace when they heard the car race off. By the time they got to the next intersection, there was no sign of a vehicle or the shooter. Stone and Chapman ran down the alley and then slowly jogged back.

They both stopped when they reached the cop.

He was squatting over his partner, who was lying behind some trash cans with his throat slit, his eyes staring blankly up.

As they knelt over the body, Chapman said, "There must have been more than one guy. He wouldn't have had time to shoot at us and then do this."

"He had backup of his own," said Stone quietly, as the cop sat on his haunches wiping tears from his eyes over the death of his partner.

"These guys are unbelievably organized," said Chapman. "I mean, who the hell are they?"

Stone put a hand on the shoulder of the cop. "I'm sorry."

The officer glanced up and nodded and then returned to staring at his dead colleague.

Stone straightened, turned and walked back down the alley as the wail of sirens reached fever pitch.

George Sykes, a D.C. police officer and a security guard were dead. They'd found the real security guard in a storage room of the lobby with a single gunshot wound burned into his forehead.

The sniper had disappeared.

Stone had given descriptions of him to Ashburn and a BOLO had gone out, but none of them were holding out much hope. The consensus was that the killer was either laying low or already on private wings heading out of the country.

Stone and Chapman were now in a car sitting outside the modest residence of George Sykes, located in Silver Spring, Maryland. It was in the middle of an ordinary neighborhood with kids on bikes, moms talking in front yards and dads cutting the grass. Or it would have been if the street hadn't been evacuated and then shut down by the FBI.

Agent Ashburn was in the front passenger seat while another agent was at the wheel.

"What do we know about him?" Stone asked.

"Wife died three years ago. Kids all grown and gone. Been with the National Park Service his entire career. No problems."

"And six grandchildren," said Stone. He glanced down at the man's file. "He's not much older than me. He must have started early."

"Money problems?" Chapman asked.

Ashburn nodded. "That was one of the first things we looked at. Didn't find anything there.

But we dug a little deeper and shook out an account that was tied to Sykes. Recent deposit of a hundred thou."

"So someone paid him off to play along."

Stone said, "What exactly did they pay him for?"

Ashburn answered. "Bomb in the root ball. What if someone started to poke around there? He would steer them clear. Make sure wherever the bomb was in the dirt that no one got close to it."

"So he betrayed his country for a hundred thousand dollars?" said Stone. "A grandfather of six?"

Ashburn shrugged. "I've seen people do it for a lot less. And six grandchildren eat a lot."

Chapman added, "And that might've only been the first payment."

"Right," said Ashburn. "And they made sure the *only* payment. MO is consistent. They're eliminating their team, closing up the tunnel. So no leads for us."

"The sniper took a risk by impersonating a guard," noted Stone. "We saw his face."

"But like we concluded, the guy is long gone. And six months from now he'll have a new face."

"Lot of money behind this," said Chapman. "That's clear."

Ashburn hiked her eyebrows. "Like a country's treasury at work?"

"Russia," said Chapman.

"I've heard that theory floated around more and more," said Ashburn. "Cartel and government maybe working hand in hand. Tough competition."

Stone nodded at Sykes's house. "So what are we waiting for? We don't need a warrant. The guy was shot. We can go to his house to investigate. He was a federal employee."

Ashburn said, "That's true, but considering that these folks employ bombs, I've sent for a bomb detection dog to go in before we do. That's also why we've evacuated the neighborhood."

The canine unit came and Stone watched as the dog methodically swept the yard and then entered the house through a back door opened by an FBI agent. Ten minutes later the search was complete and the all clear was given.

It didn't take long to go through the house, but they found very little of help. As they walked back to their car Ashburn said, "We'll send in a forensics team to give it a scrubdown, but I doubt it will yield much."

"Still have to do it," said Stone.

"Still have to," agreed Ashburn.

"Has his family been notified?" asked Chapman.

"In the process. That's another place that might get us somewhere."

"He might have let something slip to a family member, you mean," said Chapman.

"If we're real lucky."

"I'm not feeling that lucky," said Stone.

Ashburn dropped them back at their car and they drove off. Chapman was at the wheel while Stone seemed lost in thought.

"What do you think?"

"I'm thinking how much more carnage before they yank Fuat Turkekul and make him talk."

"So you think he's really guilty?"

"I don't have enough information to make that determination. But the status quo is not working for us."

"What's the alternative?"

"I haven't thought of one yet."

"So who might be the next target in the chain?"

"If Turkekul is involved?" Stone glanced at her.

Chapman said, "That's what I was thinking too. And I know she's your friend, but what about—"

"Adelphia is not part of this."

"Are you really sure? By your admission she's been out of your life for a while."

Stone gazed at her and then put a hand on her

shoulder. "How do you feel about breaking a few rules?"

"Until I met you, not too keen. But now I think I'm really getting good at it. So we're going after Turkekul?"

"No," said Stone.

"Who, then?"

"I can feel the other side leading us around again. They expect us to go left. Instead, this time we're going to the right."

CHAPTER

71

Stone made one stop to get some information he needed while Chapman waited in the car. When he climbed back in he gave the directions to her.

On the drive over he said, "They talked to one of Sykes's coworkers. They said when Sykes took the call he got very pale and ran to his car."

"What do you think happened?"

"I don't know exactly, but I have a pretty good idea."

They reached the address, a townhouse community in Chantilly, Virginia. Chapman parked where Stone told her to, but he didn't get out of the car.

"We wait," he said.

A half hour later a truck pulled up to the front of a small town house thirty feet from where they were parked and a woman got out.

Chapman recognized her immediately. "That's—"

"Yes, it is," said Stone as he opened the car door.

They reached her front door an instant before she closed it. Stone stuck his foot in the gap. The woman turned around, startled. Stone had his badge out.

"Remember us?"

Judy Donohue, who was still dressed in her National Park Service uniform, looked from him to Chapman. "I . . . Yes, I do. Are you here about poor Mr. Sykes? I heard about it. It was awful."

"Can we come in?"

"Um, why?"

"Just to ask a few more questions."

"But I told you all I know."

"In light of recent developments other questions have come to mind." Stone pushed the door all the way open and Donohue was forced to step back as Stone crossed the threshold.

"Hey," she said angrily. "You can't do that."

"I just did," said Stone. Chapman closed the door behind her and Stone moved farther into the house.

"This is illegal, isn't it?" said Donohue.

Stone glanced at Chapman and then stared at

Donohue. "I don't think so, but then again, I'm not a lawyer."

"I'd like you to leave. Right now."

"Why? Do you have something to hide?"

Donohue looked nervous and said, "Of course not."

"I found out you're leaving the Park Service. Why is that? I thought being a girl from the big outdoors that it would be the perfect career for you."

"Not that it's any of your business, but I've been thinking about it for a few months now. And after everything that happened, and Mr. Sykes being shot. It was just time."

Stone inched closer to her. "So where's your plane ticket to? A place that doesn't have extradition with this country?"

"What?"

"Let's just cut to the endgame. Where are you running to? And how much did they pay you? They plunked a hundred thou in Sykes's account. Did they match that amount for you?"

"I don't know what the hell you're talking about," exclaimed Donohue.

"So you won't mind us taking a look around for it?"

"Yes, I do mind. Now get out."

Stone ignored this and moved closer to her. "The call that Sykes got? What did they tell him to make him drive off like that? That they had one of his six grandchildren captive? That he was to contact no one or the child would be killed? That he was to drive to a certain place along a certain route. A route that would take him right in the sniper's path? And then bang, no more George Sykes?"

"Get out or I'm calling the cops."

"Sykes had nothing to do with any of this," said Stone. "The money in a secret account? Set up and planted. Easy to do. The conversation you told us you overheard between Sykes and Agent Gross? Never happened. But with Gross and Sykes dead there's no one left to question it. But you did miss one thing. An obvious one."

He looked Donohue up and down. "Would you like to hear what it is?"

Donohue's lips started to tremble but she didn't say anything.

"I'll just go ahead and tell you. You see, we can verify things. About the arborist and the reasons for the hole being left unfilled? Why do I think we'll find out that everything Sykes told the FBI was true? That the hole couldn't be filled in yet for the reasons he stated? And why do I think if we dig as deep as the hole for the tree that we're going find even bigger holes in your story?"

Donohue now looked wobbly on her feet.

Stone moved closer. "They blew a hole right through his head with a long-range rifle round." He poked her forehead with his finger. "Right there."

"Please stop."

"And with Sykes dead the investigation had to swing back to you. The arborist would be contacted too and your lie would come out. But you expected to be long gone by then, didn't you? Is that why you're home early? Pack your life up and use forged docs they provided you. Gone before we know it."

"All right, this is your last chance. Get out." Donohue held up her phone like a weapon. "Or I'm calling the cops."

Chapman took a step forward. "Keep in mind, Judy, that the people you're working with have killed everyone who's helped them. Why do you think you'll be any different?" She glanced at the door. "In fact, I wouldn't be surprised if they were waiting outside for us to leave before they come in here and tidy up this loose end."

Donohue looked like she might start sobbing. Regaining her composure, she snapped, "Last time, get out."

Stone and Chapman left.

"What now?" asked Chapman.

"Part of me says we just flushed the quail, so let's see where it takes us."

"And your other part?"

"Worried that she'll be dead before we can get her to tell the truth. Go ahead and pull out, let her think we're leaving. I know she's watching us from the window."

Chapman started the car and drove off.

Stone had her stop at a spot far enough away but that still allowed them to see Donohue's house. He pulled out his phone and called Ashburn. It took a couple of minutes of explanation and Stone nodded his head. "Make it as fast as you can." He clicked off and put the phone away.

"Well?" asked Chapman.

"She's getting the paperwork together to bring the lady in. If nothing else for her own protection."

"What if she leaves the house?"

"We're to stop her and hold her until the Bureau shows up."

Chapman eased back in her seat but almost immediately jolted up.

Stone had seen it too.

Donohue had come out of her house. She was carrying a bag and she was in a hurry.

Stone said, "Quick, let's get her before someone else does."

By the time Chapman put the car in gear, Donohue had opened her truck door.

"Block her in," ordered Stone.

"Got it." Chapman punched the gas.

Their car was twenty-five feet from Donohue's when she started her truck.

The explosion lifted her vehicle off the asphalt and the concussive wave emanating from the blast knocked Chapman's car on its side. Both their heads bloodied from impacting with metal and glass from the car, Stone and Chapman lay unconscious, still strapped in their seat belts.

CHAPTER

72

STONE WOKE. HIS MIND WAS FUZZY but his reason was slowly returning. He tried to sit up, but a hand held him back. He saw Agent Ashburn staring down at him.

"What?" he began.

"It's okay. Just take it easy," she said in a soothing voice.

Stone looked around. He was in a hospital room again. He started to close his eyes when they snapped open as he remembered.

"Chapman?"

"She's going to be okay. A few bumps and bruises. Just like you."

"Donohue's dead," he said in a low voice.

"Yes. You saw the bomb detonate?"

Stone nodded. "She was in the truck."

"Any idea where the bomb came from?"

He touched his head and grimaced. "It was either already on her vehicle when she got home or else someone put it on there while we were in the house with her."

"You saw no one?"

Stone shook his head slowly.

Ashburn eased down into a chair next to the bed. "I was surprised to get your phone call about Donohue. What pointed you in her direction?"

"A hunch."

"About her?"

"Not necessarily. About refusing to be led around by the nose this time."

"Meaning that's what you think is happening?"

Stone sat up in the bed. "Meaning I think we're being manipulated, yeah."

"Any idea by whom?"

"Maybe closer to home than we'd like. Remember what Agent Gross said. Someone was watching him."

"So what was Donohue's angle? Was she the one involved with the tree and the bomb and not George Sykes?"

"I believe so. She tried to throw suspicion his way. Did you find anything at her place?"

"No. But if she had travel docs with her in preparation for making a run they're in the wreckage and we're still sifting through it. But paper is not something that's likely to survive something like that."

"But she *had* a bag. We certainly spooked her. I think she was making a run for it."

"Not disagreeing with you." Ashburn rose. "You've had a busy day. Almost shot by an imposter security guard/sniper and now nearly blown up."

"Does anyone know I'm here?"

"You mean your friends? No, we thought it best to keep it on the QT."

"So Chapman is okay. No BS?"

"No BS."

"Can I see her?"

"I'll check. Be back in a minute."

Less than a minute later the door opened. It wasn't Ashburn. It was Chapman propelling herself into the room via a wheelchair. There was a strip of bandage across her right cheek and one on her forehead.

Stone started and sat up more. His gaze darted to the wheelchair and then back at her.

"Not to worry." Chapman grinned. "I can walk, just hospital rules for patients having gotten themselves blown up. You Americans have so many bloody regulations."

Stone sat back, relief on his features.

She stopped next to the bed. "How about you? Everything working okay?"

Stone stretched his arms and neck. "Far as I know. Sore, but functional."

"We almost caught them."

"Almost doesn't count in our business."

"What did Ashburn tell you?"

"Basic stuff. No leads." He added with a smile, "The most important thing she told me was that you were okay."

Chapman smiled back. "I'm glad to see you have your priorities right."

"You saved my life."

"That only means we're even."

"I guess that's true."

"But Donohue was the last straw. No one left to talk to."

"You're wrong. There's Fuat Turkekul."

"But he's off-limits."

"After being blown up *twice,* nothing is off-limits as far as I'm concerned."

Later, when she walked in, Stone tried to hide his surprise but really couldn't.

Marisa Friedman was dressed in a white skirt, a blue silk blouse and flats. Her makeup was immaculate, her hair was glossy and fell loosely to her shoulders. She carried a purse in one hand and a pair of sunglasses in the other. She placed a pair of penetrating eyes on Stone and sat down in the room's one chair.

"I can tell you're stunned to see me," she said.

"The last time I got near you, I was told in no uncertain terms to back the hell off."

"How much do you really know? About me, I mean?"

"Weaver was blunt but informative."

"In our line of work that's good sometimes and not so good other times."

He sat up in the bed. "So why are you here?"

"I heard about what happened to you. I wanted to see that you were okay."

"You didn't have to come here to find that out. A phone call would've done it."

She glanced at him and then quickly looked away. She rose and walked to the window. "It's a pretty day."

"I guess it is. I hadn't really thought about it."

She continued to gaze out. "When I was a kid I was fascinated with the weather. I thought I'd grow up to be a meteorologist."

"What happened?"

She turned to look at him. "I'm not sure, actually. I did all the right things. Went to all the right schools. Then I detoured to Harvard Law. After graduating I had the intention of taking a year off, traveling in Europe and then settling down to a desk job at a firm in New York City. But on a whim I attended a seminar about the CIA and the next thing I know all these years have gone by." She turned to look out the window again. "I've seen a lot of *weather*." She glanced back at him. "But not nearly as much as you, apparently."

"You've talked to Weaver about me?"

She walked to the side of the bed. "John Carr. Quite impressive."

Stone shrugged resignedly. "I hadn't heard that name in over thirty years and now it seems like I hear it all the time."

She scooted the chair closer to the bed and sat down. "I was surprised that you had gotten on to me. I had no idea you were tailing me the night I was visiting Fuat until I got the message from Weaver's people. How did you do it?"

"So that's why you're really here? To make sure there are no permanent holes in your cover?"

"Wouldn't you do the same thing?"

"Yes, I would, actually," he admitted.

"Well?"

"Process of elimination. You were at the park that night. Adelphia's story didn't hold up to scrutiny. Turkekul was there to meet someone." He pointed a finger at her. "You were the logical choice.

It took me longer than it should have, actually. But in my defense, there was a lot of smoke and mirrors thrown at me."

Friedman looked nervous. Stone easily discerned why. "You're afraid if I figured it out, so could someone else?"

"That's the story of my life, Agent Stone. Trying to figure it out before they get to me."

"How did you *figure out* Turkekul?"

"A dozen minor things that meant nothing separately but which meant everything once you put them all together. I really couldn't believe it, though. And neither at first could NIC. But once they started digging it turned out to be true. Fuat's Afghan connection was the nail in the coffin. We traced that history to ties to the former Soviet Union. His principal handler back then is now only three seats removed from the top spot in the power hierarchy over there."

"And the connection to the Russian drug cartels?"

"Cartel. There's only one, really, though it has many manifestations. And the Russian government is firmly in partnership with it. Not only is the cash flow enormous, the damage drug trafficking can do to an entire country is far more deadly than actually hitting it with one's military. In a war soldiers die along with some civilians. Most people remain completely unaffected by it. In a drug war everyone feels the pain one way or another."

"I can see that."

"Then the issue became what to do about Turkekul."

"And the solution was to give him rope to hang himself?"

"Not just that, no. We need the others. Up the chain of command. Fuat being a Trojan horse was a serious setback for us. But if we can turn that to our advantage then we can make it into a serious disadvantage for the other side."

"I wish you luck on that."

She rose and put a hand on his shoulder. "I know you're working hard to solve this case. And I know that Fuat figures into it."

"But you don't want me pushing too hard, so hard that it blows up what you're trying to do?"

"Yes."

"I'll keep that in mind. You can go back and tell Weaver your mission was accomplished today."

"He doesn't know I'm here."

"Right." There was a bite to Stone's words that surprised him.

"He doesn't," she said emphatically.

"So why are you really here? And it's not just to check your cover. Or see if I was okay."

She looked at him curiously. "A deduction based on what?"

"Based on the fact that I have you pegged as a multitasker."

She sighed. "I just wanted to see you again. Make sure you really were okay, despite what I was told. You were blown up, after all."

"And why is that important to you?"

"It just is."

"I'm not getting this."

She drew closer to him. "Well, then let me be uncharacteristically frank. We're actually a lot alike, John Carr. There aren't many people who do what we do." Her features softened and she seemed to be looking past him. "I've lived so many years of my life as someone I'm really not." She refocused on him. "I know you've done that for an even longer period of time. I've never met anyone like me. That is, until I met you." She touched his arm. "So that's why I'm here. I guess just to convince myself that I'm not alone. That there are others like me out there. I know that probably seems illogical to you."

"No, it actually doesn't. It makes a lot of sense, in fact."

She drew closer to him. "It's a lonely life."

"It can be, yes."

"I can tell you've been alone a long time."

"How?"

She slowly lifted her hand and touched it against his cheek. "It's in the face. The face doesn't lie, if you know how to look." She paused. "And we both do know how to look, don't we?"

She removed her hand and Stone looked away.

"I'm sorry if I've embarrassed you," she said. "I just wish..."

"What?"

"That we had met a long time ago."

"It wouldn't have worked a long time ago."

"Does that mean it could work now?"

Stone looked away again. "Nothing will work with me."

"You're choosy?"

"It's not that. Even if I were choosy, you would be... Well, it doesn't matter now."

"It can always matter. Even for two old warriors like us."

"I'm old. You're not."

"In this business we're all old." She paused. "If we're still alive."

She stood, slid a hand down his cheek and then bussed her lips against his face.

"Take care of yourself," she said. A moment later she was gone.

CHAPTER

73

STONE AND CHAPMAN WERE DISCHARGED from
the hospital the next day after being held for observation. Stone had to admit that he needed the extra
rest. Being knocked unconscious twice within a
short period of time would have done a number on
a young man, much less someone his age. But he
had motivation to get out of his bed and take up
the hunt once more. Things were coming to a head.
The big event was close to happening. He could feel
it in every nerve he had.

As Chapman drove off in a new ride provided
by the FBI, Stone looked across at her. "How many
stitches?"

She touched the bandage across her forehead.
"Six here and two more on the cheek. Doc said I'd
be healed in plenty of time for holiday photos." She

glanced over at him. "How'd you get off without any? I distinctly remember seeing you all bloodied before passing out."

"They probably figured what's the use? And the major cut was on my scalp. There's a Band-Aid up there but you can't see it."

"I guess we are very lucky."

"Luckier than Judy Donohue."

"So they roped her into this whole thing. How? Money?"

"I would assume so, yes. Money they never really intended on paying."

"They were going to kill her all along, you mean?"

"Clearly. The cover they built for her was flimsy at best. Only designed to hold us off a day or two. As soon as she talked to us at the church and said all those lies she was a dead woman."

"So presumably the FBI will find a deposit to an offshore account somewhere in Donohue's name that has been rescinded. Funny, she didn't strike me as the type to conspire."

"What type? The one that doesn't like money? I've run into very few of those."

"But to participate in an attack against your own country?"

"Don't be naïve. And besides, no one got hurt in that attack, except for the unfortunate Alfredo Padilla."

"But when other people started dying? She had to notice that."

"Of course she did. But by that time it was too late. If she came to us to confess, she'd be admitting to being an accessory to murder, multiple murders. She probably decided the safer course was to follow through with the plan and run with what she thought was lots of money."

"And George Sykes gets a hole in the head for doing nothing wrong at all."

"Yes. That's why I don't feel too badly about Judy Donohue."

"Your theory on how they got Sykes to drive off in a panic like that was probably close to the truth."

"Threaten his family. They might have told him where to meet. A route that would take him right into the kill zone. It was meticulously set up. Which is both informative and daunting."

"They could probably kill us anytime they wanted."

"They tried to kill me and you stopped it."

"Score one for the good guys."

"And it proves they're not infallible."

"So does that mean the whole tree farm, root ball, National Park Service angle was another red herring?"

"I think Kravitz was framed. I think Lloyd Wilder was totally innocent too."

"And the Latinos who were executed?"

"Counterparts to Judy Donohue. They were partially in on the plot, but only partially. They played their roles, received their payoff and then were eliminated."

"Okay, so we're back to Fuat Turkekul? How do you want to do this? Weaver will be all over our butts if we get caught messing around with the little Turk."

"Like I told you before, I got a wink from Sir James."

"So what? That is not going to protect you from Riley Weaver and you know it."

"So we'll bypass Turkekul and take the path slightly less traveled."

"Which is? Adelphia?"

"No."

"Who, then?"

He said nothing.

"Marisa Friedman is the only one left."

"Yes, she is."

"But the last time we tried to access her, we got nailed."

"That was last time. Now we are forewarned. And she came to see me."

"What? When?"

"Yesterday. In the hospital."

"What did she want?"

"I'm not really sure, to tell you the truth. She's a lonely woman."

"Really?" Chapman looked at him inquiringly.

"I guess we're all lonely in some way."

"All right," said Chapman uncertainly. "So how are we going to do it?"

In answer Stone pulled out his phone and punched in a number. "Annabelle? I think it's time you and Caleb had your follow-up meeting with Ms. Friedman."

CHAPTER

74

"It's good to see you again," said Friedman as she sat down at the restaurant table. Annabelle and Caleb were already seated across from her.

"We said we would be in touch," Annabelle said bluntly.

Caleb said, "We are very excited to move this forward, with your help."

Friedman slid her napkin into her lap and said, "And I'm excited to get to work on this with you. I've made some preliminary inquiries and the time is definitely ripe for your project model."

They ate and discussed more points of business. As they left the restaurant a Mercedes limo swung around the corner.

"We can give you a ride home," said Caleb.

"You don't have to do that," said Friedman. "I live out in Virginia."

He took her hand, kissed it. "It is no trouble. In fact it would be my pleasure."

Annabelle held the door open. Friedman climbed in. Annabelle shut the door behind her and the limo sped off.

Friedman jerked around and tried the door handle. The door was locked. She noticed a presence to her left and whirled in that direction.

A man was staring at her.

"What the hell is going on?" demanded Friedman. She stopped, caught her breath as she focused on him. "Stone?"

Stone said, "That's my partner up there, Mary Chapman. I'm sure you've been briefed on her too." He motioned to the driver. Chapman gave a small wave before turning onto the next street.

"You're . . . you're kidnapping me?"

"No, we're meeting with you."

She frowned. "People who want to meet with me usually make an appointment."

"We need your help and we wanted to ask for it quietly."

"I thought you'd been forbidden by Director Weaver to come near me."

"That's why we're asking quietly."

Friedman sat back, taking all of this in. There

was no fear in her eyes. "So Weaver knows nothing about this?"

"Need to know. And right now he doesn't need to know."

"Interesting theory considering he runs the country's intelligence services."

"As you know, we have great interest in Turkekul."

"You're not alone in that regard."

"You told me you figured out he was a traitor, but when exactly did you learn he was a double agent?"

"You know, you can tell me that Riley Weaver has filled you in, but that doesn't mean I have to believe it."

"People are dying at an alarming clip," he pointed out.

She shrugged. "It's a dangerous business."

"And we believe that Turkekul is at the epicenter of that business."

Friedman hesitated. "I wouldn't disagree with that assessment. But—"

Chapman spoke up. "And yet he just keeps walking along, no troubles."

Friedman glanced at her and then at Stone. "I follow orders. I might not agree with them all the time, but I follow them."

"All the time?" asked Stone.

"I wouldn't last long in this line of work if I didn't."

"Didn't you learn to exercise some independence in order to get the job done?"

Friedman crossed her legs and folded her arms over her chest. "Any place in particular where we're going?"

"Just seeing the city. Having a nice chat."

"What do you have in mind?"

"So you are concerned?"

She snapped, "Who the hell wouldn't be concerned! A dozen people have died at least by my count. Snipers, bombers, executions. All on American soil."

"So you'll help us?"

"I can't commit to that," she said frankly. "Until I know what your plan is. You know that."

"We need Turkekul to talk to us."

"He'll talk to you all right. About everything you don't want to know about. He's the most tight-lipped, aggravatingly secretive person I've ever met, and that's saying something."

"He's just trying to survive. And you do that by not trusting anyone," said Stone.

"Well, then pray tell how do you propose getting him to talk? Because I haven't come close."

"With your help I think we can."

"I haven't agreed to anything. By all rights I should report this contact right away. And if Weaver finds out—"

"But you won't report it."

She looked at him with a superior expression. "And how do you know that?"

"Because I can tell you want to get this guy."

"I've always wanted to get this guy. But it's the people behind him that my superiors want. I explained that to you. Without them Turkekul isn't worth anything. If it were just Turkekul it wouldn't be a problem. He'd be dead."

Chapman said, "And you're sure if you take him out it wouldn't help matters?"

"Not in the least. The Russians have a dozen Fuat Turkekuls spread around the globe. And if we show our hand we blow an opportunity that will likely never come along again. That's been the rub with this whole mission. If we can follow Fuat right back to Moscow and show a clear connection between the government there and the Russian drug cartel then I think even the citizens of Russia would sit up and take notice. The UN certainly would as well as the rest of the free world. And Russia would have no choice but to back the hell off its grandiose plans to dominate the planet again, using cocaine and heroin as opposed to guns and tanks."

"I can see his value more clearly now. You expressed the situation very well," said Stone.

She glanced up and their gazes locked.

Friedman said, "Would you care to guess how old I am?"

Stone appraised her. "Thirty-five?"

"Add ten years to that."

He looked surprised. "For such a high-risk profession you've aged remarkably well."

"Outside, perhaps," she replied. "Inside it's a different matter." She gazed at him. "Why do I believe you're in the same boat?"

"I think I look my age."

"Most men your age are fat and bowed. You look like you could do the Marine obstacle course at Quantico without breaking a sweat."

Friedman continued to stare at Stone. "Without breaking a sweat," she said again.

In the rearview mirror Chapman gazed anxiously between the pair. "So getting back to the matter at hand," she said quickly as the two continued to stare at each other.

Friedman ignored her and said, "Did I mention that I checked out John Carr's military and CIA career? The most unbelievable parts I found the most believable for some reason."

"I did my job. Just like you are."

"Few people did their job like you did. You're more than a legend, John Carr. You're more like a myth."

"I'm actually flesh and blood. That's been very apparent to me from the start." He touched the bandage on his head. "And never more apparent than right now."

"Your missions and methods were actually taught in the classroom at CIA, did you know that?"

"No, I didn't."

"Not by name, of course, or else I would've heard of John Carr much earlier. But I did some digging. Triple Six. Always got a kick out of that name. You never failed."

"Sure I did."

"Modesty."

"Truth."

"I don't believe you."

Chapman blurted out, "Okay, we bloody well need to get back to the matter at hand, if you two don't mind."

Stone asked, "Will you work with us? I need that commitment before I explain my plan."

"You're basically asking me to risk my career over this. If it backfires I'm gone. With nothing left."

"But if we don't stop this, there'll be a lot more gone, won't there? Not just people, maybe a city or two?" He paused. "Nanobots? The Russians back on the global warpath. And if my plan works then your goal may be realized too. This entire mess laid at the doorstep of Moscow."

She said coolly, "I'm fully aware of the situation."

"Then you know the stakes. And I do need your help."

"Turkekul spent time in Afghanistan. They like to carve their enemies up there, one slice of skin at a time. And then he'll turn me over to the Russians. And I can't believe they're any better."

"I'll protect your life with mine."

She looked out the window again. Stone watched as the woman's expression changed continually until he could tell her mind had been made up. She turned back to him.

"I'll help you."

"Thank you."

"But for the record, you could've just come to me directly and not stooped to a snatch operation. I think I deserve better than that."

"You do," said Stone. "You actually do."

CHAPTER

75

A DAY LATER STONE SAT in a restaurant overlooking Fourteenth Street. He was dressed in a black jacket, white shirt and jeans. He had his gun but not his badge. In his mind, right now the former was critical and the latter was worthless. In a far corner of the restaurant with a clear view of the front door sat Harry Finn sipping on a glass of ginger ale and casually studying the menu. His 9mm rode in a shoulder holster against his chest.

Mary Chapman had the other end of the restaurant. Perched on a barstool, she sipped on a Coke. Her Walther was in her handbag.

Three guns awaiting their quarry.

Stone rose when they entered. Fuat Turkekul looked somewhat inconsequential next to the glamorous Friedman. The woman wore a dark pantsuit and her hair fell flawlessly around her shoulders. She was a beautiful lady, thought Stone. Which in her profession was a good thing. It attracted certain men and also made such men focus on the woman's physical assets as opposed to what could really hurt them, which was her brain.

Stone shook hands with Turkekul and they all sat down. The Turk's gaze roamed the room before falling back on Stone. He took a moment to slide the napkin in his lap before speaking.

"I was most surprised when Ms. Friedman asked me to meet with you. I did not presume that you would be in the...how do you say...?"

"The loop?" suggested Stone.

"Yes."

"I get around," Stone said vaguely. His gaze pinged off all corners of the restaurant and he came away satisfied. Two guards in suits had followed Turkekul and Friedman in and were waiting near the coat check. Friedman had told Stone that the security detail had standing orders that when she was with the man they were to keep a respectful distance. Riley Weaver's men looked alert but relaxed. Stone kept out of their line of sight just in case they recognized him.

"And what did you wish to meet about?" asked Turkekul.

"How are things going with Adelphia?"

"We work well together. I am getting my feet wet, so to speak. And Ms. Friedman is a good partner as well."

"Fuat hopes to make some progress in the next several months," volunteered Friedman. She stared at Stone perhaps a beat too long before breaking off and picking up the menu the waiter had just dropped off.

Turkekul put up a hand. "These things take time. Americans want everything done yesterday." He chuckled.

"We have that reputation, yes," agreed Stone. "But recent events are troubling."

Turkekul broke off a piece of bread from the basket in the center of the table and bit into it. He brushed the crumbs off the cloth and onto the floor. "You speak of the bomb and such?"

"The death of an FBI agent. The second bombing. The murder of the Park Service man. We have to stop it."

"Yes, yes, but what does that have to do with me?"

"A group in Yemen with known ties to Al-Qaeda has claimed responsibility, so I think it has a lot to do with you. You are tasked with finding the head of that organization."

Turkekul was already shaking his head. "I told

you before that the Yemeni group is unreliable. I do not believe that they are behind the bombing or any of the other criminal acts."

"Why?" asked Stone evenly.

Turkekul held up one finger. "First, they are not sophisticated enough. This sort of long-term planning and execution is not their forte. They will put a bomb in a car and blow it up, but that is all." He held up another finger. "And second, they simply do not have the assets required to do such a mission here. You speak of many deaths but all through separate incidents. No, it is not them."

"Okay, then who do you think it is?" Stone paused and glanced at Friedman. "Your old friend Osama? He certainly has the long-term planning skills. And the assets."

Turkekul smiled and shook his head. "I think not."

"And your reasons?"

"He has other, how do you say, fish to fry."

"And what are those fish?"

"I am not prepared to say at the moment."

Stone sat forward. "I wanted to meet with you to make a deal of sorts."

Turkekul looked surprised. He glanced at Friedman before staring back at Stone. "I already have a deal with your government."

"I didn't say it was with my government."

Turkekul looked taken aback. "I do not understand." He gazed again at Friedman when he said this.

"We need to step things up a bit," said Friedman. "And I think we now have the intel to do it." She nodded at Stone.

Stone picked up this choreographed "tag" from the woman and said, "We've discovered that there's a mole."

Turkekul gazed in surprise at him. "A mole?" He shot Friedman another anxious look. "Where exactly?"

"Very close," answered Stone. "We don't have the person's exact identity, but we do know that a significant event is being planned."

"But how can you do anything about it if you don't know the person's identity?" Turkekul said with deliberate calm.

"That status is very near to changing," said Stone. "For the last month we've had a source that we have been in the process of flipping. That's principally why they brought me on, actually. And that's why I was so interested in your presence, Fuat. I can call you Fuat, can't I?"

"Of course. But I don't understand why you would be interested in me in connection with this matter."

Stone sat forward and dropped his voice. "Do you mind if we carry on this conversation elsewhere, somewhere more private?"

Turkekul again looked at Friedman, who nodded. "You really need to hear this, Fuat. It's directly connected to you."

The Turk glanced behind him, in the direction of his guards. "As Marisa knows, I do not travel alone."

"It can be arranged," said Stone.

"How?" Turkekul asked nervously.

"It can be arranged," Stone said again. He motioned with his eyes in the direction of Chapman and Finn. Each nodded back when Turkekul glanced at them.

"Can't you tell me here?" Turkekul asked.

Stone sat back. "You trust Marisa. And Marisa trusts me, or she wouldn't have brought you here."

"I do trust her."

"Then what is the problem?"

"You obviously have never lived in the Middle East."

"On the contrary, I have."

When Stone next spoke it was in Pashto. Then he switched to Farsi. The effect on Turkekul was immediate.

"How do you know these languages?"

"My hair is white. I've been in this business a long time. But you're referring to not trusting anyone because your friend is only a friend until he is your enemy?"

"Precisely."

"Then I will chance being overheard and tell you why you need to be involved."

"Yes?"

"A fatwa has been issued. A private one."

"A fatwa? Against whom?"

"Against you."

Turkekul looked stricken. "Against me? I do not understand."

"Someone has found out you're assisting the Americans, Fuat. They want to eliminate that assistance."

Turkekul's gaze swung between Stone and Friedman. "A fatwa? But I am an academic. I am no threat to anyone."

"Someone has found out what you're really doing. That is clear. The mole I spoke of? His target, it seems, was you. They know of your treachery."

"This is...preposterous."

"No, our information is rock solid. As you know, we've vastly improved our intelligence resources in that part of the world."

"Who issued the fatwa?"

Stone said a name and the man's face turned gray.

"They are..."

"Yes. And the group they have assigned to execute the fatwa have the reputation of never missing. I won't mention their name, but trust me, you would recognize it."

Turkekul looked shrunken now as he fidgeted with his hands.

Stone studied him. "I know your faith does not allow for the imbibing of alcohol, but perhaps an exception in this case? Then we can talk about what we would like for you to do."

"Yes, I think. Perhaps some wine," he said quickly.

Friedman motioned for a waiter.

Ten minutes later Turkekul left with Friedman. After he had gone, Stone and Chapman departed by a rear exit and climbed into a black Yukon with bulletproof windows and armor plating.

"Well done, Oliver," said a booming voice from the backseat.

James McElroy was sitting there. "The audio feed was loud and clear. I heard everything."

Stone sat back against the leather seat. "Well, let's see if the man takes the bait."

CHAPTER

76

"HE'S ON THE MOVE," Agent Ashburn said. She was sitting in the front seat of the SUV wearing a headset. She turned to look at Stone and Chapman. "I hope this works."

"If it doesn't, we'll know soon enough," said Stone.

"How about his security?" asked Chapman.

"They were told to give him an out."

"He won't get suspicious?"

"Their job is to protect him from others. Not from himself. He said he was going to bed. They're not expecting him to sneak out, which he just did."

A voice came over Ashburn's headset. "Okay, he just got in a cab. He must've called for one from his apartment. He's heading west."

"West?" said Stone. "Out of the city?"

Ashburn nodded. "He just crossed the Key

Bridge. Okay, he's turning right onto the GW Parkway and heading into Virginia." She tapped the driver. "Let's roll."

The truck sped off and crossed the river and then hung a right onto the parkway.

"Keep back a bit," Ashburn instructed the driver. "We've got assets all around. There's no way we'll lose him."

Stone did not seem convinced of this. He glanced at Chapman with an uneasy expression.

Ashburn looked back. "Riley Weaver gets wind of what we're doing he will throw a hissy. You know that."

"It won't be the first time," replied Stone.

He was peering out the windows into the darkness. The GW Parkway was one of the most beautiful stretches of road in the D.C. metro area. There were thick woods on both sides of the asphalt, stone walls lining the road, steep terrain heading down to the Potomac River and the lighted expanse of Georgetown north of the water. Stone wasn't focused on this aspect of the trip, however. He was watching the distant taillights of the cab that had just now come into view.

"He's pulling off," Ashburn said a minute later. "Onto the scenic overlook."

Stone had already seen this. The lights of the cab vanished as it made the turn.

"Pull past and then slow down," Ashburn ordered the driver. She gave this same command into her headset.

Stone didn't know how many vehicles the FBI had on the scene, but the Bureau typically brought overwhelming force to any task. However, the mission here was not to arrest Turkekul and anyone he was meeting with, but to follow the person he was meeting with and hope that trail led them up the chain of command. Perhaps all the way to the president of Russia himself.

"We've got infrared eyes on the entire scene," said Ashburn. "He's getting out of the cab and walking over to the wall fronting the parking area."

"Is there another vehicle there?" asked Stone. "I didn't see one when we drove past."

Ashburn looked confused and spoke into her headset. "Well, how is he meeting with someone, then? Are they flying up here?"

She flinched. "A light just came on in the woods near the wall."

Stone said, "They could have hiked up from the riverbank."

"Quite a hike," said Ashburn. She spoke into

her headset. "Everyone stand by. Do not intervene. Repeat, do not intervene. This is a—"

The sound of the shot made them all jump. Stone grabbed the driver's shoulder. "Go! Go!"

The SUV whipped around, plowed across the median and sped back toward the pull-off.

"Move in," Ashburn called into her headset. "All positions move in!"

SUVs poured into the parking lot. Stone and Chapman were out of the truck before it even stopped. Stone ran toward the still figure sprawled on the asphalt. He knelt down next to Turkekul. Chapman stood next to him.

"He's dead," said Stone. "Exit wound from the front. He was facing the river. That means the shot came from the other side of the road."

Ashburn was already screaming instructions at her troops. A pack of agents raced toward the woods on the other side of the road where the shot had originated. Two other agents were pulling a terrified cab driver from his ride. Chapman slipped over the wall and looked down.

"The light was from a battery-operated lantern with a timer switch," she said.

She rejoined Stone and looked down at Turkekul.

"Could there really have been a fatwa on him?" she asked.

Stone just shook his head. "We got played. Again," he added bitterly.

"What happens now?"

"We're screwed," he muttered. "That's what happens now. We're completely and totally screwed."

CHAPTER

77

THERE WAS NO ONE LEFT STANDING after the NIC chief found out about an unauthorized operation that had cost him his sole asset in the biggest counterintelligence investigation of his brief career as the nation's head spy. If Weaver could have issued a hit on Stone, Chapman and Ashburn and gotten away with it, he would have. Even Sir James McElroy, who immediately owned up to his part in the fiasco, was not spared.

When Stone and Chapman met with him later at the British embassy McElroy looked older and frailer than before. The spark that was usually in his eye had receded. Chapman looked crushed at having let the man down. Stone's expression was unfathomable. There were few who could discern the smoldering anger within him.

"No leads on the shooter?" asked McElroy quietly as he held his side tightly.

Chapman answered, "None. By the time the FBI got there the sniper was long gone. There's a road near the location. Takes a minute for a car to disappear into a dozen different directions."

"Well, MI6 has been officially taken off the case," said McElroy. He looked at Chapman. "I'm on the next flight out. Care to ride with me?"

Chapman glanced at Stone, who was looking at the wall, obviously lost in thought.

"If I could follow you a bit later, sir, just to wrap up a few things here."

McElroy said, "Could you excuse us for a minute, Mary?"

Chapman shot Stone another look and quickly left the room.

When the door closed Stone focused on the Brit.

"Quite a cock-up," said McElroy.

"Quite."

"I still believe it was worth the effort. The status quo was letting people die left and right."

"Well, we just added another to that list."

"Now that Turkekul is gone the matter might be closed."

Stone sat down across from him. "How so?"

"Turkekul was their point man."

"If so, why kill him?"

"You flushed him out."

"How did they know I did?"

McElroy spread his hands. "How have these chaps known anything? They just do."

"My commission has been revoked," said Stone. "The president's loyalties have their limits. Not that I can blame him."

"How about our FBI agent?"

"Ashburn? Couple black marks and a desk job for a while. She was smart enough to get some backing higher up before this all went down. Her landing will be relatively soft. But it's still not what she wanted to happen."

"Of course not." McElroy patted Stone on the shoulder. "It's no use sitting around lamenting about things we can't change. Some missions go according to plan and everyone's happy. And some unfortunately don't."

"Well, I'm not convinced this mission is over yet."

"It is for us, Oliver. I've been known to buck the system on occasion. Last night was one of those occasions. But I also know when to toss in the towel. Otherwise I wouldn't have lasted this long."

He rose, holding on to the table for support. Stone looked up at him.

"Maybe it's true. Even though I was the one who said it, I'm not sure I really believed it."

"What?"

"That I'm not what I once was."

"None of us are, Oliver. None of us are."

After McElroy left, Chapman came back in and sat down next to Stone.

"I thought it was a good try, and for what it's worth I'd do it again," she said. "Better than sitting on our hands looking for somebody else to do something."

"Thanks," Stone said curtly. "So what do you have to wrap up over here that you're not flying back with your boss?"

"I'm not sure. I thought you could tell me."

Stone cocked his head. "Not following."

"You're not going to just leave it like this, are you?"

"What else am I supposed to do? I'm officially out of the investigation."

"Officially just means technically. And from what I've seen of how you operate, technicalities don't matter much."

"I screwed up big-time. Weaver is trying to figure out a way to put me behind bars."

"Forget him. We still have a case to solve. Because I don't think Turkekul going down means anything."

Stone now looked interested. "What do you mean?"

"Come on, I was eavesdropping at the door. I heard you tell Sir James that you didn't believe the mission was over."

"I don't. I just don't see how much good I can do."

"Because you're not what you were?"

"You really were listening at the keyhole."

"Yeah, I really was."

Stone hesitated for a moment and then said, "I'm done, Mary. Fly back to London. Get the hell away from me. Right now, I'm professional poison. You've got a long career ahead of you."

He rose to leave. She snagged his arm.

"John Carr would never walk away from this."

"No, he wouldn't. But I'm not John Carr. Not anymore."

The door closed behind him.

CHAPTER

78

"I JUST CAME BY TO SAY I'm sorry."

Stone was standing on the threshold of Marisa
Friedman's office in Jackson Place. The woman
stared back at him. She was dressed in jeans, a T-
shirt and sandals. Her hair was disheveled and
there was a smudge of dirt on her left cheek. Over
her shoulder Stone could see packing boxes.

"Okay," she said. "But that wasn't necessary.
Op went wrong. Heads roll. That's the nature of
the beast. I anted in, and the pot went to someone
else."

"Unauthorized op," Stone corrected her.
"Because of me."

She shrugged. "Doesn't matter now, does it?"

"You moving?"

"Going out of business."

"Higher orders?"

"It was never really my business to begin with. Uncle Sam was footing the bill. *And* keeping all the profits. If I'd really been in business for myself, I'd be retired on a cushy income by now."

She fell silent and the two stared at each other. "I've got some fresh coffee brewing. You up for a cup?"

"All right, but I'm a little surprised you're not pulling a gun on me instead."

"Believe me, I thought about it."

They sat at her desk. As Stone drank his coffee he said, "What now?"

"What now? Good question. My ticket got pulled."

Stone's mouth fell open. "Not permanently?"

"Yes," she said quietly. "Fuat Turkekul was our only link to what my superiors referred to as the second coming of Stalin. And I lost him."

"No, *I* lost him. And I told Weaver that to his face."

"Doesn't matter. I let you take him. Same difference. And I didn't get the necessary clearance, principally because it would never have been given."

Stone looked around the office. "What will you do now?"

"Well, I'll spend about the next year of my life writing exit briefs and defending my indefensible actions to a top secret government panel that will be doing its best to find a way to do more than fire me."

"What, prison?"

"Why not?"

Stone put his cup down. "You have any options in the private sector?"

She shook her head. "Damaged goods. All the guys that are hiring people like me used to work on the government side. They need to stay in their good graces. I'm persona non grata."

"You have something else to worry about," said Stone.

She nodded. "I've been outed. They knew what we were trying to do with Fuat. If they know that, they know about me. The Russians will try to kill me, if for no other reason than professional satisfaction."

"And you have no tail coverage?"

"None. Agency cut all ties to me as soon as our little Bay of Pigs came to light. All those years of outstanding service didn't provide me with a sliver of support when things went bad." She smiled resignedly. "Why should I have expected anything more?"

Stone said nothing. He sipped his coffee and watched the woman.

She gazed around her office. "You know, as crazy as it sounds, I'm going to miss this place."

"Doesn't sound crazy."

"I was a spy, but I was also a businesswoman. And I was actually a pretty good lobbyist."

"I'm sure you were."

She looked at him. "What about you?"

"What about me?"

"Come on, I could hear Riley Weaver's screams all the way from Virginia."

Stone shrugged. "I was out of the business a long time. So I'll be out of it again. For good this time."

"Weaver's going to come after you."

"I know that."

"He will make your life a living hell."

"I know that too."

"I'm thinking about going to a deserted island where he and the Russians can't find me."

"Is there such a place?"

"Worth finding out."

"That takes money."

"I've saved well."

"I haven't."

She eyed him. "So you want to tag along?"

"I'm definitely baggage you don't need."

"You never know. Us against the world."

"I'd probably slow you down."

"Something tells me that you wouldn't. Two old spies on the road."

"You're not old, Marisa."

"Neither are you, John."

"Oliver."

She rose and slid over next to him. "Right now, just let it be John."

"Why?"

She kissed him.

Stone pulled back in surprise. "I just cost you your career," he said.

"No. Maybe you just opened my eyes to the future."

She pressed her body against his, nearly pushing him off the chair. Her scent wafted into his nostrils, and it was like a welder's spark had gone off in the part of his brain that dealt with the senses.

He moved away from her and shook his head. "I've been all over the world and I don't think I've ever smelled anything like that before. I actually felt a pop in my head."

She smiled. "It's a perfume I found in Thailand. Unavailable in the States. The English translation is roughly 'two hearts as one.' It's supposed to have a visceral effect on men. And I'm not talking in the obvious place. More emotional."

"Well I can attest to that."

She leaned closer. "Don't dismiss my offer so lightly."

"I'm not. But frankly it would be pretty crazy."

"Nothing is crazy if you want it badly enough." She sat back up. "Don't you think you deserve a little happiness? A little peace after everything you've been through?"

Stone hesitated. "I'll think about it."

She touched his cheek. "That's all I'm asking, John. I've waited a long time for someone like you. I've lost my career. But maybe I've found something else to replace it."

"You could have just about anyone you wanted. Why me?"

"Because you're just like me."

CHAPTER

79

STONE WOKE AND LOOKED AROUND. He was in his cottage, lying in his old army cot. He checked his watch. Two a.m. He got up, showered, scrubbing his skin and hair especially hard for a reason he couldn't really fathom. He dried off and slipped on his pants, shirt and shoes. After leaving Marisa Friedman's office and before coming home he'd walked for hours, until his legs were sore from smacking into the concrete sidewalks. Then he'd come here, falling asleep almost right away simply because he was exhausted.

He took some Advil, sat on the side of his cot and waited for the dull ache in his head to subside. Two concussions in a short period of time. At twenty he could shrug that off. Now he could not. It was all taking its toll. The next one might just do him in.

Maybe I can blame all the mistakes on being blown up twice.

His thoughts once more turned to Marisa Friedman. A deserted island. Two old spies. He touched his lips where she'd kissed him. He couldn't say he hadn't felt...something. In fact, she had made it clear that she would go much farther than a kiss.

And her offer to leave together? A beautiful woman. An intelligent lady. A woman who had worked in the world he had. At first Stone had thought it ridiculous. He had only told her he would think about it to appease her.

Now? Now maybe he really was thinking about it. What was left for him here? He had his friends. But right now anyone close to him would suffer too. Riley Weaver would see to that. It had all disintegrated with surprising speed.

The headache finally weakened and he put on a jacket, left the cottage and walked around the familiar grounds of Mt. Zion. Even in the dark he knew where each tombstone was, every path, every tree. He stopped in front of a few graves of the long dead. He would sometimes talk to these folks, by name. He never got an answer, but it still helped. Allowed him to think through a particularly difficult problem.

And I've got a few of those right now.

The slight crack of a stick made him turn and stare down the path.

"I take it you never sleep?"

Chapman walked toward him. Dark slacks, white blouse, leather jacket. The Walther underneath.

"Can say the same about you," he said.

"Been looking for you."

"Why?"

"You hungry?"

Stone hadn't realized how hungry he was until she asked. He couldn't even remember the last time he'd eaten. "Yeah, I am."

"Me too."

He held up his watch. "D.C. is not a late-night town. Everything's closed."

"I know a place. All-night restaurant. On the Virginia side."

"How?"

"I'm an insomniac. So I always do a recon for late-night eateries in whatever area I'm in."

"Let's go."

She drove across the river, taking the GW Parkway and turning off onto Route 123 heading toward Tysons Corner. There was no traffic and the lights were all green, so very shortly they were pulling into the Amphora restaurant parking lot in the suburb of Vienna. There were over a dozen other cars there. Stone looked around in surprise. "Never knew this was here. And it looks popular."

Chapman opened her door and got out. "You should get out more." She smacked the door closed with her hip.

They went in and both ordered breakfast. The coffee and food came fast and was delivered by a white-jacketed and black-bow-tied waiter who had astonishing enthusiasm for nearly three o'clock in the morning.

"Came by to see you earlier," Chapman said. "You weren't home."

Stone ate some of his scrambled eggs. "I was out."

"Out where?"

"Does it matter?"

"You tell me."

"You have something you want to say, say it."

Chapman swallowed a bite of bacon. "So you're really just giving up?" she said. "Doesn't sound like the John Carr I've heard about."

"I'm getting a little tired of people throwing the name 'John Carr' around like I'm supposed to suddenly put on a cape and solve the world's problems. In case you hadn't noticed, that was a long time ago and I have enough of my own problems to deal with."

Chapman abruptly stood. "Well excuse me. I thought you still gave a shit."

Stone clamped a hand around her wrist and pulled her back down into her seat.

"I'll give you a fight if that's what you want," she snapped.

"What I want is a little bit of reason and logic."

"Hey, buddy!"

Stone turned to see a large, broad-shouldered man standing next to the table. The man said, "If I were you I'd leave the lady alone." He put a hand on Stone's shoulder.

Chapman glanced quickly at Stone and saw the look in his eye and then watched as his arms tensed to strike.

"It's okay." She opened her jacket to show her gun and then held up her badge. "We were just arguing over who was going to pay the check. But thanks for coming to a lady's aid, love."

"You sure?" said the man.

Stone ripped the man's hand off his shoulder. "Yeah, she's sure, *love*."

They finished their meal and drove back to Stone's cottage. Stone made no move to get out of the car. Chapman glanced over at him but kept silent.

"Thanks for breakfast," he said.

"You're welcome."

A chunk of silence passed as the darkest part of the night drifted past them and the edge of the sky began to lighten.

"I don't like being beaten," Stone said.

"I can understand that. Neither do I. That's why when I start something I want to finish it. I'm sure you feel that way too."

"I didn't have much choice about starting this case."

"What do you mean?"

"Nothing."

"Tell me, Oliver."

"It's complicated."

"It's always bloody complicated."

Stone glanced out the window as though he expected to see someone watching. "It was my penance, I guess."

"Penance? I take it other people suffered because of something you did?"

"I sincerely hope so," Stone said.

"And now that the mission went to hell?"

"I don't know, Mary. I really don't know what that means for me."

"So go out on your terms."

He looked at her. "How?"

"Let's finish the bloody case, that's how."

"I'm not sure where to start."

"Usually at the beginning is a good spot."

"We tried that."

"So they expect us to go left, we go right."

"We did that last time and look what happened."

"So we just go right a little bit harder and farther," she said. "Any ideas on that?"

Stone thought for a minute or two while Chapman continued to watch him. "Not really, no."

"Well, I've got one," she said. "Tom Gross."

"The dead can't talk."

"Not what I mean."

"What, then?"

"Remember when we were sitting in that coffee shop and he told us about being watched?"

"Yes, so?"

"So he told us something. He said there was only one person he trusted."

It only took Stone a couple of seconds to recall this. "His wife," he said.

"So I wonder if he trusted her enough to tell her something that could help us?"

"There's only one way to find out."

"So you're back on the hunt?"

He took a few moments to answer. "Unofficially. Which is actually right where I belong."

CHAPTER

80

CHAPMAN PHONED THE BEREAVED ALICE GROSS at 9 a.m. that morning and asked to see her. Stone and Chapman arrived at the modest two-story house in Centreville, Virginia, early in the afternoon. Alice Gross certainly looked like a woman who'd just lost her husband. Her skin was naturally pale but with a gray pallor lurking just below the surface. Her eyes were red, her hair in disarray. She held a crumpled tissue in one hand and a bottle of water in the other as she led them into her small living room.

Stone saw a coloring book on the coffee table, a baseball bat and some cleats in one corner. When his gaze lighted on a photo of the Gross family showing the dead agent with his wife and four kids ranging in age from three to fourteen, Stone grimaced and quickly looked away. He glanced at Chapman and saw that she'd had the same reaction.

They sat on the couch while Alice Gross took a chair opposite.

Stone said, "Your husband was a terrific agent, Mrs. Gross. We all feel his loss."

"Thank you. You know they're holding a memorial service for Tom?"

"Yes, we heard about that. He certainly deserves it."

"He'd be embarrassed about it, though. He never liked to draw attention to himself. Just wasn't his way. He just did his job. Didn't care who ended up getting the credit."

Stone had been concerned that Alice Gross had been briefed by the FBI on the exact circumstances of her husband's death. And the role Stone had played in it. But apparently they hadn't done that.

"We're doing all we can to catch the people responsible," added Chapman.

"I appreciate that," sniffled Gross. "He really did care about his job. He worked such long hours."

Stone said, "He told me that he'd had some concerns, about people watching him."

Gross nodded. "His own people. They asked me about that, the Bureau I mean."

"And what did you tell them?" asked Stone.

Gross looked confused. "Aren't you with the Bureau?"

Stone hesitated. "We're working with them."

Chapman said quickly, "I'm actually with MI6. Your husband might've mentioned that."

"Oh yes, that's right. You're the Englishwoman. Tom talked about you. He thought you were very good."

"I appreciate that."

Gross drew a short breath. "Well, the Bureau was very upset about that. I mean about Tom believing his own people were spying on him. I don't think they believed it."

"Did you believe it?" asked Stone.

"Tom believed it and that was good enough for me," she said staunchly.

"Brilliant," said Chapman. "I think you're spot-on with that."

Stone leaned forward. "Tom told us something. Something about you."

"About me?" she said in surprise.

"Yes. He said the only person he trusted was you."

Tears crept into Alice Gross's eyes. She lifted the tissue up and wiped them away. "We were always so close. He loved being an FBI agent but he loved me more. I know he wasn't supposed to really talk to me about his cases, but he did, and I would give him my opinion. And sometimes I'd turn out to be right."

"I'm sure you were a great asset to him," said Chapman.

Stone said, "Since we know he trusted you, did he happen to mention anything to you about this case? Something he was concerned about? Anything you can remember?"

Gross put her hands in her lap and furrowed her brow. "I can't recall anything specific other than thinking someone was watching him."

"Nothing?" prompted Chapman. "It might have seemed insignificant at the time, but anything you can remember? No matter how seemingly trivial?"

Gross shook her head but then stopped. She looked up. "He did say something one night."

Stone and Chapman leaned forward.

"Yes?" said Stone.

"That ATF agent that was working with him?"

"Stephen Garchik?" replied Stone.

"Right."

"What did he say about him?" asked Chapman.

"Well, it was late and we were getting ready to go to bed. He was brushing his teeth and he came out of the bathroom and said that he needed to check on something that Garchik had told him."

"Did he say what it was?"

Gross half closed her eyes, obviously struggling to remember. "Just something he had said about the bomb, what it was made of."

Chapman and Stone looked at each other.

Gross continued, "And he also wanted to check out something to do with that nano business."

Stone looked surprised. "He told you about the nanobots?"

"Well, he tried to, but I didn't really understand any of it."

"Did he think there was a connection between what he wanted to talk to Garchik about and the nanobots?" asked Chapman.

"He didn't say. Just that he needed to check those two things out. That it might be important. Because of something he remembered. Only he didn't tell me what."

"Something he remembered?" mused Stone. "Do you know if he followed up on it?"

"I doubt it."

"Why?"

Her eyes filled with tears. "Because he was killed the next day."

CHAPTER

81

"So how do we get to Garchik?" asked Chapman as they drove away from Gross's house. "We're not official anymore. I'm supposed to be on my way to London and you..."

"Right," said Stone. "Me." He pulled out his phone. "Well, I can always try calling him." He hit the numbers.

Chapman said, "If they have him stashed somewhere he might not answer. Especially if they've told him what happened. We could be off-limits."

A voice came on Stone's phone.

"Hello, Steve, Agent Stone here. Right. I know you disappeared right off the case. We were worried about you until we got the heads-up." Stone paused as Garchik said something.

"Well, we'd like to meet with you, if that's okay."

Garchik said something else.

"I understand, but if I could just ask you about something Agent Gross was—"

Chapman cut the car to the right and nearly slammed into the curb. Stone was jerked sideways in his seat and his head would have hit the window glass if it hadn't already been down.

Stone looked in front and behind at the vehicles that had boxed them in. The men were already out of their SUVs and striding toward them.

Not again.

One of the men passed a paper through the window and into Stone's hands.

"What's this?" Stone asked in surprise.

"Congressional subpoena. Courtesy of Director Weaver. And if you're really smart, you'll never go near Tom Gross's family again."

A few seconds later the men were gone.

Stone looked down at the subpoena. He heard chatter. He realized he'd dropped his phone on the car's floor and snatched it up.

"Steve? Right, sorry about that. Little problem on our end. Look, can you— Hello? Hello?"

Stone clicked off. "Line went dead."

Chapman put the car in gear again. "Weaver's people must've gotten to him too."

"Must've."

"Now we can't find out what Garchik told Gross."

"What if what he told Gross is something he told us too? As far as I know we were with him pretty much every time he spoke to Garchik."

"I can't remember anything critical off the top of my head." She glanced at the paper. "When do you have to appear?"

Stone read through the document. "Tomorrow. Before the House subcommittee on intelligence."

"Not a lot of notice. Can they do that?"

Stone read over the document some more. "National security apparently trumps even due process."

"Lucky you."

"Yeah," Stone said dryly. "Lucky me."

"Do you need a solicitor?"

"Probably, but I can't afford one."

"Want me to see what Sir James can do?"

"I think Sir James is pretty much done with me."

"I think he's pretty much done with me too. So is there a silver lining here somewhere?"

"We have to start from square one. Go over everything."

"Well, I've got extensive notes and the video of the park on my laptop still. And before we fell out of favor Agent Ashburn provided me with electronic files for a lot of the other video feeds."

"Let's go."

They drove to her hotel and set up a mini command center. For the next several hours they pored over the notes of the case and the video feeds from Chapman's laptop.

"Well, one thing's figured out," said Stone as he stared at the screen.

Chapman joined him. "What?"

"The homeless woman who poured the bottle of water on the tree and killed it?" He pointed at the screen showing the image.

"What about it? That's one of the few things we can be reasonably sure about."

Stone hit some keys and zoomed in on the image of the woman. "I was puzzled that they'd bring someone in for such a minimal task."

"It wasn't minimal," Chapman pointed out. "It was the catalyst that set everything else in motion."

"I wasn't talking about poisoning the tree. I meant Judy Donohue. Why bring her in just to lie about Sykes and increase our suspicion of him? They could've come at it some other way. Now I know."

"I'm not following."

"Look at the back of the woman's hand."

Chapman hit some keys and zoomed into the image even more.

"Her hand is pretty dirty, but if you look at the bottom right."

Chapman gasped. "That's a bird's foot. The tattoo Donohue had on her hand. What was it? The western meadowlark. *She* was the homeless woman in disguise."

"They used her for that and then got her to try and implicate Sykes. I don't think her bosses cared whether she succeeded or not. Sykes was a dead man, and they always intended to kill her too."

Chapman sat back down and went over some notes. "You know, Garchik said that bombers like to do trial runs to make sure their equipment is working properly."

"But usually they'll do it in someplace inconspicuous. At least to the extent you can be inconspicuous when you're setting off a bomb."

"And Lafayette Park is hardly inconspicuous. Which means it wasn't a trial run. It was the mission, albeit part of a larger one."

Stone looked thoughtful. "Right. The bombing at Lafayette had to take place in order for some other event to occur."

"We have that list of upcoming events at the park."

"I don't think the answer lies there."

"I agree," said Chapman. "The bad guys won't know where the event is going to be, or if the event will even be held."

"Right."

She said, "The nanobot thing that has everyone's knickers in a knot. They occur at the molecular level, which means they can get into anything."

"And they apparently can be manufactured into just about any bio- or chemical contagion. Synthetic plague or anthrax or ricin maybe. In large quantities."

"But again, you load all that into a root ball in a tree across from the bloody White House with a bomb attached and you don't put the plague or another deadly microbe on it? Makes no sense."

"It's never made any sense," agreed Stone. "At least it doesn't the way we've been looking at it."

Chapman perked up. "Maybe we go back to where it all started."

"You mean Lafayette Park?"

"Let's call it for what it is. Hell's Corner. In fact, I can't think of it any other way now. Might've known."

"What do you mean?"

"It's named after a bloody Frenchman," snapped Chapman.

CHAPTER

82

They walked over every inch of the park for several hours. Stone and Chapman tried to look at things in a new light, but it always resulted in old conclusions. Old and wrong conclusions. Stone was actually a little surprised that no one came over and asked what they were doing here, or else simply escorted them out of the park. But apparently Riley Weaver could not be burdened with such insignificant details. Stone figured he was probably right now at NIC headquarters going over with his own legal staff and that of the congressional committee members how best to crucify him.

Stone paced the park again and again, looking at things from every angle he could think of. Chapman was doing the same thing on the other side of the park. They had passed each other several times during this exercise. At first their expressions had been hopeful, but now—now there was no hope left in either of their faces.

Stone looked at the government building where the shots had come from. And then at the Hay-Adams Hotel from where they had been meant to believe the shots had come. Then he looked at the places where the four people in the park had been that night. In his mind's eye he walked or in some instances ran them through their paces. Friedman and Turkekul sitting and standing respectively, and then walking away. Padilla running for his life. The British security guard shadowing Stone and ending up losing a tooth. The explosion. Stone being blown off his feet. Now Turkekul and Padilla were dead. Friedman was disgraced and unemployed. The British agent had long since gone home. He had never even known the man's name. He probably should have questioned the fellow directly, but what could he really have added to the account?

He stopped a short distance from Marisa Friedman's office, or former office, in Jackson Place. Staring at the front of the old town house, Stone recalled his last encounter there with her. It could have gone very differently if he'd been willing. And right now he was wondering why he hadn't been . . . willing.

"Got something?"

He turned to see Chapman staring at him. She looked over at the building and then at him.

"Friedman's career in the intelligence field is over," he said. "Thanks to me."

"She's a big girl. Nobody made her agree to go along."

"She actually didn't have much of a choice."

"Everyone has choices. You make them and then you live with the consequences." She paused. "Do you plan to see her again?"

Stone shot her a glance. "What do you mean?"

"The last time we were together with her. It doesn't take a genius to see."

"To see what?"

She turned away, directing her attention to the hole in the ground where the bomb had gone off, starting their collective nightmare.

"I don't plan on seeing her again, no," said Stone. He seemed surprised by this sudden decision.

Where did that come from? Instinct?

Chapman turned back around. "I think that's wise."

As it started to get dark Stone and Chapman drove back to his cottage. They sat in the car by the wrought-iron gates for a few minutes.

"I'll come with you tomorrow," she said. "If just for moral support."

"No," Stone said decisively. "That would not be good for your career."

"What career?"

He looked at her. "What do you mean?"

"Friedman wasn't the only one who lost her professional ride. I got a notice from the Home Office yesterday. I'm basically being ordered to resign from MI6."

Stone looked anguished. "I'm sorry, Mary."

She shrugged. "Probably time to try something else. After this cock-up I figure things can only go up."

"Can't McElroy help you?"

"No. He's taken his lumps too over this. It's out of his hands." She looked around. "I no longer have access to the British embassy. And my credit card has been revoked. I've got passage back on an American military plane leaving for London tomorrow night."

"I would advise you to be on it."

She looked up at the cottage. "Mind if I crash at your place for tonight?"

"All right," said Stone.

"And shouldn't you prepare for the hearing tomorrow?" she asked. "I can help."

"I just plan on telling the truth. If I try and prepare, it'll just make things more complicated."

"They're going to come after you with everything they have."

"I know."

"You think you'll come out okay?"

"I doubt it."

They rose the next morning early and took turns showering. Stone put on his only suit. Then they had breakfast at the same outlet servicing the construction workers. Stone threw away his meal wrapper, finished off his coffee and checked his watch.

"It's time," he said.

"I'm coming," replied Chapman.

"You're not on the subpoena. They won't let you in."

"Then I'll wait outside."

"You don't have to do this."

"Yes I do, Oliver. I really do."

The interrogation was to be conducted in the secure hearing room of the House Permanent Select Committee on Intelligence. It was in an underground room beneath the U.S. Capitol's Rotunda, and accessed by a secret elevator. They grabbed a cab and then got out and made their way toward the main entrance.

"Did you get any sleep?" she asked.

"I actually slept remarkably well. I'm getting used to my desk chair."

"I didn't."

"My cot is an acquired taste, I'm afraid."

"Yeah, next time I try it, I'll have to be drunk. Slept like a baby that time. Do you know what you're going to say?"

"I told you, the truth."

"But you need some plan. Some strategy. And not just the bloody truth. Lawyers can twist that all around."

"What do you suggest?"

"That you were doing your best. You took a calculated risk based on conditions on the ground. A dozen people had died. The investigation was getting nowhere. You had to try something. The FBI and MI6 signed off on it. The only one whose feelings are hurt is Riley Weaver. And he had produced exactly nothing on the case. And they asked you to come back to work for them. You were doing the best you could under difficult circumstances. And before the hearing even starts I'd pull the government lawyer aside and mention that there are lots of things you can tell the committee that Weaver won't want them to hear."

"Such as?"

"Such as NIC withholding critical evidence from the FBI on an international terrorism case? Remember the video from the park? And it also wouldn't hurt to remind him that your president was, or maybe still is, on your side."

"So the reason you didn't get any sleep last night was because you were up thinking about all this?"

"I didn't want you to go in there and get ambushed. You don't deserve that."

"Thank you. I think I'll take your advice."

Chapman noted all the uniformed security. "Pretty tight around here."

"Well, this area is on every terrorist's wish list."

They were walking up the steps leading into the building when a uniformed guard strolled by with his black Lab bomb detection canine. The dog sniffed around Stone's and Chapman's ankles and then proceeded on.

"At least that's one sure thing in an uncertain world," remarked Stone.

"Right. What did Garchik say? The dogs can detect nineteen thousand types of explosive material?"

"And also that there's not even a machine sophisticated enough to measure how powerful a dog's nose is. If I—"

Stone froze.

Chapman looked at him. She was holding open the door for him. "You okay?"

Stone didn't answer. He turned and ran in the other direction.

Chapman called after him, "What the hell are you doing?"

She let go of the door and ran after him. The police frowned on sudden movement at this location. And people running away were even more frowned on. However, Stone was across the street with Chapman right on his heels before any of the uniforms could react.

She caught up to him and grabbed his arm. "I didn't figure you to chicken out on your hearing. Better to just get it over with."

"It's not the hearing, Mary."

"What then."

"It's the dogs."

"What about them?"

Stone started to sprint. She ran after him.

"Where are we going?"

"To where it all began."

"We already did that."

"It'll be different this time, trust me."

CHAPTER

83

STONE CLOSED HIS EYES and sent his mind back to that night. For the second time in twenty-four hours he assembled the pieces in his head, but this time the images were even more vivid. He realized clearly this would be his last chance.

First up, Friedman on the bench. Dozing and then chatting with her fake lover on the phone. Then Alfredo Padilla in his jogging suit and iPod walking into the park from the northeast. Next, there was Fuat Turkekul lurking on the northwest side of the park examining a statue and actually waiting to meet with Friedman. Finally Stone recalled his exact steps in the park. Hearing the motorcade coming, starting to walk through the park, looking at the other people there.

The British security agent in the cammie jacket and seemingly walking in quicksand. He was behind Stone when the gunfire started. Now Stone opened his eyes and stared north, toward the Hay-Adams Hotel and then beyond it. Up floor after floor until his gaze reached the location of the shooters. U.S. government building. Didn't know how they got in, but they did. They wanted Stone to stumble on things that appeared to be the truth, yet weren't. But they hadn't wanted him to find the U.S. government building connection. He'd unconsciously gone right instead of the left they had expected. That was why an attempt had been made to kill him and Chapman soon afterward.

Which also meant they were always watching.

Now Stone closed his eyes again and envisioned the first bullet hitting several feet to his left. Then more rounds pounding the dirt. Pings and zings everywhere. He'd dropped to his belly. The Brit behind him had done the same. Friedman and Turkekul were already gone from the park. Padilla began the slow zigzag run for his life and ended up in the tree hole.

Boom.

Stone opened his eyes again and looked over at Chapman, who'd been standing there staring at him the whole time, her arms folded over her chest.

"Can they arrest you for not showing up for the hearing?" she asked.

"Probably," said Stone in a clearly uninterested tone. "All the shots were on the western side of the park," he said.

"Right, you mentioned that all the white tents were on the left side but didn't explain what you meant by it."

"That's because I didn't know what it meant. But why? Why were all the shots on that side?"

In response Chapman pointed to the government building. "Just the location of the shooter. It was a clear field of fire from there. They could see over the trees."

"They could see over the trees on the right side too. They could fire through the tree canopy for that matter. Why did they need a clear field of fire? They obviously weren't aiming at anyone."

Chapman started to say something and then stopped.

"But that's not the most important question," he said.

"Okay, what is the most important question?" she asked.

"What was the test?"

She looked confused. "What test?"

"I think I know what Tom Gross was going to ask Steve Garchik. Garchik said bombers like to test their equipment, to make sure it works. I think

Lafayette Park was the test. But what was tested? We originally thought the bomb was meant for another time, another event, but was accidentally triggered. Then we thought it might have been a test run. But those two hypotheses are incompatible. It's either one or the other. Not both."

Chapman started to say something again, but once more stopped.

"A test run? Like Garchik said, the bomb part always works. It's the connections that fail. But would you risk detonating in Lafayette Park just to test your connections?"

"No," said Chapman automatically. "They went to way too much trouble."

"That's right, way too much trouble."

"So what then? You mentioned it was about the dogs. I'm assuming you meant the bomb sniffers."

"I did. Where's your laptop?"

Chapman pulled open her bag and slid it out. They walked over to a bench and sat down.

"Bring up the video from the night of the bombing," he instructed.

She did so.

"Run the feed that happened before the gunfire started."

Chapman pushed some keys and brought that image up.

"Hold it right there."

She hit the pause button.

Stone rose and pointed to the northeast corner of the park. "Padilla entered the park at that spot."

Chapman glanced down at the screen and then at where he was pointing. "That's right."

"Why that spot?"

"Why not that spot?"

"There are lots of places to enter the park. Remember Carmen Escalante said that her uncle was going to eat at a favorite restaurant on Sixteenth Street. That's on the west side of the White House, not the east. If he were walking from Sixteenth Street he would have reached the west side of the park first, not the east. So why did he come in on the east side?"

"Maybe he went somewhere else. We never followed up on the restaurant where he actually ate. Or maybe he did eat there and then went somewhere else for a drink that was on the east side of the park."

"Or maybe," said Stone as he pointed at the screen. "Or maybe he had to enter the park on the east side because of that."

Chapman looked where his finger was. "Because that's where the police were stationed, you mean?"

"No, because that's where the bomb dog was stationed. Run the video."

Chapman hit the play button. Padilla walked within a foot of the dog. In fact it seemed as though he went out of his way to walk near the dog.

"But why would that matter? The dog didn't do anything."

"You're a Brit. Ever read the Sherlock Holmes story entitled 'Silver Blaze'?"

"Sorry, never got around to those."

"Well, in that story Holmes was able to make much of the fact of the curious incident of the dog in the nighttime."

"Why, what did the dog do?"

"Absolutely nothing. And as Holmes pointed out, *that* was the curious incident."

"You're only making me more confused."

"The test, Mary, was to walk past that dog and not have it react. To have it do nothing, in fact."

It took a moment, but the look on Chapman's face turned to astonishment. "Are you saying that the bomb was on Padilla and not in the root ball?"

"Yes. A couple of pounds of Semtex would've caused the damage that occurred. He could've easily had that on his person."

"But the leather bits from the basketball?"

"There was never any basketball. He had the leather bits already in his pocket. The tree farm, George Sykes, the hoop, John Kravitz—all were misdirection." He added, "Carefully researched misdirection. When they discovered the tree was coming from Pennsylvania they also learned of Kravitz's shady past." He looked to the office building where the shots had come from. "And that explains why the gunfire was only on the west side. They couldn't chance hitting Padilla. If the dog were on the right side, Padilla would have walked past it and then made his way to the east side. Because that's where the hole was. Which was the other critical piece."

"Are you saying he threw himself in that hole and then blew himself up?"

"The only plausible reason for him to run and throw himself in the hole in the first place was because it seemed that he was running for his life. The hole was in essence his foxhole. The gunfire was the catalyst. He would have no other reason to do it. That was why they needed to have the gunfire. To give him a reason to run and jump in that hole. Otherwise, if he simply detonated aboveground, we would all know the source of the explosive. Diving in the tree hole made us all look at the maple as being the source. Donohue told them when the hole would be covered. They had that one night to do it. Then we discovered all the planted evidence."

"But hang on. Garchik said that dogs could

never be fooled. How could Padilla get past that dog with a bomb on his person?"

"Garchik already told us. That was probably the other thing Gross wanted to ask him. What did Garchik tell us about smells?"

"That you couldn't cover them up from a dog."

"And he also said that smells were *molecular*. That's the reason nothing can contain them. That's why dogs can sniff out things locked in steel containers, covered in smelly fish and wrapped in miles of plastic."

"Right."

"And what did we learn about nanobots?"

"That they're nasty buggers." She paused, her jaw slowly descending. "And that they're molecular too."

"Exactly. They're *molecular* too."

"Are you saying that they used the nanobots to create a new type of explosive? The nineteen thousandth and first, if you will?"

"No. The ATF apparently found the usual type of explosive debris. Nothing revolutionary at all, which makes the whole thing even more brilliant. They used the nanobots to molecularly change the smell that traditional explosive materials give off. They would still make the thing go boom, but they wouldn't smell like anything the dogs have been trained to ferret out. That's how Padilla got past the dog. *That* was the test. Get past the dog's nose with a bomb strapped right on your person. And they did it."

"But why would he do it? He's not Russian. He's from Mexico."

"Mary, where was all the evidence we found pointing to the Russians?"

"The gun and the funny language being spoken. And—" She stopped. "It was all fabricated. To make it look like the Russians were involved."

"Yes."

"But he blew himself up. Why? What reason would he have? You said it yourself. They penetrated the most guarded space on earth, for no reason."

"No, they did it for a reason. A very good one. Let's go."

"Where?"

"To see Carmen Escalante. And let's get there before they kill her too."

CHAPTER

84

No one answered the knocks at Carmen Escalante's home. Chapman backed away from the front door and eyed the windows. "Do you think she's gone for good? Or someone's taken her?"

Stone peered through the window on the left side of the door. "The place still looks lived in. She might have just gone somewhere."

"So Padilla blew himself up. Why?"

"That's why I'm here. To ask Carmen if she might know why."

"So you think she's in on it?"

Stone didn't answer right away, principally because he didn't know how to answer. "I don't think so, but there's no guarantee."

"But if she's not in on it she won't be able to help us."

"Not necessarily."

Stone moved around to the rear of the house and Chapman followed.

"What do you mean?" she asked.

"Now we know or at least strongly suspect Padilla was the bomber. We can ask her questions we couldn't before. If she's involved, we'll know pretty quickly. Then we can take her into custody and question her officially. If she's not involved she may be able to tell us something helpful. Something her uncle mentioned. Something she overheard. Visitors he might have had here."

Stone tried the back door but it was locked.

Chapman put her face to the rear window and looked inside. "Nothing. But she could be lying dead and out of sight. Do we break in?"

Stone already had two slender instruments out of his pocket. "It's a deadbolt. It'll take a little time."

Chapman put her elbow through the glass, reached through the broken pane and turned the lock. "My way's quicker."

Stone slowly put away his lock-pick tools. "You break and enter a lot in your line of work?"

"Only when I'm bored."

They passed through the door and into the small kitchen.

"Food in the fridge and dirty plates in the sink," said Chapman as she looked around.

Stone looked at the dried food. "Breakfast, probably from today."

Guns out, they moved into the hall and quickly searched the main level.

"Okay, no bodies on this floor," said Chapman. "Let's try upstairs."

A two-minute search there turned up nothing.

Chapman flicked through the clothes in the young woman's closet. "Some nice things in here. Maybe she got paid off. That story about donations might have been bullshit."

Stone pointed to the set of braces in the corner. "How can she walk without those?"

Chapman examined them. "These are her old ones. Remember she said she was getting a new pair?"

Stone looked around the room. "Okay, Padilla was involved. We have the Latinos in Pennsylvania involved."

"And they're dead too. Whoever their employer is, he's not too loyal."

"Or he simply demands the ultimate sacrifice from his people," replied Stone.

They went back downstairs.

"Do we wait for her to come back?" asked Chapman.

Stone shook his head. "I've got a feeling this

place is being watched. So they know we're interested in her again."

"So you're saying we might have just signed her death warrant, you mean?"

"If we could only find out where she's gone."

They went out the back door and walked around to the front. Stone looked up and down the street.

Chapman said, "It seems this might be a neighborhood where some nice old lady might be peering out her window to see what's going on."

"Good idea. You take this side of the street and I'll take the other."

At the fourth house Chapman tried, a tiny black woman in her seventies with white hair answered the door.

"Saw you poking around. About to call the police but then it struck me you might *be* the police," she said matter-of-factly. "Not too many folks look like you wandering around here."

Chapman showed her badge and called Stone over.

"This is my partner," she told the older woman. "We're trying to find out where Carmen Escalante is. She's the woman with the braces whose uncle—"

The woman cut her off. "I watch the news. I've seen Carmen around. But she's not home now."

"Any idea where she might be?" asked Stone.

"Left around nine this morning," said the woman. "They come for her in the big black truck."

Stone and Chapman exchanged glances. "Who came for her?" asked Chapman.

"Government folks. You know, in suits and such. With sunglasses. She's got some memorial service to go to today." She paused and eyed them suspiciously. "Don't you two watch the news?"

Stone said, "Do you know where the memorial service is being held?"

"You don't know that, maybe you ain't the police."

"We *are* the police," insisted Stone. "Do you know where the memorial service is being held?" he asked again, in a more urgent tone.

"Why don't you just call into headquarters or some such and find out?"

She closed the door in their faces.

Stone pulled out his phone as they hustled back to the car.

"Oliver, what is going on?"

"We talked about how the bomb going off would cause events to be moved elsewhere, away from the park."

"Right, but that got us nowhere."

"That's because it's not an event that was *scheduled* that they're going to hit."

Chapman sucked in a breath and said, "They *created* the event that they're going to hit. The bombing led to the memorial service."

"With the U.S. president and the president of Mexico in attendance."

As Chapman drove Stone called everyone he could think of.

"No one's answering."

"Caller ID. They know it's you and aren't picking up. Should we just call the police?"

"And tell them what? 'I'm Oliver Stone. I used to work for the government before I got sacked for screwing up'? 'There's a bomb at the memorial service. Go get it'? They'll hang up on me before I even finish."

They stopped at a traffic light and Chapman glanced to her left. "Look," she exclaimed.

They were next to a bar. Through the window there was visible a TV hanging from the ceiling. It was turned to a news channel. And on the screen was the memorial service being broadcast live. Stone read the scroll line at the bottom.

"It's at Arlington National Cemetery."

"Point the way."

"Wait a minute!" Stone snapped. He was staring at the TV screen as the camera panned the area.

"That's Alex," he exclaimed.

Chapman turned to look. Sure enough, there was Alex Ford at the ceremony, obviously on protection duty for the president.

"Hold on," said Chapman. "Even if you get through to him, you don't know where the bomb is located."

"I think I do know."

Chapman punched the gas while Stone fingered in the number, praying that his friend would answer.

CHAPTER

85

ALEX FORD STOICALLY SURVEYED the surroundings even as he felt the buzzing in his pocket. He ignored it. No calls or emails on protection duty. They set the ringer to vibrate when around the president. And the texting function had been taken away from their phones altogether. He should have just turned his phone off. He eyed the guests coming through the magnetometer. But before they got there they had to pass through a series of checkpoints and bomb-scanning machines. His gaze swiveled to the bomb detection canines that were examining every person coming to the event. After the explosion in Lafayette Park, the dogs were everywhere and constituted their best line of defense because they were mobile.

His phone buzzed again. He ignored it again. If his boss saw him on the phone when he was supposed to have eyes on possible threats it would not be a pleasant day for him. In fact it would probably be his last day on protection detail.

He eyed the president as he took his seat in the front row. The Mexican president sat down on his left. There were two chairs in between the leaders. Alex watched as Carmen Escalante was escorted down the aisle, her new braces making virtually no noise when they plunked against the soft earth. Alice Gross, dressed all in black with a veil covering her face, walked behind Escalante. Gross's four children were sitting in the row immediately behind the U.S. president.

The two presidents rose as Escalante and Gross came down the row. Each man spoke a few words of condolence to the women and then everyone took their seats.

Alex said a small curse as his phone buzzed yet again. He could tell by the tone that this time an email had been posted to his account. He looked around, spotting each member of the protection detail. They were just like him. Impassive features, shades, ear buds, rigid, hands in front, staring, sweeping, trying to ferret out even the possibility of a threat before it could turn into something else, like a bullet or a bomb.

His phone buzzed again. He cursed again, a bit

more audibly. He looked around. He could manage it, if he took his time. He edged his hand in his pants pocket, slid the phone slowly upward until just the screen appeared. He thumbed his email icon.

"Great," he muttered when he saw two new ones, delivered less than a minute apart. Then he saw whom the messages were from.

Oliver Stone.

He glanced up, to make sure no one was watching him. He looked down again, pushed a couple of buttons. He edged the phone out a little more. He was able to see the screen. The messages popped up. They were each the same. By the time he finished reading one of them the blood had drained from his face and he felt queasy. His fingers hit two keys, o and k. He hit the send key and let the phone fall back in his pocket.

He took a long breath as his gaze slid back to the president, the man he was sworn to protect. He had taken an oath, just like all Secret Service agents, that he would sacrifice his life for this man. A bead of sweat appeared on his forehead and slid down his face.

If his friend was wrong? If he acted and it turned out to be a mistake? His career was probably over. Not because Alex had tried to protect the president.

But because he had acted on the intelligence provided by a now disgraced field agent.

Yet sometimes, Alex concluded, you just had to trust your friends. And he did trust Oliver Stone, like he did no one else.

He spoke into his radio, relaying word for word what he had just learned, leaving out only the source. Then he added the warning that Stone had provided in his text. "It's probable that it will be a remote detonation. Any sudden moves on our part and the bomb goes off. We need a distraction or some cover to do this. Otherwise we have no chance to pull this off."

His supervisor's voice came through his ear bud. "Ford, are you damn sure about this?"

Alex's gut clenched as he replied, "Even if I were half sure, we can't take a risk, sir, can we?"

He heard the man let out a long, tortured breath. He was no doubt doing what Alex had just done, namely contemplate what this might do to his career if it turned out to be wrong.

"God help us all, Ford."

"Yes sir."

One minute later the plan was sent across the secure line to every agent. Alex checked his watch. Sixty seconds. He did his best to look calm and professional. Whoever was behind this could easily see where all the agents were. Any hint of something wrong and the bomb could go off.

Since this had all been at Alex's initiation he had been given the honor of performing the ultimate task. He steeled himself. A routine protection detail had just turned into something else—something all agents had to prepare for and hoped with all their hearts they would never have to face.

Alex counted down the seconds, his gaze moving across the rows of guests, but always flitting back to the president. At the thirty-second mark in the one-minute countdown he started to move. He made his way down the side of the seating areas, as though he were simply doing a perimeter patrol. To his left a pair of agents walked down the other aisle. The plan had been put together on the fly, of course, and they all had to hope it was good enough. Alex eyed the large crypt immediately behind the temporary stage set up for the ceremony. He took another quick breath, trying to keep the adrenaline from ruining his motor skills.

Twenty-second mark.

Alex picked up his pace. He was nearing the row where the president was sitting, but his eyes weren't on the man. They were on someone else.

At the ten-second mark it happened.

With a yell, a woman who had been walking

down the aisle to her seat clutched her chest and fell to the ground. A crush of people immediately surrounded her. The spot of her collapse had been carefully planned. She was in fact a Secret Service agent held in reserve who had been hustled into duty just so she could collapse on cue right next to the president's row.

The crowd of people gathered around her allowed the inner core protection detail to build a wall around the president, which was normal procedure and would arouse no suspicion. They could do nothing if the bomber decided to detonate at this point, but they didn't have much choice. There was one gap in this wall and Alex ducked through it by prearrangement. Several agents glanced at him, their jaws locked in both concentration and concern, but Alex's focus was only on his target.

Carmen Escalante looked frightened. That was a bit reassuring to Alex. If she wasn't the bomber they might all survive. If she was the bomber she would surely detonate in the next two seconds.

Carmen screamed as he ripped the braces from her arms, but her screams were drowned by the agents yelling out instructions to each other while securing the president and the crowd reacting to this latest development.

Like a rugby player exiting a scrum, Alex

emerged from the wall of agents, the braces partly hidden under his jacket. He walked at first, and then when fairly clear of the president's immediate area he broke into a run. He bulled his way past people in his path, cleared the stage area, pulled the braces from underneath his jacket, wound up and threw them as hard as he could. His target was the area behind the large crypt, which was the best shield they had.

Without looking behind him he knew his colleagues were carrying the president as fast as possible in the opposite direction, running over people if necessary.

Unfortunately, the braces never reached the area behind the crypt. The concussive force of the bomb detonating in midair was enough to collapse the stage. Smoke, dirt and flames hurtled outward from the bomb seat, engulfing the first few rows of seats, which by that time had been emptied. People screamed and ran as debris rained down.

The president was already in his limo and the motorcade had screeched off down the asphalt road out of the cemetery.

Mission accomplished. That life had not ended. Not today. Not on their watch.

Due to Alex's heroic actions, no one in the crowd was killed, though many were seriously injured.

The agents converged on the man lying near the destroyed stage. Their focus shifted to the bloodied head, the piece of granite sticking into it.

"Ambulance over here, now!" one of them screamed.

Alex Ford had done his duty.

He had saved the life of the president of the United States.

At perhaps the cost of his own.

CHAPTER

86

OLIVER STONE SAT IN THE WAITING ROOM of the hospital, the other members of the Camel Club and Mary Chapman surrounding him. No one spoke. They all just stared off, contemplating the possible loss of another friend.

Annabelle's eyes were a dull red, her face puffy and a tissue clutched in her hand. Caleb and Reuben, his arm and leg bandaged, sat huddled together, heads bowed. Harry Finn leaned against the wall next to the door. He hadn't known Alex Ford as well as the others, but he had known him well enough to be deeply distressed by what had happened to the man.

Alex was in intensive care after emergency surgery. The doctors said the head trauma had been severe, his skull fractured by the chunk of crypt blasted off by the explosion. The hemorrhaging had nearly killed him. As it was, he was now in a coma and not one of the doctors could tell them if he would ever come out of it.

Stone went to each of his friends, speaking in a low voice, offering words of comfort. When he got to Annabelle she rose and went outside. Stone started to follow her.

Chapman snagged him by the arm. "Maybe she needs some time alone."

"Right now that's the last thing she needs," he answered as he pulled the door open and left the waiting room.

He caught up to Annabelle as she reached a window and looked out at the setting sun.

"I really can't believe this, Oliver," she said in a trembling voice. "Wake me up and tell me this is not real."

"But he's still with us. He's tough. We just have to keep believing that he will come out of this."

She sat down in a chair. Stone stood next to her. When she started to cry, he handed her a wad of tissues he'd grabbed before following her.

When the sobs subsided, she looked up at him. "The doctors didn't seem very optimistic."

"Doctors never do. Their job is to dampen hopes, not heighten expectations. Then if the patient comes out of it, they look more competent than they actually are. But they don't know Alex like we do."

"He's a hero. As brave as anyone I've ever met."

"Yes," agreed Stone.

"So you emailed him? Told him about the bomb?"

Stone nodded and with each motion of his head his guilt deepened. *I emailed him. I made him confront the problem. I'm the reason he's lying in that coma.*

He sat down next to her. "I...I wasn't very forthcoming with Alex during this whole thing." He thought back to when he and Chapman were leaving Friedman's office that night. Alex had approached, obviously wanted to talk.

And I basically blew him off. And now he's lying in a coma.

While putting on a brave front to Annabelle, Stone had had a private chat with the doctors. They were not hopeful of recovery.

"Is there brain damage?" Stone had asked.

"Too early to tell," replied one of them. "We're just trying to keep him alive."

"Oliver?"

He turned to see Annabelle staring at him. "What were you thinking just now?"

"That I failed my friend. That he deserved better than me."

"If you hadn't gotten that message to him, the bomb would have gone off in the crowd. So many people would have died."

"The logical part of me realizes that." He touched his chest. "But not this part." He paused. "Milton. And now Alex. It has to stop, Annabelle. It has to."

"We all knew what we were getting into."

"No, I don't think anyone really knew. But it doesn't matter."

"I want to find who did this, Oliver. I want them to pay for what they did."

"They will, Annabelle. That I swear to you."

She glanced sharply at him. "You're going after them?"

"It'll either be me or them who walks away. I owe Alex that. I at least owe him that."

Stone looked off down the hallway. He seemed to sense it before it even happened.

Annabelle noted this. "What is it?"

"They're coming."

"Who's coming?"

He helped her to her feet and hugged her. "I promise you that I will find who did this. I promise you."

"You can't do it alone, Oliver."

"This time I have to."

When he stepped back from her there were tears in his eyes. They slid down his narrow cheeks. Annabelle looked stunned by this. She had never seen Oliver Stone cry before.

"Oliver?"

He kissed her on the forehead, turned and walked away just as the men in suits rounded the corner and headed toward him.

87

Two minutes later Stone and Chapman were in a government sedan heading downtown. From the car they were escorted to a small conference room at the FBI's WFO. Stone was not surprised to see the FBI director there or Agent Ashburn. Or even Agent Garchik and the director of ATF. But he was surprised to see Riley Weaver walk in and sit down next to the FBI chief.

"I've already given my report to Agent Ashburn," Stone said.

"I'm aware that you and Agent Ford are friends," began the director, who had clearly picked up on Stone's uncooperative tone.

"One of my *best* friends, actually," replied Stone.

Ashburn interjected, "We just need to understand this better, Agent Stone."

"I'm no longer an agent." He glanced at Riley Weaver. "My commission was taken away."

The FBI director cleared his throat. "Yes, well, that can be addressed later. Right now we need to focus on where we stand."

Stone made no move to speak. He simply stared at Weaver until the man looked so uncomfortable that he eyed the door as though he wanted to flee.

Finally Chapman said, "I'll give it a go. If I miss something I'm sure *Agent* Stone will fill it in."

Over the next twenty minutes she told them everything that had happened, from Stone's realization of the source of the bomb to their visit to Escalante's home to Stone's frantic messages to Alex Ford.

"Nifty piece of investigation and deduction, Stone," said the FBI director as Ashburn nodded in agreement. The director added, "If you hadn't acted as you did, the nation would be mourning its president. You saved his life."

"You have Alex Ford to thank for that, not me."

"We all realize that," said Weaver curtly.

Stone eyed him. "Good. I'm glad we're all on the same page there."

When the explanation turned to the nanobots being used to change the molecular makeup of the bomb's trace signature, both the ATF director and

Agent Garchik looked like they might be sick. "If that's true it changes everything," Garchik said. "Everything." He looked at his director, who was glumly nodding in agreement.

Weaver looked at the FBI director. "And we're sure this is the case?"

"Carmen Escalante passed by two bomb detection canines and a bomb scanner at the ceremony today," said Ashburn. "Neither animal nor machine reacted."

"And we checked the video feed on Padilla entering the park. Same thing. Walked within a foot of the dog and nothing," added the ATF director. "Whatever they did with this nano stuff, it worked. Altered the scent and chem footprint."

The FBI director cleared his throat again. "That will have to be dealt with, certainly. But right now we need to find out who is behind this."

Chapman said, "You've interviewed Carmen Escalante?"

"Interrogated her, more like it," replied Ashburn. "Unless she's a great actress she was a total dupe. She knew nothing of the bomb in her braces."

"Perfect place for it, actually," said the director. "Going through the magnetometer they of course caused it to go off, but they're metal. And we didn't have her put them through the X-ray because, well, it would have looked pretty callous."

"But Padilla *was* part of the bombing," said Chapman. "Even if Escalante is innocent. I can't believe the guy would show up at the park wearing a bomb, pass by the canine to see if it detected said bomb and then jump in the hole when the guns started going off. He had to know he was going to die."

"We've done a lot more digging on him," said Ashburn. "The accident on the bus that led to the deaths of Carmen's parents and her leg injuries? The bus was actually sabotaged. Now we suspect that Carmen's father used to work for one of the Mexican drug cartels. He might've wanted out. They didn't like that. So they messed with the brakes on a bus. Willing to kill a hundred people to get one."

"That explains the Latinos in Pennsylvania," said the FBI director. "This wasn't the Russians, which we were led to believe it was. It was probably the Mexican drug cartels. Or more likely Carlos Montoya wanting to get back on top."

Ashburn said, "So Montoya gets the U.S. and Mexican presidents in one shot." She looked at the director. "And you too, sir."

The director nodded. "Makes sense. We thought

Montoya was out of business or even dead. But maybe he fooled us all and was looking to make a move to get back his empire and have us blame the Russians. In the power vacuum that would inevitably come, the Mexican cartels would be back on top. And if Montoya is indeed behind this, that would mean he would be back on top too."

"So the whole piece with Fuat Turkekul was a sham?" asked Ashburn. "He wasn't a traitor?"

Chapman answered. "Probably not. It's likely he was sacrificed."

"And the tree farm, John Kravitz and George Sykes?" said the FBI director.

"All innocent and all sacrificed too," said Chapman. "To reinforce the Russian angle. But Judy Donohue was in on it. Paid off and then killed."

Garchik said, "But this technology? With the nanobots. Are you saying drug cartels have the wherewithal to do this?"

Ashburn said, "I talked to my counterpart at DEA. He gave me a down-and-dirty lesson on the current state of the drug business. Even though the Mexicans have been muscled out by the Russians, they still have billions of dollars in cash flow. And some of the best scientists in the business to do their drug lab work. And the experts they didn't have they could easily have hired or forced them to work on this. This is not just about bombs. Like my friend at the DEA said, if they can change the scent of bombs, they can change the scent of *drugs*. They can walk shit right through all our defenses. It's a whole other paradigm at that point. A game-changer. The Border Patrol, DEA and the rest of us will be defenseless."

"And why didn't we know this before?" asked Riley Weaver, speaking for the first time. "I mean about Escalante's father being in the cartel?"

Ashburn said, "Padilla wasn't a person of interest—well, at least not for very long. We all figured him for the victim not the perp, so we had no reason to dig deeper. And even this latest report coming out of Mexico is speculative. No hard proof. We can't legally demonstrate Montoya is behind this. At least not yet."

Chapman said, "So they killed Carmen's parents. Where does Padilla come in? Did he work for the cartel too?"

Ashburn responded, "Doubtful, at least from the little we know. That was another reason we didn't dig deep on Padilla. Our preliminary inquiries turned up nothing."

The director said, "He might have fled here to get Carmen away from them. The cartel might have discovered them here, though."

Ashburn added, "And maybe blackmailed Padilla to work with them. Threatened to kill Carmen if he didn't. He might not have even known he was carrying a bomb that night. Maybe he was just told when the guns started up to run and jump in the hole. The cleverest part for me is they used the deaths of Padilla and Tom Gross to their own ends, knowing that there would be a memorial service for the victims."

"Right," said Chapman. "They created the event they wanted to attack." She glanced at Stone. "He already figured that one out too."

Riley Weaver slapped his hand on the table. "Okay, that's very interesting. But we still don't know how the bomb was detonated. Or who their source was in this country. Okay, so maybe it wasn't the Russians. Maybe it is Montoya and the Mexicans. But they had to have a link here. There is no way they got all this done without a traitor in the ranks. If it wasn't Turkekul, who was it?"

Finally, Stone stirred. He looked at Weaver. "The traitor is pretty obvious at this point, don't you think, *Director*?"

He stared so hard at Weaver that the man finally turned red. "You better not be accusing me of—"

Stone broke in. "I take the simple answer when it presents itself."

"Meaning what?" asked the FBI director quietly.

"Meaning it's the only person left standing."

The others in the room looked at him curiously.

Chapman spoke up. "Okay, you lot, the man means Marisa Friedman."

The room became silent as each person stared first at Chapman and then at Stone. The FBI director and Ashburn looked to be in shock.

Riley Weaver appeared markedly pale. When Stone glanced at him, he turned sharply away. "That is preposterous," he sputtered.

Chapman said, "Remember the government building used for the sniper's nest? When Stone and I discovered that, we were very nearly killed. There were a number of red herrings they wanted us to find out, to point the finger at the Russians. But the connection to the government building was not one of them. That was the one thing they didn't want us to connect to all this. Why? Because it had to be someone who knew about that building. It had to be someone who could gain access to that building. It had to be someone on the inside."

Stone pointed at Weaver. "On your side. Someone like Friedman."

Weaver started to say something but then just sat there glaring at Stone.

"And Friedman was at the park that night. She

could have detonated the bomb using her cell phone after she left. She was on the east side of the park away from the shooters. And she could have been the one to phone Turkekul and lure him out to be shot along the GW Parkway, while she was pretending to work with us to nail him and whoever he was working with. If you recall, it was Friedman who made the initial discoveries about Turkekul, which led to all of you suspecting him of being a mole and a traitor in the first place."

"And," said Stone, looking at Weaver again, "she was dismissed by the intelligence service because of her complicity in Turkekul's death. Which gave her the perfect opportunity to retire from the field with no questions asked. She played *all* of us perfectly."

"You have no proof of that," growled Weaver.

Ashburn spoke up. "Director Weaver, have you tried to get in touch with Marisa Friedman lately?"

All gazes swiveled to the NIC chief.

He said defensively, "I had no reason to try and reach her."

"I would suggest that you now *do* have a reason," said the FBI director firmly.

Weaver slowly pulled out his phone and drilled in a number with his thick index finger. Five, ten, twenty seconds went by. He left a message for her to call him.

He put away his phone. "Okay, she didn't answer her phone. That proves nothing."

"But if I'm right," said Stone, "what do you think she's doing right now?"

"Running like hell," said Chapman.

"If you're right. And it's a big if," replied Weaver.

The FBI director said to Ashburn, "We need to find Friedman. Right now."

"Yes sir." Ashburn picked up her phone and left the room.

Weaver shook his head and looked at the FBI director. "We cannot simply accept this man's word for it. Friedman was one of the best field agents I've ever worked with."

"I think she's actually *the* best," said Stone. "The only problem is she's not working for us anymore."

"Well, if you are right then she's probably long gone," said Weaver. "She would have her exit strategy down to the last detail."

Stone turned to him. "She would, except for one little thing."

The man looked contemptuously at him. "Really? And what's that?"

"The presidents are still alive. Which means she *failed*. I doubt her employer is too happy about that. But it also gives us a shot at getting to her."

CHAPTER

88

SEVERAL HOURS LATER they had a lead on Friedman. They were all still at the WFO when Ashburn came back into the conference room waving a piece of paper.

"Visual ID on Friedman getting on a train bound for Miami from Union Station in Washington. We checked the passenger manifest. She's traveling under an alias, obviously. No Friedman on the list. Guess that confirms her complicity."

They all looked at Weaver, who sat sullen-faced in a corner of the room.

Ashburn said, "I take it she never called you back, sir?"

Weaver didn't even bother to answer.

Ashburn said, "Miami makes sense. She's presumably working for a Mexican cartel. She gets to Miami and hops on a private plane headed west to Mexico. And her taking the train was a smart move. She probably thought we'd expect her to use wings to get away fast."

Stone looked at Ashburn. "Visual ID? Did someone actually see her?"

"We have surveillance cameras set up at all the airports and train stations. We programmed her features into the loop and got a hit at Union Station."

"Did you look at the video?" he asked. "To check to make sure it was her?"

"I did. It wasn't a clear shot and she was obviously in disguise, but the computer can pick up on factors the human eye can't. And the match came back. We're going to hold the train at the next stop, go through it passenger by passenger and take her."

They all hurried out of the room. Weaver was the last to leave.

He turned to Stone. "I guess I owe you an apology."

"You don't owe me anything. It's complicated. I've been in the dark almost as long as everyone else."

"You saved the president's life." He added, "Fair winds and following seas I believe are in your future permanently."

Stone said nothing. He simply watched the man turn and go.

Chapman was eyeing him closely. "What was all that about?"

"Ancient history."

"You keep saying that."

"I keep saying it because it's true."

"Okay, you're not buying the train theory, are you?"

Stone recalled the things Marisa Friedman had said to him. They were all lies of course. But that was how spies survived.

"She said she wanted to go to a desert island," he said quietly.

Chapman perked up. "Really? When did she say that?"

"When I went to her office, to tell her I was sorry for destroying her career," he added. "She said she wanted me to go with her. That we were so much alike."

Chapman put a hand on his shoulder. "For what it's worth, I don't think you two could be more different. She's a cold-blooded, ruthless bitch just interested in the money. And you, well, you're obviously not that." She looked away, perhaps embarrassed at her words.

"A desert island," he said.

"Right, where she really wanted to go."

"She's a spy. She lies for a living."

Chapman looked at him with renewed interest. "So not a desert island then?"

"Facial recognition software," said Stone abruptly.

"I've heard the stuff is really very accurate."

"It's a machine doing it, so it's only as good as what's fed into the machine. Which makes me wonder something."

"What's that?"

"I wonder what database they used to compare the picture to?"

"You mean someone as obviously smart as Friedman would have thought of that? She would have known they'd use that measure against her?"

"And if she got into the right databases and fed slightly different parameters into them, that would register a hit on someone else that she made sure was at the train station on the way to Miami."

"And the police stop the train and search it but don't find Friedman, so that person isn't even questioned. Home free."

"Home free," said Stone.

"So where is Friedman?"

"What's the opposite of a desert island?"

"The opposite?" Chapman thought for a moment. "A place with lots of people. A big city?"

"Yes. And she didn't go south. She wouldn't go to Mexico."

"Why?"

"She failed. Why would she go running to the likes of Carlos Montoya if she didn't get the job done? He'd just put a bullet in her head."

Chapman sat back. "That's right, he would."

"So her 'double' headed south to lead us on a fruitless chase."

"Opposite of south is north. But why would she go to a big city at all?"

"Best place to hide. Yes, you have lots of cops and cameras, but she's too smart to get tripped up by that. She'll lose herself among millions of people. She'll wait to see how it falls out. Once she gets a read on that her options grow."

"So how do we catch her? We can't go running off to every big city that's north of here to look for the woman. Or maybe she's already out of the country. Maybe Canada."

"I don't think so. She runs too fast, she'll make a mistake even with a prearranged exit strategy. And remember, her exit plan was predicated on a successful ending to her mission. No, she'll take her time now."

"And if she is on the train to Miami and the Feds bust her?"

"Then more power to them. But I really don't think that's going to happen."

"Okay, but where do *we* start looking?"

"We need information."

"What sort?"

Stone thought about what Friedman had said. About the CIA keeping all the profits from her lucrative lobbying practice. That she could have retired in style if it had truly been her business. "She didn't do this for free. Which means we have to follow the money." He added cryptically, "And the muscle."

"Muscle?"

"If she has someone like Carlos Montoya after her now, she'll have a wall of pros around her. For protection. So to get to her we have to go through them."

Chapman smiled. "Now that's more my cup of tea."

CHAPTER

89

ANNABELLE SAT DOWN across from Stone at his cottage.

"They let me see him," she said, her voice barely above a whisper.

"Alex?"

She nodded as she traced her forehead with one of her fingers. "Piece of granite hit him right about here. An inch to the left it would have missed him and he wouldn't be lying in that hospital bed in a coma."

"Is his condition the same?"

"A bit worse, actually." She stifled a sob. "His vitals aren't as good today."

Stone reached across his desk and gripped her hand. "All we can do is hope and pray, Annabelle. That's all."

"He's such a good guy, Oliver. Solid as a rock.

Always there even when I acted like a bitch to him."

"We all have regrets, probably me more than anyone, when it comes to Alex." He took his hand away and sat back in his chair.

"We have to get her, Oliver," said Annabelle. Her eyes were no longer moist. She was staring earnestly at her friend.

"I know. And we will."

She pulled some pieces of paper from her bag. "After you called me with your questions about the money trail I spoke with my contact in Bermuda."

"Was he helpful?"

"You know the amount of illegal monies that are funneled around the Caribbean banks on a daily basis? Literally hundreds of billions."

"Needle in a haystack, then," said Stone doubtfully.

"It would have been except for one thing." She looked at one of the papers. "Five hundred million dollars was wired into an account one month ago at a bank in the Caymans. It just sat there with a hold on it. A little over one week ago it was released. One hour after that another five hundred million was wired to the same account. It sat there for the full week. Then it was released. But it didn't go forward into another account. It went backwards."

"Return to sender?"

"Exactly. It was rescinded."

"What day exactly?"

"The day Alex nearly died."

"When they knew Friedman had failed?"

"That's right."

"So she got half the money when certain goals were met. Probably the explosion in Lafayette, the death of Tom Gross and cleaning up the loose ends like Sykes, Donohue and the Latinos."

"What about Turkekul?" asked Annabelle.

"He's a special case. At first I just thought that she had seized an opportunity that had presented itself, but now I'm not so sure."

"I'm not getting what you mean."

"I'm not sure I do either. We'll just have to see how that plays out. Any way to see where the money went?"

She shook her head. "The cops have put pressure on Swiss banks to open up their records and they've complied. That's pushed a lot of the illegal transactions to the Caribbean. And the islanders have not been as compliant as the Swiss. We'll need some more expertise to get those answers."

"I think I might have a way to find some," said Stone.

"But Friedman has half a billion dollars at her disposal. That will fund an excellent escape plan."

"Yes, it will. But she has some problems."

"Her employer?"

"She tries to run now it puts up signals they can intercept. She may think if she bides her time they'll lose their focus on her and move on to other matters."

"But she may also be able to finger one or more of the cartels with the assassination attempts," replied Annabelle. "They aren't going to let that hang out there. Now she's become a potential witness against them."

"She's a very smart woman and she's undoubtedly thought the very same thing. All the more reason for her to take it slow. And that's only one side of the equation."

"Meaning the cops coming after her on the other end."

"Yes. I'm sure by now Friedman knows we're on to her."

As Annabelle gathered her things in preparation to leave she said, "If Alex doesn't make it, how are we going to get on without him, Oliver?"

She looked like she was going to start crying again. Stone put his arms around her, held her tightly. He let Annabelle Conroy, possibly the most gifted con artist of her generation, but a woman with a huge heart and a rock-solid understanding of loyalty, sob quietly into his shoulder.

When she was done Stone said, "We can never get on without him, Annabelle. All we can do is just survive each day as it comes. I think you and I have a better understanding of that than most people."

She nodded dumbly and then left. Stone watched her drive off and then went back inside his cottage.

Stone made a call to someone he'd only recently met, but with whom he'd formed a permanent alliance.

Joe Knox said hello on the other end of the phone.

"Joe, it's Oliver Stone."

The man's response was classic Joe Knox. "I was wondering how long it was going to take before you called me in on this. I'll be at your place in an hour."

CHAPTER

90

JOE KNOX WAS A BURLY MAN who at age fifty still had the build of the college linebacker he had once been. He and Stone had spent time in a max security prison together, without having had the benefit of a trial much less a conviction. Knox had been assigned to hunt Stone down by what turned out to be a rogue superior at the CIA. But having survived the prison ordeal largely by trusting each other, Knox and Stone had developed a strong friendship.

"I've followed it all," Knox told Stone as they sat across from each other in Stone's caretaker's cottage. "Either in the papers or else scuttlebutt, official or otherwise, at the Agency." Alex Ford had helped Knox's daughter find her father when he'd been kidnapped and slapped in that prison, and Knox had never forgotten that. The expression on the man's face clearly revealed his desire to bring in the people who'd put Alex near death.

"Let's not waste time then," replied Stone. "Which Mexican cartel has recently moved large amounts of money in the Caribbean bank chains and then rescinded a half-billon-dollar payment?"

"It's not good, Oliver."

"Carlos Montoya?"

Knox nodded. "When the Russians came in they sliced up his mother and his wife and his three kids and left them in a ditch. So no love lost there. He's based on the outskirts of Mexico City. And even though his business has shrunk by about ninety percent he still has muscle and reach all over the world."

"That's actually good for our purposes. Friedman will have to exercise maximum caution. Which will slow her escape down."

Knox thought about this. "She also has another problem."

"She needs protection."

"Obviously, but she won't get it from the Latinos. None of them will side with her against a man like Montoya. And American muscle will probably stay away from her. They don't like to get mixed up in presidential assassination attempts. The penalties are too stiff and the Feds coming after you are too many. She could go to the Eastern Europeans—the Russians don't give a damn who they take on—or else the Far East Asians maybe."

"Which means we have to find out if, say, a half dozen of them or more have slipped into the country in the last few days. Think you can find that out?"

"Even on a bad day," said Knox. He paused, studying his hands. "So what's the prognosis on Alex?"

"Not great," admitted Stone.

"He's a first-class agent and man."

"Yes," said Stone, "he is."

"Saved our butts."

"Which means we have to finish this the right way. For him."

Knox rose. "I'll have something for you within six hours."

After his friend left, Stone walked out of his cottage and strolled along the paths between the graves. He reached a bench under a sprawling oak and sat down. He had already lost one close friend. Any moment now it could become two.

He eyed one of the old tombstones. In a cemetery not too far from here Milton Farb lay under the earth. Soon Alex Ford might be occupying a similar position.

It would either be Friedman or him. Both would not survive this. Not after what the lady had done.

Either he would walk away from this. Or she would.

There was no other way it could be.

CHAPTER

91

THEY HAD SEARCHED THE WOMAN'S OFFICE and found nothing. That wasn't surprising, since she had officially been fired and had moved out of the space. But when they went through her home in Falls Church, they found nothing there either, and she clearly hadn't moved out from there. But it was certain she'd left in a hurry, her timetable no doubt disrupted by the fast-acting Secret Service after being tipped off by Stone.

Stone and Chapman looked around one more time through the three-level end-unit town home that had been built in the early 1980s and where Marisa Friedman had lived since the year 2000.

"Ashburn gave me an inventory of what they took from here and it was pretty minimal," said Stone to Chapman as the latter sat down in a chair and surveyed the room. "But there isn't one personal photo, no scrapbooks, old yearbooks, nothing to show she had a family. She's scrubbed herself clean."

"She's a spy, it obviously comes with the territory."

"Even spies have lives," Stone said firmly. "Much of their history might be invented, but they usually have some personal items around."

"What do we know about her background?" asked Chapman.

"She was born in San Francisco. Only child. Parents both deceased."

"How?"

"House fire."

"You don't think?"

"She was only four, so no, I don't think she killed them. Her parents had been wealthy, but the estate taxes took a real bite out of the money, and apparently the relatives who took her in weren't that generous. They couldn't deny she had brains, though. She went to Stanford undergrad. Harvard Law School. Then recruited by the CIA. She's been one of their top field agents for a long time. The lobbying firm façade was a brilliant one. It let her go to places all over the world collecting intel and no one gave it a second thought."

"Apparently none of your blokes gave it a second

thought that she had been turned either. Weaver looked ready to piss in his pants."

Stone looked around the modest confines of the town home. "Not exactly a mansion."

"So this is all about money, isn't it?" Chapman said derisively. "I knew I hated the witch the minute I first saw her."

"This is all about a *lot* of money," said Stone. "A billion dollars can make just about anyone do just about anything and worry about rationalizing it later."

"I can't believe you're defending her."

"The only thing I'm wondering is when I find her can I keep myself from killing her?"

"Do you mean that?"

Stone turned away from her. "There's nothing here that can help us."

"So where do you really think she is?"

"Every airport surveillance video has been reviewed. Every TSA agent questioned. Every piece of paper one needs to travel by air in this country examined. Which leaves car, bus or train. She doesn't have a car registered to her. A rental car is too problematic for a number of reasons. Bus the same. Besides I just don't see a near billionaire traveling by Greyhound."

"Private jet?"

"Checked. Nothing. There are holes in that arena certainly, and we can't be absolutely sure she didn't take private wings, but that's the best we can do."

"So a train somewhere *north,* to a big city? You really think that's it? But if you think she sent a lookalike by train to Miami, it seems like she'd want to stay far away from the train station."

"Friedman thinks eight moves ahead. She would have run through the analysis you just laid out, figured what we might think and done the opposite."

"Right instead of left," responded Chapman.

"Which means getting to her will not be easy. And bringing her in will be even harder."

His phone buzzed. He answered it. Joe Knox was on the other end.

Stone listened for several minutes. "Thanks, Joe, now if you can put markers on credit cards, cell phones, what? Right, I knew you'd already thought of that. And this is all between you and me, okay? Right, thanks."

He looked at Chapman. "She's even better than I thought."

"What do you mean?" Chapman asked nervously.

"I thought she would have hired muscle from either Eastern Europe or Asia."

"Okay, so what did she do?"

"She hired a team from each one. Six and six."

"Why would she hire two teams?"

"Two walls between us and her. And if one team for some reason turns on her or gets paid off by Carlos Montoya?"

"She has another team to fall back on."

"And if I'm reading her right, she'll keep each team independent and perhaps ignorant of the other."

"Outer and inner wall. Classic defensive position," said Chapman.

"We pierce one with casualties, we have another line to get through. Then maybe we don't get through at all."

"And where are these guys right now?"

"The big city to the north."

"New York?"

"Which means that's where I'm headed."

"Where *we're* headed," corrected Chapman.

"Look, I—"

"Right, you don't have a chance in hell of not taking me with you."

"This isn't your fight."

"Look, that bitch tried to kill me too. So you're not the only one wondering whether you can keep yourself from pulling the trigger."

CHAPTER

92

Six hours later a fellow named Ming, who was part of Friedman's Asian protection team, came to the surface. He was known as a highly paid mercenary who sidelined as a hired killer. No case could ever be built against him, mainly because witnesses kept disappearing. Probably against orders, Ming had used his credit card to buy some lunch at a deli in the South Bronx.

That was still a big area, but they'd managed to whittle it down some. They could trace no rental cars to anyone on the watch list Friedman might have hired. Cabs in the Bronx were not as plentiful as those in Manhattan and there was no record of Ming being in New York before, which probably stopped him from trying to figure out how to use the subway. So based on all that, Joe Knox assumed he was probably on foot when he went for his meal.

On the phone he told Stone, "Let's figure in a six-block radius with the deli as the center point. It's a lot of ground to cover, but not nearly as much as we had to check before."

"That's good work, Joe."

"So who do you have on your hunting team?"

"Harry Finn, Mary Chapman from MI6 and me."

"And me."

"No, Joe, not you."

"Alex Ford saved my life. I owe him this."

"I thought you were going to retire."

"I will, right after this. How we getting up there?"

"Private wheels. For all I know Friedman has a way to put markers in the electronic system too, so rentals are out."

"We can take my Rover. When do you want to leave?"

"You really sure about this?"

"Don't ask again. But what about the rest of the Camel Club?"

"Reuben is shot up. I don't want Annabelle going anywhere near this. And Caleb, well."

"Enough said."

They headed out at four in the morning. Knox drove. Stone rode shotgun. Finn and Chapman were in the rear seats. Stone had explained the plan to them the previous night. Except for Knox they were all disguised, just in case Friedman had scouts out doing what they were doing. Friedman might have gotten a look at Finn when he was tailing Turkekul and Stone was not willing to take any chances.

They each had a photo of Ming, and Knox also had one of Friedman, although it was doubtful the woman looked anything remotely like she had before.

"Six-block radius," Stone repeated to them as they reached the Big Apple, which was fully awake by now as millions set off to work. Knox was going to roam in his wheels after he dropped the other three off in different locations around the South Bronx. The area they were in wasn't exactly Park Avenue, but they were all armed and well capable of taking care of themselves.

Stone walked his route inward toward the deli. He had no need to look at Ming's photo again. He'd memorized each of the man's distinctive features, the most prominent of which was a pair of blank eyes. Stone knew if he weren't a hired killer Ming would have simply become a sociopath and done the same thing for free. But even sociopaths made mistakes. Ming's error had been using his credit card for a pastrami sandwich, a can of Sapporo and an order of fries.

While there were many gentrified areas of flourishing neighborhoods and retail strips, the South Bronx also contained over half of the borough's public housing projects. And despite the presence of the new billion-dollar Yankee Stadium, about fifty percent of the population lived below the poverty line. Crime was a problem and there were parts of the area one should avoid. Stone and company were in precisely one of those areas.

However, Stone was less worried about domestic criminals than about a team of imported killers. His gaze kept moving, but as the sun rose high overhead and sweat began to trickle down his neck, he understood quite clearly that it would take a minor miracle to find them.

He was only hours away from getting one.

Chapman reported the sighting. She gave the address where she was. "He's headed west, just crossing the street."

The others moved in while Chapman relayed updates via texts.

She texted one last time and then called Stone. "He just went into what looks like a machine shop on...hang on. Uh, East 149th Street is what the sign says."

"What's the cross street?" Stone asked, and Chapman told him.

He said, "Now get some cover. They might be watching the street."

She crossed over and entered an alley. She looked back at the four-story brick building. "It looks abandoned," she said into her cell phone.

"Stay put and keep watch," said Stone. "I'll be there in ten minutes."

In nine minutes Stone joined her in the alley. "I've got Knox and Finn approaching from the other side," he told her. He glanced at the building. "Seen anything else?"

"Figure at a window on the third floor. Didn't look like Ming. But I couldn't be sure."

Stone studied the area and wondered why Friedman would have chosen this spot to hide. Certainly parts of the South Bronx offered lots of space that no one else was using. Still, it was an odd choice, thought Stone. But he was coming to realize that Marisa Friedman was far more complex than he had originally believed. And he had thought she was quite talented to begin with.

He gazed southeast toward the East River where more than a few bodies had been dumped over the years. To the west was the Harlem River, beyond that upper Manhattan and beyond that the Hudson

River where Interstate 95 connected the city with New Jersey to the south and New England to the north.

"What's the plan?" asked Chapman.

"We sit on the place and observe."

"How long?"

"As long as it takes for us to figure out what they've got, who's there and how we get to them at minimal risk to ourselves."

"How about we call in NYPD and/or the FBI?"

Stone glanced back at her. "When you insisted on coming I took it for granted that you were going to follow my lead."

"I will, to a limit. We need to do everything possible to ensure that Friedman gets back alive, to stand trial."

"*You* said you were going to have a hard time not pulling the trigger."

"I only said that to make you feel better. I'll have no problem with it. She's not worth screwing my life over. But the question is, can you stop yourself from pulling it?"

"If I have to, yes."

"What's that supposed to mean?"

"It means I seriously doubt the woman will walk out with her hands up so she can be tried, convicted and executed for treason. If she tries to harm anyone of my team I'll do my best to kill her. I'm assuming you feel the same way."

"How much weapons training does she have?"

"I checked her file. She's got plenty. And all top of the grade performance-wise. Close-quarters and long-range."

"And here I was thinking she was just a pretty face."

Stone snagged her shoulder. "This is serious stuff, Chapman. No time for anything but your best game face. So cut out the wisecracks."

She pulled herself free from his grip. "I'll let my performance speak for itself. How about that?"

Stone looked away and took up surveillance on the building again.

A few minutes later he received a call from Finn. "In position. No activity back here. Two entry points. One center and one east of center. Appears to be locked and would assume watched. They might have a portable surveillance system in place too. At least I would if I were them and had picked an area like this to hole up in."

"I agree with that, Harry," said Stone. "Is Knox there?"

"Affirmative. What do you want us to do?"

"Let's sit on the place and see what we can see. When we hit it, I want it to be as clean as possible.

Any chance on getting the interior plan for this building?"

"Already downloaded it onto my phone."

"How so fast?" asked a surprised Stone.

"Got a buddy in the city planning office. We served together in the navy."

"Give me the layout."

Finn did so.

"Lot of problem areas," noted Stone.

"Agreed. Once we gain entry. That'll be the hard part. Unobserved, I mean."

"Keep watching. Report back every thirty."

Stone ended the call and turned his gaze back to the old brick structure.

Chapman stirred behind him. "What if someone notices us in this alley?"

"Then we move."

"I've never been to New York before. It's not as glamorous as I heard."

"That's Manhattan, to the west over there. That's the land of the rich and famous. The Bronx is a different experience. Some cool places and some not so cool places."

"So I take it you've been here before?"

Stone nodded.

"Business or pleasure?"

"I've never traveled for pleasure."

"So what'd you do when you were up here last?"

Stone didn't even attempt to answer her query. And from her look, it was clear Chapman didn't really expect a response.

Yet in his mind's eye it was decades ago and Stone pulled the trigger on his custom sniper rifle, ending the life of another enemy of the United States as he walked across the street with his mistress toward the luxury hotel where they were going to have sex. His downfall had been ordering the execution of two CIA personnel in Poland. Stone had put a shot through the right eyeball at the stroke of eleven p.m. from a distance of nine hundred yards on elevated ground with a breeze from the north that had given him a few anxious moments. The mistress hadn't even known what happened until her dead lover hit the pavement. The NYPD and local FBI, tipped off to what was going down, had never attempted to solve the case. That's just how it was done back then. Hell, thought Stone, maybe that was how it was still done.

He refocused on the brick building even as his index finger curved around an imaginary trigger.

CHAPTER

93

Six hours later Stone and Chapman had moved to an empty building across the street. Filthy mattresses and dirty syringes signaled this for a "prick palace" for addicts, although it didn't look like anyone had been there in a while. They'd entered through a rear door and settled themselves in for however long this would take. Stone opened his rucksack and handed Chapman a bottle of water, an apple and a hunk of hard bread.

"You know how to show a girl a good time, I'll give you that," was her only comment as she started in on her "meal."

A bit later Stone's attention was engaged when the front door of the building opposite them opened and Ming and another man came out, walked down the street and turned left. He immediately relayed this to Finn.

"You want me to follow them?" Finn asked.

"No. At this hour of the night they're probably going for something to eat. They've been in there all day. You think you can get a peek inside one of the windows? If our intel is right, there should be ten others in there plus Friedman. But I'd like to get a more accurate head count."

"The place is mostly dark, but I've got a Gen Four NV scope with me."

"Be careful, Harry. These guys know what they're doing."

"Roger that."

Twenty minutes later Finn reported back. "Got two sentries on the first floor, southwest corner. Assuming cocked and locked though no visible weapons. The others must be on the upper floors. That's the best I can do with the scope."

Knox got on the phone. "Hey, Oliver, what would you say if I could get my hands on a TI?"

"A thermal imager? How?"

"I know people here. Hell, I should have brought one with me."

"How fast can you get it?"

"One hour."

"Do it."

Within one hour two things happened. Knox returned with his thermal imager, and Ming and his colleague came back and went inside the building. They were carrying large bags of what looked to be fast food.

Two minutes later Knox buzzed Stone.

Knox said, "Okay, I just hit the building as best I could. This device is rated for penetration of most construction materials, so brick, rebar and concrete block are no problem."

"How many are you seeing?"

"I've got six images, all with SBAs," said Knox, referring to soft body armor. "It blocks the thermal signal so it stands out pretty prominently."

Stone looked perplexed. "Just six? You're sure?"

"Wait a sec. Okay, now I see it, third floor I've got a thermal with no SBA."

"Gender?"

"From the silhouette looks to be female."

"Friedman."

"Probably. But I've never met the lady. No way to do a positive ID from the TI anyway."

"Thanks, Joe, you and Harry sit tight." He looked at Chapman.

She said, "Okay, we have the players lined up, site locked down. Do we go in shooting or do we call in official reinforcements?"

"Some reason you keep harping on that theme?"

"I could say I was concerned we'll all get shot. Well, I am concerned about that. But I'm more worried that some of us will be tempted to do things that we might officially regret later. Well, I'm worried that *one* of us will be tempted." She looked at him expectantly.

"You can leave right now. No one's stopping you."

"It wasn't an ultimatum on my part, merely a passive comment."

"I don't get you sometimes."

"Just sometimes? I'm disappointed."

"How many weapons do you have?"

"My Walther and a Glock. Four extra clips. You?"

"Enough."

"A shotgun, MP-5 or TEC-9 would be nice in close-quarters combat."

"Let's hope the other guys don't think that way."

"You know they'll be loaded."

"Maybe, maybe not. You can't exactly walk through the city with an arsenal without getting some attention from the NYPD."

"Maybe they stashed it there earlier."

"Maybe they did."

"We can still call in backup."

"We don't even know if Friedman is in there for certain."

"But at least six bad guys are. In a building they're not supposed to be in."

"Well, for all we know they leased the space and have every right to be there. And in case you've forgotten, we're not supposed to be here either. Joe and Harry are doing me a favor. And I'm unofficial. You're the only one with a badge and it has the queen on it. It would take about six months to explain it all to the boys in blue and we'd probably stay in lockup that whole time."

"Well, the 'queen' has revoked my authority but I see your dilemma. So what do we do now?"

"I expect they believe a zig is coming."

"So we zag?"

"We zag."

Stone picked up his phone. "Get ready," he told Knox. "We go in one hour."

The zag did not exactly go according to plan. In fact it did not come close to going according to plan. The first indication was that neither the front nor rear doors were locked. Finn and Knox collapsed the rear entry and Stone and Chapman the front entrance at two a.m. precisely. The guards stationed there were asleep. Guns pointed at their heads woke them, but they took their time about it. By the time Stone's team hit the top floors the four other men were up and stretching.

The second indication of their plan being unsuccessful was that none of the men even had their guns in their hands. The last clue was that the woman on the third floor wasn't Friedman. She was older by about twenty years and appeared to be drunk. At least they couldn't wake her. She snored on.

Thoroughly frustrated, Stone let his anger get the better of him. He grabbed Ming by the neck and slammed him up against the wall. "Care to tell me where Friedman is?"

Ming's smile was both deliberate and superior. He replied coolly, "She anticipated your visit."

Stone slowly released the man. Ming looked around at the other three, their guns pointed at him and his team. The woman snored loudly in the corner on an old cot.

"She anticipated me? Me specifically?"

Ming nodded. "John Carr," he said. He pointed at Stone. "That is you. She gave us your picture. Even though you are disguised. The eyes give you away."

Stone glanced at Finn, then Knox and finally Chapman before bringing his gaze back to Ming.

"Why all this?" asked Stone.

"She pays us big to come here, stay in an old building, walk around, be seen. No fighting. Easiest gig I've ever been on."

Stone swore under his breath. He'd been played again.

Ming interpreted his look and his smile deepened. "She tells me you are smart. That you will not believe she has gone on the train to Miami." He paused and added, "A desert island?"

"Opposite," said Stone.

"Right," replied Ming. "When we go on a job it is usually with more cover. This job, I buy lunch with my own credit card, because she tells me to."

Another red flag that I missed because I wanted her so badly. She used every instinct I had against myself.

"To what purpose?" said Stone.

"A distraction."

Stone thought, *Two teams. Asian and Russian. I thought they were for the inner and outer walls. The fallback contingency. But they weren't. Ming was the distraction. So during the distraction what was the other team doing?*

Stone's heart began to sink.

So obvious. Now so obvious.

He steadied himself and asked, "Where did she take them?"

Chapman blurted out, "Who?"

Stone never took his eyes off Ming. "Where did she take my friends?"

Ming clapped his hands together. "You are good. She said you would probably figure it out."

"Where?" Stone edged closer to the man and leveled his pistol against Ming's forehead. "Tell me. Now."

Ming's smile was still there but behind it was a small trace of concern.

"Do you have the guts to pull that trigger, in front of all these people?"

Stone slowly pulled the hammer back on his weapon. "You'll find out in three seconds." When two seconds had passed, his finger began to descend to the trigger. "When I touch it, there's no going back. You're dead."

Ming blurted out, "She says to where it all began for you and the Triple Six. And that is where it will end. That's all she says. She says you will know what it means."

Chapman exclaimed, "Oliver, do you know what he's talking about?"

Stone slowly removed the muzzle from Ming's forehead. "Yes, unfortunately I do."

Murder Mountain. To where it all began. For me. And now where it will all end.

CHAPTER

94

WITH AGENT ASHBURN AT HIS HEEL, Stone strode down the hall at WFO like a plane gathering power to lift off the ground. He didn't stop to knock on the door. He slammed it open and walked in.

The FBI director looked up at him, stunned. Across the conference table from him was seated Riley Weaver.

The director said, "What the hell is going on?"

Stone didn't even look at him. His gaze went immediately to Weaver. "What did you tell her?"

"What?" snapped Weaver. "We're in the middle of a meeting, in case you hadn't noticed, Stone."

Stone came around the table with such a threatening look that Weaver half rose out of his seat, his hands curled into fists, his body hunched into a defensive stance in case Stone attacked.

The director barked, "Ashburn, what is going on? Why did you let him in—"

Stone shouted, "What did you tell Friedman about me, Weaver?"

"I haven't talked to the woman. I warned you before. If you start accusing me of crap—"

"I mean before I told you she was behind it all," barked Stone. "You talked to her *then,* didn't you?"

Weaver slowly sat back down in his chair. The FBI director stared over at him. Ashburn gazed at him from the doorway. Weaver looked at each of them before turning back to Stone.

"She was one of my field agents. I had every right to talk to her."

"What did you tell her about me? That I figured it out? That I was the one who warned the Secret Service? That I was the reason the plan didn't work?"

"So what if I did?" blustered Weaver. "I didn't know she was a traitor then. And frankly, I still don't know that she is. For all I know someone kidnapped her or even killed her."

Chapman walked into the room. "They didn't. And she is a traitor. She set us up. Diverted us while she had two of Stone's friends kidnapped."

"What!" exclaimed the FBI director and Ashburn in unison.

"How do you know that?" asked Weaver curiously. "We searched the train to Miami, she wasn't on it. But something tells me you already knew that." He glanced at the FBI director. "Holding out on us, Stone?"

"I'm no longer working for the government, in case you didn't get the memo."

"That's bullshit."

"What's bullshit is you talking to Friedman and not telling any of us. In fact, I bet you kept her in the loop the whole time. I wondered how they always knew what we were going to do before we even did it. Now I know. It was you, wasn't it?"

"I don't owe you or anyone else an explanation for my actions."

"I'll tell that to my friends when I find their bodies," snapped Stone.

Ashburn said, "Do you have any idea where she's holding them?"

Stone calmed and finally looked away from Weaver. "No," he lied. "I don't."

"So why'd you come here?" asked Weaver. "You want our help?"

"No. I just wanted to know who I had to thank for fingering me to Friedman."

"Damn it, I didn't do it intentionally," roared Weaver.

But Stone had already left the room. They could hear him marching rapidly down the hall.

Ashburn looked at Chapman. "What is going on?"

"He told you. His friends have gone missing and Friedman has them."

"You're sure?" asked the director.

"Heard it from the horse's mouth."

Ashburn glanced down the hall. "What is he going to do?"

"What do you think he's going to do?" replied Chapman.

"He can't do this alone."

The director added, "We have resources that he doesn't."

"That may be all well and good. But he's John Carr. And quite frankly he's got resources you lot don't have either. And there's no one on earth who has more motivation to get this woman than he does."

"And you're telling us he doesn't know where they are being held?" asked Ashburn.

"If he does he hasn't bothered to tell me."

"Where did you find this information out?"

"In the South Bronx," said Chapman.

"The South Bronx!" yelled Ashburn. "How did you get a line on the South Bronx?"

"You'll have to ask Sherlock Holmes that question. I'm just good old Watson."

"Agent Chapman," began the director.

"Sir," she said, heading him off. "If I knew something helpful I would tell you."

"Why don't I believe that?" He paused, studying her. "I think I can plainly see where your loyalties lie."

"My loyalties, sir, lie about three thousand miles from here, to a dear old lady, an ambitious PM and an old man with dandruff and a brilliant mind."

"Are you sure?" asked the director.

"I've always been sure of that," replied Chapman.

She turned to leave.

"Where are you going?" demanded Weaver.

"Holmes needs his Watson."

"Agent Chapman, this is not your fight." said the director.

"Perhaps not. But it would be awfully bad form to stop now."

"I can have you detained," said the director.

"Yes, you can. But I don't think you will."

Chapman turned and hurried after Stone.

CHAPTER

95

"So why Annabelle and Caleb?" said Harry Finn as they all drove in Knox's Range Rover west of Washington, D.C., on Route 29. The night was dark, though dawn was only a couple of hours away. The ambient light was limited and the mood in the vehicle matched the outside: black.

Stone, who was again riding shotgun, said grimly, "Because they helped me run a scam on her and I guess she didn't like it."

And I let her decoy me with a tactic a rookie should have seen through and I fell for it like the damn fool I am.

But there was something else nagging at Stone. Mere revenge didn't seem enough motivation for someone as intelligent and ambitious as Marisa Friedman. There had to be something more. He just didn't know what that was. And if he was afraid of anything, it was the unknown.

They'd quickly confirmed that both Annabelle and Caleb were missing and that no one had seen them for at least twenty-four hours. Stone had taken a few minutes to visit Alex Ford in the ICU. His condition hadn't changed, but it hadn't gotten worse either, which Stone took as a rare bit of good news. As he stared down at his friend lying on the hospital bed with thick bandages wound round his head, Stone had gripped his hand and squeezed it. "Alex, if you can hear me, it's going to be okay. I promise that everything will be okay." He paused, drawing a long breath that seemed to take forever to leave his body. "You're a hero, Alex. The president is okay. No one was hurt. You're a hero." Stone looked down at his hand. He thought he had felt the other man squeeze it. But when he looked back up at the unconscious agent he knew that was just wishful thinking. Stone let go and walked to the doorway. Something made him look back. As he stared at his friend lying in the bed and fighting for his life, he felt a measure of guilt so powerful his knees started to buckle.

He's lying there because of me. And now Caleb and Annabelle are probably dead. Again, because of me.

Stone had made one other stop, at a rare book store in Old Town Alexandria. The owner had been helped by Stone and Caleb and in return had allowed Stone to keep certain items there in a secret room underneath the old building. Those items were now in the back of the Rover.

"Murder Mountain?" said Chapman. "You mentioned it but didn't really explain it."

Knox answered when it didn't appear Stone was going to. "Old CIA training facility. Shut down before my time. Hell of a place, from what I've heard. The way the Agency used to do things during the Cold War. I thought they'd demolished it."

"No, they haven't," said Stone.

Knox eyed him curiously. "Have you been back recently?"

"Yes. Pretty recently."

"Why?" asked Chapman.

"Business," Stone replied tersely.

"What's the layout?" asked Finn, as he hunched forward in his rear seat.

In answer Stone pulled out a laminated piece of paper and handed it back to him. Finn clicked on the overhead light and he and Chapman studied it. There were annotations on the page in Stone's handwriting.

"This place looks bloody awful," exclaimed

Chapman. "A laboratory with a torture cage? A holding tank where you square off with an opponent in the dark to see who can kill the other?"

Stone glanced back at her. "It was not for the fainthearted." His look was searching. She quickly got it.

"I'm *not* fainthearted."

"Good to know," he replied.

She eyed the cargo hold of the Rover. "That's a fine set of *vintage* equipment you've got back there."

"Yes, it is."

"How are we going to do this?" asked Knox as he turned off Route 29 and onto Highway 211. They entered the tiny town of Washington, Virginia, the seat of Rappahannock County at the foothills of the Blue Ridge Mountains. Washington, Virginia, was world famous for one reason: It was the home of the Inn at Little Washington, a prestigious restaurant that had been serving world-class cuisine for over a quarter century.

As they left the town and rose higher into the mountains, Stone broke his silence. "There are a couple of entry points. One is obvious, the other is not."

"How well do you think she knows this place?" asked Chapman.

"Like Knox, it was before her time. She never would have trained there. But I can't answer your question. She obviously knew of its existence. She may have explored it thoroughly. In fact, from what I know of her now, she probably has gone over every inch of it."

"So she'll know about the secondary entrance?" said Knox.

"We have to assume she will."

But she won't know about the third way in and out, because I'm the only one who does.

Stone had discovered it in his fourth month at Murder Mountain, when he just needed to get outside the place for a few moments alone. Just to catch his breath, collect his wits. Just get out of what had become a hellhole. Worse than any prison ever could have been. That was the principal reason Stone had been able to weather the max prison he and Knox had ended up in.

Because I endured something far worse. A year at Murder Mountain.

Chapman said, "What I don't get is why she would have set up shop at this place, kidnapped Caleb and Annabelle and then basically dared you to come get her. She'll never be able to escape now."

Stone looked grim. "I don't think she intends

on escaping. She's conceded that she's going to go down for this. But she's choosing to exit on her own terms."

"Meaning she's willing to die," said Knox.

"And take us with her," replied Stone.

"Dangerous opponent," said Finn. "Someone who doesn't care if she dies. Like a suicide bomber."

"She better be thinking the same thing about me," muttered Stone.

The other three glanced at each other but said nothing.

Chapman finally broke the silence. "So front or hidden entrance? We have to get in some way."

"She'll have six guys with her. All Russian, all hard as nails. They'll kill anybody she tells them to."

"Okay, but that doesn't answer my question."

"It's a big place and they'll have to have at least one man guarding Caleb and Annabelle. Friedman will be back in a protected space. That leaves five men for perimeter duty. They can't deploy them all at the entrances. They have to hold at least three back for interior protection. That leaves one at each entrance. That's thin."

"What do you think they expect us to do?"

"Hit both entrances, and whichever team gets

through, so be it. If we did that we'd split up, making it two against one. If we hit one entrance together, it's four against one."

"I like those odds better," said Knox.

"So do I," said Stone. "But we're not going to do it that way."

"Why?" said Chapman.

"You'll see why."

CHAPTER

96

STONE WAS ALONE. He slipped among bulky rocks and narrow crevices as he made his way toward the secondary entrance into Murder Mountain. As a raw recruit to the CIA's fabled Triple Six Division, Stone had spent a full year of his life here learning new ways to hunt, new ways to kill and new ways to be something both more and less than human. He had become a magnificently skilled predator with all ordinary emotions such as compassion and empathy burned out of him. Murder Mountain had turned out the best killers ever to walk the planet. And John Carr was universally acknowledged as the best of the best.

The training became so intense that Stone and some of his fellow trainees had looked for and discovered a way out of the facility. They had done so not to run to the rural town about twenty miles distant to get drunk or bed a few farmers' daughters, but simply to sit under the stars, look at the moon, feel the breeze, see the green of the trees, feel the earth under their feet.

Stone had just wanted assurance that there was still a world going on outside Murder Mountain. Assignment to Triple Six was technically voluntary, but in all the important ways it was not. Stone still remembered clearly the day the man from the CIA had visited him in his military barracks. Stone and his company had just returned from Vietnam. Stone had performed so heroically in one firefight that there was talk of his being awarded the Medal of Honor. But that had not happened, largely because of a jealous superior officer who fudged the paperwork. If Stone had been awarded the medal his life might have turned out differently. Medal of Honor winners were rare. The army might have sent him on a publicity tour, even though by then the war was waning nearly as fast as the country's interest in waging it.

So the man in the suit had come. He had made a proposal. Come join another agency. Another unit dedicated to fighting your country's enemies. That was how he had phrased it: "Your country's enemies." Stone had been told little else. He looked to his commander for advice, but it was clear that the decision had already been made. Stone, barely twenty years old and covered in medals and commendations for his exemplary service in Vietnam, was mustered out of the army with breathtaking speed and soon found himself here, at Murder Mountain.

The light was poor along this trail, but he had no trouble traversing it. It was all mental memory at this point. When he'd come back to this place not all that long ago, it had been the same way. He had remembered it all, as if he had never been away. As if the memory of it had been lurking in a set of brain cells, sequestered from the rest and not degraded in any way, like a cancerous tumor lying dormant until it started its fatal spread. Then nothing else was safe. Every part of him was vulnerable. That could sum up his life in Triple Six quite adequately.

He slipped the pair of old NVGs over his eyes when the light became too poor to make anything out. The crevices grew smaller. It was a good thing he had remained lean all these years or he never would have fit. Although, he recalled, big Reuben Rhodes had managed to squeeze himself through the rocks when he came here with Stone to save a man's life. To save President Brennan's life.

All the men in Triple Six had been lean, nothing

but gristle and muscle. They could run all day, shoot all night without missing. They could change plans on the fly, ferret out targets no matter how deeply they had dug in. Stone could not deny that it had been exhilarating, challenging and even memorable.

"But I never wanted to come back here," he said to himself.

He paused, looked ahead. The entrance he was searching for was up ahead. It was built into the back of a kitchen cabinet on a swivel pin. Stone had always assumed that another group of trainees before his time had done that. Stone and his teammates had merely discovered it one night and followed it out. They weren't the only class of Triple Six recruits who wanted a bit of freedom, it seemed. Or maybe the people who ran Murder Mountain had done it, sensing that the recruits needed to believe they had a bit of control over their lives, that they could take a few moments rest from a hellish experience.

Maybe they were afraid we'd all go mad and kill them.

He slipped his gun from its holster and another object from his belt. The entrance was straight ahead. He assumed Friedman had given strict orders. Do not kill, at least him. Bring him to me.

Then she would kill him, probably after making him watch the deaths of Caleb and Annabelle.

He reached the outside of the entrance. Readying his gun, he held out the other object, a telescoping rod. He flipped it out to its full six-foot length. He nudged the wall in front of him that represented the back of the cabinet on the pin swivel. It had been painted to resemble black rock, but it was only wood. Rotted wood now. He pushed harder with the rod. The wood gave way, the pin swivel did its job and the wall swung inward.

Something shot out of the opening and hit the rock Stone was standing next to. This he'd expected. A dart. Paralyze, not kill. He pulled the pin on the lump of metal he'd taken from a compartment on his vest and tossed it into the opening at the same time he slid behind a large outcrop of rock.

There was a small pulse of energy followed by a dense cloud of smoke. Stone slid on his gas mask and counted. He stopped counting when he heard the man behind the wall hit the floor. He moved through the opening and looked down. The Russian was large, with a shaved head, a small goatee and a dart pistol in his hand. It was probably not in the man's nature to seek to stun instead of kill. He'd not been very good with the dart gun. Stone used two pairs of plasticuffs to immobilize the man's hands and feet. Clear of the gas, he removed his mask and moved forward into Murder Mountain.

At the front entrance to the facility, Finn, Chapman and Knox stood facing a metal door revealed in the rock face of the mountain where they'd pulled aside a curtain of kudzu that covered it. Stone had told them where the door was located and had given them a key that he said would open the portal. But there wasn't even a keyhole to try the key in. He'd also told them that he was the only one who could make it through the hidden entrance, because there was no way for someone to follow him closely enough not to get lost. He told them he would rendezvous with them at the front door.

"He snookered us," moaned Knox, who was holding the useless key. "I can't believe I fell for it. Like he'd have a damn key to this place after all these years."

"He's going it alone," said Finn.

"The hell he is," snapped Chapman. She reached inside her jacket and pulled out a slender metal object with a magnetized edge.

"What is that?" asked Knox.

"Well, love, at MI6 we call this a doorbell." She attached it to the metal door where it met the door-jamb. She motioned them to step back. She drew a remote from her pocket, slid open the protective hard plastic covering and pressed a button. "Don't look at the laser," she instructed.

They all looked away as a burst of red light erupted from the device she'd placed on the door. It cut neatly through the locking bar, and the door swung free on its hinges.

"Pretty cool technology," said Knox.

"One-time power pack, good for most secure doors, metal or otherwise," she explained.

"I see Mr. Q is still alive and well in British intelligence."

"Actually, it was a woman who invented this little toy. But you can just call her Ms. Q."

Guns out, they approached the door. With Chapman and Knox covering him, Finn slowly pulled the door all the way open. He aimed his gun into the darkness and then nodded at the others. They pulled on protective goggles, as did Finn. A second later Finn hit the opening with a pulse of blinding white light. There was a shout of pain from inside and then the light vanished.

Before the men could move, Chapman was through the opening. They hustled after her in time to see her nimbly disarm the man and then smash her foot into his face, sending him rocketing backward against an interior wall. The man, partially blinded by the light, ricocheted off the wall and came at Chapman, big arms swinging like pistons. Finn moved to step between the attacker and Chapman, but the MI6 agent had already launched off the ground. With her left foot she hit the man with a crushing blow to his right knee. They all heard the bone in his leg snap. He crumpled downward at the same time she delivered a kick to his chin, flipping him heels over ass. When he tried to rise, his gut pushing in and out with painful breaths, Chapman laid him down for good with an elbow strike to the base of his neck. She rose and placed the muzzle of her Walther against the unconscious man's temple.

"Wait a minute," snapped Knox.

"What?" she asked.

"You're just going to shoot him in cold blood?" asked Knox.

"Do we want to leave witnesses?" she asked calmly.

"Witnesses to what?"

"To whatever's going to happen here tonight. Like me killing Stone for him playing us for fools."

"We're not killing anyone unless they're in a position to kill us," Knox said firmly.

Chapman deftly cuffed the unconscious man. "Suit yourself."

Finn said, "Where'd you learn moves like that?"

"Maybe you blokes think otherwise, but MI6 is not a bloody girls' school. Now let's get going."

She turned on a flashlight and headed down the corridor.

Finn and Knox looked at each other and then quickly followed the woman.

CHAPTER

97

THOUGH THE ENTIRE FACILITY itself was quite large, with barracks, kitchens, an infirmary, a library, offices, classrooms and other specific free spaces, the most intensive training areas of Murder Mountain were set up in the form of a pair of large steel cylinders divided into parallel sections and separated by a main hall. Once you entered the first section, you had to continue on until the last section in that cylinder. The massive entry doors locked behind you and did not allow passage back. And one couldn't simply block the door open, because if one did the next door would not open. It was a way to keep reluctant recruits focused and on mission and always moving forward. Stone's plan was simple. He was going to take the section on the right and follow it through. If he didn't find his quarry there, he would exit this cylinder, walk back down the main hall and enter the other cylinder.

Stone made his way slowly down the hall to the first door. One man was down and there were five more to go, plus Friedman, whom Stone considered probably the most skilled of the bunch.

He felt no guilt about tricking his friends. If anyone was going to die trying to rescue Caleb and Annabelle it was going to be him. This ultimately was his fight, not theirs. He'd lost enough friends. He was determined not to lose any more tonight.

He ran off the order of the training sections in his head. Shooting range first, where he had fired off hundreds of thousands of rounds in the year he had been here. They threw every imaginable distraction at you while you were aiming at the targets. It had been good training, because out in the real world a perfect field of fire with accompanying idyllic conditions was impossible to find.

After the shooting range was a room outfitted like the famed Hogan's Alley at the FBI Academy. Here Stone and his teammates had practiced what they'd learned in the classroom. After that room was the lab. It was there where the psychological testing took place—really glorified torture to determine what your breaking point was. Stone had seen hard-as-steel men weep in that room, as the technicians played numbing games with their minds, which would never be as strong as their physical side, no matter how much they trained. There were proven exercises that would enlarge and strengthen muscle. The mind, on the other hand, was not so easily quantifiable. And the recruits all carried hidden mental elements with them here that would jump out at unexpected times and cause them to falter, to fail, to scream in rage. Stone had felt all those emotions. No place on earth had ever humbled him like the lab at Murder Mountain.

After the lab was a series of rooms that served as holding cells. Stone never knew what persons might have been "held" here, and he didn't want to know. If Caleb and Annabelle were not down this way he would start through the other cylinder where there were only two sections. The first was a tank full of foul liquid. One would fall into this muck if one did not know where to step on a catwalk that constituted the top of the tank. Once inside the tank it became a fight to the death. After the tank came a maze that Stone thankfully had the answer for. Or at least he thought he did. He now wondered if Friedman had built some surprise for him.

Of course she has. She's enjoying this. I ruined her plans. She has a half billion dollars she can't spend.

She's going to take it all out on me. At least she's going to try to.

But again something tugged at the back of Stone's mind, telling him there had to be more to it than that. He listened as the flap of wings evidenced that birds had gotten into Murder Mountain. That had happened when the place was operational. Stone had even made a pet of one bird that had built a nest near where he slept. It was the only tie to the outside world he'd had.

The place had been built in the 1960s, and the design reflected the era. There were even ashtrays built into metal consoles. Everywhere he looked he saw something hopelessly out of date. But when it was new, Murder Mountain was a state-of-the-art facility. The government funds to build it, Stone had been told once, had been buried in a huge spending bill that included subsidies for hog farmers and the textile industries.

What was a little governmental assassination with your ham and polyester?

He cautiously entered the firing range. It was here that he had killed the first man he'd shot in thirty years. He had done it to save himself and Reuben Rhodes. His gaze traveled to the very spot where the man had fallen and died. The fluorescent overhead lights were too weak to allow Stone to see if the man's blood was still there. At least his body wasn't. The place had been cleaned up after his last visit here. He wondered why they hadn't just imploded Murder Mountain, burying it under tons of steel and rock. Maybe they were holding on to it, in case they needed to use it again. That was a chilling thought.

The lights *were* on, though, however feebly. Which meant Friedman had figured out how to use the old generator system to create a bit of power. He crept forward, past the tattered targets, ducking under the sagging wires on pulleys that allowed the paper targets to be moved back and forth. He stopped thinking about anything other than what would be waiting for him.

The bare scrape of a shoe on the dusty floor caused him to drop low behind a wooden counter where he had once stood daily to fire his allotted rounds. The sound had come from his left, ten yards at most. He wondered if they were all using darts until the moment of truth came. It didn't really matter. If he allowed himself to be knocked unconscious by a tranquilizer round he was as good as dead anyway.

Crouching down, he circled backward, his gun covering both front and rear flanks in alternating swivels. This tactic must've confused his opponent, who probably thought Stone was moving forward and not backward with every creak of boards. When the man emerged from his hiding place to fire at a target that wasn't where it was supposed to be, Stone placed one round in the man's arm, disabling him. As he clutched for his wounded limb, Stone fired the kill shot into his neck, neatly bypassing his body armor. The man dropped on the spot, his carotid severed.

Stone studied the door, did the math in his head. It was probable that the man he'd just killed was a ruse to flush him. Sacrifice one to accomplish the mission. The landing at Normandy in 1944 had followed this same strategy, only the number of lives sacrificed had been in the thousands. On the other side of that door were probably at least two shooters waiting to take him.

So he waited. He counted off the seconds in his head. Patience. He had spent years learning that trait. There were few men who could outwait him. Ten minutes passed and the only part of Stone that moved was his chest, with each shallow breath.

The only problem was that Friedman, and thus her men, knew that one could not go back in these sections. One had to go forward. How long were they willing to wait? How long was Stone willing to wait?

We're all going to find out.

98

"WAIT A MINUTE, HOW'D YOU KNOW to bring that laser thing?" Knox asked Chapman as they crouched in the darkness.

"Like your Boy Scouts, it's the mission of MI6 to always be prepared."

"Meaning you didn't believe Stone?"

"The key?" Chapman scoffed. "Of course I didn't believe him. Reading his psychological profile was fairly easy. He wasn't going to endanger us too."

"He let us go to New York with him," Finn pointed out.

"I guess he believed the South Bronx was safer than this place," pointed out Knox.

"Murder Mountain," said Chapman. "Made for interesting reading."

Both men looked at her.

"I researched it, of course," she said. "Didn't you?"

Knox cleared his throat. "How did you know what to research? Stone didn't mention the place until we were on the way here."

"The place where it all began? Remember, that's what Ming said back in New York. So I did some digging, got my folks back in the UK doing the same. I knew that Stone started out his career in Triple Six. What I didn't know was that it began with a year's worth of training right here. Got a file emailed to me two hours before we left. Like I said, interesting reading."

Finn looked down at the laminated plan of the place Stone had given him. "Looks like multiple spots to be ambushed."

"That cuts both ways," said Knox, and Chapman nodded in agreement.

She pointed at the plan and said, "We have two choices. Go through each side together or split up."

Finn said, "I vote for getting out of the open. If we need to go through these section things, let's split up. I'll go to the left and you two to the right."

Chapman shook her head. "No, you two go right, I'll go left."

The men looked at her again. "What?" she said.

"A woman can't go it alone? She needs a precious man to hold her poor, fragile hand?"

"It's not that," said Knox uncomfortably.

"Good to hear it," she said. "I'll take the one on the left. Now here's some little tidbits you need to know about the section on the right to traverse it safely." She filled them in on particulars she'd gained from her research.

"Got it?" she said, looking at them.

"You've given this a lot of thought," said Knox.

"Why wouldn't I?" shot back Chapman. "It's my job."

"Good luck," said Finn.

"Cheers."

She left the two men standing there staring after her until she disappeared into the darkness.

Stone was still waiting in the firing range room. He considered his options. It didn't take long since there weren't many. He could stay here until he starved to death. Or he could go through the door.

Or...

He got up, grabbed the wire that the targets rode on and pulled it free. He wound one end of it around the door handle and over the existing pulleys. Then he crouched down behind the counter and wound the remainder of the wire around his hand. He counted to five and aimed his pistol at the door opening. He slowly pulled on the wire. The door handle lifted. He tugged harder. The door started to open. As soon as it was open half-way, a barrage of bullets poured through, clanging off metal surfaces in the firing range room.

Okay, probably against orders, the Russians are done playing around with stun darts.

He tugged on the door some more until it opened all the way, then tied off the wire onto a hook to keep the door open. He sidled along the counter and slid down the pair of NVGs he had brought. They were older and had a major drawback if the other side had night-vision equipment too.

He edged closer to the opening, but keeping something solid between him and the doorway at the same time. Then he did something unusual, at least to the untrained eye. He took off his goggles, but still kept them powered. He placed them on top of the counter, facing the doorway. Then he scuttled away, aimed his gun and waited for what he was pretty certain was coming.

The shots came. He counted four of them. Stone couldn't see the rounds, but he was sure they had passed an inch above the red dot revealed by his goggles to someone looking at them with NV eyewear too. That was the drawback to the old-generation goggles. While on infrared power they painted a red dot basically on your forehead, allowing a sniper to draw a fatal bead.

But by firing the Russians had revealed their position to Stone by their muzzle flashes through the open doorway. He fired rapidly, once, twice and then a third and fourth time, aiming at spots two inches above the twin flashes. Stone could tell by the weapons' discharge that they were pistols. If they were firing from classic shooting positions, Stone's target selection would coincide with their heads, bypassing their body armor.

He heard two distinct thumps as the bodies hit the floor.

He got up, snared his NVGs and kept moving.

Three Russians down, three to go. Plus Friedman.

CHAPTER

99

FINN AND KNOX MADE THEIR WAY carefully across the catwalk that was suspended over a tank of foul-smelling liquid. They knew this for two reasons. One, because they could smell it, even if they couldn't see it. And two, it was on the plan Stone had given them. But it was Chapman who'd told them the secret of passing safely over it. Stone hadn't done so, because he had never intended for them to get inside this place.

They had to keep their weight in the center of the metal walkway. If they made a misstep and touched the sides, only bad things would happen. They had nearly reached the end of the catwalk when they heard it.

A groan.

Both men looked around, guns pointed at obvious threat points.

Another groan.

Finn whispered to Knox, "Sounds like it's underneath us."

"Thinking the same thing," replied Knox.

"I recognized it."

"The groan?"

Finn nodded. "Keep a lookout." He dropped to his knees and put his face against the floor of the catwalk that was only inches from the top of the tank. "Caleb?" he said softly.

Another groan.

"Caleb?" he said in a louder voice as Knox gazed anxiously around.

Another groan and then, "Harry?" The voice was weak, the mind obviously muddled.

Drugged, was Finn's first thought.

He looked up at Knox. "Remember what Chapman told us?"

Knox nodded and glanced around. "Got an idea."

Keeping to the center of the walk, he headed back the way he had come. He couldn't go back out the door they had come in. It had locked behind them and it was thick and made of stainless steel. But there was an old packing crate set against the wall. He slipped his gun in its holster, hefted the box, which weighed about fifty pounds, and carried it back over to where Finn was, again keeping to the center of the catwalk.

Each man climbed up on the railing of the catwalk. This was difficult for Knox with the weight of the crate, but he managed it. He looked at Finn and told him his plan.

"You ready?"

Finn nodded.

Knox counted to three and then dropped the box on the side of the catwalk. The floor immediately tilted down on that side while the other side tilted up, revealing a blackened strip of empty space on each side. The crate fell through the opening on the right side and they heard a splash. The foul smell got even fouler.

Finn, still holding on to the railing, dropped down until his foot was squarely in the empty space. As the floor tilted back up and into place, he jammed his foot against it, holding it open. Knox reached into the rucksack he carried on his back and slid out a length of rope. He tied one end to the railing and let the other drop through the opening.

Knox switched places with Finn and held the floor open with his foot. Finn grabbed the rope and lowered himself through. He landed in knee-deep muck.

"Caleb?"

"Harry?" the voice said groggily.

"Are you alone?"

"Yes. At least I think I am."

Finn switched on his flashlight and quickly found Caleb trussed up and sitting in the muck, which was up to his chest. Finn cut him loose and helped him through the opening and up to the catwalk.

"You okay?" Finn asked as the three men proceeded on into the next room.

Caleb slowly nodded. "Just a little woozy. They gave me a shot. Made me fuzzy. And the stench down there. I don't think my sense of smell will ever be the same." His face paled as his mind cleared. "Annabelle? Is she all right?"

"We're still looking for her. Any idea where she might be?"

Caleb shook his head. "I just want to get out of this place. All of us."

"That's the plan," said Knox.

"Where's Oliver?" asked Caleb.

"In here somewhere," replied Finn.

Stone passed into the next section. It had a mock street, building façades, a rotting 1960s-era sedan and mannequins filling in for real people. The mannequins all had bullet holes in their heads. He cleared this space and kept going.

The next room was the last one on this section. The lab.

Stone cautiously pushed open the door and went inside. No lights here. Using his NV goggles, he checked the room methodically. He kept one hand on his goggles, ready to rip them off if he saw any hint of others using similar equipment, since the red dot would give away his position and probably his life as well.

As he looked around he noticed something odd. There were long tables set up against one wall of the lab. These tables were new. Various pieces of sophisticated-looking equipment were set up on these surfaces. Glistening metal contraptions with power cords trailing off to the floor. And test tubes in racks lining the walls. Elaborate microscopes and other equipment were centered on another table. On the floor in one corner was a metal cylinder about six feet in length. It had a digital readout screen and a square of glass in the center.

None of this was here the last time Stone had visited Murder Mountain. He had no idea what it represented or who had placed it here. And right now he didn't have time to explore the issue.

Next, his gaze went to the cage that normally hung from the ceiling but now was on the floor. The cage had fallen due entirely to Stone's marksmanship when he'd last been here and an enemy who had been trying to kill him had died when the two-ton cage had fallen on him.

But Stone had another recollection of that cage. When he'd been training here all those years ago he and three men had been placed in the cage together. A flame had been ignited under the cage and every ten seconds was increased so that it grew nearer and nearer the metal. The goal was for the men to get out before the heat became unbearable. Added to the problem was that Stone and his colleagues had seen the other team that had come before them. They had failed the test. And two men had suffered crippling burns.

While the other men in his group had started to panic as the metal grew too hot to touch, Stone had focused all his energies. Why four men in the cage at the same time? Why not three or five, or six? Four men. Four sides to the cage.

He'd barked out his orders. Each man was to take off his shirt, wrap it around his hands and simultaneously apply pressure against his side of the cage. They did so. The cage door had sprung open. His leadership actions had earned Stone the praise of his instructors. At the same time he had wanted to kill them.

But this recollection stayed with Stone for only a moment. He could hardly believe what he was seeing.

"Annabelle?"

She was inside the cage, gagged and tied up.

He moved forward, checking the room again for threats but seeing none.

The cage door wasn't locked. Stone swung it open. Annabelle's eyes were closed, and for one terrible moment Stone wasn't sure if she was alive or not. But you didn't gag and tie up a dead person. Annabelle had a pulse, and with Stone's touch against her neck she slowly came around.

He untied her, took off the gag and helped her out of the cage.

"God, is it good to see you," she said drunkenly.

"They drugged you?"

"I think so. But it's wearing off."

"Can you walk?"

"I'll crawl if it means we can get out of here."

He smiled as her feistiness returned.

"Are you alone?" she asked.

"Yes."

"Any sign of Caleb?"

"Not yet. Have you seen Marisa Friedman?"

Annabelle shook her head.

"Let's keep moving," said Stone.

"Oliver!" cried out Annabelle as the buzz of fluorescent lights came on.

Stone ripped off his goggles, turned, but was too late.

The Russian was by the door leading out of the lab. Somehow Stone had not seen him hiding. His gun was aimed right at Stone's head. Stone pushed Annabelle to the floor and pulled his weapon. The shot rang out, catching the surprised Russian in the forehead, tattooing his skin with a small black dot.

He dropped. The lights went out.

Stone looked down at his weapon. His unfired weapon. Where the hell had that shot come from? He grabbed Annabelle's arm and pulled her along beside him. They hopped over the dead man and through the door.

Four dead Russians. Two to go. Plus Friedman.

100

Stone and Annabelle reached the end of the cylinder.

The holding cells.

If Caleb wasn't in one of them Stone would have to start over from the other side. And he would have to bring Annabelle with him.

The first thing he saw brought astonishment and then relief. Knox and Finn and Caleb were waiting for them. Weak light allowed everyone to see the others.

"How did you get in here?" Stone asked as they huddled in one corner and Annabelle hugged Caleb despite his foul clothes and smell.

"Chapman's doing," said Knox as he filled Stone in on what had happened to them so far. "She told us how to get through the maze too. Said she researched it."

Stone looked behind him. "So she went to the left?"

"That's right. Any idea where she is?"

"Somewhere behind me. And she just saved my life."

"We got one Russian at the front entrance. At least Chapman got him."

"So there's only one left."

"And now there are none," said a voice.

Chapman stepped into the light.

"Guy tried to jump me as I came through to start my first section," she explained. "He either wasn't very good, or I'm better than I think I am."

When she finished speaking, Stone looked around, a curious expression on his features.

Finn said to Chapman, "Any sign of Friedman?"

"No."

"I say we get the hell out of here as fast as we can," said Knox. "We've got what we came for. Friedman can keep."

He looked at Stone, who seemed frozen to the spot.

"Oliver, are you okay?"

"Russians."

"What?" said Finn.

"Russians," Stone said again.

"Right. And we killed them all."

"Not very good Russians," said Stone. "You would have thought they would have been better."

They all looked at him.

He stared back. "We went through them very easily. Too easily. They weren't very good. And I think that was intentional."

"Why would Friedman hire not very good security?"

"Because she didn't need the A-team. The B-team was good enough."

"Good enough for what?" asked Chapman.

"To draw us here. To get us to this spot, in fact. They were expendable. She didn't care if they died or not. No, I take that back. She wanted them to die."

Knox said, "But if we killed them, that means they didn't kill us. How does that get her anywhere?"

"She's trying to redeem herself to Carlos Montoya. She failed the first time around. But now she's going again with her backup plan."

"Backup plan?" exclaimed Knox.

Stone nodded. "You always have a backup plan. And I walked right into it."

"Into what exactly?" asked Chapman nervously.

"They're going to find us all here with a pack

of Russians." Stone paused. "And there's a laboratory back there loaded with new equipment. And I think I know what that new equipment is supposed to represent."

Chapman was the first to see what he was getting at.

"Not nanobots?"

He nodded. "Yes, nanobots."

"But the Russians aren't behind it. I think we clearly established that."

"But when they find us here with all these dead Russians and a lab full of nanobot research that was probably shipped in from Montoya's facilities, what do you think the world will think?"

Caleb said nervously, "What exactly do you mean by 'when they find us here'?"

Finn answered, "We were set up. We were meant to get in here, plow through the Russians and get to this point."

"Why?" asked Annabelle.

The explosion sounded above them.

It was so powerful it shook the floor. Bits of concrete and a plate of steel fell nearby, making them all jump.

"What the hell was that?" yelled Chapman.

"That," said Stone, "was the front door being sealed off."

He grabbed Annabelle's hand. "Come on."

They all followed his lead as he guided them back to the main hall and then toward the way he had come in.

"Should we at least see if we can get out the front way?" called out Knox.

His answer came in the form of another explosion that dropped part of the mountain twenty feet behind them, effectively cutting off any access to the front entrance.

They all ran harder.

The mountain was trembling now, as one precision explosion after another detonated.

"The whole mountain is going to come down on us," screamed Annabelle.

"No it won't," said Stone as they raced along. "Just enough to kill us. But she has to allow them to be able to get in and find the pieces of evidence she wants to be found."

"That bitch!" screamed Chapman as another bomb detonated in front of them, causing Stone to veer off to the left with the others right behind.

"Oliver, what about the way you came in?" called out Finn. "She might not know about that."

"She *does* know about it but we've got no choice," Stone replied.

A section of wall toppled over, nearly crushing

Caleb. However, Finn and Knox pulled him to safety with a second to spare. But Caleb moaned and clutched his shoulder where a chunk of rock had struck.

Finn pulled open his shirt and shone a light on him. "Collarbone's cracked. But you're okay. Collarbone's the fail-safe. It breaks so another more important part doesn't."

"Makes me feel so much better," groaned Caleb.

When Stone reached the kitchen area he stopped and stared helplessly at what was in front of him. Friedman had been ahead of him on this too. She'd collapsed the entrance to the back of the kitchen with a thick wall of debris that had cascaded down from a charge no doubt having been placed in a perfect spot to accomplish this. And even if they dug through that, Stone knew they would just confront another, even thicker wall of rubble. Friedman would have seen to that.

She did her homework.

He briefly wondered how long ago she had had Murder Mountain ready to go. And was she somewhere nearby, detonating these charges? Was she somehow watching them, knowing exactly when to set off each one? And then he had no more time to wonder, as everyone looked at him.

"What now?" said Chapman breathlessly, her

face, like all the others', caked with grime from the dust and smoke.

Stone looked upward as another charge detonated, though not nearby. But more of the facility collapsed and the mountain gave another shudder.

Then the lights went completely out, plunging them into darkness.

Stone, Finn and Knox immediately powered up their NV goggles. Stone took Annabelle's hand, Knox took Caleb's and Finn clamped his hand around Chapman's wrist.

"Follow me," said Stone.

There was one more way out of here. And as far as Stone knew, he was the only person who had ever discovered it. This was their last chance.

He was very conscious of the fact that he had no idea where the next charge Friedman had placed would detonate. She had no reason to allow them to leave here alive, where they could tell people the truth. Each step they took could truly be their—

Annabelle screamed.

CHAPTER

101

JOE KNOX DISAPPEARED UNDER A PILE of rubble as a charge detonating fifty feet away collapsed the section of wall next to him. The others instantly began digging the man out. Stone was on his knees pitching chunks of debris off his friend. His fingers and arms bloodied, the sweat stinging his eyes, he frantically worked in the dark to free Knox. Finally, his fingers touched flesh. In two more minutes they had uncovered the man completely.

Knox was breathing, but unconscious.

Stone started to lift him up, but Finn said, "Let me do that."

He hoisted the two-hundred-pound Knox over his shoulder.

"The only other way out is up, Harry," said Stone.

Finn nodded, a grim look on his face. "Just lead the way."

Stone took the length of rope from Knox's knapsack that the man had used to help rescue Caleb from the tank of sludge. Each person looped the rope around their middle and then passed it on.

"Let's move," said Stone.

He prayed that Friedman had not figured out the third exit from Murder Mountain, as he had done all those years ago. He led the group across the main hall and down to the other end. Stopping in front of what looked like a sheer wall of metal, he ran his fingers up and down its surface. It was cold to the touch, still strong, seemingly impenetrable. Rivets ran up one side of the panel and down the other. Another explosion shook the building. Dirt and dust tumbled down on them from the weakening ceiling.

He pressed on one spot and the wall gave way. He slid the metal out of the way and a set of crude rock stairs was revealed. They went through the opening and headed up.

Stone wondered how long it would take for the authorities to realize what was happening. Some local would report the explosions. This would be relayed to the sheriff's department or whatever police was up here. They would send someone, probably a single officer, and that person would have no idea what they were faced with. Calls would be made. At some point, after a lengthy interval, the CIA would hear of it. They would send a team up here helter-skelter.

But what would they find?

They would find exactly what Friedman wanted them to find. Dead Russian muscle, possibly tied to the drug cartels. And a nanobot research facility where long ago the CIA had trained its assassins. That would hit the national and global news pipelines like a nuclear warhead.

And they will find us, thought Stone. *They'll find us dead.*

But how would she accomplish that last part? The explosions might seal them in here, but they could conceivably survive until rescuers arrived. They had some food, some water. There might be supplies here they could use.

She would have thought of that. There has to be something else.

They kept moving. When Finn grew tired, Stone hefted Knox over his shoulder and carried him for as long as he could. Then Finn swapped back. But as the route took them upwards, it became harder and harder to manage. Yet they kept going.

Chunks of rock now dropped from above with each detonation, since they were in parts of the facility that had never been built out, where the mountain had been left untouched.

Annabelle gasped, "Where are we headed?"

Stone pointed up. "Not much farther."

"Is it on top of the mountain?"

"Close to it."

"Is there a way down?"

Stone didn't answer right away. Actually he didn't have an answer. He had used this exit before, finding it mostly by accident one night when he couldn't sleep. But he'd never gone down the mountain. He'd just looked at the stars, had a few moments of peace before heading back and taking up his training once more. So he didn't know if there was a way down the mountain. But there had to be. He would find one.

He glanced back at Finn, who was carrying Knox. He looked at Caleb clutching his injured shoulder. He looked at exhausted Annabelle. He felt his own legs tremble from extreme exertion.

"We'll find one, Annabelle," he said. "And being outside the mountain is better than being inside it."

They traveled upward another hundred feet. Every time they came to a cross-tunnel Stone had to stop and think about which one was the right one. Twice he made the wrong decision. On the third time he went on ahead alone until he was sure of the way and then came back and got the others.

Finn said in a low voice to him, "Knox is not doing well."

Stone knelt down beside the injured man and shone his light on his face. It was gray, sweaty, but cool to the touch. Stone gently lifted one of the man's eyelids and hit the eye with the light. He let the eyelid fall back into place and rose.

Knox didn't have much time left to live.

"Let's go."

Chapman said, "Is it my imagination or is it getting harder to breathe? I didn't think the mountains in Virginia were that high."

"They're not," said Stone. He took a long breath and it caught halfway in his chest as the amount of oxygen drawn in petered out.

Now Stone had his answer. Friedman was going to suffocate them. Down below he heard machinery operating.

"Fans," he said. "Taking the air out."

He took another whiff and his features involuntarily seized up.

Finn looked at him. "And she's adding something

to the air that's still left in here. Something we don't need in our lungs. Besides all the smoke and shit from the detonations."

"Hurry," said Stone. "This way."

Another fifty feet of rocky paths like large steps made of stone. They were uneven, overly wide in some places, problematically narrow in others.

Stone looked at Finn. He knew his friend had uncommon strength and the nearly infinite endurance of the Navy SEAL he had once been. But he was operating on about half the level of oxygen one needed and the situation was getting worse.

Annabelle had her arm around Caleb, helping him up the path. But Caleb was growing tired quickly. He didn't have near the strength or stamina of the others.

Finally he stopped and sat down, his breaths coming in desperate wheezes.

"Just...go. Leave...me. Can't..."

Stone turned, put his arm under Caleb's good shoulder and hauled him to his feet. Caleb winced in pain.

"No one gets left behind," he said. "We either all stay here or we all keep going."

They struggled on.

Annabelle was the first to see it.

"Light!" she exclaimed.

They rushed forward, encouraged by perhaps the end to their journey.

It was a natural cleft in the mountaintop that decades ago Stone had enlarged and then covered with materials he had smuggled up from the facility below. The cracks of light did not lie. The dawn had broken outside. It was hard for Stone to believe that hours had passed while they'd been inside the mountain.

They reached the seam of light. Stone pushed through plywood and dislodged metal plates that he had placed there years ago. The seam became a foot-wide opening. Finn put Knox down and helped. Twelve inches became a yard. Far below they heard a single explosion, but they were now free of the mountain.

But Stone cautioned, "Be ready. I'll go first."

They all tensed. Finn picked Knox up and pulled his weapon. Chapman had her Walther in one hand and what looked like a throwing knife in the other. Annabelle held on to Caleb, who was nearly dead on his feet after the long ascent.

Stone took a step forward and then stumbled, nearly toppling to his knees. He looked down.

"Shit!"

He hadn't tripped over the uneven terrain. A wire had been stretched between the rock sides of the opening. He looked to his right. Wedged into a crevice was the last explosive. It had a counter. It was at five seconds.

"Get back," screamed Stone as he lunged forward toward the bomb. Right at the same instant Chapman darted forward too.

Annabelle yelled. Caleb moaned. Finn staggered backward under the weight of Joe Knox.

Stone glanced at the MI6 agent. She wasn't looking at him. She was staring dead at the bomb, her jaw tensed, her arms raised above her. She gained purchase with the rock floor and launched herself past him.

Stone shouted, "No, Mary!"

The counter hit one.

102

ANOTHER MEMORIAL SERVICE.

At Arlington Cemetery.

A trio of caskets was lined up side by side representing three veterans of America's military.

Harry Finn.

Joseph Knox.

And John Carr.

Security was doubly heavy considering what had happened last time. There were four circles of perimeter patrols. Bomb detection canines were everywhere. Because of what they now knew about nanobots, every bag was hand-searched, every person patted down, every cell phone, iPhone and electronic device of any kind confiscated.

The rules had definitely changed. Nothing would ever be the same again.

The president was there to give the remarks.

Important members of Congress and the military were also in attendance. The FBI director, Riley Weaver and Agents Ashburn and Garchik were all there. Sir James McElroy was also in attendance because his PM was also present. Not being in the American military or satisfying other specific criteria, Mary Chapman did not have a casket here. But the PM was scheduled to say a few heartfelt words about her sacrifice to help Britain's greatest ally.

Annabelle Conroy and Caleb Shaw were not here either for the same reason as Chapman. They didn't satisfy the criteria for burial at the exalted cemetery. But the president would mention what they had done as well.

The PM spoke first. Then came a stream of important dignitaries to the podium, including Riley Weaver. He didn't explain what Murder Mountain was, because he didn't have to. The press had been kept completely out of the loop on that. Officially, the deaths of Knox, Finn and Carr had come about by a confrontation with a team of Russian drug dealers who had fashioned a laboratory at an abandoned government facility with the aid of an American intelligence officer turned traitor. The bombing and gunfire in Lafayette Park and the subsequent murders in Pennsylvania, Virginia and D.C. had been carried out by the same group.

Speaking last, the president swore that he would do everything in his power to see that justice was done and the perpetrators of these vile acts held accountable. Tension between the Americans and Russians was understandably at an all-time high.

From nearly a half a mile away, atop a knoll at Arlington Cemetery the woman watched these proceedings while she pretended to be gazing at the faded tombstone of a long-dead general. By virtue of a PA system that broadcast across the cemetery, she could hear every word of the speeches. Most held no interest for her, but the one by the president did capture her attention. When he mentioned the American intelligence operative turned traitor, she had to smile.

She knew that the proceedings here were being carried live on all the major network and cable stations. She also knew that Carlos Montoya was watching, because she had communicated with him and told him to.

The plan had worked, even if the president of the U.S. and his counterpart in Mexico had survived. The Russians were being blamed. Her mission, against all odds, had been successful.

Her cell phone chirped. She looked at the message that had just come across the screen.

Buen trabajo.

Good work indeed.

And then the rest of the message came through. It lifted her spirits even more. The remainder of the money was being sent to her account. Carlos Montoya wished her well. She typed her reply.

Hasta luego.

But she didn't really mean it. She was done. This was it. How could she ever top this, anyway?

Marisa Friedman swiped at her new hairdo, cut exceedingly short and dyed dark brown. She had used time-tested techniques to change her facial features to the extent that not even her closest friends would know who she was. She could freely walk these grounds without worry of being recognized.

She turned away from the ceremony. If she had any regrets, it was that John Carr had not taken her up on her offer. Yet she couldn't have expected that he would. Once he found out she had been behind it all—and he was the sort that would—she would have had to kill him anyway. Yet they could have had a little time together. For someone like Friedman, alone most of her life, that would have been enough.

One billion dollars in her bank account and the rest of her life to do as she pleased. She sighed contentedly. It wasn't every day that one pulled off one of the most intricate and earth-shattering operations of all time. Her new papers were in order. A ride on private wings awaited her at Dulles Airport. She had actually purchased an island, through a straw-man transaction. And now she intended to do absolutely nothing for the next year except lie on the beach, read, sip a cool drink and decide what would be next. She passed a number of bomb detection canines. None registered on her. She hid her smile as she passed the wall of security on her way out of the cemetery.

Nanobots.

Montoya had spent years and two billion dollars engineering the transformation of smells and chemical signatures detectable by machines at the molecular level using this microscopic army of programmable soldiers. Now drugs and anything else that would normally be detected could flow freely around the globe. But mostly into America. Drugs, guns, bombs, nuclear material. This really did change everything. The possibilities for the criminal element were limitless. That was one reason Friedman had purchased her island so far away. She didn't want to hear the screams from her homeland.

Screw them.

She reached her car. A rental. She surveyed the landscape once more.

She looked down as the dog came up to her. No leash, not even a collar. A stray. She bent down to pet it, but it backed away from her.

"It's okay, sweetie. I'm not going to hurt you."

The dog drew nearer, as though to check her intent. But when she put her hand out it backed away once more, sat on its haunches and commenced howling.

A bit unnerved, Friedman put her key in the car door.

Her head whipped around when the men converged on her. There were ten of them, half in suits, half in military uniform. All had weapons out. All were pointed at her.

"What's going on?" she demanded. She slipped her sunglasses up to her forehead.

"What is going on?" she said again.

One of the suits said, "Step away from the vehicle and place both hands on your head, fingers interlocked. Now!"

Friedman did as he instructed. "Is this your dog? If so, it's made a very big mistake. You can search me. I have no bombs or drugs or anything like—"

Marisa Friedman stopped speaking when she

saw him come around the back of the SUV parked next to her car.

Oliver Stone slipped his sunglasses into the pocket of his windbreaker. Behind him Mary Chapman kept her aviators on.

Something made Friedman look to her left. There was Finn. And next to him was Joe Knox in a wheelchair, a bandage wrapped around his head and his right arm in a sling.

When Friedman looked back at Stone she flinched yet again.

Caleb Shaw, also wearing a shoulder harness, and Annabelle Conroy, looking perfectly fine, stood just behind their friend.

Friedman took her gaze off Stone long enough to look at the dog that sat just feet from her.

She smiled. "What a cute dog."

"That dog was your undoing," said Stone.

"How?" she asked.

Stone made a show of sniffing his wrist. "It's always a mistake to reveal anything true about yourself that can later be used against you."

"I don't understand."

"The Thai perfume with the visceral impact on men? Two hearts beating as one? Very rare. But not impossible to get if you have the United States government behind you." He looked down at the dog.

"And a very distinctive smell. One sniff is all this little guy needed to track you down in a place as big as Arlington."

"How did you know I'd even be here?"

"How could you not be here?" replied Stone.

"Would you have come if the positions had been reversed?"

"No."

"Why?"

"I never gloated over killing anyone."

She stopped smiling. "I wasn't gloating. I prefer to think of it as paying my respects to a worthy opponent."

"We also just intercepted Montoya's email to you and your reply back. *Hasta luego*? Nice touch. A billion dollars is a good payday. And best of all, it provided a direct link from you to him. His days are quite numbered now too."

She looked around at all the armed men. "Doesn't look like I'll be able to spend that billion dollars." She paused. "I have to commend you on figuring out the nanobots and the scents. I really thought I had that one well covered."

"You did. It was more luck than reasoning."

"I doubt that. No one is that lucky. When Montoya saw the president walk away from the bombing he was not a happy man."

"Hence your *comeback* plan?"

She nodded. "You always have a plan B, because plan A doesn't always work."

"Most people would have simply cut and run by then."

"I only had half the billion. I wanted it all. And I wanted to see the plan through. If I could. The best ones do, you know. Point of pride."

"You almost did."

"Doesn't really matter now. Can I ask how you managed it? I really thought I had all bases covered at Murder Mountain."

"You did," said Stone. "Particularly with the third exit. Can I ask how you managed that?"

"Like I said, I studied you in the classroom."

"Okay, enough of this crap," came a loud voice, and Riley Weaver made an appearance, with the FBI director and Agent Ashburn right behind.

"How did you get so totally screwed up, Friedman?" barked Weaver, pointing a stubby finger at her.

She didn't even bother responding to him. She kept her gaze on Stone and smiled. "A man like you goes his own way. I found two other Triple Sixers who knew of the exit through the kitchen. So I knew you'd have found another way, one that only you would know."

"Why?" asked Stone.

"Because you didn't trust anyone other than yourself. Not even your fellow assassins. Not really."

"What made you think that?"

"Because I never trusted anyone either. Other than myself."

"How'd you find it?"

She looked at the men holding the guns. "Do you mind if I lower my arms? I'm getting a little stiff. You can see that I'm not armed. And even if I were, I'm a bit outgunned."

"Just keep your hands where we can see them," said one of the agents.

Holding her hands in front of her, she turned back to Stone and continued. "Once I knew I'd use Murder Mountain, I went over every inch of the place. The front door was to the west. The back door was to the east. One couldn't go down. So I went up. And there it was, much like how you left it. Now I answered your question. How about mine?"

Stone looked at Chapman.

Friedman swiveled her gaze to the woman.

The MI6 agent shrugged. "Seen a bomb like that twice before in Northern Ireland. Once it was the blue wire. Once it was the red wire. My favorite color was blue. So that's the one I snipped. Cut it pretty bloody close, though. Second to spare. Not much else we could do. But we're here. That's what counts."

"Once we got safely away we detonated the bomb," explained Stone. "Just in case you had someone in the area watching. After that it was a phone call and the rest was arranged. We were all carted away in body bags. The rest of the plan you saw today. Figured it was the only way we'd have a shot at getting to you. Making you believe your plan had worked. President Brennan worked it all out with the Russian government."

"Neatly done."

Stone drew closer to her. "Was it really just about the money?"

"Partly. But it was also about the thrill. To see if I could pull it off. It was quite the challenge. Even you have to admit that. When Montoya came to me, tried to recruit me, at first I pushed back. But then I thought, why the hell not? I think even you would have been tempted." She reached out to touch his arm, but he drew back.

She looked disappointed but said, "I know that's what motivated you. The thrill. All those years at Triple Six. You certainly didn't do it for the money."

"No, I didn't."

"Why then? And don't lie and say you were merely serving your country."

Riley Weaver snapped, "I said enough of this." He strode forward. "You're going to prison. But just for a short while. Then you're going to be executed. For treason."

"Riley, you really are so tiresome," said Friedman as she shook her head. "You take the fun out of everything."

The former Marine looked apoplectic. "Fun! You call what you did fun! You are a complete psycho."

She turned back to Stone. "Why? Why did you do it?"

"I had a woman I loved. I had a daughter I cherished. I wanted to go home to them."

Friedman didn't say anything for a long moment. "Well, I didn't have any of that," she finally said.

"Okay," said Weaver. "Cuff her and read the lady her rights. Let's do this by the book. No mistakes. She's not missing out on her date with a lethal injection. In fact, I think I'll hit the trigger myself."

She looked at him disdainfully. "I'm not going to prison and I'm certainly not being executed by *you*."

Weaver smiled maliciously. "Well, lady, I'd sure as hell like to know how you're going to avoid it."

"I already did."

She staggered a bit as she said this. She reached out and steadied herself by placing a hand against the door of her rental.

Stone was the first to realize what had happened.

He rushed forward and seized her left hand. He saw the pinprick of blood on the inside of her left wrist, right in the middle of a blood vessel. He grabbed her right hand and twisted it upward. The stone on the ring she wore there was gone. In its place was a short, thin needle sticking upward.

"I would be careful around that, if I were you," Friedman said. "Nasty, extremely fast-acting stuff. Leaves old cyanide in the dust on the toxicity ladder." Her voice was slow and her words a bit garbled. She staggered again. Stone held her up and then let her slide back against the car and descend to the ground.

They all stood looking down at her. Weaver's face was a mask of fury.

"How?" he demanded.

Friedman smiled. "As soon as I saw him." She pointed at Stone. "I knew it was over. So I took care of business, Riley. A good spy to the last. And all good spies go out on their own terms. Not anyone else's."

She looked back at Stone and drew a long, painful breath. "I bought the island."

He said nothing.

Her chest started to heave. "I think we could have been happy there."

Everyone looked at Stone, and then back at Friedman.

She said, "I think we could have been. Tell me we could have been."

Stone remained silent, looking at her.

Her body clenched and then relaxed. Stone thought she had passed at that moment. But she managed to say, "We're more alike than you'll ever be willing to admit, John Carr."

Now her eyes grew still. And then glazed. And Marisa Friedman slid sideways, her lovely pale cheek coming to rest against plain gravel.

Stone didn't see this.

He had already turned and walked away.

CHAPTER

103

THE CAMEL CLUB CROWDED AROUND Alex Ford's bed to see the agent staring back at them. Annabelle was gripping his hand, tears easing down her face.

Reuben and Caleb exchanged smiles. Reuben whispered to Caleb, "Remember, no flowers for the man."

Stone moved closer to the bed and looked down at his friend. Alex still couldn't speak and the doctors had warned that the extent of his injuries was as yet unknown because part of his brain had been impacted.

"He may fully recover. He may only partially recover," the surgeon had told them.

"But he'll live," said Annabelle.

"Yes," said the doctor. "He's going to live."

Stone put a hand gently on Alex's shoulder.

"It's . . . good to have you back, Alex," he said in a faltering tone.

Alex blinked back at him, his mouth remaining a thin unmoving line.

Annabelle bent her face closer to his. "We'll be with you every step of the way, Alex, every step."

He squeezed her hand.

Late that night Stone sat at his desk at his cottage. He had a lot to think about but really didn't want to dwell on any of it. He had a standing offer to return to work for the government in any capacity he wanted. He'd told the FBI director he'd get back to him on that, without saying when.

Carmen Escalante had been put into WITSEC just in case Carlos Montoya decided to take out his anger on her. Stone doubted she had much to worry about. The world now knew the truth about Montoya being behind Lafayette Park and all the rest. Stone assumed the man would not be alive that much longer. Either someone in his organization would seize the opportunity and take over his cartel, the Russians would murder him for trying to pin all these crimes on them, or else the Americans would take him out.

In the end, Stone didn't care who killed him.

And the nanobots that could change the trace footprints of bombs and drugs? Well, it would give the ATF and the rest of the crime-fighting world many a sleepless night.

Finally, despite not wanting to do so, his thoughts turned to Marisa Friedman.

A desert island she'd bought for them.

We're more alike than you'll ever be willing to admit, John Carr.

She was wrong about that. They were not alike at all.

Or are we?

As he gazed at his desktop, his mind reeling with the implications of these sudden doubts, he saw the little red dot skitter across the old, scarred wood, like a gnat ablaze. It continued to skip across the wood until it reached him. He looked down and watched it climb his chest, scurry across his face and then stop, he presumed, in the middle of his forehead.

He said calmly into the darkness, "I was actually expecting you earlier."

Chapman appeared in front of him, her Walther with attached laser sight pointed at him.

"Sorry, I'm usually punctual. When did you figure it out?"

"I know that MI6 does not have the luxury of their best agent loitering abroad for no good reason.

You should have been reassigned a long time ago and gone home. The fact that you weren't told me you had another assignment. And it wasn't just keeping an eye on me. There are plenty of others here who could do that."

"Well done. But I also hung around to help you solve the case, and keep you from harm. Wasn't that Watson's role with Holmes? To carry the gun and shoot the occasional shady character? And offer up oohs and ahhs over the master's deductions?"

"You said you hadn't read the stories."

"I lied. I actually loved them. But I do have to tell you, in all sincerity, I enjoyed playing Watson to your Holmes."

"Who assigned you to kill me? McElroy?"

"Sir James genuinely likes you. He believed I was simply watching you. I have to keep some things even from my godfather. No, I'd try closer to home if you're looking for those responsible. We and the Yanks do play well together. You know that."

"So Weaver then?"

"What do you Americans say? That's neither a confirm nor deny. But I won't deny it all that hard."

"So the NIC chief contracted with British intelligence to kill an American citizen?"

"Don't you love how the bloody world works these days?"

"How about the president? Does he know about this?"

Did the man lie to my face at Camp David? And after I saved his life? Again?

"That I truly don't know. But if Weaver is doing it without his knowledge or consent it's pretty ballsy. You must've been a really bad boy."

"I give as good as I get."

"I don't blame you in the least."

"So you're an official assassin on the other side of the pond?"

"Sort of like you were. I do the occasional investigation or saving the world for the queen sort of thing from time to time, but mostly I do the bang-bang on a troublesome opponent."

"I'm sure you're good at it."

"So were you. Maybe the best there ever was." She cocked her head and smiled at him.

She said, "Tell me something. You ever disobey a direct order?"

Stone didn't hesitate. "Only once in my career. When I was in the army."

"Are you glad you did?"

"Yes."

"Ever disobey an order when you were at Triple Six?"

"No."

"Are you glad you didn't?"

"No. It's one of the biggest regrets of my life."

She lowered her gun and then holstered it. "Well, this is my one time."

Stone looked surprised. "Why?"

"For a lot of reasons I don't care to discuss right now."

"But won't you suffer for not carrying out the mission?"

"I'm a lady who likes to take her chances in the face of adversity."

"You'll have to watch your back now."

"I've been doing that ever since I joined up."

"Will I see you again?"

"The future is promised to no one."

She turned and walked to the door but then looked back. "Take care of yourself, Oliver Stone. Oh, one more thing, you can put your gun away. You won't need it now. At least not with me. But don't turn your back on Riley Weaver. That would be a mistake. Cheers."

A moment later Mary Chapman was gone.

Stone slowly put his gun back in the desk drawer and closed it. As soon as he'd seen the dot on his desk he'd aimed his gun toward the kneehole. He was glad he hadn't had to fire. Chances were very good they each would have killed the other.

He was not tired though the hour was very late. He didn't need as much sleep as he used to. Age, he supposed, did that to you. He waited a bit and then got up and walked. He walked so far that he reached the spot where it all began.

Not Murder Mountain. That's where it all began for John Carr.

He looked around the confines of Lafayette Park. This is where it all began for Oliver Stone. And for many reasons he knew this was also where he belonged. He looked across at the White House where the president was no doubt sleeping soundly even after narrowly avoiding an assassination attempt.

Stone paced the grounds of the park, nodding to security personnel who knew him well. He wondered if Alex Ford would ever be standing out here again on protection duty. He would now be a revered legend at the Service, a hero to his president and his country. Stone would have preferred simply having his friend whole again.

His thoughts next turned to Chapman, who would finally be returning to her little island. Maybe he would make a trip across the pond to see her. Just maybe. He sat down at the same bench where Marisa Friedman had perched that night when an explosion rocked Lafayette. That had started everything in motion. Now it was calm once more.

Stone looked over at the maple tree freshly planted in its new home. It looked like it had always belonged here.

Just like some people.

Just like me.

Oliver Stone sat back, drew a long breath and continued to admire the view.

ACKNOWLEDGMENTS

To Mitch Hoffman, who knew "hell" could be so much fun;

To David Young, Jamie Raab, Emi Battaglia, Jennifer Romanello, Tom Maciag, Martha Otis, Anthony Goff, Kim Hoffman, Bob Castillo, Roland Ottewell and all at Grand Central Publishing, who support me every day;

To Aaron and Arleen Priest, Lucy Childs Baker, Lisa Erbach Vance, Nicole James, Frances Jalet-Miller and John Richmond, for keeping me straight and true;

A special shout-out to Maja Thomas, for taking my digital world to a whole new level;

To Maria Rejt, Trisha Jackson and Katie James at Pan Macmillan, for helping me rock across the pond;

To Grace McQuade and Lynn Goldberg, for superb publicity;

To Donna, to whom I owe the title;

To Scot, thanks for the assist;

To Neal Schiff, for all your help on Bureau procedures;

To Bob Scule, for your eagle eye and lobbying insight;

To Frank Verrastro and John Hamre, for the D.C. details;

To Marisa Friedman, Stephen Garchik, the family of Dr. Fuat Turkekul and Tom Gross, hope you enjoyed your roles, and the various charities you contributed to certainly benefited;

To Lynette, Deborah and Natasha, and you know why.